P9-CRA-969

THE
PREDATORS

By F.M. Parker:

SKINNER
NIGHTHAWK
COLDIRON
THE SEARCHER
SHADOW OF THE WOLF
THE HIGHBINDERS
THE SHANGHIERS
THE FAR BATTLEGROUND
THE SHADOW MAN
THE SLAVERS
THE ASSASSINS

F. M. PARKER

THE

PREDATORS

NAL BOOKS

NAL BOOKS
Published by the Penguin Group
Penguin Books USA Inc., 375 Hudson Street,
New York, New York 10014, U.S.A.
Penguin Books Ltd, 27 Wrights Lane,
London W8 5TZ, England
Penguin Books Australia Ltd, Ringwood,
Victoria, Australia
Penguin Books Canada Ltd, 2801 John Street,
Markham, Ontario, Canada L3R 1B4
Penguin Books (N.Z.) Ltd, 182-190 Wairau Road,
Auckland 10, New Zealand

Penguin Books Ltd, Registered Offices:
Harmondsworth, Middlesex, England

First published by NAL Books, an imprint of Penguin Books USA Inc.

First Printing, July, 1990
10 9 8 7 6 5 4 3 2 1

Copyright © F.M. Parker, 1990
All rights reserved

 REGISTERED TRADEMARK—MARCA REGISTRADA

Library of Congress Cataloging-in-Publication Data

Parker, F. M.
    The predators / by F.M. Parker.
      p.   cm.
    ISBN 0-453-00734-1
    1. Mormons—History—Fiction.   I. Title.
PS3566.A768P7 1990
813'.54—dc20
                                           90-30815
                                              CIP

PRINTED IN THE UNITED STATES OF AMERICA
Set in Times Roman

PUBLISHER'S NOTE
This is a work of fiction. Names, characters, places, and incidents either
are the product of the author's imagination or, if real, are used fictitiously.

PROLOGUE
The Making of the Great Plains

O NLY THE PRIMEVAL SUN SAW THE BIRTH OF THE mountains in that ancient time of orogeny on the northern continent of the Earth.

A compressive force of unimaginable power ushered in that age of mountain building. For a time span of millions of years, the crust of the continent was squeezed from the east and west, and the thick rock layers arched upward, bending until they stood at steep angles. In places the mighty force completely overturned the rocks so that they lay upside down. A giant range of mountains was formed, stretching some three thousand miles north to south and spanning the continent. Stony mountain peaks stabbed four, five miles high, wounding the sky in scores of places.

As the mountains rose, streams of a thousand sizes came to life and tumbled with awesome violence down from the high ramparts. The myriad currents cut and tore at the steep flanks of the mountains, grinding the rock to sand and silt and rushing away with it to the lowlands. Where the grade became less steep on the lower reaches of the streams, the currents slowed and wandered in meandering courses, dropping their load of eroded mountain debris. The valleys of the streams became choked with swamps and shallow lakes as thousands of cubic miles of sediment were spread in flat, ever-thickening layers.

Time ticked off the millennia, one after another, adding to millions of years. During the long epoch of erosion a broad plain grew at the base of the mountain range and extended toward the rising sun for many hundreds of miles.

So flat was the land surface that the larger animals could see each other for long distances, to the limits of their vision.

Far away at the extreme eastern edge of the plains, the streams coalesced to form a grand river. This stupendous flow poured in a never-ending current to the south, finally debauching into the salty brine of one of the great oceans of the world.

As time continued to whisper its passing, the climate of the Earth began to cool. Glaciers thousands of feet thick formed and advanced across the northern portion of the plains, each time to retreat and die. In the harsh, frozen part of the cycles, the land was buried under an unbelievably large expanse of ice and swept by hurricane winds that never ended. Wet, warm, pluvial times, the interglacial periods, melted the ice, creating torrents that scoured the mountains and plains and sped off to add their volume to the prodigious south-flowing river.

A dramatic change occurred in the climatic cycles of the Earth. The continental glacier retreated and the deluge came, but the next phase of the cycle did not arrive. Instead the land grew drier and drier. Broad forest died and the plains became a prairie, a sea of tall grass.

The great animals that had lived and thrived during the rugged glacial period, the wooly mammoth, the wide-horned bison, the saber-toothed tiger, and the vulture condor all died. However, the bison left a legacy, for in its genes there existed the potential for change. As the plains became ever more dry, each succeeding generation of the bison grew smaller and smaller, adapting to the changing climate and the decreased availability of food. It became a miniaturized replica of its ancestor, weighing a mere ton or less. This new breed of bison flourished by the millions on the grassy prairie.

In this warmer, drier time, a brown-skinned man came onto the plains and stalked the bison herds. The man was skilled and killed what animals he needed. Only the white buffalo wolf competed with the brown man as he journeyed where the buffalo journeyed and lived in harmony with the herds for twelve millennia.

Then a new clan of man, one with white skin, came onto

the broad prairie. The quiet tread of the moccasined foot and the silent bow of the Indian were joined by the hobnailed boot and thunderous rifle of the white man.

The two clans of man became enemies and pursued each other across the prairie. They fought savage battles. The victor slew the vanquished without mercy.

The white man won most of the battles, relentlessly extending his domain. He began to build permanent villages on the eastern edge of the prairie.

A new sect of man, adhering to a religion never before seen upon the earth, came from many countries and gathered on the edge of the prairie at a place called St. Joseph. These people, formed into groups and held together by their religious faith, marched out almost totally unarmed from the border settlement and into the wilderness. They were searching for a place they called Zion.

This story takes place during the time of the migration of those religious men and women—Saints, they called themselves—of that latter-day religion.

— • ◆ **1** ◆ • —

Red River, Texas—March 3, 1859

THE MAN CAME OUT OF THE STONE HOUSE ON THE bluff above the Red River while the cold dawn was still too black for shooting. A tall, ghostly figure, he walked swiftly to the corral, caught and saddled a horse, and rode off. He spurred the horse to a gallop across the two hundred yards of meadow surrounding the house. The oak woods on the hillside swallowed rider and mount into its gloomy depths.

"Goddamn," cursed Santell, lowering the telescope from his eye.

"I told you we should've got closer." Kunzel's voice came

from the brush near Santell. "If the range had been shorter, I could've killed him even in this poor light."

"Shut up," growled Santell. "This is the closest we could get and still have cover in the woods." The ranch man had been very lucky by leaving so early in the day. But that made no difference in the final outcome. When the man returned, he would die, for Santell and his two men would still be there waiting. Santell raised the telescope and focused the round field of magnification back on the house.

"What now?" asked Cotter from Santell's other side.

"There should be one more man," replied Santell. "We'll kill him when he comes outside."

"It's a hell of a shame one of them don't have a woman," Kunzel said. "Are you sure they don't? I could use some lovin' today."

"You're always ready for a woman," Santell said. "But you'll find none here. There's only the two Tolliver brothers. You'll have to be satisfied with your share of their land and cows. When we're done here, we'll ride to Austin and you can buy all the women you can handle."

"You had better be certain that you have the correct information about these Tollivers," Cotter said. "We don't want any relatives showing up and asking questions about their disappearance, or our claim of ownership to their land."

"I got it straight. There'll be no problems," Santell said. Cotter was a worrier and an aggravating man. However, he had a skill with a pen that was worth a fortune. He could prepare a deed or bill of sale and forge a dead man's signature that no one could tell was false.

Santell had no doubt that his plan would succeed in taking the ranch from the Tollivers. He was in possession of four other ranches and had not paid a cent for any of them. Soon he would be very rich. He chuckled low in his chest at the thought.

"Did you say something?" asked Cotter.

"No," said Santell. He watched the door by which the first man had left the house.

Three days before in the early-evening dusk, Santell and his men had crossed the Salt Fork of Red River and located the ranch headquarters. They had stolen through the woods and spied upon the house until full darkness. After spending the night in a hidden camp they had begun to prowl the land, counting the cattle and riding the boundaries marked with stone monuments. The grass was dense and tall. The Salt Fork and several springs provided abundant water. Though they had found but three hundred head of cattle, the land easily could support a herd of five thousand. By nightfall today, the Tolliver land, buildings, and cattle would become Santell's, and his men's. And later Santell's alone, for he had a second plan.

As Santell lay watching the building in the meadow, he tried to recall all the isolated ranches and farms in Oklahoma and Texas that he and his men had plundered. The number was too large. The images of dead men, and raped and slain women, were blurred and intermingled. He could clearly remember only the last four. Those were ranches they had carefully selected, killed the owners, forged deeds, and now claimed as their own property.

In the east, the gray morning turned hard blue and welled up to fill half the sky. The dull yellow orb of the sun rose up from its hiding place in the pit below the horizon. The sun's rays struck the valley of the Red, drove the last night shadows into the low hollows and crevices of the earth, and killed them there.

In the brighter light, Santell examined more closely the large single-story house and the round corral lying some one hundred yards upstream from it. The uncountable back-breaking tons of stone that had gone into the walls of both structures had been laid true and plumb. The work of a true craftsman.

"Damn fine headquarters buildings," Santell said. "Made of stone like that, they'll last the lifetimes of two men. Add that to the excellent grazing land, and this is the best ranch we've stolen. All of this was done by the Tollivers, hardly more than kids, in just two years."

"Mighty nice of them to build it for us," said Cotter.

Santell agreed. Now he would take it away from the Tollivers with a couple of bullets. He would then move on along the frontier and take a dozen or two such properties for his own. It was a grand country where a man could get rich so easily.

"There's the second fellow just coming out the door," said Kunzel in a low voice.

A tall, young man stepped out of the house and stood in the yard. He stretched hugely, reaching up high, and then far out to the side. He glanced over his shoulder at the sun and then moved off toward a walled spring. Partway there, he halted and scooped up a rock. With a long, looping swing of his arm he sent the missile sailing out over the bluff in the direction of the river, lying some two hundred feet below. Whistling, he walked on toward the spring.

"Doesn't seem to have a worry in the world," Cotter said.

"He sure won't be able to worry about anything in a minute," said Kunzel, rubbing the stock of his .50-caliber rifle. "Want me to shoot him now, Santell?"

"I haven't seen a hanging for a spell," Cotter said. "Why can't we hang this fellow and watch him kick his way to hell?"

Santell scratched his bearded jaw. "That's a good idea. And we'll let him continue to swing after he's dead. When his brother sees him dangling by the neck, he'll think he might still be alive and come hurrying to cut him down. That'll bring him into easy gun range without fail."

Santell stood up. "Let's ride down there. Act friendly until we get close enough to jump him. We'll do this quick, because we're going to be out there in the open and the other man could ride back at any time."

Jason Tolliver spotted the three horsemen the moment they broke free of the woods. He raised his hand in greeting. "Hi!" he shouted out to the men.

"Hello, yourself," Santell called back. "Can we get a drink from your spring?"

"There's plenty of water, and it's good and cold," Jason said, and smiled broadly. It had been many days since Nathan and he had had visitors. His brother was often gone for long periods of time, and it was lonely.

Santell reined his horse close to Jason and swung down to the ground. Kunzel and Cotter dismounted on the opposite side of Jason.

"Your name Tolliver?" asked Santell.

"Tolliver, that's right. Jason Tolliver." He bobbed his head and continued to smile in a happy, childish way at the new arrivals.

He was pleased by the fact the man knew his name. "What's your name?" he asked.

Santell did not reply. The friendliness of the young man was strange. He should have been wary of three unknown men riding up and surrounding him. Tolliver wasn't armed, not even with a belt knife.

Jason cocked his head, waiting for the expected answer to his question. Finally he asked, "Why have you come to visit me and Nathan?"

"To kill you and take your ranch," Santell said. He raised his hand, signaling to Kunzel and Cotter.

Cotter sprang forward and pinioned Jason's arms to his side in a bear hug. Kunzel moved quickly upon the startled young man and slugged him savagely in the face. Then swiftly struck him again.

Dazed, Jason slumped, hanging in Cotter's arms. Blood began to stream from his nose and mouth.

"Tie his hands behind him," Santell directed. "Hurry now before he can start a fight."

Kunzel dug a length of rawhide from a pocket and roughly bound Jason's hands. "He's ready for the hanging," Kunzel said.

Jason straightened, his eyes coming back into focus. He shook his head, flinging the blood from his face in a spray of red droplets. With an uncomprehending expression he looked at the man who had hit him, and then at the man who gave orders to the others.

"This should be a good show," said Cotter. "He's strong and won't die fast."

"Put him on your horse," Santell said. "Move, dammit. Let's get this over with."

The men hoisted Jason up on the horse. "Keep your damn legs astraddle the horse," growled Cotter as Jason started to lift a leg to dismount.

"That big oak tree on the edge of the bluff has a good limb for hanging him," Kunzel said, pointing.

"Take him over there while I tie a hangman's knot," Santell said. He took his lariat from his saddle and followed along behind Jason and the two men holding him on the horse. Expertly he made a loop and tied the slipknot. When the men stopped beneath the limb of the oak, Santell walked close to Jason and dropped the noose over his head.

Jason looked at the outlaw leader with wide eyes. "Please don't hurt me anymore."

Santell laughed. "We're only going to hang you." Cotter was right, Tolliver appeared very strong. Why hadn't the fellow fought? Damn odd.

Santell tossed the loose end of the lariat over the limb of the tree. "Cotter, draw that tight and make it fast to the oak."

Cotter grinned in anticipation of the hanging. He jerked the lariat taut with a sharp pull.

Jason cried out at the painful tightening of the noose around his neck. His hands began to wrench and tear at the ties that bound him. "Let me go!" he pleaded. Tears started to flow down his cheeks.

"He's ready for hanging," Cotter said. "So let's hang the crybaby."

Santell looked at Jason. "Tolliver, do you have any last words to say before we let you walk on air?"

Jason tried to speak but could not. He sat taller in the saddle to loosen the choking rope. That did not give enough slack. He stood up in the stirrups of the saddle.

Jason swallowed. He spoke in a small, frightened child's voice. "Nathan won't like you for hurting me."

Santell threw back his head and laughed uproariously. Cotter and Kunzel joined in, slapping their thighs and glancing at each other in great mirth. Their loud laughter swept out across the bluff above the river. An evil, contorted echo bounced back from the vertical stone walls of the house.

"I don't give a damn what Nathan likes," Santell said. "He'll soon be joining you in hell."

Santell grabbed the bridle of the horse and led the animal from under Jason.

Nathan dismounted from his horse and squatted in the meadow near the edge of the woods. Clouds were scudding down fast from the north. Blustery winds rushed out ahead of the approaching storm front and whipped the dry reeds of the previous year's dead wild grass. He reached out to part the grass and hold it still so that he could study the tracks of the three shod horses in the dirt.

Several times during the last two days he had found the same sets of hoofprints. At first he thought they had been made by a group of horsemen merely passing through. Now he sensed danger from the riders.

He swung back astride and followed the trail at a trot. It was time to run the men down and discover their purpose for being here on his land.

The hoofprints led around the border of a large meadow, then swerved to pass near a cattle loafing area among a clump of large trees. The sign continued on up and across a string of hills to a spring. There the men had sat their horses for a time.

Nathan nodded to himself. The strange riders were counting cows. His cows.

A mile farther on, the horsemen had left the meadow and entered the woods. In a low swale full of a dense stand of trees they had made a hidden camp. The fire had been small, leaving few ashes.

Nathan felt a chill, as if a feather had been drawn along his spine. He twisted in the saddle to look in the direction of his home on the bank of the Salt Fork of the Red River. A sudden premonition surged over him that Jason needed his help.

He pivoted the horse and spoke sharply to it. The mount sprang away in a gallop, darting through the woods and dodging the trees like a big cat.

The horse broke free of the woods and struck a large meadow. Nathan leaned over the neck of the beast and slapped the outstretched neck a stinging blow with his hand.

"Go!" he shouted into the animal's pointed ears. The horse took the command, its legs stretched, and the iron-shod hooves beat a rapid drumlike tattoo on the ground.

At a dead run the horse carried Nathan over the meadow, then through a finger of trees and into a long grass-covered area studded with boulders lying between wooded hills. Half a mile farther along a rimrock blocked Nathan's course. He reined the mustang in a series of left and right switchback jumps down a broken, rock-filled gully through the massive rock outcrop.

Horse and rider broke free of the rocks and raced out into a wide, flat section of land sloping down toward the Red River. Nathan spurred. Two miles and he would be home.

They left the meadow and plunged into thick woods. Nathan pulled the mustang down to a walk and went on quietly toward the clearing where the ranch house sat.

He halted in the fringe of the trees and stared ahead, searching. The corral was nearest to him. The six head of horses were still there. Beyond was the house. No one stirred in the yard, and no smoke came from the chimney.

Nathan's view jumped past the house to the big oak tree on the edge of the bluff. Something hung to its thick lower limb.

Oh God! Jason.

Nathan screamed a wild cry full of pain and terror. He raked the sharp rowels of his spurs brutally across the ribs of the mustang. The animal burst into the clearing.

◆ 2 ◆

"**T**HERE HE COMES," KUNZEL SAID IN A GLEE-ful voice as he watched Nathan race the horse across the clearing toward Jason. "Just as you said, Santell. Tell me when you want me to shoot."

"Don't be in a hurry," replied the outlaw leader. "We've got plenty of time."

"Let's see the show for a while," Cotter said. "Damn. This should be a good one."

The rider reined his horse to a sliding stop beside the body swaying in the wind. Swiftly he clasped the figure to him. He snatched a knife from a sheath on his belt and slashed the rope.

Clutching Jason tightly in his arms, Nathan threw his leg over the saddle horn and slid from the horse's back to the ground. He dropped to his knees and laid Jason on his back. He yanked the choking noose loose from his brother's neck and flung it aside. The shirt was ripped open with a popping of buttons.

Nathan pressed his ear to the still chest. With every particle of his being, he willed that there should be a heartbeat. His brother must not be dead. He strained to hear.

Not one sound, not one flutter of a heart struggling to live came from within the quiet body. Nathan raised his fist and struck the center of the broad chest. And hammered down again, and again. The heart must start. He dropped his ear against the pale chest. There was not one whisper of life.

Nathan examined Jason more closely and saw that the

11

blood on his face was congealed, almost dry. The body held little warmth. He was an hour too late to save his brother.

He remained kneeling and closed Jason's shirt. He untied the bound hands and folded them across the chest. The long legs were straightened.

The blue eyes were open and staring out from the face, burned brown by sun and wind. Never had the eyes seemed more innocent. Why had harm come to somebody so free of violence himself? With a thumb and forefinger Nathan closed the cold lids, holding them shut for a moment before removing his hand.

Jason's neck was unnaturally bent to the side and ringed with a red wound, caused by the noose that had choked away his life. A raw rope burn was on his jaw and the side of his face, made by the dying man's struggles against the hanging rope. Tears pooled in Nathan's eyes at the cruelty and pain that had been inflicted upon his brother.

His teeth clenched and he climbed to his feet. God damn the murderous bastards who had slain Jason! He would find them and send them all to the blackness of everlasting death.

A blast of wind buffeted Nathan and he looked up to survey the sky. Dense black storm clouds were speeding close upon the valley of the Salt Fork of the Red. The wind was growing stronger, and it had cold teeth that nipped at him. A norther was hurrying straight from the birthplace of blizzards. Jason had to be properly buried before the storm struck. Nathan strode off hastily along the bench and entered the stone walls of the house.

He tossed aside the buffalo sleeping robe from Jason's bed and stripped away the blue Indian blanket beneath. Taking the blanket and a length of twine, he returned to Jason's still body. Here on the bluff where a man could see for many miles along the beautiful valley of the Red River, he would bury his brother. Nathan began to dig a grave.

As he labored, the temperature fell steadily. The wind increased in strength, howling a dismal dirge through the brush and rocks on the face of the bluff. The sun dimmed, then vanished, as the leaden clouds drove in beneath it to hide all of the sky.

Nathan held tight rein on his bitter sorrow. He concentrated his thoughts on the short-handled shovel, the iron blade ringing harshly with each blow upon the hard, stony earth. He would mourn his brother later.

When the excavation was chest deep, he encountered a hard layer of sandstone. He could dig no deeper. *Jason, your grave is ready.*

Tenderly Nathan wrapped the body in the Indian blanket and tied it in place with the twine. He climbed into the grave and, drawing the body into his arms, lowered it to the bottom at his feet. He positioned the blanket-shrouded form and straightened.

He started to hoist himself out of the grave, then halted. He untied one strand of the twine and reopened the blanket at Jason's head. And as he had done a thousand times before to quiet his brother and drive away his nightmares so he could sleep, Nathan ran his hand twice through the thick mop of reddish hair and then over the brow.

His brother's brow was cold. Smooth and cold, like a river rock.

"Be at peace in your long sleep," Nathan whispered.

Nathan felt the full impact of the loss of his brother. Only Nathan, of his lineage of Tollivers, now remained alive in all the world. Never again would he enjoy the presence of Jason, gentle Jason who played at work and asked childish questions and who had the most pleasant and joyous laugh ever uttered by man.

Nathan felt the gathering in of his memories, time falling away, going back to his deepest recollection. He journeyed again through the few short childhood years with his mother and father, far away to the east in the mountains of Virginia. Then suddenly both of those loving people were gone, swept away by the deadly disease—cholera.

Cut loose from family, the gangly twelve-year-old twin brothers drifted off along the mud roads through the never-ending forest of giant oak, beech, maple, and chestnut trees. It was only natural to travel in the same direction that the tide of immigrating people moved with their animals and wagons—to the west.

The raggedy boys worked for handouts of food and permission to come out of the rain and sleep in barns. Dry hay for bedding was a luxury.

Nathan often fought in those early days with the bully boys of the towns Jason and he passed through. The loudmouths poked fun at Jason, calling him feebleminded and a half-wit. A terrible fever had struck Jason at the age of seven, holding him in a wild delirium for three days. Thereafter his body grew to be that of a man, but his mind did not develop. Jason had been doomed to live forever in the simple world of a child.

When Jason cried at the cruel, taunting words of the bully boys, Nathan charged them with swinging fists. He lost many of those first battles with the larger boys. However, he grew tougher with each fight and lost fewer and fewer.

The two brothers would halt their wandering and work for a week, or a month, then Nathan would grow restless and would gather their scant possessions and, with Jason in tow, strike out again along the frontier byways.

The cold winters and hot summers passed as Nathan and Jason drifted. When they were fifteen, their travels brought them across Tennessee to the banks of the Mississippi River. Nathan worked for a year there, chopping wood by the scores of cords for the boilers of the steamboats that plied the river from New Orleans, north to Cincinnati and a hundred other cities. That year, swinging the iron-headed ax, Nathan grew to the full size of a man.

Using the hard-earned chopping money, Nathan bought sturdy buckskin clothing and horses for the two of them, and firearms for himself, a Navy Colt revolver .36-caliber and a Sharps carbine .52-caliber. Jason and he crossed the Mississippi into Arkansas and, riding onward for days, passed into Texas.

During the year Jason turned eighteen, he rode guard on the stage line between Houston and the rapidly growing capital city of Austin. That year fell during a turbulent period in Texas. Highwaymen struck at the stage many

times. During those attempted robberies Nathan killed some
of the bandits. The stage was successfully taken only one
time, and that while Nathan lay wounded and unconscious
in the dirt of the road. The following year found him working on the Satterlee Ranch, a large land holding located
astride the headwaters of the Tongue and Pease Rivers in
northwest Texas.

While on a buffalo hunt north of the Salt Fork of the
Red, Nathan discovered a band of wild cows, thirty or so
and their calves. He told Billy Valentine, with whom he
rode while doing ranch tasks, of his find.

The old rustler, now turned honest cowboy in his last
years, had slapped his leg and laughed. "Boy," he said,
"you've got a God-sent chance to become a rancher in your
own right and not have to work and take orders from any
other man."

"What do you mean?" asked Nathan.

"Do you know how most men start becoming ranchers on
the frontier?"

"Tell me." Nathan sensed a tale about to be told.

"Well, he buys a few cows and drives them out past the
farthest white settlement and into Indian country. Then,
over the next few years, he occasionally sneaks back and
picks up unbranded calves from the more established ranchers, those with the biggest herds, and drives them off. He
puts his own brand on them. So in a very short time he has a
three- or four-hundred-head outfit. Then he stops his stealing and lets his herd just grow naturally.

"Of course, the ranchers that lose the calves call that
rustling. They hire tough riders, like Satterlee did with those
three hombres that live in a wing of the big house. They're
good with guns and would hang a man quick if they caught
him with a stolen calf."

"Satterlee's spread is damn big," Nathan said. "Is that
how he first got his start?"

"He got started while I was still up in the Oklahoma
Territory. But I've heard that for the first few years after he
came to the Pease River country, his herd sometimes grew
by two hundred percent in a year, and he never bought one
of the animals."

Valentine studied Nathan. "You're strong and a hard worker. You know cattle. Out there, away from other men, Jason wouldn't be bothered by all the mean talk said to him."

The old rustler swung his arm to the north. "The land is free for the taking beyond the Red River. But the Comanche are there and they'll kill some of your cows, and maybe you too. So if you go, be careful. And be damn certain you don't get caught stealing calves. Take only a few from each rancher so he'll not know that his losses ain't from wolves and lions.

Within the week Nathan had quit his job on the Satterlee Ranch. Jason and he loaded their possessions on two packhorses. Tucked away among the items was a branding iron Nathan had made at the ranch forge. Half a day's ride brought them to the North Fork of the Pease River. They made camp in the edge of the night and slept to the sound of the river's song.

Morning sun found them pushing northwest. In the late afternoon they forded the North Fork of the Red River and passed into the wildland claimed by the fierce Comanche.

Nathan and Jason explored the broad valley of the Red River with its braided stream channel and many marshes. Giant cottonwoods and thickets of willow, and tall water-loving grasses grew in dense abundance on the rich bottomland. On the rolling hills above the river, broad grassy meadows, interspersed with stretches of brush and trees, extended for miles.

Finally Nathan selected the land he wanted. He built tall stone cairns to mark the boundaries of his new ranch. The area was fifteen miles on a side, the Red River being the south limit. On the top stone of each cairn he chiseled his brand, TT, for two Tollivers. He roped and branded the wild cows and their calves that he had seen in the days before. The orphan brothers were now men of property.

Nathan labored from daylight to dark. Even Jason seemed to sense that something new and good, and perhaps permanent, had come into their lives. He worked doggedly beside Nathan. A generous-sized ranch house began to rise on a tall bluff above the Red River.

All the exterior walls were constructed of stone with mud mortar, and had been completed by the end of the second autumn. The construction of a round stone corral followed. All this last winter the brothers had lived snuggly sitting in the snowy evenings before a fire in the huge fireplace.

At times, as the months passed, Nathan would cease his labor on the house and ride away, leading five horses with special packsaddles he had built. He had taken Jason with him at first, afraid his brother would wander off or that the Comanche would come and harm him. However, Jason did not like the hard riding, and after a few trips Nathan allowed him to remain behind.

Nathan traveled swiftly far beyond the ranch, a hundred miles, sometimes a hundred and fifty miles. There in the woods and brush thickets that abound, he would rope the half-wild calves and tie them upon the backs of the packhorses. Journeying at night and covering forty to fifty miles in the darkness, he returned stealthily home. The Double T brand was burned onto the flanks of the calves and the animals turned loose. Never once did Nathan take a Satterlee calf.

Nathan shook himself and roughly dashed away his tears. Why had the bandits killed gentle Jason? He was no threat to them, regardless of what they did. Why hadn't they simply taken the cattle or whatever they wanted and left?

He again shrouded Jason's face with the Indian blanket. *Rest easy, my brother, for soon I'll send your murderers to their graves.* He grabbed the top of the excavation and jumped out.

◆ 3 ◆

"WHAT'S HE DOING THERE SO STILL?" Kunzel asked, staring across the meadow at Tolliver, standing in the grave with only the top part of his body showing.

"Just looking down at the corpse," said Santell, watching through his telescope. "But he's dug the hole deep enough to hold two men. That's what we've been waiting for, so get ready to shoot." Kunzel was the best rifle shot of the three of them. However, there must be no misses. Santell would fire also. He cocked his rifle.

In the meadow, Tolliver sprang up out the excavation. Now for the killing, thought Santell.

He raised his rifle and aimed with Kunzel down at the tall young man. Santell's finger tightened on the trigger. "Shoot," hissed the outlaw leader.

Santell's rifle bucked against his shoulder. Kunzel's gun crashed at the same instant. The thunder of the double explosions roared out across the meadow.

Santell knew his bullet had gone exactly to his point of aim. But Tolliver had abruptly stooped to reach for the shovel on the ground. Santell's and Kunzel's bullets had merely torn holes in the air where Tolliver had been a moment before.

Tolliver, bent at the waist, flung a startled look up at the source of the gunshots. Then, unbelievably fast, he spun and hurled himself toward the brink of the bluff. He vanished downward, out of sight.

"Run! Catch him! Shoot him before he can hide in the brush and escape," shouted Santell, recalling the dense growth of vegetation on the steep slope extending down to merge with the even thicker growth along the river.

Kunzel, shifting his empty rifle to his left hand and pulling his pistol, sprang from hiding. Cotter, trailing his rifle, rushed pell-mell beside him toward the spot where Nathan had disappeared. Santell ran close behind. The three raced past the open grave and slid to a stop on the edge of the bluff.

Nathan heard the buzz of the bullets streaking past, like small deadly hornets, and the boom of the rifles from the woods. In a scuttling run he leapt away from the grave and over the lip of the bluff.

The brush slowed his wild, stumbling run down the steep incline. His flailing arms caught hold of a stout oak limb and stopped him. He scrambled off to the side, and then, with legs driving, fought his way back up almost to the top of the embankment. Hunkering down out of view in the concealing brush, he drew his revolver. Cocked it. He ordered his pumping lungs and pounding heart to slow. He had some killing to do.

More than one man had fired a rifle at him. Since they outnumbered Nathan, they might think themselves safe and make a mistake. He needed an advantage if he was to live through the next few minutes of battle.

Two men appeared sky-lined above Nathan. A second later a third came into view and stopped. Nathan felt his terrible hate boiling. These men must be responsible for Jason's hanging. And they had tried to kill Nathan. He wanted to start shooting, to blast holes through them. But he would wait a couple of seconds. He must know how many foes he had. Then the gunfight would begin.

"I don't see him," one of the men said. "Where in the hell could he have gone so fast?"

Nathan grinned flintily. They had thought he would run. They were wrong.

Two seconds passed . . . five. The outlaws craned their necks to spot him. Nathan made his judgment. There were only three men.

He raised his revolver and pointed it through an opening in the brush. The feel of the iron gun in his hand was grand. The sights came into alignment on the face of the nearest outlaw. Nathan squeezed the trigger.

The gun jumped like a live thing in his hand. The head of the outlaw was slammed backward by the punch of the bullet. His rifle fell with a clatter on the stony ground.

Nathan swung the barrel of his pistol and found the chest of a second bandit. Killed him with a ball of lead to the heart.

The last man threw a quick shot at the smoke of Nathan's gun and darted out of view. Brambles shattered close beside Nathan's head, flinging splinters into his cheek like a handful of darts. Nathan fired back but knew he had missed.

He sprang from the protective cover of the bushes and scrambled directly up the slope. He was making the same mistake the outlaws had made, charging at an enemy whose location was unknown. But not one of the Jason's killers must escape.

Nathan caught himself at the last step and peered cautiously over the top of the bluff. The killer, running hard, was nearly to the woods. Nathan sprang up the last few feet.

Racing swiftly at an angle to intercept the course of the outlaw, Nathan crossed the clearing and entered the woods. He stopped immediately, listening for some noise the man might make.

Almost immediately the sound of a horse's hooves sped away to the right. Nathan turned and followed at the peak of his strength. The sound of iron striking rocks came as the rider and mount began their descent on the stony trail down to the river.

Nathan broke free of the trees. Below him, the outlaw lashed his mount in long, splasing lunges through the shallow ford of the Red River. The horse tore up out of the water and raced due south.

Nathan pivoted around and hastened back to the house. He filled in his brother's grave, tamping the dirt down firmly as he did so. Nothing must be able to dig down and disturb the body. He finished the final shaping of the earth mound. When he returned after slaying the last murderer, he would prepare a fitting monument to place at Jason's head.

He glanced once at the bodies of the two dead men. After the buzzards and coyotes had cleaned the bones, Nathan might bury what was left. Better yet, and more fitting, he could merely throw them over the bluff into the brush. But now he must hurry, for his foe was getting farther and farther away.

He trotted to the corrals and dropped the bars. The horses must be free to forage for themselves, because Nathan knew he might be gone for days. Perhaps he would never return, for he might be the one to die when he finally caught the last hangman.

He glanced up at the dark gray clouds that had lowered to hang just above his head. He studied their swollen black bellies. There was cold snow in them. And a lot of it. He gathered up an armload of hay from the stack near the corral and led his saddle horse to the ranch house.

The mustang fed on the hay by the door while Nathan prepared for the hunt. Shortly, he emerged wearing his wolfskin coat and carrying a packet of food and a second Colt revolver. The items were stored away in the saddlebag. His buffalo-hide sleeping robe and slicker were already tied behind the saddle. The Sharps rifle was in its scabbard.

With one yank of his arms Nathan swung astride his mount. The animal went off willingly and was soon clattering down the steep trail on the front of the bluff.

The horse forded the cold current of the Red and climbed the far bank. Nathan touched the mount with sharp spurs, and the animal broke into a ground-devouring gallop to the south, on the trail of the fleeing outlaw.

Miles of low, choppy hills and many wooded stream channels fell away behind Nathan and the running horse. Always the tracks of the outlaw's mount stretched ahead. The man must have ridden the land before, because he avoided the brush-choked breaks and the rimrocks that would have slowed his escape.

As Nathan rode down into the valley of the North Fork of the Pease River, the night caught him. The norther arrived with the night, hurling diamond ice out of the darkness to sting his face like fire. He turned up the collar of his wolfskin coat and turtled his neck down into its furry depth.

The snow quickly covered the ground and swirled around Nathan in a haze of tumbling ground currents. The tracks of the outlaw became hidden and lost beneath a blanket of white. But the loss of the sign did not slow Nathan. The knowledge the man had of the land and the frigid violence of the storm would drive him to only one destination.

The wind would blow from the north for hours. Nathan had but to hold it on his back. When he struck the main stem of the Pease River, he would turn east. A few miles downstream he would find the man and kill him.

The storm gathered madness as the night deepened. The black world was full of swift wind and flying currents of snow. The temperature fell hour by hour. Wind tears came, and turned to ice upon Nathan's cheeks. He and the horse became plastered with snow, a phantom man upon a phantom horse.

The mustang waded the rivers of streaming ground snow, flowing so deep as to reach its chest. Now and again the beast stumbled, blinded by the snow, buffeted by the hurricane winds, and weary from the long miles its master had driven it. Nathan spoke to the valiant animal, coaxing the miles from it.

He made the easterly turn along the heavily wooded Pease River. After a time he slowed, coming upon a bend of the river that he recognized. His frozen eyes stared hard out through the night and the blizzard.

In a momentary break in the wall of snow he saw a small patch of pale yellow light coming from the tiny window of a log cabin squatting in the edge of a grove of trees. This was one of Satterlee's line shacks. Nathan had once stayed there with Old Billy Valentine.

The horse came to an exhausted halt of its own volition. Man and animal sat in the lonely gloom of the snowstorm. The feeling of anger and hate at the man within the cabin ran through Nathan's mind, colder than the arctic storm that raged around him. He reined the horse to the left into the woods, dismounted, and tied the animal.

He dug the pistol from the saddlebag and checked it for the set of the lead balls against the powder and the caps on their nipples. The weapon was shoved into the waistband of his trousers. The second pistol was examined. His eyes wrestling with the darkness, Nathan stole upon his foe.

Nathan moved warily, a pistol ready in his hand. All around him the woods were full of whistling winds that made the trees buck and bow. The limbs seemed to strike at him as he crept upon the cabin.

The outlaw had traveled many miles through a driving snowstorm. Perhaps he would not be on guard, thinking his trail could not be followed and was safe. Still, Nathan was cautious, and he veered off, swung away into the night, circling the cabin.

He came downwind and smelled the sooty odor of wood smoke. Slowly continuing on, he found the makeshift pole corral behind the cabin. A single animal, its rump turned to the norther, stood within the enclosure.

Nathan stole along the wall, turned the corner, and drew

close to the only window in the cabin. The single pane of glass was rimmed with frost. He pressed close to see inside.

The cabin was small, with barely enough space for two crude cots and a table. A stone fireplace was set into the end wall. A man rested on the end of one of the cots and faced the leaping flames in the fireplace. He lifted an iron pot from the fire, removed the lid to look inside, then set it back at the edge of the fire.

Nathan recognized the bearded, hawklike face of the outlaw from the fight at Jason's grave. The pursuit was ended.

The man was armed with a pistol strapped to his side and a knife on his belt. His rifle leaned against the wall near the fireplace. A saddle lay on the floor by the door.

Nathan stepped back from the window. This was the last of the men who had murdered Jason. Now it was his time to die.

Silently Nathan moved to the door. He pulled his second Colt revolver from his belt. Both weapons were eared back to full cock. The sound was whipped away by the wind.

Strangely, just for a short heartbeat of time as Nathan prepared to kill, he felt a tinge of sadness. Not for the man, for he deserved to die. But for himself, for what he must do. Then the anger and hate that had driven him through the snow in pursuit of the outlaw welled up like a tide that washed away all thoughts except getting the hangman in the sights of his guns and pulling the triggers.

Nathan sucked in a deep breath of the snow-filled air. He raised his foot and kicked the door with all his strength.

The door sprang open, half ripped from its leather hinges, and slammed back against the wall. The latch flew across the room.

Nathan leapt into the room. His pistols swung to point directly at the outlaw.

Santell spun off the cot and into a half-crouching position. With amazing swiftness his hand snapped his pistol from its holster. He abruptly halted, his weapon only partially lifted, pointing at the floor between Nathan and himself. Santell stared into the twin black bores of Nathan's pistols, locked on his face.

Santell's eyes jumped up to look at the man holding the

guns. The man he had hung stood in front of him. "But you are dead!" Santell exclaimed.

Santell jerked himself up short. The brothers had been twins, identical twins. Nobody had told him that.

"Jason is dead," said Nathan. "Why did you kill him?"

Santell started to straighten to a standing position. The young man had not shot him at once, as he should have. There was still a chance to win this fight.

"Back down, hangman," Nathan snarled.

Santell lowered himself back to his prior half-crouched stance.

"Why did you kill my brother?" Nathan's words hit like iron.

"So there would be no one left alive," said Santell.

"And why was that so important? Why not take the cattle and go?"

"I planned to take the land too."

Nathan nodded his understanding. "So that was the reason. What did my brother say before you hung him? Did he leave a message for me?"

"There was no message for you. He told me that you would not like me if I hurt him."

"My brother told you the truth, for he did not know how to lie," Nathan said.

He pressed the triggers on both pistols. Thunder filled the confined space of the cabin. Twin plumes of flame and smoke lanced out toward Santell's face. Two round black holes appeared in the outlaw's forehead, one just above each eye.

The outlaw was hurled backward against the fireplace. He crumpled slackly to the floor of the cabin.

Nathan stood without moving, holding his pistols and watching the body of the outlaw through the tumbling gunsmoke. Then the gunsmoke was gone, sucked out the open door and between the logs of the ill-built cabin.

The pot began to boil over the fire. At the sound Nathan stirred. He grabbed the corpse by the collar and roughly dragged it outside. Unceremoniously he dumped the loose-jointed body in the snow.

Nathan raised his head and looked to the north in the

direction of Jason's grave on the high ground above the Red River. *Jason, I've taken the full measure of revenge for your murder. Now rest in peace.* Nathan knew that statement was empty. Jason would not know what revenge was. The revenge was for Nathan alone.

Nathan walked off in the snow. He returned with his horse and put it in the corral with the mount of the dead man.

After carrying his buffalo robe and saddle inside the cabin, he propped the door back into its frame to keep out the wind and snow. One of the bunks was dragged against the door to hold it in place.

Nathan spread his sleeping robe on the second bunk and pulled off his boots. Placing his pistols close to his hand, he slid into his simple bed.

As he lay listening to the cold cough of the wind around the eaves of the cabin, a sense of overwhelming emptiness and a terrible aloneness fell heavily upon him. He knew nothing of kinship other than the presence of his brother. For the twenty years of their lives, Jason had been his constant companion. In his childishness Jason saw a score of things each day that brought him to laughter. And he shared those thoughts and laughter with his brother. So different from Nathan, who seldom ever smiled. Nathan's heart yawned empty and bare.

The fire died. The cabin became black. The warmth of the sleeping robe, soft as heavy velvet, finally took Nathan off in sleep.

He awoke in the early hours of the morning, shoved aside the robe, and walked to the window. He scraped the frost off the glass and looked outside. The night lay cold as iron in the woods. Overhead, a white moon, round and frozen and wintry wan, glared down from a cloudless sky.

Nathan crawled back into his bed and again let the robe fall over his face.

---◆ **4** ◆---

Missouri River, Dakota Territory—March 6, 1859

THE NOISE OF THE RISING MISSOURI RIVER HAD grown steadily louder over the last two days. The sound was now a deep, wet rumble, like a sullen monster awakening after a long sleep.

In the winter flow of low water, the river had been full of large sandbars with the snags of trees partially buried in the stream bottom. Now the obstructions had been drowned by the swelling brown current, and the river ran nearly brim-full.

In one place on a straight mile stretch of river, a finger of land extended some two hundred feet into the current. At the extreme outer end of the projecting land a huge mass of tangled tree trunks and brush was piled against a huge cottonwood, thrown there by the river in one of its wild rampages.

DeBreen sat on the end of a log protruding from the mound of driftwood. He watched steadily upstream. The location was well suited for his need; he wanted to be as close as possible to the first rafts when they came floating down the Missouri.

The driftwood pile served a second purpose. It hid his three men, who sat on the downstream side. Speaking in low voices, they played cards with a tattered deck on a blanket. Their rifles, together with two extras, lay ready beside them.

DeBreen and his band had spent the long, cold winter trapping mink, marten, fox, and other fur-bearing animals, high in the Rocky Mountains. Heavy snow had fallen in mid-November and grew deeper day after day. By December, the men had been forced to start using snowshoes to cross the high drifts to run their trap lines. DeBreen's catch of pelts had been one of the smallest in his sixteen years of trapping.

The frigid temperatures of the winter had proven beneficial in one important way: The animals of the mountains had grown dense, luxurious coats of fur to protect themselves from the great cold. Never had DeBreen seen pelts of such excellent quality. Those they had caught would bring a premium price in St. Joe.

DeBreen felt cheated that the rich days of the beaver trade had ended just as he had gone into the mountains and begun to trap. Those were the grand days of the mountain rendezvous, when the fur buyers—bringing everything a man needed, from lead and powder to sugar and women— came to the trappers. In those times a man could earn four, five thousand dollars in a few months of trapping. Now the trap lines were twice as long, and with several species of animals to catch, the set of each trap had to be specially designed. Still, DeBreen liked his life in the mountains. With no law west of St. Joe, the rifle and knife made it possible to take what he wanted. And DeBreen was very good with both weapons.

He and his men had pulled their traps early, for they wanted to be first on the river. They had packed their furs upon the backs of the horses and fought their way down from the mountains through a driving snowstorm. With the fierce wind pounding their backs and snow frozen to the tails of the horses, the men had struck the plains.

The band headed due east, passing through the land of the Crow Indian, who liked to make war, and reached the Missouri River in ten days. A camp had been made and the horses staked out in a low swale, back from the river and hidden from view.

For the past four days DeBreen and his band had lain in wait for the weather to change. Now the sun's rays had finally gained some warmth. The snow in the mountains was melting and the spring runoff had commenced.

During the period DeBreen had trapped in the Rocky Mountains the best fur areas had moved ever farther north up the great string of peaks. He estimated there were one hundred and fifty white trappers in the mountains north of

Denver City. Sometimes he would encounter a group of them in the high valleys, or low on the broad plains, going east to the fur markets, their horses loaded with bundles of valuable pelts.

As the distance had increased between the trapping areas and the major fur-buying companies in St. Joe, some of the trappers stopped using horses to transport their catches across the plains to market. Instead they would strike out for the nearest reach of the Missouri River, and there build rafts from the plentiful logs found in the driftwood piles. Lying lazily on their crude crafts, the trappers would float their furs down to St. Joe on the head of the spring runoff from the mountains.

The Missouri River would carry them along at six, seven, sometimes eight miles per hour, faster than a horse could walk. By keeping their crafts in the center of the current and away from the banks, the men were reasonably safe from attack by Indians, the Sioux on the upper stretches and, farther down river, the Pawnee.

The river travelers were much safer than the trappers who journeyed by horseback—at least until they encountered DeBreen and his men.

"You cheated." Gossard's angry voice came from behind the pile of driftwood. "That's the only way you could have beat my hand of cards."

"Oh, hell, Gossard, you've been saying that all winter to account for your lousy playing," replied Hammler in a testy voice. "I'm getting tired of your complaining."

"I say you cheated this time for sure," retorted Gossard.

"I'll show you who cheated," said Hammler. He started to climb to his feet.

"Hammler, sit down," ordered DeBreen. "And you, Gossard, shut your mouth. I don't want any more noise out of either of you. I'll come down there and stomp the next loudmouth."

DeBreen glared down at the two men. They were becoming harder to control as the long weeks passed. To pass the time, the gang members spent much time playing cards. They had few coins or bills with which to bet. The third man, the silent Stanker, had carved wooden chips of several sizes. With values assigned to the chips, they played for each other's furs. Now Hammler and DeBreen owned nearly every pelt the group had trapped.

However, the finances of the losers, and the winners alike, would soon be immensely increased. Any day now, furs worth several thousands of dollars would come drifting past them on the river. DeBreen and his men would do a little killing and take that fortune for themselves.

Still watching Hammler and Gossard, DeBreen spoke in a surly tone. "Do either one of you want to argue with me?"

Neither man answered. DeBreen spoke again, this time in a mollifying voice. "Sound travels far across water. There could be a raft with men just up there beyond the bend of the river. Even with the water noise they might hear you. So watch yourselves."

The two men nodded reluctantly, their angry eyes turned down at the ground.

"Good," said DeBreen. "Stanker, check the loads in those two extra rifles. We may need them."

"Sure," said Stanker. He reached to pick up the nearest weapon.

Stanker was DeBreen's second in command. He had traveled with DeBreen for ten years. He went a little crazy when drunk and totally wild in a fight. However, he was the best man with a knife that DeBreen had ever encountered. Almost as skilled as DeBreen himself.

DeBreen had taken Gossard and Hammler into his band after the deaths of two prior members. The two were expendable, as every band of men must have an expendable element to throw into unknown and possibly quite dangerous situations. DeBreen hoped the men never figured out why they had been allowed to join up with him. Stanker knew. But he would never tell them.

DeBreen faced back upriver. He sat without moving. The hours slid by. Nothing moved on the two-hundred-yard-wide river except the muddy water. Once a flock of crows cawing loudly to each other flapped past overhead. The black gang drove off to the north, their raucous voices finally fading away to nothing.

The sun rolled up its ancient path, touched the zenith,

and started its long, falling trajectory toward the western horizon. DeBreen stood up and stretched, his huge chest expanding, his thick arms reaching above his head. He reseated himself and became motionless again. His slate-gray eyes, small and deeply set in bony sockets, watched the rolling water.

"Here they come." DeBreen's voice was hard yet joyous. A brown object nearly the same color as the river water had come into sight at the bend of the river. A second raft trailing the first came into view.

"All of you keep your heads down until I give the word. Pick your targets carefully and shoot every last man. Don't get in a hurry and miss. The rafts will be moving slow, and you'll have plenty of time." He knew there would be few, if any, misses. All the men were deadly with a rifle.

He glanced down at his own rifle, leaning against the log on which he sat. There should be sufficient time to reload once, maybe twice. The men on the exposed deck of the raft wouldn't have much of a chance to fight back. And no chance to survive.

The rafts steadily drew nearer, growing in size. The second one tagged along about a hundred feet behind the first. A man worked slowly and leisurely at the long arms of each of the crude sweeps used for steering, and located at the rear end of the rafts. DeBreen strained to see how many men they would have to fight.

"I count six men," said Stanker in a whisper as he peered out through an opening in the pile of driftwood. "Three on each raft. God Almighty, look at the number and size of those bales of furs! They've got ten times as much fur as we got. They musta found a virgin valley to trap."

"Quiet," DeBreen whispered back. "If the men try to hide behind the furs, shoot right through them. They won't stop a bullet."

He jumped down from the log and, leaving his rifle behind, stepped out to the very point of the peninsula, where he would be most visible. He began to wave his arms over his head. There were six men on the rafts to his four, yet a surprise attack from a protected position would more than even the odds.

"Help! Help!" DeBreen shouted in a stentorian voice. "Come get me. Indians have killed my horses. I don't have a gun."

At DeBreen's first movement the men on the rafts instantly picked up their rifles. They looked across the water at DeBreen a few seconds, and then along the riverbank. They began to call back and forth between the rafts.

DeBreen guessed the range at two hundred yards. If the rafts continued on their present courses, some of them might escape the ambush. They had to be lured closer.

DeBreen quickly stripped off his buckskin shirt. His naked body was startlingly white.

He waved the shirt in large arcs above his head. "I'm a white man," he yelled at the top of his voice. "For God's sake, help me. Don't leave me here."

The man on the lead raft vigorously began to swing his sweep. The craft started to inch across the current toward the point of land where DeBreen stood. The second raft also began to crab across the river but at less of an angle, gradually falling farther astern.

DeBreen recognized the strategy of the trappers. The men on the second raft would hold some distance off the land, and in the event of an attack they could support their comrades and fire upon the enemy. DeBreen's plan could fail.

He backed up, close to his rifle. He whispered over his shoulder. "You three shoot the men on the far raft first. Then, when all those fellows are dead, help me with the others. Do you hear me?"

"Okay. We all hear you" came Stanker's voice from the pile of driftwood.

"We're not stopping," called the man at the sweep of the closer craft. "I don't want to get pinned against the shore by the current. You'll have to swim out and climb aboard as we pass."

"I can't swim," lied DeBreen.

"Fella, that's your problem," called the man on the raft. "We're not stopping for any reason."

DeBreen studied the raft, still above the point of land and moving diagonally in his direction. It was being carried very swiftly downstream by the current. The distance was barely thirty yards.

"Come in close so that I can wade out." DeBreen brought a pleading tone into his voice. He threw a quick glance at the second raft. It had come to within a hundred yards. The men would be easy targets, every one. But the craft was nearly even with the point of land. In a moment the trappers on the river would be able to see DeBreen's men behind the driftwood pile.

DeBreen pivoted around, scooped up his rifle, and jumped behind the driftwood. He snapped up his rifle, sighted down the long barrel, and shot the man at the sweep of the nearer raft.

The man was knocked backward, his hands torn loose from the handle of the sweep. He screamed a harrowing pitch, instantly silenced as he tumbled into the rolling brown water of the river.

As DeBreen ducked down out of danger, a bullet struck the log in front of him with a savage thud. He was surprised that one of the men on the river could return his fire so quickly. Then he grinned at the crashing volley of rifle fire from his men.

DeBreen speedily reloaded as he moved to a new location behind the pile of river debris. He peered cautiously out at the first raft. A man crouched low behind a bale of furs. DeBreen raised up, thrust out his rifle, and fired. The man fell into the river with a bullet in his brain.

Three more shots rang out from his men. No answering fire came from either raft.

"They're all down, or in the river," Stanker called. He came out of hiding and stood on the narrow beach in front of the driftwood. "We got to catch the rafts or they'll soon be in St. Joe," he said.

Gossard and Hammler walked out to stand beside Stanker. DeBreen finished reloading his rifle and joined his men near the water's edge.

Only one man remained on the nearer raft. The trapper that one of DeBreen's men had shot lay flat on his back where he had fallen. On the more distant raft, a man lay draped over a bale of furs. Another hung with his legs dragging in the river. Neither moved.

"Where's the third man that was on the far raft?" asked DeBreen.

"I shot him," said Stanker. "Knocked him over the side. He never came to the surface."

"Then that accounts for all of them," said DeBreen. "Gossard, you're the best swimmer. You catch that furthest raft and bring it in to shore as fast as you can. Hammler, you get the closer one."

"That water's god-awful cold," replied Gossard. "But for all those furs I'd go into hell to get them."

Gossard and Hammler stripped off their clothing. They waded into the water to their waists.

Hammler shivered. "This is the first bath I've had in six months and it's got to be in ice water . . ." He dived into the river.

Gossard pushed out into the water until it reached his shoulders. "The current is damn strong," he said. He kicked off into the brown flow. He swam skillfully, slicing through the water with little apparent effort. He rapidly overtook the bobbing raft. He reached up to catch hold of the edge of the craft.

The man that hung over the bale of furs abruptly jumped erect and sprang across the raft. He grabbed Gossard by the hair of his head and jerked his chin up. A long skinning knife flashed as it was plunged into Gossard's throat.

The man shoved Gossard back into the water. Hastily he sheathed his knife and moved to the sweep handle.

DeBreen saw the killing of his man. One of the trappers was a trickster. DeBreen's rifle jumped to his shoulder. The range to the speeding raft was long, very long. But he would allow for that. The rifle roared.

The man on the raft spun to the side, his arms flinging out. Still spinning, he tumbled into the river. The brown current of the Missouri took him with but a ripple.

◆ 5 ◆

SAM WILDE FELT THE BULLET TEAR THROUGH HIS stomach. Then he was spinning out of control, falling. An instant later the water of the river engulfed him. Down, down he sank, a sickening blackness drawing across his mind.

Sam's muscles were like wet strings, refusing to respond to the frantic commands of his weakening mind. He could not prevent the current of the river from rolling and tumbling him with its twisting, wet current. He concentrated his last ounce of strength on fighting to hold at bay the terrible pain and invading darkness. To become unconscious was to allow the icy water to drown him.

He partially won the battle. One corner of his mind remained clear and functioning. He struck feebly upward through the slippery water that encased him in its frigid embrace. His lungs screamed for air. He reached high up, but there was only more water above his head. Then a down-dipping current caught Sam and drove him to the bottom of the river.

His feet touched the gravelly bottom and he kicked upward. He broke the surface and gulped a huge draft of the life-giving air. God! How sweet.

He hastily looked around on all sides. One of the rafts, propelled by a naked man at the sweep, was just reaching the land some one hundred yards upstream from Sam. Downriver, the decoy man ran at full speed along the bank. He came parallel to the second raft and then slightly ahead of it. He jerked off his trousers and moccasins and lunged into the river. He swam strongly in the direction of the raft.

Holding low in the water, Sam began to stroke weakly

34

toward the shore. He was in the center of the river more than a hundred yards from land. Wounded, and with the water so cold and swift, he doubted he could swim the long distance.

Sam made slow headway toward the distant, brush-covered bank. The river was all powerful, rushing speedily downstream with him. He seemed little more than part of the flotsam and jetsam that went where the river willed.

He struggled on across the tide of water. His muscles had weakened to almost nothing, sapped by the loss of blood and the water, which still held winter in its depths. Then abruptly the wild current slackened as Sam broke free and into almost still water behind a point of land.

He pulled himself out of the deep water and into the shallows. Here, the muddy fingers of the rising river swirled and flowed around the stems of the brush that grew along the edge of the shore. He tried to stand up but was too weak to rise to his feet. He crawled, wounded creature that he was, up on the bank.

He lifted his buckskin shirt. The bullet had struck him in the back just below the rib cage and had continued onward, plowing through the flesh of his stomach and tearing free at the front. He could put a finger in the hellish holes— .50-caliber at least. Blood leaked steadily from the hideous injury.

He cursed Farrow, the chief of the party, now dead, who had argued so strenuously that the trapper who called from the shore must be helped. Sam had sensed a trap and had tried to convince the others of his group not to stop. But he had been the most inexperienced of the lot and the others had not been swayed by his argument. Now they were all dead. He had seen them fall.

When the attack commenced, Sam had fired at the man who had decoyed them in toward the shore. Sam wanted to put a bullet through the white skin that had betrayed them, but the man moved too speedily. The bullet missed.

Sam had known he was doomed on the exposed deck of the raft. When the bullet had nicked him on the shoulder, he had exaggerated the tiny wound, dropping his empty rifle and falling across a bale of furs. When the robber started to crawl out of the water to take the raft, Sam had killed him. But that was only partial payment for what they had done.

Sam dragged himself a little farther from the rising river. His head dropped as total blackness caught him.

Sam slowly came to consciousness. He lay in some tall grass above the fringe of brush that bordered the river's edge. He could hear the wet, watery rumble of the river nearby. He was cold but not freezing. The westering sun, shining fully upon him, was half warm.

Cautiously he lifted his head to look around. He jerked, startled. A tall man with a long horse face stood upstream not two hundred feet away from Sam. He held a rifle ready in his hands. The man was staring toward the river and had not seen Sam raise up in the grass.

Sam immediately dropped flat and hugged the ground. If the man should come only a little closer, he could not help but spot Sam in the grass.

He felt the terrible ache in his stomach. Without rising, he twisted to look. A large patch of dirt beneath him was soaked with his blood. However, the gaping wound was now seeping only a little blood and lymph. It seemed he might have had some luck that the bullet had not struck a major vein or artery. He hoped it had not punctured his intestines. He had once seen a gut-shot man. It had taken many days full of the worst kind of pain for him to die.

Sam remained motionless watching the man through a break in the grass. He would conserve his strength until the man left. If Sam had to fight him, knife against a rifle, the outcome would be predictable.

Sam heard the thud of horses' hooves. They grew louder and louder, coming directly at him. Sam lifted his head slightly.

Two mounted men leading three packhorses loaded with bundles of furs pulled their animals to a halt. One of the men spoke to the man with the rifle. "We don't need a lookout anymore. Come and get one of these packhorses and take the furs to the raft." He gestured in the direction of the craft down river.

"Okay, I'm coming," replied the man.

The man on foot took the reins of one of the packhorses and headed along the river. The river pirates had brought their own pelts to add to the ones they had killed for. They passed well away from Sam. When the sound of the horses faded, Sam raised higher to look.

The two men had ridden up river to the second raft that was tied to a bush on the edge of the water. They began to carry the furs aboard the craft. When the last bale was loaded, and lashed down, the men removed the packsaddles and dropped them on the ground. The remainder of their possessions, saddles and other personal gear, were brought onto the raft.

One man shoved the raft away from the bank. He sprang on board as the second man began to swing the sweep to propel them out into the current of the river. The horses stood watching after the men.

Sam saw the last man load his furs and take his personal items onto the raft. He left the horses and worked his craft into the river. He joined with his comrades as they floated past.

The two crafts grew smaller and smaller until they were but mere dots upon the back of the Missouri River. The rafts vanished around a bend and were lost to view.

Sam checked the height of the sun above the horizon. The yellow ball had fallen only a couple of finger widths since he had looked at it while still on the raft. The deaths of six men and the theft of many thousands of dollars in furs had all occurred in less than an hour. He had gone from a relatively wealthy young man bound for the delights of St. Joe to a man badly wounded and a thousand miles deep in Indian country.

The four horses left behind on the river shore upstream from Sam had seen him sitting in the grass. They began to drift in his direction. Occasionally one would lower its head and crop a bite of grass. Then it would continue on with its mates.

Sam painfully climbed to his feet. He held out his hand to the horses and whistled low and soft. The closest horse, a good-looking gray animal, increased its pace toward him.

So someone has been hand-feeding you, thought Sam. "Come on, old fella," he said gently to the horse.

The gray reached Sam and began to nuzzle his fingers. Sam stroked the long bony jaw. The horse watched him with large gold-flecked brown eyes.

Sam could fashion a halter and perhaps a crude saddle out of the packsaddles left behind by the thieves. However, with his wound, it would be cruel punishment to try to ride the horse south across the plains. There was a second option. His party had passed two trappers beginning to build a raft at the junction of the Knife River and the Missouri. If the Indians did not kill the men, or they did not drown in the swift current, they should be coming downriver in two or three days. Sam had a better chance to heal lying on the raft than riding on the jarring back of the horse for days.

Could he get the men on the raft to stop for him? He grinned without humor. His skin was as white as the thief's. Sam would take off his shirt and show his skin to the men.

He pulled his skinning knife. "Sorry, old fella," he said in a sad voice. He slashed the horse across the vulnerable underside of its neck with the keen-edged knife.

The blade cut deeply into the soft neck. The white ends of the severed jugular vein showed just for an instant. Then the bright red blood throbbed out in a great crimson geyser. The hot blood fell upon Sam and the brown grass on the ground.

The gray horse screamed in agony. It spun away from the man who had hurt it so horribly. Its hard hooves threw clods of grass and dirt as it bolted. The other horses followed in a wild, snorting stampede.

Sam did not follow. The horse could go but only a short distance. He hated what he had done.

The wounded horse halted. It looked back at Sam for a handful of seconds, as if trying to understand why the man had hurt it. The blood still spouted from the gaping neck wound, jetting out with each beat of the strong heart. In the sunlight Sam could see the red stream rapidly weakening.

The dying horse splayed its legs to keep from falling. The proud head began to droop. A moment later the animal began to tremble, every muscle straining to hold the heavy body upright.

The horse fell to its knees, tried to steady itself but failed. It collapsed onto its side.

Sam made his way to the horse. Wincing with each stroke of his knife, he began to skin the animal. Blood started to flow from both the entrance and exit holes of Sam's wounds. He halted and cut a strip from the tail of his buckskin shirt. This he tied tightly around his waist to close the wounds and lessen the loss of blood.

He recommenced the skinning of the horse. It was going to be a long and difficult chore with his injury.

Near dark he finished, taking the hide only from the back, one side, and the stomach, for he could not turn the heavy body. There was one more chore to do. He cut the flesh of the horse along the backbone and took a three-foot strip of tenderloin.

With the length of meat hanging over a shoulder and dragging the wet horse hide, Sam slowly made his way down onto the point of land and out to the driftwood pile.

As darkness of night fell upon the valley of the Missouri River, the little heat that had accumulated leaked away into the sky. A chilly wind began to blow down from the north. Sam wrapped himself in the green hide, the hairy side to his body. The night would be cold.

He started to tremble, as the horse had trembled from loss of blood. The horse had died. Would he?

His trembling increased. Unconsciousness swept over him. He was falling and spinning as he plunged down into a bottomless pit of blackness.

Hours later Sam awoke fuzzy headed and weak. But he no longer trembled. He was even slightly warm. He shoved back the horsehide. The high dome of the sky arched sapphire blue overhead. The sun was halfway to its zenith.

The river had risen another three or four inches during the night. It gurgled wetly as it poured past the bank. The sound brought Sam's thirst quickly to his attention. He crawled down the river's edge and drank deeply of the muddy water.

Sam remained by the edge of the water for a time and watched upstream. There was only some brush and patches of brown foam floating on the current. Growing weary, he crawled back to the horsehide. The trappers could not yet have come this far downriver. He let himself slide off into sleep.

On the morning of the second day Sam unbound his wound. The ragged gunshot holes were red and ugly. They started to bleed slightly. He was troubled by the thought of infection. He turned to let the sun shine on the wounds.

After an hour or so, he replaced the binding around his waist. Painfully propping himself into a sitting position against a driftwood log, he watched the river for the balance of the morning. The only living thing he saw was a blue jay that flew in to perch above his head and study him with bright liquid eyes. In the afternoon a herd of forty-seven buffalo— Sam counted them as they unhurriedly filed down the riverbank—came and drank from the brown Missouri. Then they climbed back up to the level of the prairie and disappeared.

Sam tried to eat a piece of the horse meat in the late afternoon. But he spit it out. He had eaten raw meat before, and his lack of appetite was not caused by that. His body simply rejected the food. He knew he was badly hurt and might never leave the riverbank.

Those were bad thoughts. He must prepare for the future. He cut the rest of the meat into thin strips and hung them over the limbs of the cottonwood that grew close to the ground. He would have a fair supply of jerky in a few days. He would need every bit if he should have to travel overland by himself.

Sam studied the drying meat. He should have cut it for jerky the day before. He thought ruefully of yesterday. Then he was just trying to live.

On the third day Sam felt weaker and more light-headed. He thought his wound was infected. He again tried to eat a little of the half-dry horse meat but could not. He propped himself up to watch the river. Come on, somebody—anybody.

His eyes grew heavy and he fell asleep in the afternoon sun. He dreamed that the two trappers he and his partners had seen working on the raft along the river were floating by, just off the end of the point of land. They were sitting on bales of furs and looking downriver. They did not see him.

He jerked and called out in his sleep. The pain of his sudden movement brought him instantly awake. He flung a scanning look out over the river.

A raft with two men sitting on bales of fur was on the river. Sam shook his head, not believing that reality was exactly the same as his dream, that there were in truth two men on a raft on the river. One of the men idly turned to glance toward the point of land.

Sam weakly climbed erect. He gasped at the pain from his wound. Holding his stomach, he staggered to the edge of the water.

"Miller!" Sam shouted. His voice was but a croak. He tried again, raising his voice above the noise of the river. "Miller! Over here! Hey! Over here!" They must see him. He must not be left behind!

The man spotted Sam. He spoke quickly to his comrade. The second man turned to stare toward Sam.

Sam called at the top of his voice. "Miller, Stamper, it's Sam Wilde. We met upriver a few days back." He waded out into the river up to his crotch. "Stop. Pull into shore."

Stamper stepped to the sweep and vigorously began to swing it. The raft, still speeding downstream, angled across the current.

Sam watched for a few seconds longer to be certain the raft was indeed pulling in the direction of the riverbank. Then he turned and, in a stumbling walk, made his way slowly off the point of land and downstream.

The raft made shore two hundred yards below Sam. Miller hopped out and stood near the water's edge, holding the raft by a rope. Stamper climbed to the top of the bank with his rifle

"What in God's name happened to you?" Stamper asked as Sam drew near.

"River pirates. They tricked us into coming close to land and then shot the hell out of us. Everybody but me is dead. They got every fur we had."

"How long ago?" Miller called up from the river.

"Three days now."

"How many of them?" asked Stamper.

"There was four but now only three. I knifed one."

"Well, come on and get aboard the raft," Miller said. "Let's shove off. You can tell the story as we go. If they should have some trouble that slows them down, we might catch up."

Sam went down the bank and climbed out on the raft. Miller moved to the sweep. Stamper shoved them away from the bank.

Sam was dizzy from the exertion and pain. He thought he was going to faint.

"You'd better lay down," said Miller. "You look awfully peaked. How bad are you hurt?"

"Bullet in the stomach. Went clear through."

"Well, let Stamper look at it. He's doctored some bad wounds in his time and is fair at it."

Stamper snorted through his nose. "I haven't let anyone die yet," he said.

Sam stretched out on the deck of the raft. Stamper knelt beside him and removed the buckskin wrap.

"Awful bad to get shot through the guts," said Stamper, examining the wound.

"It feels like I'm burning up inside," said Sam.

Stamper's face was creased with his concern. "Just lay there and rest. It's good that I won't have to dig for a bullet. I'll get some of my herbs and make a poultice. It might take you a few tomorrows of healing before you can hunt down those fur thieves."

Sam closed his eyes. He just wanted to live to see the first tomorrow.

◆ 6 ◆

Liverpool, England—March 9, 1859

CAROLINE SHEPHERD STUMBLED, EXHAUSTED AND shivery. She had been walking for three days, from daylight to black night. For every minute of that long, dreary time, an icy, drizzly rain had fallen upon her without letup.

The watery mud came in through the holes in the sides of her shoes. It squished cold and slick between her toes and around her feet. Her thin coat and every thread of the clothing beneath, down to her skin, were soaked. The bundle on her back containing her scant belongings was heavy with the water it had absorbed. The straps Caroline had fastened to the bundle to make it easier to carry painfully cut into her bony shoulders.

She raised her eyes from the road and looked to the front along the line of plodding people that traveled with her. Not one person spoke. There was only the sloppy, sucking sound of their feet in the muddy road.

The people were part of the recent converts to the new religion, The Church of Jesus Christ of Latter-day Saints. The Mormon missionary had sent word that he was returning to America. He had asked those who could to join him on the return trip. He had promised to guide them and, with the help of the other church officials, arrange transportation. A few had decided to make the exodus from England. They had been waiting, some in nearly every town and village he would pass through along his route. He had greeted them as brother and sister, and they had replied, calling him Elder Rowley, and had fallen in behind him in the march to the sea.

Caroline had come the farthest, eighty footsore miles

from her village in the interior of the country. That distance
was barely a step in the five-thousand-mile journey that lay
before her.

In the line ahead of Caroline, a baby began to cry. A
woman's voice rose to comfort the child. The crying faded,
weakening to a whimper, then ceased altogether. Again the
only sound was the feet of the people in the mud.

"Ellen's baby is very sick," said the girl who walked near
Caroline.

"Yes. I saw it at noon," said Caroline.

"I think it may die soon. Perhaps in the rain before we
can find shelter."

"I know," said Caroline. "The missionary has told us the
ship will leave us behind if we are late." She did not want to
talk. She felt light-headed. She had spent sparingly of the
few coins she possessed, stopping but once each day at one
of the markets in the towns they passed to purchase a little
food. Still, only one sixpence remained in her pocket. However, now she and the other one hundred and fifty-six converts of the Mormon Church had finally reached the outskirts
of Liverpool. The ship that would transport them to America would be waiting.

She had already paid for her passage. The fare of six
pounds and five shillings provided for both a berth and food
for the lengthy voyage. The fare had also been purchased
for the railroad that would carry her from the east coast of
America and inland to the center of the continent. A one-
quarter ownership had been bought in something the missionary called a handcart. In that vehicle she and three
other people would haul their possessions from the end of
the railroad and across the wilderness to a place the missionary called Zion. Now she had but to endure, and in a few
weeks she would reach that wondrous land.

She looked past the trudging forms of her fellow travelers. The gray, drippy twilight of the evening was closing in
swiftly. There was hardly a discernible break where the
rain-filled sky ended and the mist-shrouded city of Liverpool began.

Somewhere there, surely not too far, they should reach
the waterfront. The Mormon missionary, Mathias Rowley,

could see the pitiful condition of the people. He would take them straight on board the ship and out of the rain and have the captain provide a warm meal for the starved folk. Caroline's step lightened somewhat at the prospect of food to fill her empty, shrunken stomach.

"Out of the way! Get off the road!" shouted the driver of the "dead wagon" hurrying along the road. He was a huge man sitting high on the wagon seat. A greatcoat protected him from the rain. He reached out and popped his whip near the face of one of the women converts, who was slow in yielding the right-of-way.

"Make way," the driver shouted again. He yanked on the reins of the lone horse that pulled the wagon. The animal leaned against the shafts of the vehicle and guided it off the road and through the line of people and in the direction of the nearby paupers' graveyard.

Caroline moved hastily aside as the wagon swung close. The bed of the vehicle brushed her clothing, and the iron-rimmed wheels missed her feet by only inches.

She cast a look into the wagon as it passed by. The bed of the wagon was crowded with eight corpses, the dead paupers from the poorhouse, and men, women, and one child, cadavers gathered up from the street, victims of disease and starvation. The wagon could haul so many corpses because they were so skinny. Not one body had a casket, not even a death wrap. They lay on their backs, their pale white faces and open, unseeing eyes turned upward into the falling rain.

"Ain't you seen dead people before, missy," the driver called down in a coarse, amused voice to Caroline.

She shuddered and did not reply. The wagon rolled on and entered the graveyard.

The dead wagon approached the two grave diggers standing and holding their shovels near the raw yellow dirt of a freshly dug trench. One of the men yelled at the driver of the wagon. "Hurry your arse so we can get this grave filled in before dark."

Caroline heard the converts moving onward along the road, but she could not prevent herself from delaying, looking into the cemetery. There were no individual graves for the dead; only a long shallow excavation half filled with water awaited the corpses. She had heard of these "poor holes" for the penniless dead of the cities. Her village, though very poor, still provided each person who died with his or her own grave. As it should be.

The driver climbed down from his seat on the wagon. "Hurry your own arses," he said to the grave diggers. "Help me put the buggers in the hole so we can get out of the rain."

The grave diggers dropped their shovels and, grabbing hold of the corpses, lifted them from the wagon. The bodies were roughly tossed into the common grave, the water splashing and then settling back to nearly submerge the still forms.

"Now cover them," said the driver, climbing back up on his seat.

The grave diggers hastily began to shovel the sodden dirt upon the corpses. The driver of the dead wagon wheeled his horse around and lashed the clumsy-footed beast out of the graveyard and into a slipping, sliding trot toward the center of Liverpool.

Caroline turned and hurried through the cold rain plummeting out of the gray heavens. As she caught up with the rear of the group of converts, she suddenly realized that not one person would have missed her had she not returned to join them. She was a stranger to all of them. Every face was turned in but one direction—to the ocean, and beyond to America.

She thought of her home and family. She was the fourth daughter of seven of a poor farmer. There, too, in that house, she would not be missed. Indeed, ever since her conversion to this new religion her father and mother had treated her as half a stranger. She thought her father wished her gone before she, in some manner, contaminated her sisters with the religion. Well, she *had* left, deciding to abandon the Anglican Church and search for a more full and prosperous life in America with the new Mormon Church.

The crowd of religious converts left the outlying area of Liverpool and entered the ancient, four-hundred-year-old congested central section. In every direction, thousands upon thousands of smoldering fireplaces in the houses, multi-story tenements, and factories belched out their smoke. The poisonous, lung-burning vapors, beaten down to the earth by the rain, lay like a murky, stagnant liquid in the narrow canyons of the streets.

The black wave of the night came stalking, and the blackness mixed with the smoke and mist to completely smother the city. Here and there a gas streetlight became visible, its flames casting a dull yellow stain on the dismal night.

The streets were deserted except for a few figures, bundled in coats and hastening along. Most carried oil lanterns to light the way. Some of the nightwalkers lifted their lanterns to stare at the muddy line of people following along behind the young missionary.

Mathias Rowley brought his religious followers onto the stone-paved quay between the row of warehouses and the piers of Liverpool. He led on, to the office of the Mersey Steamship Company, where George Cluff was to meet him. Rowley was late by several hours but he knew Cluff would still be waiting, and he would have kept the captain of their chartered ship from sailing.

Rowley smelled the salt water of the ocean and the multitude of odors coming from the docks and warehouses. He could see deck lights and distinguish the outlines of several berthed merchantmen, a mixture of tall-masted sailing ships and squat steamships. A constant creaking noise came from the docks as the vessels wallowed at their moorings.

Soon he would be sailing home on one of those ships, his four-year mission to serve his Lord and his Church completed.

On the water, bobbing lights moved as several small boats were rowed toward the shore. Off-duty sailors were heading for a night of liberty in the pubs and brothels of Liverpool. Rain would not prevent the seamen from swilling alcoholic drinks and taking their carnal pleasure with the whores.

Rowley halted at the door of the steamship company. He turned around and, raising his voice, called out, "Wait here, brothers and sisters, until I can find out which ship is ours."

Caroline shrugged wearily out of the straps of her pack. With several other people she pressed tightly against the side of the building. The overhang of the eave was just wide enough to give her shelter from the falling rain and the cascade of water falling from the roof. She closed her eyes and leaned her head on the wall. So awfully tired. Soon she would fall and not be able to rise.

The door of the office opened and Mathias and a second young man came outside to stand on the stoop in the rain. The second man carried a large, brightly flaming storm lantern. He held it up high and peered out at the group of people.

"Gather around, brothers and sisters," Mathias said, and motioned with his hands for the people to come close.

"This man is Brother George Cluff. He is our Church's representative here in Liverpool. He has given me very bad news. The ship that is to take us to America has not yet arrived and will not for another five or six days. And perhaps longer if the weather is bad."

A groan went up from the gathering of people. A woman began to sob.

"You have our money," called a man. "Get us space on another ship that is leaving right away."

"George, is that possible?" asked Mathias.

"I wish I could," said Cluff. "But we have contracted for a certain vessel. We have paid the price and can't change."

"If the ship is not here to carry out its part of the arrangement, then why can't we break the contract and buy passage on another one?" asked the man who had spoken before.

"Weather on the ocean, as on the land, can't be controlled. Our contract allows for delays in the ship's scheduled arrival and departure."

Rowley looked out at his converts. They stood hunched, their hands in the pockets of their coats and their heads pulled down between their shoulders, as if the shape of their bodies could ward off the cold rain. They wore but the flimsiest of clothing. He felt a deep sorrow for them.

His proselytizing in England had gone better than his greatest expectations. He had converted three thousand and forty-one people to his religion. However, he did not mislead himself. His strong belief in his calling helped him to sway the men and women to accept his religion. But there was a more important reason for the large number of conversions. England was a land of wretched poverty and famine, and the price of provisions was sinful. There was also much oppression from the priestcraft, and a terrible inequity in land ownership. The people wanted—nay, searched desperately—for something better than what they had. Still, only about one in twenty of his converts, often the most destitute, had the courage and will to tear up their roots and follow him to America. That will and courage would be sorely tested if they were to survive the tremendous hardships that lay ahead.

Most of the faces staring back at him were those of very young women, some hardly more than girls. The females were the easiest to sway from their prior belief. They would gaze into his face as he told them about his religion, and their eyes would widen to his words and they'd agree to be baptized in the name of the Lord so they could enter his Church. The young men were very difficult, and often belligerent. Of the one hundred and fifty-seven people there in the rain, one hundred and nine were young, unmarried women. The remaining were married couples, several with children.

The sight of his wet and hungry converts stirred Mathias. He lifted his handsome head and thrust his hands high in the air. "Brothers and Sisters, I have brought you bad news. But do not despair. Ye all have felt the calling to come to the True Church for your salvation and to gather together and journey with me. And I shall lead you to the most joyous place upon the face of the earth. The glory of the Lord shall be there, and it is called Zion. It is a place of promise, and that City of Zion is on the shore of the great salt lake in the heart of the mountains in the land called America. That country surely has been reserved by the Almighty as a sure asylum for the poor and oppressed. There ye shall be in the Kingdom of God on Earth."

A chorus of amens came from the crowd. There was a movement of the people and a nodding of heads.

"Now Brother Cluff has some different news," said Mathias.

"I have reserved all the rooms of a boardinghouse for you," Cluff said. "The charge is one shilling for a bed and a meal. That is a fair price. Those of you with a family will have to double up in the beds. If you will follow me, I'll lead you there. It is just a few blocks from here."

Cluff and Rowley moved off with the lantern. The people fell in at their rear, crowding each other, trying to hang close so that they could walk in the light of the lantern.

Caroline remained standing under the eave of the building. She felt betrayed and dismayed. She could not go with the others, for she had no shilling. And she would not beg.

The darkness thickened and congealed around her as the lantern moved farther and farther away.

7

THE BREEZE COMING OFF THE NORTH SEA cut through Caroline's wet, almost useless clothing. She was cold to the very core. Her teeth started to chatter and she clamped her jaws together to quiet them.

She had to find shelter, a place to sit, hopefully to lie down. She wearily pulled on the pack and moved out into the rain. Dejectedly she walked back the way she had come.

The buildings loomed above her. Now and then, the dark form of another person caught out in the night went by her in the darkness. A horse-drawn cart lumbered past.

As she passed in front of an alehouse, the door was flung wide and a man stepped outside. He halted, staggering slightly. He saw Caroline in the light coming from the open door.

"Well, little lady, you're out in god-awful weather to hope to find any business. But you're in luck. I haven't had a girl tonight. So come inside. There's a room in the rear the owner will let us use. There's no bed, but we can unroll your mattress on the floor." The man winked and crooked his finger for her to come with him.

Caroline began to back away from the drunken man. She knew what he meant. She had heard of the girls who walked the streets of the cities and carried thin, rolled mattresses or pieces of carpet on their backs. In any half-hidden place they could lie down and earn a coin.

"Wait, don't go," said the man. "I'll give you a shilling for five minutes of fun." He dug a handful of coins from his pocket and jingled them in his hand. "A whole shilling," he said, chuckling. "That's a fair price for a street girl."

Caroline was in the edge of the light and retreating speedily. She would not beg for a shilling, nor would she whore for one. She spun around and hastened off along the street.

"Go on, you little slut." The man's angry words chased after Caroline. "You're too damn dirty, anyway. And so skinny, it'd be like laying on a bag of bones."

Caroline welcomed the concealing darkness of the night. Her heart throbbed against the ribs of her chest like a frightened bird beating itself on the bars of a cage. She looked back. The man was still standing and staring after her.

She slowed as her fright lessened, and walked wearily onward.

Half a block ahead, a square of lamplight from a window fought with the rainy gloom of the night. As she came even with the window she glanced inside. Several loaves of bread lay on a table. A bakery.

Nobody was within sight inside. There was only the golden brown, round, or rectangular loaves of bread on the display table. And some sweet rolls piled in a precise little pyramid. The sprinkle of sugar on the rolls was like a thin covering of snow.

Caroline tried the door, but it would not open. The bakery was closed and locked for the day. As she started to turn away, she felt a warm draft of air escaping around the ill-fitting door. She pressed her face to the crack and breathed the heated air into her lungs. Riding on the air was the delicious aroma of bread and sweet rolls and tangy cinnamon.

She removed her pack and sat down in the shallow alcove

of the doorway. She pulled her feet in out of the rain. Leaning against the door, she closed her eyes. A weary, drugged sleep overtook her almost at once.

Caroline awoke as she fell. Her head struck the floor of the bakery with a thump.

"Girl, are you hurt?" cried the baker. He set the candle lantern he held in his hand on the floor and knelt quickly beside Caroline.

"What happened?" asked Caroline. She sat up rubbing her aching head.

"You fell inside when I opened the door to go out," said the baker. "What were you doing there?"

"Trying to sleep. I'm very sorry to have caused you trouble." Caroline climbed shakily to her feet.

She looked at the baker as he stood erect beside her. He was old, his hair white. At the moment his brow was furrowed with a hundred wrinkles of worry and astonishment. Somehow he seemed familiar to Caroline. Yet she had never seen him before.

"I'll get my belongings and leave," she said.

The baker stared at the young woman. She was gaunt, her bones showing painfully sharp through her white skin. Her large green eyes were sunken deeply in their sockets. Exhaustion and cold pinched her face.

Wet mud covered her to her knees. Both of her shoes gaped open along the soles. Her hair was a wet, tawny tangle hanging to her shoulders.

But it was the color of the eyes that held the old baker's attention. And the way she looked at him so piercingly, as if trying to read his innermost thoughts. The eye color and the expression on her face brought back memories from long ago. Sad memories that squeezed his heart, memories that he never wanted to forget.

His daughter would look at him in that manner, wanting to anticipate his wishes before he spoke. When he told her what he wanted, she would smile and run, laughing, to do his bidding in the bakery or to go down the street to run an errand for him.

How many years had it been since her death? Thirty-five,

maybe thirty-six. Time passed so swiftly now in the last years of his life.

His wife had died at the birth of their daughter. From that day on, the baker had put all his love into the growing girl. Then, at the age of ten, the plague had taken her. She had died in the evening while it was raining. Like the rain tonight. Was that a sign?

Caroline gathered up her pack and slipped her arms through the straps. She cast a last look at the baker. "I'm truly sorry that I bothered you," she said.

The baker felt his heart jump. There was his daughter's look again from those green eyes. Could it be possible? Tales were told of instances where the souls of those who died young and innocent were born again in a new body. Had that happened here? Was his daughter a joint resident within this girl's body?

"Your eyes are green," the baker said. "I once knew another girl with green eyes."

Caroline fastened her sight on the old man, wondering about the meaning of the strange, hopeful expression on his face.

"And so are yours," Caroline answered.

"Are there two of you?" asked the baker.

"I don't understand. What do you mean, two of us?"

"Nothing. Nothing," said the baker quickly. "Where will you go in the rain?"

"I don't know. Maybe I'll find another doorway to sleep in."

"Would you want to stay here? It is quite warm because of the oven." He gestured at the big brick oven occupying one end of the small bakery.

"What is your name?"

"Caroline Shepherd."

"Well, Caroline Shepherd, my name is John Bradshaw. You are most welcome to stay here," said the baker. "I mean you no harm. I can give you some blankets and you could sleep there on the floor by the oven. It'll stay warm all night. However, I do have to rise early to start baking for the new day."

Caroline glanced out the open door. The rain streaked

down cold and wet in the lamplight. She shivered at the sight. Could she survive the night out there? She looked back at the oven and then at the baker.

"It would be very pleasant to have someone to talk with," said the baker encouragingly. "I have a potato and some meat left from supper. I can warm that in the oven. And I believe I can find some cheese, and of course there is bread and cake." He smiled in a hesitant, uncertain manner.

"Why are you so generous to me?" Caroline asked.

Because you are so like my long-dead daughter, thought the old man. *And, oh, I'm so terribly lonely.*

He spoke. "Because we green-eyed people are few in number and we must stick together." He tried to keep the sadness out of his voice.

"Yes, we green-eyed people must help each other," agreed Caroline. She began to take off her pack.

The baker smiled broadly. He closed the door against the cold rain.

"I'll heat some food for you. While I'm doing that you are welcome to take a bath." He pointed at an inside doorway. "Just through there is a bathtub. It sits against the rear of the oven. The water will be warm. Take a bath and then come and eat."

"That is a most kind offer, and I accept."

"Here, take this," said the baker, and handed the candle-lantern to Caroline. "This will light your way. You will find soft soap in the jar on the floor beside the tub."

"Thank you," said Caroline.

She went through the door and found the rectangular metal tub sitting with one of its long sides touching the back of the oven. She dipped her hand into the water. It was wonderfully warm.

Caroline took a clean dress from her pack and hung it on a nail she found driven into the mortar between the rows of bricks. The garment was a much-worn thin cotton. Near the oven, the dress would partly dry while she bathed. She stripped and stepped into the tub. The touch of the water on her skin was a caress that made her tremble with delight.

She soaked, her cold feet tingling as they warmed. After a time her hunger and tiredness drove her from the bath. She dried her body and hair and slipped into the dress. She glanced once at the muddy, dilapidated shoes, and shook her head. Barefoot, she padded out to the kitchen just off the bakery.

"Your food is ready," said the baker.

Caroline looked at the table. She almost cried out with pleasure. Two whole potatoes and a slice of meat as large as her hand was on a plate. A wedge of cheese and a half loaf of bread lay beside it. One of the little sweet rolls from the window was there for dessert. Her mouth moistened in anticipation.

"Would you want cider or wine?" asked the old baker.

"Cider, thank you."

"Cider it shall be."

Caroline ate, chewing slowly, savoring every morsel of the food. Her tongue delighted in the flavor and texture of the meat, the crust of the bread, and the coarse, chunky cheese. She sipped some of the cider, letting it glide cool and fragrant down her throat.

The baker could not help but smile at the expression of rapture on the girl's face. And the beauty of her, for what could be more enchanting than a freshly scrubbed young woman with green eyes who just might possess his daughter's soul within her.

Caroline reached up and tucked her damp hair back behind her ears. The baker's breath caught at the gesture. His daughter used to do that after a bath. The baker felt his certainty increase.

Caroline finished eating. It seemed that the moment she swallowed the last bite, her eyelids began to droop. She tried vainly to hold them open. "I'm so sleepy," she said.

"Don't fall," said the baker. "I can have your bed fixed in a jiffy."

He hastened into the adjoining room and returned immediately. He spread a heavy comforter on the floor near the base of the oven.

"Come and lie down," he said.

Caroline did as the old man bid, sinking down and stretching out. Her eyes closed tightly. She felt a cover being placed over her. She slipped away in the slumber of sheer exhaustion.

"Rest well, my daughter," said the baker.

Caroline only mumbled. The baker smiled and picked up the lamp. He glanced once more at the girl who had fallen out of the storm and into his life. Then he silently left the room.

As the night wore on, the storm intensified, strong winds driving heavy rains in off the North Sea. Caroline woke when a brittle burst of raindrops rattled noisily on the pane of glass in the front window of the bakery. She jerked to a sitting position. Was she dreaming? Was the warmth false and but a prelude to freezing to death? Her hand shot out in the darkness to press on the bricks of the oven, just to be certain they were there. The bricks were real and warm, and she was fully awake.

She sank back down on the comforter and pulled the blanket up snugly under her chin. She said her nightly prayers, which she had neglected earlier when she had fallen asleep, thanking the Lord for his blessing this night.

"Thank you too," she said softly to the old bakerman somewhere out there in the darkness of the house.

She slept.

8

THE TWO RAFTS, HEAVILY LOADED WITH BALES of furs, rose and ducked as they swept downstream on the rolling waves of the swollen Missouri River. On the lead raft, DeBreen swung his sweep to halt the beginning spin of his craft. He scanned the flat plains on the west side of the river and the hills on the east side. The land was familiar.

The gray smoke from the fires of St. Joseph became visible first, rising up in scores of columns above the bleak, leafless trees covering the hills. A mile later the city itself came into DeBreen's view.

"Stanker, let's take the rafts in closer to land," DeBreen called across the yellowish-brown stretch of water separating the two river craft.

"Right," Stanker replied.

Both men worked the long arms of their wooden sweeps and in the next half mile had driven the laden rafts out of the swift current of the Missouri and into the sluggish eddies along the shore. They turned the clumsy crafts and, skimming the bank, drifted down upon the city.

St. Joseph sprawled along the east shore of the Missouri for three miles. The city, though barely twenty years old, had a permanent population of nine thousand people. It had outgrown the cove's flat land that had once been called St. Michael's Meadow and now overflowed onto the surrounding hills. The large whitewashed homes of the wealthy were like late-winter snowdrifts upon the highland.

More than twenty large steamboats were tied up at the two miles of rickety wooden docks that stretched along the river. Some of the steamboat captains had been unwilling to trust the docks to hold their vessels against the strong current of the Missouri and had run lines onto the land, where they were tied to the trunks of trees.

A broad-beamed ferry, its decks full of wagons, draft animals—and men, women, and children—was pulling away from the shore. A second ferry, nearly empty, was docking. The railroad coming from the east ended at St. Joseph. Immigrants and traders, bound outward to the plains, organized their wagon trains on the far side of the river opposite the town.

As the rafts floated past the landings DeBreen looked ahead, reading the signs stating the owners of the piers. At last he shouted at Stanker and pointed at a pier extending seventy-five yards or more along the shore. "That's Crandall's landing. Make for it."

Both men began to swing their sweeps. The blades bit strongly into the river water. Carried by the current, the rafts angled down on the dock.

"Hammler, stand ready with the rope," DeBreen said.

"I'm ready," replied Hammler, coiling the rope in his hand.

DeBreen's raft closed the gap and bumped the dock. Hammler instantly leapt ashore. He threw two quick hitches of the tie rope around a wooden piling.

DeBreen stepped ashore and cast a quick look to see how Stanker was faring in landing his craft. As DeBreen looked, Stanker reached the shore and jumped onto the dock to snub the second raft down. It swung in to lay against the dock.

"Well done," called a man who had watched the landing from the high seat of his freight wagon. "Do you need any hauling done? I'm empty and available."

"I'll give you two dollars to haul my furs up to Crandall's," replied DeBreen.

"That's a fair price and agreeable to me," said the driver. He wheeled his team and brought the wagon alongside DeBreen's raft, which lay closest.

"Ain't you DeBreen?" asked the driver.

"Yes. Why do you ask?"

"No special reason. Just thought I recognized you from that fight last summer in Garveen's Saloon. You sure did slice those two fellows up real nice."

"That was a good fight," said DeBreen. "Help us load the furs on your wagon."

"Sure," said the driver. He climbed down over the front wheel of his wagon to the ground.

The driver stopped and surveyed the bales of pelts stacked on the rafts. "That's the biggest catch of furs I've ever seen at one time," he said. "Did you fellows trap all of them yourselves?"

"What the hell's it to you?" DeBreen growled angrily. "I hired you to haul my furs up the hill. Now shut your trap and earn your two dollars."

"Yeah. Sure. I didn't mean anything," the driver hastily replied. He stepped aboard the raft, hoisted a bale of pelts, and carried it to the wagon.

The four men quickly transferred the furs. DeBreen stalked off ahead up the slanting grade of Francis Street. Stanker and Hammler climbed aboard the wagon as it fell in behind DeBreen.

"Pull up there in front of Crandall's Fur & Hides," DeBreen said, directing the driver. "Stanker, you and Hammler wait here until I see if Crandall's buying."

DeBreen turned and looked along Main Street, lined with two- and three-story brick, stone, and wood-frame buildings crowding each other wall against wall. He checked the faces of the men moving on the sidewalk and the occupants of the red-and-white omnibus coming from the waterfront. He had made enemies in St. Joe. That did not worry him, but it did make him cautious.

He saw nobody he knew and turned back to Crandall's. The huge building stretched for half a block along the street. The structure housed not only Crandall's Fur & Hides but also his large general mercantile store. The remaining portion of the block was an open yard full of canvas-covered, Pittsburgh-built wagons. A large sign proclaimed it to be CRANDALL'S OUTFITTING COMPANY. The fur buyer was a prosperous businessman.

Albert Crandall saw the men and wagon halt on the street in front of his building. He remembered the trapper DeBreen, a surly man given to fits of savage violence. He was a most difficult person to do business with; however, he always came back from the mountains with many furs. Tales were told that the man was a river pirate and murderer. Crandall believed it. No charges had ever been brought against DeBreen, but then what happened out on the plains or in the wilderness of the mountains had little meaning to the law, which had jurisdiction only in the city.

DeBreen pushed open the door and came inside. "Hello, Crandall," he said.

"Hello, DeBreen," Crandall said, returning the greeting.

"I've got a few bales of pelts to sell. Are you buying?"

"I'm always in the market if there are good furs to buy."

"I've got the very best furs you'll see come out of the mountains this year," said DeBreen.

"Then let's examine them."

DeBreen started to turn around, then halted when he

noticed the young woman working over ledgers at a desk on
the far side of the room. He recognized Ruth Crandall,
daughter of the fur buyer. She was even more beautiful than
DeBreen remembered from the previous autumn. He felt
the surge of hot blood that a desirable woman always sent
through his big body.

Ruth raised her head and saw DeBreen watching her. His
wide, round head was cocked in her direction. The gray
eyes, staring out from the deep sockets under the heavy
black eyebrows, seemed to be prying into her. His body was
tensed within his filthy buckskin clothing, as if he were
ready to charge across the room and pounce upon her. The
lust in the man was a palpable thing, ageless and frightening.

Ruth hastily dropped her head. She dipped her pen in the
inkwell and began to write in the ledger.

DeBreen chuckled low in his beard. He enjoyed seeing
women react to his thoughts alone, no word spoken. But
now there were furs to be sold. Later the pleasures offered
by St. Joe would be taken in great quantities.

DeBreen called out the door to Stanker and Hammler,
"Bring the pelts inside."

One hour slid past, and then another, as Crandall and
DeBreen sat on opposite sides of the long counter and
inspected the pelts. They discussed the softness, density,
and length of the hair of each skin, and the care with which
the skins had been scraped of the flesh and then dried. They
dickered over the value until an agreement was reached.
Crandall kept a running tally sheet of the species from
which the fur came, and the price.

The last fur was sold and laid aside. Crandall added the
prices on the tally sheet and recorded the total.

"Your furs have brought twenty-eight thousand dollars.
That is the largest amount I've ever paid for the winter
catch of three trappers."

You mean, the work of ten men, thought DeBreen. He
believed some explanation should be given to allay the
suspicion of the experienced fur buyer as to why three men
had so many furs. He said, "There were four of us. Gossard
got killed. And we took several pelts from some Indians we
came on to."

Crandall knew DeBreen was lying about taking part of the furs from Indians. Crandall's practiced eyes had seen many thousands of furs, some skinned and cured by Indians and others by white men. The professional white trapper was the very best in taking care of his pelts. He thought all of DeBreen's had received the handiwork of skilled white men.

Crandall kept his face impassive and said nothing. He did not want to risk a violent confrontation with the man. To accuse, or even to hint that he was a thief, would bring an instant challenge to a duel. No one had ever won against DeBreen. Besides, Crandall did not care whether or not the furs were stolen.

"I'll write you a bank draft on the Merchant and Trader's Bank, located just down Main Street. It's still open and you can get your money today."

"Write the bank draft," DeBreen said impatiently. "There's whiskey to drink, cards to play, and pretty women to make love to."

"Hammler, your share is thirty-five hundred dollars," DeBreen said. He counted bills and gold coins into the man's outstretched hand.

"I should get some of Gossard's share," said Hammler. "He can't claim it from hell."

"Bullshit!" exclaimed DeBreen. "You've got what I promised you and that's all you're gettin'."

Hammler opened his mouth to argue with DeBreen. Then he saw the threatening expression on the big man's face. "Oh, hell, I'll be broke by the end of the summer even if I had *all* the money the furs brought." He hustled off down the street.

DeBreen and Stanker watched Hammler's retreating back. Then Stanker spoke. "What do you want to do about him?"

"Kill him," DeBreen said. "We don't need him anymore."

"I like the idea. I don't want to get hung for something he might tell."

"Do you want to do it?" asked DeBreen.

"Sure. I can use his money."

"Do it tonight."

"Okay."

"Good. Your share of the fur money is seven thousand dollars, plus a quarter of Gossard's."

Stanker's hand closed tightly on the money when DeBreen finished counting. "Now I'm going to find that widow woman and see if she's still got my clothes saved for me."

"She's probably thrown them in the street and taken up with another man," DeBreen said.

Stanker laughed. "Doesn't make a whole lot of difference," he said. "I'd simply cut the bastard into ribbons with my knife, slap the woman around some, and then everything would be back the way it was when I left."

DeBreen registered at the three-story, one-hundred-ten-room Patee House, located at Twelfth and Pennsylvania Streets. He retrieved his large leather-and-wood trunk from the hotel storage. Then, kneeling in the lobby in his dirty buckskin, he dug a black suit and hat from the trunk. He handed the clothing to one of the young bellhops.

"Take this suit and get it pressed, and have the dents blocked out of the hat." He flipped a silver dollar, and then a second, at the bellhop.

The young bellhop expertly caught the coins.

"One is for you and one for the presser," DeBreen said. "Wait for him to finish, then bring everything back to me by the time I take a bath."

"Yes, sir," said the bellhop.

The trapper swiftly stepped forward, and his long arm snaked out to catch the bellhop by the shoulder. The bellhop winced in pain as DeBreen clamped a powerful hold on him.

"You've taken my money. Now be back before I'm ready for my clothing or I'll give you a thump on the side of your head that you won't soon forget." The trapper's lips smiled, but his eyes didn't. He released his hold.

The bellhop rubbed his bruised shoulder. Then, clutching DeBreen's clothing, he sped away at a trot.

"Bring one of those portable bathtubs up to my room," DeBreen told the second bellhop. "Fill it with five full buckets of hot water. Do it now." He flipped the boy a dollar.

DeBreen closed and latched the trunk. Hoisting it to his back, he went across the lobby and up the stairs to his room.

He soaked in the large tub of hot water and lazily looked at the ceiling. He would spend a month, maybe two, in St. Joe. Then he would catch the train to St. Louis, or a river packet down the Missouri to the Mississippi and on to New Orleans. Either of those grand cities would provide entertainment for him until autumn, when he would return once again to St. Joe to outfit himself and head off to the mountains.

The bellhop came with DeBreen's clothing. He sighed in relief when he saw the trapper still in the tub. He placed the suit and hat carefully on a chair and hastily left.

DeBreen dried off, then dressed in the freshly pressed suit. He took a black shiny pair of boots from the trunk and pulled them on. The hat was set on his head at a jaunty angle. The dirty, torn buckskin shirt and pants, together with the worn moccasins, were thrown in a pile on the floor.

He returned to the front of the hotel. "Go take the tub out of my room," he told the first bellhop. "Burn the buckskin clothing."

"Yes, sir," said the bellhop, who went sprightfully off toward the stairs.

DeBreen walked out to the sidewalk. The day had ended while he bathed, and dusk was crowding in from the east to fill the streets. He went off toward Garveen's Saloon, his shoulders squared and rolling in a swaggering, pugnacious motion. He laughed in the full knowledge of his strength and the joy of anticipation of the pleasures the night would bring.

9

THE SUN WAS A FLAMING FIREBALL BURNING DOWN on the flat prairie that stretched away from Sam Wilde without end in every direction. The yellow orb was impossibly close to him, hanging overhead within easy reach. He would knock the damn hot sun back into its proper place in the high sky.

He started to lift his arm to strike, but it would not move. He strained mightily; still, he could not budge the arm from where it rested on the ground. Oh, hell, he thought, and ceased his effort to hit the sun.

He stared around. He lay on the prairie on his back with the shriveled buffalo grass standing motionless all around. Strangely the blades of grass cast no shadow in the bright sunlight. Sam marveled at that oddity.

His clothing was soaked with the sweat that boiled out of every pore of his skin. The salty brine was puddled in the sockets of his eyes, and he felt the sting of the salt on his eyeballs.

Sam could not move the sun farther away, but he could at least turn to keep the sweat out of his eyes. He started to roll to his side. Instantly something caught him by the shoulders and pressed him back down.

Sam struggled against the restricting force. But it was always stronger than he, increasing to match his strength, and then more.

He felt the edge of a growing panic. He summoned all his energy and tried to rise. His shoulders cleared the ground hardly an inch before they were shoved down.

"Easy, Sam," a woman's gentle voice said. "Don't fight. You're all right."

Sam halted in amazement at the sound of the female voice. There was somebody with him on the prairie. A woman who could talk but could not be seen.

"Can you hear me, Sam?" The woman's voice came again. "Lay still or you will tear open your wounds."

Sam began to chuckle at the thought of an invisible woman holding him down on the ground. Was he going crazy? His chuckle increased as he contemplated being an insane man.

A moment passed and the woman spoke again. "Doctor, I believe his fever is starting to break."

"Keep bathing him down with the cold water," a man's voice said.

The force that had held Sam was removed. The wonderful coolness of a damp cloth was placed on his forehead. Then someone began to bathe his chest and arms.

A fresh cold cloth was laid on Sam's forehead. The delightful coolness penetrated his skull and caressed his feverish brain. The flaming yellow sun began to withdraw, spiraling swiftly upward, diminshing to a tiny, twinkling star in the far-distant reach of the heavens. The wild hallucinations were gone and reality came flooding in.

Sam opened his eyes. Everything around him was blurred, formless. He squinted to see, concentrating on something hovering over him. His eyes came into focus. A heavyset, middle-aged woman was looking down at him.

"Hello," Sam said in a cracked, raspy voice.

"Hello, yourself," the nurse said. She looked closely at Sam. "Can you tell me your name?"

"Sam Wilde." He could barely whisper, for his throat was dry as dust.

The nurse smiled brightly. "Exactly right." She looked across Sam. "Doctor, our patient seems clearheaded."

"So I see," said the doctor.

Sam rolled his eyes to look in the same direction as the nurse. An elderly, stooped-shouldered man stood on Sam's other side.

"I'm Dr. Byington," said the man. "And she is Nurse Hanson. Welcome back to the land of the living."

"The land of the living is a good place to be," Sam replied. His head felt woolly and he wished he could talk

louder than a whisper. "I'm pleased to meet both of you.
Where am I?"

"In the hospital in St. Joe. Two trappers brought you in."

"So Miller and Stamper got me here. How long ago was
that?"

"More than a week," said the doctor.

"Nine days to be exact," Nurse Hanson added.

"Nine days," Sam said in surprise. He remembered none
of the stay in the hospital, nor the last days that had passed
while he floated down the Missouri with the trappers.

"I'm awfully thirsty," Sam said.

Nurse Hanson immediately stepped to a nearby stand and
poured water from a pitcher into a glass. She offered it to
Sam.

He lifted his hand to take the glass, and stopped in sharp
surprise. The skeleton hand could not be his. The thing was
nothing but skin stretched over bones. "What has happened
to me?" he asked, turning his hand to view it from several
angles.

"You have been feverish and delirious for a very long
time," the doctor said. "You almost starved to death."

"How bad is my wound?"

"You should have died with a wound that completely
passed through your body, and that was made worse by a
terrible infection. Both the entry and exit holes have healed
closed. But there is a lump in your stomach. I think a very
large cyst is developing, one that is full of pus and the
leakage from an intestine that was punctured by the bullet."

Sam felt of the hard object. It was as large as two fists and
bulged up the skin. "Will I live?" he asked.

"Perhaps. Unless the cyst continues to grow and ruptures
and poisons you. Now you must begin to take nourishment.
An important factor will be whether or not your stomach
can handle food."

Sam noted the doubtful expression on Dr. Byington's
face. He had said Sam should have died. But he had not.

"I'll not die," Sam said. He took the glass of water from
the nurse and drank every drop.

"Nurse, bring Sam clear broth, but just a little," directed
the doctor. He spoke to Sam. "Eat very sparingly at first.

You have a very long ways to go before you'll be completely healed."

"Give him laudanum if he has pain," said Dr. Byington as he walked from the room.

Sam slowly sipped the half cup of beef broth Nurse Hanson brought him. Simply holding the cup sapped his strength. He finished and lay back. "Thank you," he told her.

"You are very welcome," the nurse said, and left.

Sam rolled his head to look around. He was in a room by himself. He must have been a very noisy patient because of his fever, and had been isolated from others. Half asleep and half unconscious, he floated away on a giant black wave.

Sam awoke with a fire raging within his stomach, as if a blacksmith's forge was stoked to the limit there with red-hot burning coals. He clamped his jaws to keep from screaming. The doctor may have been correct that Sam's intestines had been injured by the thief's bullet. He felt a foreboding that he might yet die.

But if he died, then the men who had murdered his comrades and shot him would go unpunished. That must not be allowed to happen.

"Nurse Hanson, bring me some laudanum," Sam called.

He heard hurrying footsteps approach along the hallway. Then the nurse's lamp was floating toward his bed.

The days, stretching endlessly for Sam, had crawled into another week. A burning pain rose in his stomach within hours each time he ate. The nights after the evening meal were the worst, his sleep cruel, even with the potent narcotic circulating in his blood.

After one especially bad night he surfaced to wakefulness and lay listening to the black wind moaning along the street just outside his window.

He turned his head so that he could look out the window of his room. The hospital had been built on a high bluff above the Missouri River. In the deep darkness the river was invisible. He could see the lights of several of the nearer steamboats tied up at the wharves. The small points of light faded at times, as if they were losing their battle to hold the darkness at bay.

Sam felt that the ebb of his lifetide was something like the lights of the steamboats, struggling to hold a place in the universe and not be shredded to nothingness. His recent luck had been bad. However, he had no regrets as he reflected upon the events that had put him on the Missouri River and in front of the rifles of the thieves. That had been arranged by Old Man Fate and nothing more. He had freely chosen the frontier, leaving his father's farmstead in Pennsylvania and traveling west. Danger went with that decision.

Nor did Sam have regrets about joining with Farrow and his band of trappers. He grinned as he recalled that he had earned only a one-quarter share that first winter trapping pelts in the Rockies. He had learned from that rowdy, tough band of men how to set a trap, skin an animal, to track and shoot with the best of them. Coming down from the mountains in the spring of that first year, the group had been attacked by Blackfoot Indians. Sam had killed two men that day and grew from boy to man. There had been more battles during the next four years, and Sam had brought death to other men. Now he lay on the threshold of being one of those who died.

The swiftly flowing Missouri came out of hiding as the morning dusk arrived. Sam could see the west end of the Blacksnake Hills, which lay north of St. Michael's Meadow. He recalled the legends of the hills. Before the white man came, the Indians forbade bloodshed and weapons there because several tribes believed that God once dwelt on the hills, making the soil sacred. Ailing Indian chiefs of the different tribes were brought great distances by travois to die there. They would be buried on the summits of the hills facing west over the valley of the Great River. The sunsets from the hills were so fine that the Indians believed the rays of the setting sun provided an invisible bridge over which the souls of the departed took a direct road to the next world. This place, called Wah-Wah-Lanawa, was holy, a place of peace and plenty, a refuge and a sanctuary. The Platte Indians acted as custodians of the Blacksnake Hills until the white man crowded them out and built homes on the sacred hills.

Sam rested, dozing. When he again looked, enough light had come streaking in from the east to allow objects to throw off their colorless night shades of gray and show their true hues. The river was still high and running a muddy brown.

As daylight brightened, a certain amount of satisfaction came to Sam. If he died within the next few hours, it would be in the sunlight of a day and not the sour darkness of night. And if he died at sunset, he might see the Indians' road to the next world.

Sam watched the activity of the riverfront increase. Many wagons came and lined up in a long string on Francis Street, awaiting their turns to be ferried across the Missouri. Children played around the high, spoked wheels of the vehicles. Men and women had congregated in groups and stood talking.

A side-wheeler ferry arrived from the west shore. It tooted its steam whistle three cheery notes as it landed and dropped its gangway onto the dock. The knots of immigrants split, and the people began to move to their wagons. A group of black slaves stirred. Missouri had been a slave state since 1821. The men picked up heavy loads of lengths wood and carried them aboard. The fuel was stacked near the boiler and the blacks filed off the ferry.

The whistle tooted again and the line of wagons inched forward as eight of them were driven onto the ferry. The ferry pulled away from the dock and tackled the swift Missouri again. Sam envied the people on the ferry.

Noontime came and Sam ate a little food. He took a dose of the laudanum and slid off into a troubled, jerky sleep. He dreamed he was slashing the throat of the gray horse, and the red blood was pumping out to splash upon the ground. In his dream state his sorrow for the dying horse made him cry. The crying made his wound ache terribly.

Sam came awake to the whispering voice of Nurse Hanson from near the door. "Dr. Byington, do you think he will recover?"

"I see no sign of that," the doctor replied in an equally low tone. "He may well die."

"That's too bad," the nurse said in a sad voice. "He seems like such a nice young fellow."

Sam kept his eyes closed as the doctor and nurse moved away. The words of the doctor, pronouncing his probable death, careened around his mind like ricocheting bullets. He turned to look out the window, to see all the life and activity just beyond the glass.

The two ferryboats were meeting in mid-river. Each sent a blast of steam-driven noise at the other. The endless stream of wagons was still lined up on Francis Street. The wood-carrying slaves sat waiting. Two boys were chucking rocks into the water of the river.

Sam knew he must go and join the living, and do it now.

If he was to soon die, then he must find the murderous fur thieves and kill them now. He steeled himself for the pain he knew would come when he sat up. He slid a leg toward the edge of the bed. The tensing of his stomach muscles sent a surge of pain through him. The leg came free of the sheet and hung over the side of the bed. The second leg followed. He sat up, his teeth clenched.

The room spun with a rocking motion around Sam. He braced himself with his arms to keep from falling. The weakness caused by the wound and lying in bed so many days had destroyed his sense of balance.

The room finally came to rest. Sam caught hold of the bedstead and gingerly stood erect. The pain in his stomach rocketed to a crescendo of torment that took his breath. But he stood.

He found his buckskin clothing in the closet of the room. The garments had been cleaned. He silently thanked the kind person who had done that for him. He dressed, almost fainting when he lifted his arms to slide into the buckskin blouse. Bent forward like a very old man, Sam left the room and went along the hallway.

"Where are you going?" cried Nurse Hanson, catching sight of Sam.

"Out there," Sam said, pointing to a door that opened to the outside.

"But you are not well enough."

"Will I ever be well enough?"

"Certainly," said the nurse. She took Sam by the arm. "Let me help you back to bed."

He pulled free. "I have something to do that has waited far too long. And it can only be done out there where men live. Thanks for all your help, but now I must say good-bye to you and leave this place."

Sam pushed through the door and into the sunlight of the afternoon. The fresh breeze struck him like a tonic. Gone was the smell of medicines, of liniments and salves. A hundred familiar odors flooded his senses. The strongest of all were the scents of the river water and mud, and the pungent horse turds on the street. He moved off, bent forward, stepping gently, his shoulders slumped.

He withdrew the total amount of money he had in the bank: seven hundred and twenty-six dollars. Surely not a fortune but hopefully enough to feed and shelter him and purchase a gun and horse to use to find and kill his enemies.

Sam returned the few blocks to the hospital and paid his bill. As Sam was leaving, Dr. Byington called out to him. "Wait a minute, Sam, I've got something for you." He held out a half-pint bottle. "This holds laudanum. It will deaden your pain. But it's a narcotic and you can become addicted to it, so use it sparingly."

"Thank you. I shall."

"Come back when you need more."

"I'll do that."

"Good luck to you," said Byington.

"I'll need some," Sam replied. He could hardly walk, yet he had three men to find and kill. A crazy thing to attempt. But even a dying man had responsibilities.

Sam fell as he crossed the short distance from the door to the bed. He hurt awfully. He had used up every ounce of his limited strength. He crawled on his hands and knees to the bed and pulled himself up on it. He took a small taste of the laudanum and recorked the bottle. Rest. Just a little rest. But exhausted as he was, he was pleased for he had lasted out the day, and on his feet.

He had purchased a Colt revolver and ammunition at a gun shop, and a long-bladed skinning knife in a sheath at a hardware store. Then a room had been rented, one that had a window and door opening out onto Main Street. Sam had planned to sit and inspect the men passing by in front. But that would have to wait.

The pain lessened as the laudanum was absorbed into his blood. However, the strong opiate could not remove Sam's black hate for his foes, as well as his dread of dying before he could discover them.

Tomorrow he would begin his search. St. Joe was not so large that he couldn't find the river pirates if they were there. He recalled the few short seconds during which he had seen the decoy man and the other two on the shore of the river. The decoy man was large, barrel-chested, with black hair and beard. And that damnable snow-white skin that had drawn Farrow and the others to their deaths. The horse-faced man would be easy to identify. The third man was different in that he was ordinary, of average height and build, and had a brown beard. Even now Sam was not certain he could pick him out of a crowd. He did not want to kill the wrong man.

He put his hand on his stomach and felt the bulge of the cyst. The thing was round and hard, like a small green melon. The physician had said that when it burst the poison it contained would kill Sam.

He removed his hand from the cyst and lay watching a small brown spider hanging suspended from the ceiling on a single thread of web. "I'll die one day," Sam said to the spider. "But not right away, for I also hang by a tough thread and I know there's a little more of it for me to spin out."

10

HARTZELL, A TEXAS RANGER, RODE HIS HORSE from the woods and crossed the meadow to the stone house sitting on the high bench above the Red River. The door was closed. The man and horse tracks on the ground were old and wind blown.

The dirt mound of a fresh grave was beneath a large oak tree off a distance to the left of the house. The end of a rope hung from a thick limb of the oak. The Ranger wondered what story lay behind the rope and the grave.

"Hello, the house," Hartzell called.

He listened and watched for some sign of another human being. Only the echo of his own voice replied. He felt that indefinable sense of emptiness that lay about a vacant house.

"Anybody home?" Hartzell called in a louder voice. The echo of his words came again.

"Appears we are alone," he said to his horse, and swung down to the ground. He stepped to the door, pulled the latchstring, and entered the house.

A table and two chairs sat near the fireplace of the big room. Four well-thumbed books were stacked on one end of the table. Someone knew how to read. A small assortment of dishes and cutlery was neatly arrayed on the other end of the table. A pair of handmade bunks made up the only other furnishings. Three saddles with saddlebags lay by the door. Three rifles leaned against the wall. An equal number of holstered pistols lay on the dirt floor near the rifles. A double handful of gold and silver coins were scattered beside the pistols, as if the money had been carelessly thrown there. Hartzell shook his head in puzzlement at the presence of the money.

He wandered the remaining rooms of the house. The dirt of the floor was packed and perfectly level. The interior walls had been expertly plastered with light-colored mud, and gave a pleasing appearance. Someone had put considerable labor into the house. Every room except for the big front one, was barren, without one item of decoration. It was obvious no woman lived here.

Hartzell left, closing the door of the house. He mounted and rode upriver along the bench.

The Ranger spent the remainder of the day roaming over several square miles of land, surrounding the house. In the evening he returned. Again he found the ranch house empty.

He stood for a time in the doorway of the house and looked at the gold and silver coins that lay glinting in the last of the day's sunlight. Why was money worth several months of a man's salary lying so openly in view? He left the house and rode into the woods.

Something tapped Nathan Tolliver on the forehead. He came instantly awake but did not stir. The gentle strike of something hard, but lightly wielded, landed again on his forehead. And yet a third time.

The precise intervals between the blows told Nathan that they had been struck by a human hand. He waited for the next one. None came. He opened his eyes and looked out into the dusk of evening.

An old Comanche with a burnt-copper face and white-streaked hair squatted on his haunches a few feet distant. He was dressed in worn buckskin, an outfit that once had been splendid, with much quill and colored needlework. A single black crow's feather was tied to a lock of hair and hung behind his right ear. He held a wooden rod, some three quarters of an inch in diameter and three feet long, extended in Nathan's direction. The stick was painted with alternating bands of red, yellow, and black from the end and down to a short section wrapped with buckskin. The buckskin section was used as a handhold.

Nathan realized the Indian had tapped him on the head with the end of the rod. No, not just a rod, but a treasured coup stick. A warrior could show his great courage by creeping upon a foe while he slept, to count coup by touching him with the special stick. Then he would leave, taking one of the sleeping man's possessions to prove to his comrades what he had done.

Nathan thought the trick was to count coup stealthily, without waking the enemy. Why had the Comanche tapped him awake?

"You sleep like the possum and hear nothing," said the Indian in a coarse, rumbly voice. His English was passably spoken.

A half-amused expression was on the face of the Comanche as he stared at Nathan with piercing black eyes. He was old and wrinkled, yet the leanly sinewed body appeared strong. He was still a formidable warrior and could have killed Nathan with the powerful war bow that lay at his feet, or the knife in his belt. A U.S. Army carbine was in a scabbard on the Comanche's mustang. To Nathan's surprise a calf was tied across the back of the mount.

Nathan sat upright on his bedroll. He was returning to his home on the bank of the Red River. He had been gone seven days. When the morning daylight had overtaken him, he had halted in a small meadow surrounded by woods and staked out his six horses, and the five calves he had stolen. Weary from the long travel, he had slept. At noon he had moved the animals to fresh grass and then slept again. Until the Comanche had awakened him.

Nathan glanced down at his rifle and pistol, both still lying where he had placed them within easy reach. The Comanche had not taken them.

"You could have killed me while I slept but you didn't. What do you want?"

"You have built yourself a stone tepee by the spring on the land above the Red River." The Indian pointed west, directly at Nathan's house.

"How do you know that?"

"I often visit that place. I have watched you there. I first saw you in the season of the last great heat. Another man was with you, one who looked very much as you do. I sometimes thought of slaying both of you but decided not to and always went on my way, leaving you unharmed."

The Comanche looked closely at Nathan. "During the last
months of cold and snow I lived with my people in a place
far away, toward the place where the sun comes up. It is a
great canyon slashed into the plains, a beautiful place of
sweet springs, streams, and waterfalls, the willows and buffalo grass tall and good for the horses. It is all sunken below
the flat plains and hidden from the frigid winds that blow
down from the north. The place is called Palo Duro Canyon."
   The old Comanche was silent, his thoughts turned inward
and far away. Then his eyes fastened back on Nathan.
   "I had a woman to keep me warm, but still I became very
ill. I was long in recovering my strength, so that once again I
could draw my strong bow. I knew that my days among the
living were growing short. Though that wintering place is
grand, I do not want to die there."
   "Where do you want to die?" asked Nathan, caught up in
the old Comanche's tale.
   "I once had a tepee by the spring near your stone house.
My first woman and I built it there more than half a hundred winters ago. She first spread her legs for me there and
we made our man-woman pleasure act on the new grass by
the spring. I can still feel the warmth and softness of her
flesh." The Indian's eyes half closed and he smiled to himself as he recalled the long-ago lovemaking of two young
people.
   "I have had many other women but none as beautiful and
pleasing as she."
   "She is no longer with you?"
   "I had her only a year. The Kiowa found our tepee by the
spring. They killed her while I was gone and not there to
protect her. For that I killed fifty Kiowa and made that a
sad day for them also. Even now I go north and slay one
Kiowa each year. For as long as I live, they shall not live in
peace. And I have killed many white men. No enemy has
ever heard me when I steal upon him with my bow or
knife."
   "You did not kill me," said Nathan.
   "You are a brave warrior. I saw three men hang the man
who looked like you. And then you came and fought them.
When you returned back across the snow after the storm

with the extra horse, I knew the last man was dead. I thought much about you and me. I believe you and other white men will soon have all the land along the Red River and the Comanche will be driven away. I want to live the last few days of my life there by the spring. To do that you and I must make a treaty."

"Make a treaty?" Nathan said in surprise, staring through the growing darkness at the old Comanche.

The man nodded. "That is a dangerous place for an Indian. Also, it is a dangerous place for a white man because the Comanche come there, as I came. Our treaty would be that I keep you safe from the Comanche and you keep me safe from the white men. I will not be a trouble to you, for I will build my own tepee. Perhaps when it is so very cold that the hearts of the trees freeze and burst open, you might let me come inside and sleep by the fire in your stone tepee. I want nothing else except to be buried in a place where I can see the the water of the spring."

The Indian gestured at the five stolen calves. "You are a good thief. But you do not have to journey so long a distance to find something to steal. Look, I have brought you one as a gift, and from just the other side of the river." His hand swung to point at the calf tied across the back of his mustang.

"That's a Satterlee calf," Nathan said. "You'll have to take it back."

"This Satterlee is a friend?"

"Something like that. I don't steal from him."

"I shall take it back where I found it."

"Good."

The Indian fastened his penetrating, black-eyed stare on Nathan again. "Then you and I have a treaty and you will let me build my tepee near the spring?"

"Yes. I hope you live for many years."

"I feel it will not be long."

"What is your name?"

"Crow."

"Mine is Nathan Tolliver."

"That is a good name," Crow said.

"How did you come to be able to speak English?" asked Nathan.

"When one has lived as many years as I have, he can learn many useful things if he tries. I once guided your white soldiers. At another time, the soldiers of the Spanish. I listen and learn both languages."

The Comanche climbed to his feet and walked to his horse. Lithely, like a young warrior, he leapt astride.

You shall live forever, thought Nathan.

"I will catch you by the time you reach the stone tepee," Crow said.

In the deepening night Nathan fastened the packsaddles upon the backs of the horses. The feet of the calves were bound and the heavy animals hoisted up with a back straining lift and secured to the packsaddles. He mounted his riding horse and headed into the darkness.

He halted hours later in the cold predawn light. He had passed the border of his land many miles ago. He was now in the north portion of his land. He built a fire and shoved his branding iron into the center of the bright flames.

One calf after another was marked on the flank with his hot TT branding iron. The hurt and bawling animals vanished at a run into the darkness as Nathan jerked the tie ropes loose.

He traveled south. By the time he had reached the woods surrounding the meadow and his house, a drop of dawn had made a hole in the dark eastern horizon.

He dumped the specially designed packsaddles in a pile and covered them with brush. A man with a keen eye might interpret the use of the gear. He released the packhorses and slapped them away to graze.

Nathan left the woods and crossed the meadow to the house. The saddle was removed from the back of the horse and the animal turned loose to forage where it willed. It would not wander from the meadow.

He tripped the latch of the door and, leaving the portal open to let in the growing daylight, entered the house. His pistol was tossed on a bunk. He stripped off his clothing. This was the first time he had removed the garments for many days. Now for a bath and a long sleep.

"Leave your gun on the cot and turn around." The voice

of a man came from the doorway behind Nathan. "Make no sudden moves and you won't get shot," continued the man.

Nathan pivoted slowly. A ruggedly built man with a ruddy face was in the doorway. His hand rested lightly on the butt of his pistol.

"My name is Hartzell. I'm a Texas Ranger. Are you Nathan Tolliver?"

"I'm Tolliver."

"Then I want to ask you some questions."

"Is this the way a Ranger asks questions? Waits until a man is naked?"

"It was your idea to take off your clothes. I just want to talk."

"Then I can put my clothes back on?"

"Sure," said Hartzell. "But first, step away from your gun. I don't want to tempt you and then have to kill you. After we're done talking, then I might let you have the gun back."

"What've I done that the law would want me for?" Nathan asked as he moved to the center of the room with his clothes.

"Perhaps nothing," said Hartzell, stepping inside the house. "Dress if you want," he said.

Nathan slid into his pants and shirt. "What're your questions?"

"How long have you lived here on the Red River?" The Ranger's hand remained resting on his revolver as he talked.

"Almost two years."

"How many of you live here?"

"Just my brother and me, until the last few days. He's dead now."

"You got a big herd of cattle?"

"No. Actually it's quite small. But I'm getting started."

"Uh-huh. I saw some of your stock. Lot of young animals."

Nathan remained quiet. The Ranger stood ready to fight. What did he want? Was it the stolen calves? Or the dead outlaws?

"The body of a dead man was found in the yard of Satterlee's line shack on the Pease River. Outside of Satterlee and his men, you live the closest. I've talked to all of them and they know nothing of the dead man. Do you know anything?''

"I killed a man there about three weeks ago," Nathan said. "But it was a fair fight."

The Ranger's eyes hardened. "How do you figure that?"

"Three men hung my brother Jason out there on the oak tree. His grave is close to there. The rope is still tied to the tree. When I came to cut him down and bury him, they tried to shoot me. But they failed to get the job done. I killed two of them by the edge of the bluff. The other fellow ran. I caught him at Satterlee's place."

"Why'd they hang your brother and try to shoot you?"

"That last man told me they planned to lay claim to my ranch after Jason and I were dead."

"So you killed three men. Where are the other two?"

"Out there in the meadow. I dug a hole and threw them in. I can show you."

"Why didn't you report what had happened?"

"I saw no reason to tell anybody. They deserved to die. My brother never hurt anybody in his life, yet they hung him. Those guns and saddles belonged to the three of them. And that gold and silver was theirs." Nathan pointed at the coins on the floor. "I found papers on the men that told who they were. They're in that saddlebag." His finger swung to indicate the correct one. "You can take everything. I don't want it."

The Ranger's sight stayed locked on the young man. His story of how he came into possession of the money would explain why it was thrown on the floor. "I'll take the papers and coins. And I am going to take you to Austin for a hearing. Maybe you'll have to stand trial, or the judge might believe what you say and turn you loose. That's for him to decide, not me."

Nathan shook his head, all desire to be agreeable gone. "I'm not riding three hundred miles to stand trial for killing men who murdered Jason and tried to shoot me. I told you the truth. With their deaths all is now even, or as even as anything can be in this world. Surely you can see that. Make your report that it was a justified killing."

Crow came stealthily in the door. Nathan saw the Comanche pull his knife.

"I could do that," Hartzell said. "But for one man to kill three looks odd. It's better for me to take you to Austin." He took a grip on his pistol and started to draw it from the holster.

"Don't pull your gun on me," Nathan said quickly. "Crow! No! Don't kill him. He's a lawman."

Hartzell hesitated, focusing his senses behind him. Tricks had been tried on him before. He heard nothing. Again he started to lift his weapon.

The sharp point of a knife pricked his back. It stung, and he knew it had drawn blood. A hand wrenched the pistol from his grip.

"You lied to me about there being only you and your brother here," Hartzell said angrily.

"I just met Crow a few hours ago. He and I have made a treaty of peace between us."

"Once I knew a Comanche named Crow," said the Ranger. He pivoted to look behind him. "Yes, you are the same man."

Crow's face was like stone. His black eyes glittered. "You and I, with our comrades, fought the big battle on the Canadian River."

"We defeated you," Hartzell said.

"No," Crow said, shaking his head. "You killed many of my people, but you did not defeat us."

"Have it your way." Hartzell shrugged his shoulders.

"Now I have you to kill," Crow said, sounding pleased.

"There'll be no killing," said Nathan.

"Why not?" asked Crow. "He is your enemy, as he is mine. We can bury his body and no one will ever find him."

"I think you want to live here without war. I know that I do. We must let him go safely back to Austin."

Crow held the knife and pistol and stared at Hartzell. His muscles were tensed, ready to launch him upon the Ranger. "Are you very sure, Nathan? I would like very much to slay this white man."

"I'm certain, Crow."

The Comanche remained taut, poised, the desire to strike with the knife burning within him. His voice came like rocks hitting rocks.

"Hartzell, you owe Nathan your life. He is a peaceful man and I'll do as he asks. But I'll tell you, if it was not for him, I would surely kill you at this moment."

Nathan stepped to Crow and took the pistol from his hand. He gave the weapon to the Ranger. "Crow and I will obey the law. But we'll always defend ourselves. Go to Austin and tell the officials that Nathan Tolliver killed in self-defense."

Hartzell held his revolver and looked from the white man to the Comanche's bitter countenance. He thought Tolliver told the truth. If, on the other hand, he took Tolliver and started for Austin, the Comanche would pursue him. Someplace during those many days, Hartzell would have to sleep. Crow would kill him.

"Perhaps it is best that way," Hartzell said. "I'll do what I can to convince the judge that the killing was justified. That you freely admitted to doing it and told why. I'll say I believe you." He looked at Nathan. "Their horses, saddles, and guns must be turned over to the Rangers. You killed the men, so you bring their belongings to Austin."

"I'll do that in the summer," said Nathan. "That's the soonest I plan to go there."

The Ranger scooped up the saddlebags containing the dead men's identification, and the coins from the floor. He moved to the door, then turned back to face Nathan. "When I come this way again, I'll ask to see a bill of sale for all the calves that ain't trailing a cow. I'll surely take you to Austin if things ain't right." He stepped through the door and was gone.

Crow and Nathan followed outside. They watched the Ranger walk to the woods and, a short moment later, reappear on his horse. He headed across the meadow. Not once did he look back.

"Crow, we shall never steal another calf," Nathan said.

"That is a very great sorrow to me," Crow said.

THE STEAMSHIP *AFRICAN BLACKBIRD* PLOWED westward across the Atlantic. Thirteen days had passed since the ship had pulled away from the rocky bone of the English coast at Liverpool. She was making eight knots and bound for New York.

Deep within the bowls of the rusty hulk, the steam engines hissed and grumbled as they strained to spin the screw that drove the ship. A school of several hundred mullet, frightened by the unnatural noise, scooted away through the green, rolling waves. A shark that had been on the verge of striking the mullet leisurely followed their smell and noise in the water.

On the fantail of the steamship, Mathias Rowley led the evening service for the Mormon converts. His face held a smile as he described the land of Zion in the mountain heartland of America. He focused his attention for a second on one of his followers after another, assuring that person with his eyes that he spoke the total truth.

Caroline sensed the magic of the Mormon missionary, for she, too, was caught up in his words. However, there was more to his power over the people, especially the women, than his words. He was very handsome, tall and fair. His manly appearance, as well as his complete conviction of the rightness of the faith of the Latter-day Saints, drew and held the converts. Caroline turned to study the spellbound congregation around her.

The people sat on blankets brought from their beds below deck. The fifteen men with their wives and children were on the edge of the gathering. The single women occupied the rest of the ship's stern. Caroline saw the people's rapt concentration, their eyes never straying from the face of Mathias. She judged that nearly every unmarried woman was in love with the man. He had said that he intended to marry when he returned home. Each woman hoped that he would choose her as his wife.

Caroline wondered what her answer would be if Mathias should ask her to marry him. She glanced back to the front. Mathias was looking straight at her. Her cheeks reddened with a blush, even though she knew he could not read her thoughts.

She dropped her sight to the deck of the ship as Mathias continued to speak to the congregation. He spoke of the Church's tenet of Celestial Marriage, a marriage for earth and beyond, for all eternity. Her mind began to stray, for she had heard it all before. Was religion merely a restatement of the same dogma over and over again? Her eyes drifted off to the side toward a pair of sailors working on the lifeline that rimmed the ship.

From the first day the Mormons had boarded the ship, the crew of sailors had found various reasons to come and go near the stern of the ship, where the women often gathered. They would walk slowly past the women, clustered in groups to talk or to wash and mend their clothing. The two young sailors working so casually nearby were especially daring. It seemed they always had a vantage point from which they could see the women.

The two seamen—hardly more than boys, with soft, sparse beards—did not appear to be the kind that would be part of a crew of slavers. For indeed the *African Blackbird* was a slave ship. The Mormons had not known that at first. Had they been wiser, the name would have alerted them, for slave ships were called blackbirders.

The ship that George Cluff originally had contracted had run aground just outside the harbor of Liverpool during the severe storm that had thrashed the English coast. She was badly damaged. Repairs would take weeks. The shipping company had no other vessel bound for America for another month. Cluff had demanded the return of the money he had paid for the ocean passages of his charges. Grudgingly the sum had been given back.

Cluff and Rowley had searched the waterfront for another ship to transport the converts to America. They'd found a ship that was leaving in a reasonably short time and had space available for the large number of passengers. Varick, captain of the *African Blackbird,* agreed to alter his usual course to Africa and make a port call in New York. Arrangements were quickly made with the captain and the Mormons boarded the ship. The *African Blackbird* steamed promptly out of Liverpool.

Two days later Rowley chanced upon a locker room full of leg irons, manacles, and chains. When he had asked the captain about his discovery, Varick had described the three-legged voyage his ship had made. Thousands of bales of cotton were purchased in New Orleans and transported to the spinning mills in Liverpool. Arms and other provisions were then taken aboard at London for delivery to the English garrisons in the conquered lands on the west coat of Africa. Once the holds of the *African Blackbird* were again empty, she would anchor off some remote African shore and Varick would lead his men inland for raids on native villages. They took many black men, women, and children prisoners. The dark holds of the ship were jammed with the black people and hauled to the slave market in New Orleans.

One of the young sailors spied Caroline looking at him. He winked at her and smiled. He seemed so much a mischievous boy that Caroline half smiled before she caught herself. It would not be wise to encourage the pair. They were brash enough.

"Timson, Hobbs, get forward and do some useful work before I take the cat to you," Captain Varick's bull voice roared down from the wheelhouse. The two seamen jumped, spun around, and looked toward the source of the command. They hurried forward.

The captain's eyes bored into Caroline. She felt as if the slaver had somehow reached out and touched her with foul hands. She quickly jerked her sight back to the front.

Mathias finished his sermon and the congregation began to break up. He moved through the milling crowd and approached Caroline. He stroked his short beard in a contemplative manner.

"Caroline, I noticed you were restless during the evening service. Your thoughts seemed on other things. Is something the matter that I can help you with?"

"No, Mathias. It is the strangeness of the ship and the ocean. And the crew is a rough lot, except for the two young seamen."

"Would you like to talk? We can sit over there near the rail of the ship."

"All right."

Caroline was somehow pleased that Mathias had sorted her out. She knew several other women watched as she and Mathias found a place and spread her blanket. She did not care if they envied her.

Mathias allowed her to seat herself and then dropped down to face her from the opposite side of the blanket. She folded her legs and spread her dress over them.

"What would you like to talk about?" asked Mathias.

"You have told me about the wonders of the place you call Zion. I understand it is called Utah Territory by the United States government."

"Yes. That is what non-Mormons, and also some Mormons, call it. Salt Lake City is the center of it. Our people are expanding outward in every direction, making settlements in one mountain valley after another. There they level the land and dam the streams for irrigation water. Grain fields and vegetable gardens and orchards are started. They are reaping bountiful harvests."

"Can women own land? Can they be self-sufficient?"

"What do you mean? There are many men. Those of you women who want to marry can easily find husbands. Every young woman marries. You are quite pretty, and men will ask you."

Mathias's answers were not satisfactory to Caroline. She wanted to own land in her own right. However, she let the subject go and went back to her original comment. "I understand the United States government sent an army to invade Utah a year ago. What happened?"

"An army was sent. We were ready to fight the soldiers and there were skirmishes, but our leader, Brigham Young, is a wise man. He met with leaders of the United States government and the invasion was halted. We agreed to have a United States judge installed to hold court in Salt Lake City. He is there now. But that was a small price to pay for the right to peacefully go on with our life as we like."

"Tell me of our leader, Brigham Young," Caroline said.

Mathias smiled at Caroline's use of the words *our leader*. "He is our high priest, a truly great Saint," Mathias began.

Caroline sat on her thin cotton mattress, which lay upon the steel deck of the ship. She removed the sturdy shoes John Bradshaw, the bakerman, had bought for her. She ran her hand over the tough leather as she thought of the old man. He had proved to be a kind and generous person.

She had worked with John in the bakery for six days, helping to mix the bread and cake dough and tend the oven. In the evening they sat and talked while she nibbled on a sweet roll or drank tea with him. She had never been hungry once in all those days.

He had spoken briefly about a daughter, and asked her about her family. He especially wanted to know whether or not her family had green eyes, as she did. She had told him all their eyes were shades of brown and that she must be a throwback to some ancient ancestor.

John had nodded at those words and his eyes had glistened with moisture. He always called her daughter thereafter.

Caroline routinely walked to the docks to inquire of the missionaries whether or not the ship had arrived that would carry them to America. One day she returned to the bakery with the news that a ship was ready to sail and that the Mormon converts should assemble on the waterfront with their possessions. John had asked her to remain in England and help him in the bakery.

Caroline had declined the kind offer, explaining she must continue on the journey with the Mormon converts. That she must see this fabulous land of America. John had said no more. He took her to a clothier and purchased boy's heavy shoes, pants, and shirts for her. "To wear when you begin the trip through the wilderness of America," he had said. He gave her several shillings.

Caroline had waved from the deck of the ship as it left the

dock in Liverpool. The old bakerman had shed tears, which he'd tried to hide with his hand. Caroline also had cried at their parting.

Now she set her shoes aside and reclined on her bed. The flames of the single oil lantern that lit the compartment waved and flickered as the ship rolled steeply to a beam sea. Shadows, distorted black caricatures of the women preparing for bed, moved on the steel bulkheads. The women were unnaturally quiet as they let down their hair and spread their blankets.

The family groups had been given cabins on the port side of the ship. The single women were assigned five large compartments on the starboard side, aft of the smokestacks.

Caroline shared the space of one compartment with nineteen other girls. She slept near the rear and farthest from the hatchway that opened out into the main starboard passageway of the ship. A smaller hatchway, locked and never used, was near her feet. That exit led into a cargo storage area.

One of the women pried up the globe of the lantern and blew out the flame. A Stygian darkness engulfed the compartment. Caroline heard a few calls of good night between friends. Then the only sound was of low stirring as the women settled down to sleep.

Caroline lay staring upward into the blackness for a long time. Now that the women were quiet, she could hear the creaking noise of cargo shifting in the hold beyond the hatchway. That noise had begun the first day the ship had left harbor and caught the taller waves of the open sea.

She let her mind drift back to recall the years her family worked the small rocky farm on the side of a hill in England. Those long years had been bad, a time of backbreaking labor and near starvation. The future, perhaps, would be better. She had been told there was land, rich land, without limit in America. That people could claim all the land they could plow and sow. She would need a husband to help with the work. She was eighteen years old, and no one had ever asked her to be his wife. Maybe no one ever would. What then? She went to sleep with that worrisome thought in her mind.

* * *

Caroline jerked awake. Something was wrong. She breathed lightly through her mouth, listening.

The creaking noise from the cargo hold was louder; that was what had awakened her. She rose up silently. In the total darkness she could see nothing. She cocked her ear, straining to hear.

A hand swept across her bed. The fingers touched her leg just above the knee. The hand hesitated but for an instant only, and then long, callused fingers closed like a vise nearly encircling her leg. The other hand of the man shot out and caught her by the neck. Quickly it shifted up and clamped tightly over her mouth. The scream in Caroline's throat was stifled to nothing.

The hand that held her leg released its grip and jumped to catch hold of the front of her clothing. The man began to crawl upon her. Before his body could block the lifting of her knees, Caroline bent her legs and jerked them up. She kicked out with all of her strength, driving her feet at the place where she judged the man's head would be.

One of her heels crashed into the face of the man. She felt the crush of flesh and the coarse beard. The hold upon her loosened slightly. She tore free and began to scuttle backward on her rump.

The man uttered not a sound as he struck out. His hard hand caught Caroline a stinging blow to the side of the face, rolling her like a doll.

Caroline added her own impetus to her roll, tumbling over the girl that slept beside her. She rolled again and came to a stop against a second sleeper.

Caroline sobbed as she sucked in a breath of air. Her heart was nearly bursting as it pumped large pulses of blood.

A startled cry, swiftly cut off, came out of the darkness. There was a dragging sound that went out through the hatchway into the cargo hold. Caroline heard clothing rip. A low, rhythmic thumping sound began.

"Light the lantern," Caroline screamed at the top of her voice. "A man's broke in. He's taken one of the girls."

An instant hubbub of voices arose. "What's happening?" an excited voice demanded to know. "You're tramping on me," another girl cried out. Others yelled. "Shut up." "Get off me." "Who yelled?"

"Light the lantern," Caroline shouted into the bedlam of noise.

No light came to life. Fearfully Caroline crawled to the hatchway. Just barely out of her reach in the darkness, the tempo and violence of the thumping increased. Now she heard a grunting sound, like a hog rooting.

"Make a light!" she cried out in desperation. "For God's sake, make a light."

The thumping ceased. There was a moment's pause, and then a large body moved away in the blackness of the cargo hold.

The lantern flared to life. Was lifted. The hubbub slackened.

"Over here," called Caroline. "Hurry!"

A girl crawled in through the hatchway on her hands and knees. Her face was bloody and her eyes filled with a horrible fright.

The woman holding the lantern pushed through to stare down at the girl on the floor. "Oh! My God! What happened?"

"He raped me!" cried the girl as she huddled on the floor. "A man pulled me in there and raped me." She pulled a blanket over her half-naked body and began to sob.

"Here's Mathias," someone said.

"I heard the screaming," Mathias said, hurrying into the compartment. "What's wrong?"

"A man came through there," said Caroline, pointing at the small hatchway. "He hit and raped Esther."

Mathias' face took on an angry expression. "Damnation. Do what you can for her," he said. "I'll get the ship's doctor and the captain." He hastened out into the passageway.

The doctor and the captain arrived as Caroline talked and tried to comfort Esther.

"Move aside, young woman, and let me take a look," the doctor said to Caroline. He bent over Esther.

"Bad blow to the cheek," said the doctor. "Come down to sick bay so I can treat you and get you cleaned up. Can you walk?" he asked her.

"Yes, I think so," said Esther.

"Very well," said the doctor. "Lean on me as much as you need to." Supporting the shaken young woman, he left the compartment.

"Caroline, did you say the man came in through that hatchway?" asked Mathias.

"Yes, and then he dragged Esther out the same way."

The captain spoke. "That hatch is supposed to be secured on the other side by a padlock. Only the storekeeper has a key. I'll get to the bottom of this. Someone will pay."

Looking neither left nor right, the captain strode from the women's compartment.

•◢ 12 ◣•

THE DAYLIGHT ARRIVED AND THE ENTIRE CREW of the *African Blackbird,* except those seamen on duty watch and operating the ship, stood at muster amidships on the main deck. They had been there since the dark morning hours when the captain had rousted them from their hammocks.

Varick and Rowley were searching the crew's quarters for the key to the hatchway from the cargo hold to the women's compartment. The captain had insisted Rowley accompany him in the search when the key had been found missing from the storekeeper's cabin.

The Mormon converts had gathered on the stern and watched the assembled seamen. Caroline was wrapped in her coat and leaning against one of the iron stanchions that supported the upper deck. The cold sea wind seemed to blow through her, and her face ached where the rapist had hit her.

She looked ahead, beyond the ship. A line of tall, gray

clouds showed on the far wet horizon. One cloud was strangely shaped, resembling the head of a great bull with long pointed horns. The *African Blackbird* steamed directly at those horns.

Varick and Rowley came along the starboard side of the ship. The big captain led, walking swiftly. He reached the ranks of the crewmen and halted to stand bleak-faced in front of them.

"There is a criminal among you," the captain said in a stinging voice. "He is a man who beats women and rapes them." He held up the padlock key for all to see. "The missionary and I have found the stolen key."

Varick ceased talking and ranged gimlet eyes over the crew. "The guilty man must be severely punished," he said. "Timson, come forward," the captain ordered.

To Caroline's surprise one of the two youthful sailors she had observed before stepped from the ranks of the seamen. An uncertain, questioning expression was upon his face. He stopped in front of the captain.

"Timson, you were on bow lookout from midnight to eight bells, isn't that right?" said the captain.

"Yes, sir," replied Timson.

"Did you leave your post at any time?"

"No, sir."

"Then how do you explain this being found in your locker?" Varick held up the padlock key for all to see.

"It couldn't have been found there," Timson said.

"Are you calling me a liar?" roared Varick.

"No, sir," the young seamen said hastily. "I'm saying that if you found it there in my locker, then somebody had to have put it there."

"Timson, you lie. I've seen you watching the women many times. Then last night you left your post, stole the key from the storekeeper's cabin, and went to the women's quarters. You entered and raped one of them. I'm placing you under arrest until we reach port. There you'll be turned over to the authorities."

"I didn't do it," cried Timson, his face taut and scared.

Varick motioned at the first mate. "Lock Timson in number-three hold forward," he directed.

"No, you're not," Timson said. "I'm innocent. Somebody put the key there." He balled his fist and pivoted to confront the mate bearing down upon him.

Varick moved suddenly forward from Timson's side. A pleased smile came to his face as he swung a wicked blow into Timson's head. The seaman fell to the deck with a thud.

The captain bent over the nearly unconscious Timson, and his large hand caught the seaman's jacket. He jerked the seaman's slack form erect. His bony fist crashed again into Timson's head, snapping it cruelly to the side. Varick struck again and again at the limp form that hung in his hand.

"Captain, that's enough," said the first mate, catching Varick by the shoulder. "You'll kill him."

"Get your damn hand off me," the captain said with a snarl.

The mate backed hurriedly away.

"He deserves to be killed," said the captain. He slugged Timson one last time and let him fall to the iron deck. "Now take him and lock him up."

Varick turned to the gathering of women. "You will now be safe for the rest of the trip to New York."

The Mormon women stared back, their faces pale at the violent beating of the sailor.

Caroline felt horrified. She was looking directly at the captain. His lips, swollen and cut, protruded from the coarse, heavy beard on his face. She knew without doubt that in the struggle in the darkness of the compartment her foot had struck that ugly face. The captain was the rapist, not Timson, with his boyish beard. She broke from her trance and hastened through the women to Rowley.

"Mathias," she said, catching him by the arm, "Timson was not the man who hurt Esther or me."

"What do you mean?" asked Mathias. "How do you know that?"

"Look at the captain's face. See the bruises on his mouth? I kicked the attacker in the face. And awfully hard. Timson's face was not injured before the captain beat him. But the captain's has been hurt. And the face I kicked had a coarse beard, like the captain's."

Mathias wheeled about to look at Varick. Caroline also turned.

The captain was intently watching them. His eyes locked with Caroline's across the distance separating them. Caroline tried to break her sight free, but it seemed as if she were bound to the captain with a band of steel. And time was frozen, continuing for an age. Then Varick wheeled and walked forward along the ship's deck.

"Oh! Oh!" Caroline whispered in a frightened voice. "Now he realizes that I know he is the guilty one and not Timson." Her fear was a cold lump in her breast.

"You could be wrong about him," said Mathias. "He did find the key in among Timson's clothing."

"Was the locker locked?"

"No."

"Then anyone could have put the key there. Or Varick could have had it in his hand and only pretended to find it. Isn't that possible?"

"Yes. But I still say you could be mistaken. After all, he *is* the master of the ship."

"Yes, a slave ship. And are men of position less likely to be wicked than others?"

"No. Surely not."

"I'm not wrong about the captain. And you know it too. You saw his face and the look in his eyes."

"Even if you are right, there is nothing I can do now. Nor you, either. You can tell your story to the authorities when we land in New York."

"If I live that long," said Caroline. "He is an evil, violent man. He did that terrible thing to Esther. And he enjoyed hitting poor Timson. Didn't you see his expression? He will try to find a way to silence me."

"You must be very careful," said Mathias. "Don't be alone at any time."

Caroline gripped Mathias's arm. "Kill him. You of all the people can get close to him. You are strong. Catch him when he's not looking and shove him into the ocean. Kill him before he kills me or hurts some other member of our people."

Mathias backed away, breaking Caroline's hold on his arm. "What are you saying? Kill him? I've never killed anybody. God forbids that most unholy crime."

"Yes! I want you to kill him, unholy or not."

"Never. I could never do that."

Caroline studied the handsome face. "No, I see that you couldn't."

She turned from the missionary and walked away from him and across the deck to the far side of the ship. She watched the heaving waves of the dark sea. She trembled with her fear.

Caroline held to the stanchion that supported the upper deck and stared out into the sea from the fantail of the *African Blackbird*. She was deeply disappointed in the response Mathias had given her about killing Varick. Had she been a man, she would surely strike at the captain before he could harm her.

She released her hold on the metal column for a moment and pulled her coat more tightly around her body. The wind was increasing as the ship drove ever closer to the storm lying dead ahead. The waves were building, cresting higher and higher. The seabirds were gone, hiding from the danger of the storm. Caroline wished she could as easily hide from the murderous captain.

One of the waves broke under the thrust of the wind and sprayed across the deck to strike Caroline. She caught her breath at the sudden dousing of cold salt water. She turned to go below. It would be safer and warmer in the women's quarters.

Caroline saw Hobbs, Timson's young friend, making his way along the deck. He walked straddle-legged to keep his balance on the pitching ship. A comical walk, but his face held only gloom and sadness.

He called out to Caroline. "I hoped you might be on deck so that I could talk with you."

"I'm sorry about your friend," Caroline said.

"He did not do what the captain said."

"I know that."

The youth looked sharply at Caroline. "You do?"

Caroline nodded. "The captain did it. Did you see his bruised mouth? I kicked him in the face when he grabbed me in the dark. I got loose. But then poor Esther got caught."

"The bastard," cursed the seamen. "The goddamn bastard. He killed Tim for a crime he committed.

"Your friend is dead?"

"Yes. I just came from talking with the doctor. The captain beat him to death."

"I'm sorry for you," said Caroline. "And I'm afraid for my own life too. Varick knows I'm aware that he is the guilty one. I believe he will try to kill me so that I can't tell what I know to the authorities."

"You must protect yourself. I'll do what I can to keep an eye on the captain, but I'll be on watch some of the time. Usually I won't be able to get close enough to you to be of much help."

Caroline pointed at the knife on the seamen's belt. "I need a weapon. Would you sell me your knife?"

"No, but I'll give it to you." He unbuckled the belt holding the sheathed knife. "You must carry it on you all the time," he said.

"I will. Every minute."

"Let me tell you how to use a blade. The captain is a big, thick-boned man. Don't try to stab him through the chest. You could hit a bone and only lightly wound him. Stab straight for his neck—or his stomach, just below the ribs." The seaman pulled the knife from the sheath and made two motions with it to show Caroline how. "If you go for his stomach, point the knife slightly upward. Maybe that way you can reach his lungs or, if you're real lucky, his heart."

The seaman grinned wickedly at Caroline. "Then slice sideways. The knife is damn sharp. It'll cut a mean hole. Spill his guts on the deck."

"I understand." Caroline shivered as he placed the handle of the weapon in her hand and pressed her fingers around it.

"If he comes close, don't think, just stab and kill him," said the seaman.

"I'll try, but he's awfully big."

"The knife, if you use it quick, will make you almost as big as he is," said the seaman.

The storm came with uncanny speed, seeming to jump from the horizon toward them. A great, dark, slate-gray cloud killed the sun and drove upon the *African Blackbird*. The plunging ship was hurled into a twilight world drained of all color.

The rolling waves became peaked and frothed with white sea foam. The spumy crests grew, building to run level with the ship's smokestacks. One of the waves, taller than the others, broke against the side of the ship and poured across the deck. Some of the water tumbled down an open hatchway.

The cold water fell upon Caroline and two other women as they made their way along a passageway leading to the food locker that contained the Mormons' provisions. The women darted from under the open hatchway and hurried on down the dimly lit passageway with their baskets. Cold wind and wetness, and the rolling, pitching ship, were now commonplace and no longer spoken of. There was only the food that must be taken to the compartments and prepared for the people.

The women filled their baskets with foodstuffs and filed out of the locker. Caroline was last to leave. The task of closing the hatch fell to her. She set her basket down and started to pull on the dog arms, one after the other, to secure the hatch. The other two women continued on with their loads.

Caroline finished closing the hatch of the locker. Again she hoisted her basket and went on, bracing herself against the plunging ship with her elbows on the metal bulkheads.

At an open side portal Caroline drew in her elbow, planning to use the opposite bulkhead for support to hold her on her feet. As she leaned away, a pair of long arms shot out and grabbed her. Before she could utter a sound, a huge hand clamped her mouth and she was jerked toward the open hatchway. An arm of the man encircled her waist, lifted her bodily, and swept her into the side compartment.

Caroline dropped her basket of foodstuff. Her hands

jumped up to pry away the hand that covered her mouth. She must scream for help. The man's hand was unmovable, locked to her face.

"Gotcha, Miss Green Eyes," Varick whispered in her ear. He kicked the hatch closed.

A thunderous wave rammed the ship. The vessel rolled far starboard. Varick grew tense, waiting for the ship to right herself. Slowly the tons of iron ballast in her keel brought the ship back to her feet.

Varick spun Caroline to face him. "Don't yell and I'll release your mouth," he said. "Do you understand?" Even if she screamed, no one could hear her through the steel door and above the roar of the sea.

Caroline nodded against his hand. She could barely see his face in the weak light coming from the single porthole.

The captain removed his hand. Immediately he slapped her a stinging blow to the side of the head. "Just to show you I mean for you to obey," he growled.

Caroline staggered, then caught herself. "Please don't hit me again," she said in a trembly voice. The tremble in her voice was real, for she was deathly afraid of the huge captain, who stood swaying easily to the roll of the ship. Her mind raced to devise a plan to escape alive.

"I'll let you do what you did to Esther, and I'll never tell anybody what you've done."

You dumb little bitch, thought Varick. *Don't you know that I'm going to break your little neck regardless of what you give me.* "That's a bargain," he said.

"Let me take off my coat and dress first," said Caroline.

Varick took one step backward. His face split open to smile in evil anticipation.

Caroline slid out of her coat and dropped it on the deck. Her hands went to the buttons on the side of her dress. She turned that side slightly away from Varick. Her legs were wobbly. Her heart thrashed like a crazy thing. Her fingers fumbled at the buttons. Could she go through with it? She must if she was to live.

Her hand slid inside her dress. Her fingers encircled the handle of the sailor's knife, the weapon awkward in her grasp. She had asked someone to kill Varick. Did she have the courage to try to do it herself?

She glanced at the large bulk of the man. He was like a giant to her.

Caroline slid the knife from the waist of her dress. Perhaps the captain would not immediately recognize what it was in the dim light. The man's neck was too high for her to reach easily. The stomach had to be the target. She lunged forward, stabbing out, plunging the knife to the hilt in the man's shirtfront. Instantly she cut sideways as the seaman had told her to do. She felt the keenly honed blade slice muscle and intestines. She jerked the knife free.

Varick reacted by instinct. His fist lashed out, landing a stunning blow to her face. She crashed backward into the bulkhead. Varick started for her.

Abruptly the captain halted. He put his hand against his stomach and looked down. A surprised, disbelieving expression poured into his eyes.

Caroline gained her feet. She had expected to see the captain fall. But he seemed unhurt. She must cut him again, before he attacked her. She tightened her grip on the knife and leapt forward. She thrust out savagely with the weapon.

The blade caught for an instant on the captain's belt buckle. She felt the edge of her panic, for she was within easy reach of his big hands. Then the knife slid past the obstruction and into the burly body of the man. She jumped hurriedly back before he could hit her again.

Varick looked up at Caroline and his mouth came open, as if he wanted to say something. He stepped toward her. As he came closer he leaned forward, farther and farther. He fell, his face smashing into the iron plates of the ship's deck at Caroline's feet.

She backed against the bulkhead and stared down at the captain. She must get away. She moved to the hatch, yanked it open, and stepped into the passageway.

A hand touched her arm. Caroline whirled and crouched, the knife extended.

The young seaman, Hobbs, threw up his hands and backed away hastily.

"I didn't mean to scare you," Hobbs said quickly. "I saw the captain coming aft toward the women's quarters and followed him. I was worried about you."

"I killed him!" Caroline gasped, straightening.

"The captain?"

"Yes, he's in there." Caroline's voice was as thin as a ghost's.

"Good for you," said Hobbs. He glanced hastily along the passageway, then back at Caroline. "You're sure he's dead?"

"I'm pretty sure. I stabbed him twice. He fell hard. What'll I do?"

"Throw the son of a bitch to the sharks."

"You're right. No one must ever find his body."

"I'll carry him topside and dump him overboard."

"Won't you be seen?"

"The storm is bad. There'll be nobody on deck."

"He's twice your size. Can you carry him up the ladder?"

"You just watch for someone who might see us. I'll do the rest."

The seaman stepped into the compartment. A moment later he emerged with the large body of Varick slung over his shoulder. "He's sure dead. You did a good job on him," he told Caroline.

He walked a few paces along the passageway to the nearest ladder leading up to the main deck. He stopped and looked back at Caroline, who followed close behind him.

"You go up topside and tell me if its clear," said the seaman.

Caroline hastily climbed to the deck above. The cold sea spray stung her face as she scanned about through the weak light of the storm.

"No one in sight," she called down the hatchway.

The seaman had climbed behind Caroline. Now he clambered out of the hatchway with his heavy load. Immediately he headed for the ship's starboard side. As he moved, the ship rolled dangerously, slanting the deck at a steep angle. The seaman's pace increased to a trot as he headed straight for the railing.

Caroline thought for an instant that both Hobbs and his

burden were going over the side. However, at the last possible second, the seaman's hand flashed out and snagged hold of one of the guy wires angling down from the smokestacks. At the same time he heaved with his shoulder. The body of Varick sailed away, twisting, the arms flinging out. The corpse fell into a trough at the base of a huge wave. The wave collapsed upon Varick, driving him down. Then there was only the storm-tossed, foam-crested water remaining.

Hobbs laughed a wild laugh as he returned to Caroline. "The stinking murderer is gone to the fishes. He's beat my friend Timson there."

He stopped laughing and quietly watched Caroline. "You did the right thing. But never tell a living soul what we did today or we'll both hang. Go get your provisions and act like nothing has happened. I'll clean up the blood on the deck of the compartment." His eyes studied Caroline's strained face. "Do you hear me? You did the right thing. He deserved to die. He surely would have killed you."

"I know you are correct," Caroline said with a shudder. She went back down the hatchway ahead of Hobbs.

◆ 13 ◆

ON THE MORNING OF THE TWENTY-EIGHTH DAY AT sea the *African Blackbird* sailed into the port of New York, riding in on the spring tide as it inexorably invaded the coastline. Caroline stood on the deck and looked ahead at the teeming, bustling wharf and the tall stone-and-brick buildings of the city as the ship slowed and crept up to the dock.

The steel side of the vessel nudged the pilings with a grating noise. At an order from the second mate, thick hemp hawsers snaked down from the deck of the ship. The men onshore scrambled to catch the lines and make them fast to iron cleats on the dock. The *African Blackbird* was once again tied to the land of the earth.

"All secure," the second mate shouted up to the first mate, who was on the bridge of the ship.

The engines died. As the vibration and noise ceased, a surging surf of voices, raised in joyous approval, broke from the Mormon converts.

Caroline hurried below deck and gathered her possessions. She climbed back topside and filed along with the men, women, and children toward the gangway.

Seaman Hobbs was near the gangway as Caroline left carrying her bundle. He winked at her and smiled in his mischievous, boyish way. She smiled back at him. They had spoken but half a dozen times together in the days since the death of Varick, and then only a few words.

Every cabin, hold, and locker had been searched for the captain. When he could not be found, the first mate had declared him lost at sea and took command of the ship.

Mathias had tried to discuss the death of the captain with Caroline, telling her that she no longer had anything to fear. She had merely shrugged her shoulders and said, "Perhaps the Lord saw fit to destroy my enemy." She walked away. Mathias stared after her with a perplexed expression on his handsome face.

As Caroline passed by Hobbs a sense of sadness came over her. He was the second good friend she had lost in less than a month. Though she traveled with more than a hundred and fifty people, she felt alone, prey to events far beyond her or the entire group to control.

She came off the gangway and onto the dock. After nearly a month at sea she was once again on firm footing. To her surprise the dock seemed to heave beneath her legs. It was not until she had taken several steps that her mind accepted the fact she did not walk upon a pitching ship's deck.

The New York Port Authority officials questioned Caroline and the other Mormons about the rape of one of the women, the death of Timson, and the mysterious disappearance of the ship's captain. Caroline told the investigator that she did not believe Timson was the rapist. She wanted to clear his name of the crime, if she could. But she did not tell the investigator about Varick. She feared the official might tie her to the captain's disappearance. The interrogation ended on the second day, and the Mormons were told they were free to leave the city.

The next morning, as the sun floated up out of the sea, the converts purchased passage on a steam-powered river packet and sailed up the Hudson River to Albany. One night was spent in that river town. The following morning, the travelers boarded a train especially chartered from the Hannibal and St. Joseph Railroad by the Mormon Church's representative in Albany. The trip inland commenced.

Every railroad car was jammed with people and baggage. Cooking and eating were done in shifts. The flat-topped, coal-fired heating stove located in the center of each car was used to prepare food. Men, women, and children ate in their seats. They also slept in their seats, except for those few who could find space to lie down in the narrow aisles. The train made no stops, except to take on coal and water or to go onto a siding to allow a train of a higher priority to pass going in the opposite direction.

Caroline was surprised that Mathias continued to hold his morning and evening religious services for the converts. He would come into the end of the swaying car and, bracing himself, speak to the people, raising his voice above the clank and rattle of the train. Always he closed the brief ceremony by leading the people in a song. Caroline thought he had a very pleasant voice. She knew he gave the people new heart for the crowded, tiring journey.

Ellen's little baby girl died in Pennsylvania. Mathias could not delay the schedule of the chartered train to halt for a funeral and burial. Tearfully Ellen passed the little body to a black porter at the next station. "Bury her, kind sir," she said. She broke away crying.

Mathias gave the man money. "Please do as the woman asks," he said.

The train chugged west day and night and passed into Ohio. At a refueling stop in Cincinnati on the Ohio River, Esther, who rode in the car with Caroline, gathered up her possessions and stepped from the train. She walked off among the people on the station platform. She did not return. The train left without her.

Mathias sadly shook his head when Caroline informed him of the girl's action. "That makes eleven apostates that have deserted us," he said. "Some of our brothers and sisters grow weary, and their belief in our religion is not strong enough to carry them over all the many hundreds of miles to our land. I'm surprised more of them haven't abandoned us along the way."

Caroline shook her head. "I believe Esther wanted to get away from the people who knew what happened to her on the ship."

For hours at a stretch Caroline sat and watched the hills and valleys of the new land go past the window of the train. Many small villages were strung along the railroad. Between the towns, thousands upon thousands of clearings had been made in the great forests, which seemed never-ending. Homes had been built in the openings among the tall trees, and fields laid out and encircled by split-rail fences. Farmers were already in their fields with yokes of oxen or teams of horses plowing the black soil. The children, in the yards of the homes, would stop their play and run to a vantage point to wave and shout at the people on the train.

The villages became farther and farther apart as the train rolled ever westward. Long stretches of land held only an unbroken forest, seemingly unused by man. Perhaps the land was not claimed by anyone, thought Caroline.

She began to hum a low tune to herself. Her hand closed into a small, tight fist of determination. She was about to escape the grinding poverty that had been her lot in England. She would become the owner of many acres of rich land, even if she never had a husband to help her.

Several people became ill on the train. John Carlson's wife died in western Illinois. The trainmen helped the Mormons bury the body in a meadow beside the railroad tracks while the train sat on a siding. The widower climbed back on the train. He lifted his little boy onto his lap and continued on with the people.

The train pulled into the railroad station at St. Joseph,

Missouri, on the evening of the sixth day after leaving New York. The Mormons poured out of the cars. Mathias called them together in the park across the street from the station.

As the people assembled, two young men in pressed suits and fresh white shirts swept up in a horse-drawn buggy. "Mathias, hello!" one of the men shouted. Both men leapt down from the vehicle and walked toward Mathias.

"Booth, glad to see you," Mathias called.

"I believe those men are two more missionaries," said Sophia, who stood near Caroline. "Are all the Mormon men handsome?"

"All that I've seen are," replied Caroline with a smile. "This land of Zion, or Utah, or whatever it's name is, should be an interesting place to live."

"Let's move closer so we can hear what they're saying."

"All right," agreed Caroline.

The two girls lifted their bundles and gathered with the other converts near Mathias and the two new arrivals.

"We've been expecting you," Booth said to Mathias. "Word came two days ago that you had arrived in New York." Booth gestured at the man beside him. "This is Anton Lund. He has been on a mission to Sweden. He reached St. Joe with one hundred and eighteen brothers and sisters two weeks ago, or maybe a little longer."

"Glad to meet you, Anton," said Mathias, and shook the man's hand. "Why are you and your people still here in St. Joe?"

"The handcarts aren't built yet, and Deacon Moeller has directed me to wait here a few more days."

"We can talk about that later," said Booth. "We have a camp set up just outside town for Anton and his group. When we heard you were coming, we set up tents for you also. Come, let us guide you there. After you have your brothers and sisters settled, we must meet and talk with Deacon Moeller."

Mathias turned to the women and men standing expectantly watching him and the other two men. "This is Brother Anton Lund. He has just returned from Sweden. He and his people will travel on with us. Booth Clark is here in St. Joe to help all our brothers and sisters with their journey to Salt

Lake City. A camp has been fixed for us outside of town. We shall soon have a place to rest. Follow us."

"I would follow him anyplace," Sophia said with a low laugh to Caroline.

Mathias placed four ill people in the buggy. Then he, Booth, and Lund struck off, leading the horse that pulled the vehicle.

Caroline looked around at the town as Sophia and she trailed along at the rear of the file of converts. Men in all manner of dress went by on the street. There were city dwellers in suits, trappers in buckskin, river men in sun-faded cotton and wool, and immigrants in a dozen different types of strange outfits. A few women in clean, brightly colored dresses could be seen here and there, making Caroline more aware of her own dirty body and clothing.

Two- and three-story commercial buildings, stores, small factories, boardinghouses, and hotels lined the dirt streets. Here and there, warehouses stood with big doors gaping wide open. Caroline saw men loading wagons within the cavernous interiors. Saloons were liberally dispersed among the businesses.

A large river, the Missouri, Mathias had called it, flowed past a hundred yards distant at the end of a down-sloping street. The quarter-mile-wide flow of brown water dominated the view to the west. Wharves and piers extended for more than two miles along the bank of the river. Heavily loaded drays with breaks grinding against iron-rimmed wheels went down the sloping street. A broad-beamed, side-wheeler river ferry waited, steam escaping from its relief valve.

A wagon train rumbled past, the drivers popping their bullwhips over the ears of their teams and cursing the animals for no apparent reason. Two blacksmiths working their trade, one on each side of the street, struck ringing blows with their hammers and unknowingly made a musical duet in iron. The ferry blasted a shrill whistle, loud enough to tell the whole town that it was leaving the pier.

"People of St. Joe, look at the number of innocents that have fallen into the hands of the devil," cried a man standing on a street corner. He gripped a Bible in one hand and pointed with the other. As the female converts drew even with the man, he excitedly began to wave his Bible above his head. He shouted out in a loud voice, "I give ye warning, oh, young women. Be not taken in by the promises of the devil Mormon missionaries. Don't believe that their Zion is a heaven here on earth. Their religion is false. Ye shall be but one wife of the dozen each man has. Ye shall be living in sin for the rest of your life. Ye shall surely sink down to hell." The man's voice rose almost to a screech. "Hell awaits you!"

Caroline was taken aback by the man's heated words. Mathias had not discussed the church's tenet on plural wives. However, she had heard the female converts speak of it in whispers. What would she do if a man who already had wives asked her to marry him?

"Repent!" cried the man with the Bible as the Mormons moved away from him. "Repent and halt your march to damnation and certain destruction."

Caroline was glad when the shouting man no longer could be heard or seen. However, other men had stopped to stare at the parade of young women passing by on the street.

Caroline saw two men looking directly at her and Sophia. The hungry, animallike looks in their eyes sent a chill along her spine.

One of the men was thick-shouldered and had a black beard. A pistol showed in a holster on his belt, inside the unbuttoned coat of his black suit. The second man was in buckskin. A skinning knife and a pistol was at his side.

Caroline was surprised that men so different should be together. Then, as their penetrating eyes lingered longer on her, she knew they were not different, except in the clothing they wore.

DeBreen studied the last two girls in the line of Mormons. Their clothes were rumpled and soiled and they, themselves, obviously needed baths. Still, their feminine beauty showed plain. Clean them up and they would stand out in any assemblage of women.

DeBreen moved away from Stanker and into the street to fall in beside Caroline and Sophia. He lifted his hat and smiled at the girls. "Good day, young ladies," he said. "My name is Emile DeBreen."

"Good day to you, Emile DeBreen," Sophia said in a jaunty tone.

Caroline smiled at the man. She glanced at his clean black boots and city clothes. The big pistol seemed to her to be out of place with the suit.

"You like my outfit?" DeBreen asked, seeing Caroline's close scrutiny of him.

"I think it very strange that you should wear a pistol in the city," replied Caroline.

DeBreen laughed. "It's useful even in St. Joe. We are not as civilized as you might think, and besides, where I spend most of my time, a gun is absolutely necessary."

"Where is that place?" asked Caroline.

"About a thousand miles northwest of here," DeBreen pointed. "In the mountains. I've heard that you are from England. Is that so?"

"That's right," said Sophia.

"We're falling behind the others," Caroline said. Something about the man repelled her. "We must go on. Good-bye, Mr. DeBreen."

"I will walk with you," said DeBreen.

"No," said Caroline. "We must hurry. There are many things we have to do."

At Caroline's words a shadow of anger flared in DeBreen's eyes. He quickly masked his thoughts. He lifted his hat and bent forward in an exaggerated bow. He straightened and stared directly into Caroline's eyes.

"Good-bye," he said. A crooked smile came and went across his face. "I should tell you that you should stay here in St. Joe instead of going to that polygamist land."

Caroline and Sophia looked at each other. Then, without responding to DeBreen, they hastened to catch up with their fellow converts.

DeBreen watched until the two girls had disappeared among the people and vehicles on the street. He stepped back up on the sidewalk near Stanker.

"You scared them, DeBreen," said Stanker with a laugh. "Did you see them run?"

DeBreen turned and looked at Stanker. The man fell instantly silent.

*   *   *

"We are in danger here in St. Joseph, as we are in many other places we go outside Utah," said Deacon Moeller. He turned his long, somber face from one of the three young missionaries to the other. "However, we must remain here to help our new converts provision themselves for the difficult journey westward toward Salt Lake City."

"Why is there danger?" asked Mathias. "The United States Army has withdrawn from the borders of our land. I would think we would be at peace now."

"You have been away four years," said the deacon. "The ill will—no, call it hate—of the nonbelievers for us has grown. The invasion by the United States Army was only the outward sign of the hate our enemies have for us. Though the Army is gone, the hidden danger may be even greater."

Booth spoke. "Mathias, you saw the man on the street shouting that craziness at the women. Well, he said what many believe. That we are devils and our wives are bound for hell."

"The women have come to America of their own free will," said Matthias. "And they marry of their own free will."

"We know that," said Deacon Moeller. "But that makes little difference to the nonbelievers, who see the young, single women, many quite beautiful, going in large numbers to Salt Lake City. Booth, it was not wise to bring them through the main section of St. Joseph."

"The railroad station is in the center of town and we had no choice," said Booth, a tinge of irritation in his voice. Deacon Moeller knew that fact.

"I wish we could leave at once for Salt Lake City," said Anton. "When will the handcarts be ready?"

"I've received word today from the workmen Brigham Young sent out to Florence to build the handcarts. Thirty carts have been finished now. All fifty-five should be ready in less than a week."

Mathias watched Deacon Moeller thoughtfully pull at his long chin. He knew the deacon. The church official had come to St. Joseph from Salt Lake City with the group of

Mormon missionaries Mathias had traveled with on his way to England. Deacon Moeller had brought only one wife, his favorite, with him to St. Joseph. The remaining six wives were operating the deacon's large farm in the Sevier Valley, south of Salt Lake City. What would the rowdy citizens of St. Joseph have done to the deacon had they known about his several wives?

The deacon spoke. "When Anton reached St. Joe, I sent a messenger to Brigham Young. I told him that I thought any group of our people that set out westward this year could be in danger from the Indians and white renegades. I requested he send armed men to escort the people safely to Salt Lake City."

"Will he send men a thousand miles into enemy country to guard us?" asked Anton.

"Without a doubt. He will order men on their way within a day after he gets my message."

"I hope he sends Orrin Grueling," said Booth. "Of all the men he would be the one to keep the handcart company safe."

"Yes," agreed the Deacon. "Grueling would be the best choice. He is a hard man and knows weapons."

"I remember Grueling," said Mathias. "He and his tough friends are an embarrassment to the church. It is said he has killed men."

Deacon Moeller studied Mathias. "Grueling is indeed an embarrassment. But an embarrassment we can't do without at this time. He and his kind are necessary to fend off the enemies of the church. And I don't mean just outside enemies. There are those malcontents inside who meet with representatives of the eastern newspapers and tell them untrue stories. Those stories, when printed, increase the resentment against us. They contributed very much to the United States Army marching against Salt Lake City."

"He and his Sons of Dan followers must be watched very carefully," said Mathias.

"Don't use that name," Deacon Moeller said sternly. "There is no such organization as the Sons of Dan."

Mathias was surprised by the elder's statement. Perhaps there was not a formal organization sanctioned by the church, but a loosely knit group of self-appointed avengers visited people and—in a quite harsh, sometimes cruel way—pointed out the errors of their actions.

"When can we leave for Salt Lake City?" asked Anton.

"Make plans to steam upriver to Florence in five days. I'll have all the provisions you'll be taking with you sent on ahead. There'll be three wagons with mules to carry food-stuff and water. Everything else must be transported by the people on their handcarts. Spend as little time in Florence as possible. The citizens there do not like us any better than here in St. Joe. You should be safe from the renegade nonbelievers and the Indians for the first few days of travel through the outlying farmsteads west of Florence. By that time the men Brigham Young has sent to guard you should have met you on the trail."

"If your messenger got through to Salt Lake City," said Booth.

"Let's pray that he does," said the deacon, looking at Mathias and Anton. "Otherwise you and your converts could be in great peril."

•◆ 14 ◆•

CAROLINE WAS ANGERED BY THE NOISY CROWD of St. Joseph townspeople gathered on the border of the grove of oak trees. Today there were sixty, maybe seventy, people gawking at the Mormons as they assembled for the evening devotional service. She could see others, mostly young men, coming along the road from the town. If the spectators continued to increase at the present rate, they would outnumber the Mormons in two days. Disgusted, she turned her back to the throng and sat down on the grass beneath one of the large oaks.

Mathias Rowley and Anton Lund came striding from the tent village the Mormons had constructed in the narrow meadow between the woods and the Missouri River. Anton veered off and approached the congregation of Swedish converts. Mathias joined his English followers. He was smiling in a pleased way.

Mathias ignored the mustering of the noisy St. Joseph people watching them. He raised his voice and it rang out over his followers. "Zion is there beyond the Missouri, beyond the broad prairie and in the heart of the Rockies." He swept his arm west at the yellow sun hanging a finger's width above the flat horizon. "The construction of our handcarts is nearly completed in Florence. In three days we shall leave this city of St. Joseph. You must endure the laughter and scorn of the nonbelievers of this place until then. Tell them of your faith, and in your testimony your voice shall sound like brass horns and tinkling cymbals to the wicked around you. We have journeyed four thousand miles together, many of you with but a few shillings. Now, together, we shall go up into the mountains to the beautiful shore of the Great Salt Lake."

He lifted both arms to the sky. "There you can live a righteous life and serve our God. You shall surely go to his Celestial Kingdom when your time here on earth is finished."

As Mathias ceased speaking, a puff of wind sprang into life, as if it had been waiting for the pronouncement. It swept upon the missionary's back and lifted his hair and flared it around his head. The low, slanting rays of the sun caught the strands of his hair and for a few seconds turned the strands into golden, flaming filaments, as if a golden halo had been placed upon his head.

A murmur of astonishment rose from the converts as they saw the sudden flash of radiance around the missionary's head. Several of the people jumped to their feet.

"Look! Look!" a young woman cried out.

Mathias heard the surging rise of voices. He stared at his converts in an uncomprehending manner, a man with a temporary halo upon his head and a perplexed expression upon his face.

The wind died, and a limb of a tree resumed its position

and blocked out the sun. The missionary stood in deep shadow. The people's voices quieted.

A rough-looking man shouted out in a strident voice from the crowd of townspeople. "Preacher, you promise the women your Celestial Heaven in the hereafter, but I have a different plan for them. I'll take half a dozen of them for wives. No, make that an even dozen, half blond and half dark heads. I'll give them heaven right here on earth." He laughed in a coarse, ribald tone.

An uproar of laughter erupted from the townsfolk.

"You tell them, Jack," a man shouted. "I'd take a pretty one myself, but my wife would kill me if I did."

A bedlam of hoots and shouts broke from the crowd. Some of the men began to stomp the ground in a crude, drumlike rhythm.

Mathias looked stonily at the troublesome throng until the hubbub finally stilled. He began to speak again to his followers. "There'll be a meeting of the leaders of the groups of ten later this evening. Much must be planned for our journey. But now we shall sing 'Come, Come Ye Saints' to open the regular evening service."

Caroline was one of the leaders of the groups of ten. She had not sought the position. Mathias had simply told her on the day of their arrival at the camp that she was to represent the other nine girls who shared a tent with her. He had looked steadily into her eyes for a moment after his announcement, then pivoted on his heel and left. His abrupt, dictatorial manner had bothered Caroline. Yet there was something else in his eyes, something that had stirred her blood.

As Caroline sang with the others she pondered the meaning of the momentary halo that had appeared around Mathias's head. Was that a sign the man held some religious, perhaps divine, power? She thought not, for in all her short, hard life she had witnessed nothing but the tough knot of everyday reality. What had occurred was a mere coincidence of time and circumstance, of wind and sunshine. But others of the converts might disagree with her. There would be much discussion of the event in the tent that night. The song ended and Mathias began a discussion of the Book of Mormon.

Caroline found her mind wandering, as so often happened
during the religious ceremonies. From nearby, faintly heard,
came the voice of Anton talking to his converts in their
strange tongue. The English and Swedes tended to remain
apart because of the language difference. But soon they
would all be joined together in one caravan for the long trek
west over the plains.

"May I sit beside you?" asked a young woman who had
drawn near, unnoticed by Caroline.

"Of course," Caroline replied, glancing up. The girl was a
stranger, not one of the converts. She was about Caroline's
age. A shy expression was on her pretty face. She was
dressed in a blue silk dress with many ribbons and bows. A
blue hat with a small thatch of feathers sat primly upon the
brown curls of her head.

The girl dropped down beside Caroline, seemingly uncon-
cerned about the stains the ground might make on her fine
clothing. Caroline ruefully reflected upon her own cheap
cotton dress.

The girl spoke to Caroline. "I heard there were Mormons
camped near town and just had to come and see for myself."

Caroline was not sure how she should interpret the girl's
statement. Did she think Mormons were something strange,
like a a freak show in a circus?

"I'm Ruth Crandall," the girl said.

"My name is Caroline Shepherd."

"Are you one of those who came from England?"

"Yes. But we should not talk while Elder Rowley is
conducting the service."

"Oh, yes. Of course, you are right." Ruth turned to face
Mathias.

Mathias had noted the arrival of the well-clothed young
woman. As he went on with his sermon his attention and
words were often directed at her. His voice deepened, its
timbre becoming more solemn.

Caroline remembered back to the first time she had heard
Mathias preach. His voice was now like that other day. She
looked at Ruth.

The girl was leaning forward. Her face had lost its shy

expression. Her lips were parted and her eyes were locked upon the missionary's handsome countenance.

Caroline saw Ruth drinking in the words of the missionary. She knew the fervor and power of Mathias to sway people to his religion. He might gain another convert in Ruth. Caroline should have been pleased with the thought. However, for some unexplainable reason, she was not. Should she say something to the girl? Foolish thought, there was nothing to say. Fate would take the girl wherever it willed.

Mathias finished speaking. His last look was at the new girl. Then he began to talk with members of the congregation as they drew close with comments or questions.

"My, he's a wonderful speaker," Ruth said to Caroline.

"Very eloquent and very persuasive," Caroline said.

"I understand all of you will soon be going on to Salt Lake City," Ruth said.

"In three more days. The handcarts are almost all built."

"Handcarts? What are handcarts?"

"I'm not certain exactly what they look like. I've been told they have two high wheels and can be pulled by four or five people. We'll use them to carry our possessions with us across the prairie."

"There are no wagons or horses?"

"Only to haul the heavy items, such as part of the supplies of food, water, and those who become too ill to walk."

"How many miles must you pull the handcarts?"

"More than a thousand."

"A thousand miles would be difficult to walk, let alone pulling handcarts."

"I don't think it will be easy. But others have done it before us. We can too."

"Do you live there in those tents?" Ruth asked, and pointed at the canvas structures beyond the trees.

"Yes. There are ten girls to a tent. Or two families with children in each."

"Your religion must be very strong for you to travel all that long distance across the ocean from England."

Ruth's statement brought remembrances to Caroline of the ocean and the *African Blackbird*. She recalled again the rape of Esther and the beating death of Seaman Timson.

She shivered as the face of Captain Varick came into her mind. The feel of the knife in her hands as she stabbed and cut the man's flesh would never leave her. Sometimes she awoke at night in terror, the captain reaching for her.

Caroline wondered if she could still be a good Christian, a good Mormon, after committing murder. A very troubling question.

"Are you married?" Ruth asked.

"No."

"Will you get married in Salt Lake City?"

"Maybe."

"Do the Mormon men have several wives?"

"I believe many of them do."

"What do you think of that?"

Caroline folded her hands in her lap and looked at Ruth. "What do you think of it?" she asked.

Ruth was silent, pondering the question turned back upon her. At last she spoke. "It would depend on the man."

"Exactly," Caroline said.

Somewhat flustered at the turn of the conversation, Ruth rose to her feet. "Well, I've asked far too many questions. You have been kind to talk with me. I must go."

Ruth walked a few steps, then whirled around to look back at Caroline. "What time is your morning service? You do have services twice a day?"

"Yes, morning and evening. Morning service is at eight o'clock, at least while we are in camp here."

"Thank you. Good-bye."

"Good-bye," Caroline said.

She watched after Ruth for a moment, then went through the grove of trees toward the tent village. Sophia fell in beside her.

"Who was that girl who sat beside you?" Sophia asked.

"A girl from St. Joseph named Ruth Crandall. She was curious and came to see what we were like."

"I saw her face as she looked at Mathias. She will be back."

"I think so too," Caroline said.

"I've heard Mathias and Booth Clark talking. The resentment against the Mormons is increasing day by day as we stay here in St. Joe," Sophia said. "He should not try to convert anyone, especially one of the town girls. That could bring trouble to all of us."

Caroline gestured at the group of men and large boys still lingering and watching. "I agree. They could get mean about that. However, if Mathias gets the opportunity, he will try to persuade the girl to give up her religion and accept his. I don't think he can help himself." She felt a premonition that the pretty girl in the expensive clothing would bring tragedy to the Mormons.

Rain drummed with a dismal sound on the tarpaulin of the tent. Caroline had heard the storm come in during the night. The rain had not slackened at all. She doubted Mathias would hold a morning ceremony.

She rose from the cot and made her way through the women and down the narrow aisle in the middle of the tent. She lifted the flap and peered out into the downpour.

To her surprise a woman stood in the rain at the edge of the trees and watched the camp of the Mormons. A black umbrella was held low over the person's head to keep off the rain. Still she was wet from the waist down.

The woman shifted the umbrella and Caroline recognized Ruth Crandall. The girl saw Caroline and lifted her hand timidly in greeting.

"For goodness sakes, come in out of the storm," Caroline called, and made a sweep of her hand to emphasize her words.

Ruth left the trees and hurried over the short stretch of meadow. She ducked her head and entered the tent.

"What were you doing out there?" Caroline asked.

"I didn't want to miss your religious ceremony," Ruth said. "Will there be one?

"I don't think so, not in this rain. We have no tent large enough to hold all the people."

"That's too bad. I enjoyed listening to Elder Rowley yesterday."

"You came out in this rainstorm to hear him preach?"

Ruth's cheeks turned crimson through their wetness. "To hear him tell the truths of his religion."

"Don't you have a church to go to?" asked Caroline.

"I do. I'm a Baptist, but our church is so dry. They do nothing exciting like the Mormons do. Even our revival meetings are dull and long." Ruth's voice quickened. "The Mormons are the talk of everybody, how their missionaries go all over the world and bring back converts. I want to be part of an adventure. Like your coming thousands of miles from England."

Ruth's excited speech silenced Caroline. She did not consider her journey from England an adventure. It was a necessity if she was to better her lot in life. And she had been forced to kill a man. Would Ruth think that killing somebody was an adventure?

"So you came out into the rain to see the Mormons because they do exciting things?" Caroline said.

"I'm not sugar, that a little rain will melt me," Ruth came back tartly.

"All right, you'll not melt. Are you also thinking about hooking yourself to one of the handcarts and dragging it for three or four months across a thousand miles of plains and mountains that have no road?"

"Maybe I will," replied Ruth, her tone sharper.

"May I come in?" Mathias's voice came from outside the tent entrance.

"We're all decent, so come in," Caroline replied.

The tent flap parted and Mathias's tall form appeared in the opening. He stepped inside and straightened. His head brushed the ridgepole of the tent. He removed his hat. "I wanted to inform you that there'll be no services held until the rain stops."

He noticed Ruth sitting among the other young women. "Hello," he said. "I saw you yesterday. I'm Mathias Rowley."

"I know," Ruth said. "Caroline told me. I'm Ruth Crandall. I thought your sermon was excellent."

Mathias inclined his head in acceptance of her compliment. His eyes brightened. "Perhaps sometime I may talk with you about our religion," he said.

"I would like that," Ruth said.

"It is raining now and there's nothing much that can be done. Would this be a suitable time?"

"Now would be fine," Ruth said.

"I have my Bible and the Book of Mormon in my tent. If you will wait here, I'll go get them and then we can have a discussion about the two great books and how they complement each other." He spoke to Caroline. "If that is okay with Caroline and the other women that we use their tent."

Caroline checked with the other occupants of the tent. They all nodded in the affirmative. Sophia had a knowing expression on her face.

"We are all agreeable to that," Caroline said.

"Good. I'll be back in a moment." Mathias shoved aside the flap of canvas and left.

Caroline saw the glow of anticipation in Ruth's eyes. What was the girl thinking? Was it a search for true religion or a young girl's attraction to a handsome man?

Caroline picked up her coat and threw it over head. She left, crossing the meadow through the wetness toward Ellen's tent. She did not want to be present while Mathias talked with Ruth. Caroline had already experienced his fervor to convert a new disciple for his Mormon religion. In England that was expected of him. Somehow here in St. Joseph, with the dislike of the townsfolk so prevalent, his unbridled enthusiasm could be very dangerous. For had not Joseph Smith, founder of the Mormon religion, been slain, his followers driven into the wilderness because of their beliefs?

Caroline caught herself up. She had thought of the Mormon religion as Mathias's; however, it was also hers. But even the acknowledgment of a joint religious belief did not lessen her concern that Mathias's actions would bring harm to the people.

◆▶ 15 ◀◆

THE RIVER STEAMER *SIOUX*, A LARGE STERN-wheeler, heeled far to the side as the winds of the storm front caught it broadside. The thick oak siding of the boat slammed the wharf with a thunderous, pile-driving bang. The gangway fastened to the boat and resting on the dock instantly dropped nearly four feet.

Caroline's knees almost buckled beneath her as the gangway stopped its fall with a spine-jarring jolt. She grabbed the safety rail and held on fiercely to keep from being thrown into the river. With her other hand she tightly clutched her blanket-wrapped bundle of personal possessions to her.

The *Sioux* rolled back onto its keel. The gangway accelerated upward to its original position.

"Oh, my God!" cried Sophia, hanging half over the handrail against which she had been thrown. She pulled herself back from the precarious position above the water and stood erect. She shuddered. "I can't swim," she said to Caroline.

"That was a terrible wind," said Caroline. "Are you hurt?"

"My ribs feel broken from hitting the railing," said Sophia as she rubbed her side. She grinned at Caroline. "But I'll live."

Other people were catching their balance on the gangway. A man shouted to those in the line ahead of him. "Hurry, move on! Get off the gangway before the boat rolls again and breaks it!" The men and women hastened on.

"More bad things are on the way," Caroline said, spotting the curtain of white sweeping down the river under the heavy gray overcast of clouds that filled the sky. "Looks like a snowstorm is coming. Will winter ever end?"

She hunched her shoulders and ducked her head as the storm pounced upon the steamboat and the people. She had been wrong. The whiteness of the storm was not soft snowflakes but hard balls of sleet streaking down like arrows. A hissing, popping sound immediately filled the air as the ice balls struck the deck and bounced across the wooden planking.

Driven by the added impetus of the stinging sleet, the people scampered even faster up the slanting gangway. Their feet slipped and slid on the slick, ice-covered wood. A woman cried out as she dropped her package of belongings into the river. A man on the dock ran to the edge of the water and fished the sodden bundle out before it could sink. More people entered onto the gangway.

Mathias moved about on the dock, encouraging his people to hurry on board the *Sioux*. He saw Anton gathering the last of his Swedish converts. Several of the families were carrying a very large number of items. They were bringing far too many possessions. Most of it would have to be thrown away in Florence. Anton should have told them that much earlier, rather than let them bring it the long distance from their homes in Europe and then have to discard it.

He ranged his sight over the decks of the steamboat. Caroline was in the lee of the deckhouse with Sophia. Caroline had selected the most protected spot on the open deck. As Mathias watched, the other girls of her tent of ten were winding their way through the people to cluster around her. Caroline had no responsibility for them on the boat. They were drawn by her quiet certainty of purpose. With her as a solid, competent leader, though he knew she was a reluctant leader, he would not have to worry much about that group of girls.

The captain of the *Sioux* came out on the little foredeck of the wheelhouse, the third deck and highest part of the boat. He lifted his cone-shaped megaphone to his mouth and shouted down at the dock. "Get your people on board, Mr. Rowley."

Mathias cupped his hand around his mouth and called back. "Don't you want to wait for the storm to slacken?"

"No. The *Sioux* is used to storms on the river. Let's get on our way."

"Right, Captain. Another five minutes should do it." Mathias would be very glad when all the Mormons were gone from the hostile Gentiles of St. Joseph.

"Look who's coming down Francis Street," Sophia said, gesturing across the dock toward town.

Caroline glanced in the direction in which Sophia pointed. "It's Ruth Crandall. Mathias went and did it. He's recruited a girl from St. Joseph."

"Since she's joining just as we're leaving, he might get away with it without having angry brothers or a father searching for her with guns."

"Or a hundred St. Joe men coming to look for her. That could be very great trouble."

Ruth, clothed in a long-tailed dress, coat, and hat, hastened past a group of men who had gathered at the foot of Francis Street to watch the Mormons leave. One of the men called out to Ruth. She did not turn or answer but continued on, a blanket roll under her arm and a valise swinging in her hand.

She climbed the gangway and cast a look about through the converts already on the boat. She saw Caroline and came across the deck toward her.

"I'm going with you," Ruth said as she drew near.

"Why?" asked Sophia.

Ruth was taken aback by the question. Disconcerted, she looked around at the girls watching her. Ignoring Sophia, Ruth spoke to Caroline. "Mathias told me all about the religion of the Latter-day Saints. And I believe his religion is the true one. I want to be one of you. So here I am."

"Ready for that big adventure you told Caroline about?" Sophia said.

Ruth squarely faced Sophia. "I suppose you could say that," she said with a hint of anger. "But am I any different than you?"

Caroline spoke in a soft voice to Ruth. "Where are your folks, your brothers, your father? What do they have to say about you leaving with us?"

"My mother is dead. I am an only child. My father is in New York selling furs. I left him a note explaining my decision."

"What will he do when he finds out you have run off with Mormons?" Caroline asked.

"He will understand. And, anyway, I'm eighteen and can do as I please. May I travel with you?"

"Why don't you go back home," Caroline said gently. "You still have time to leave the boat. Think about what you are doing. We are going to drag handcarts to Salt Lake City because we have no other way to get there. But you have money. If later you still want to go, then pay for a ride on a wagon."

"No. I'm going now. Making the thousand-mile journey with the handcarts will be a test of my faith in the Mormon religion. If you don't want me to travel with you, I'll find another group of girls."

"If you must go, then you may travel with us," Caroline said.

"Oh, thank you!" cried Ruth.

"In a day or so you won't be thanking me. More than likely you'll be cursing all of us. Put your belongings down there on the deck with ours."

Caroline turned from Ruth and spoke to Sophia. "Would you please watch my things? I'm going forward for a while."

"Sure," Sophia said.

Caroline removed one of the two blankets from her pack and wrapped it around her. The thin coat she wore gave little protection from the falling sleet and cold. The blanket helped.

She walked across the deck, winding a course through the throng of more than two hundred and fifty converts standing or sitting elbow to elbow, and their bundles, boxes, and suitcases. She saw the excited faces of the children, who, together with their mothers, had been given the small enclosed deck cabin for shelter. The youngsters stared out big-eyed through the glass windows at the falling sleet and the people huddled in their worn clothing.

The fire beneath the twin boilers of the steamboat had been stoked to the limit with wood. Caroline saw the smoke

and sparks fly from the two smokestacks and sail off with
the wind. The trip up the Missouri was one hundred and
seventy miles. With the current fighting against the *Sioux*,
the trip would take nearly two days. When black night came
and the captain could no longer see the snags and sandbars
in the river, he would tie up to the bank and wait for the
light of day.

The captain shouted with his megaphone from the wheelhouse. "Up gangway. Prepare to cast off."

On the deck the riverboat men pushed through the passengers to their duty stations. Two crewmen took hold of
the arms of the windlass that raised the gangway and heaved
mightily to turn it.

The lines were cast off. The *Sioux* began to rumble and
vibrate. The giant paddle wheel groaned and started to
revolve, clawing for a hold on the slippery brown water.

Caroline reached the bow of the steamboat. The cold
storm winds blew fiercely. The sleet peppered the river,
wounding it a million times a second. The river instantly
swallowed the ice pellets and healed the wounds.

Caroline stared up the river. The brown current was hidden beyond a quarter of a mile by the white, masking
shroud of sleet. She pulled the blanket more tightly around
her. There was much danger on the river: floating logs to
bash in the hull and sink the boat and sandbars upon which
to run aground; or the boilers could explode, as she heard
they often did. Beyond the river lay the great prairie, with
its hostile Indians; and still farther away the tall mountains
and their steep, nearly impossible grades. And always another tribe of Indians. She must drag a handcart a thousand
miles over all that land. She vowed she would never turn
back. Her destiny was out there somewhere, waiting for
her. She knew it.

She raised her head and faced the storm and all the
unknown hazards ahead. The wind-driven sleet bit and tore
at her cheeks and froze her face into a stiff mask. She did
not flinch.

◆ 16 ◆

CAROLINE STRAINED FORWARD INTO THE HARNESS and her feet drove hard against the dusty ground. Sweat coursed down her face and funneled into a tiny stream between her breasts.

The leather straps of the harness that had chafed her shoulders so raw at first now rode on callused skin. Her hands had become toughened to the crossbar and no longer pained as she pushed. During the past eight days every muscle of her body had hardened with the torturous labor of pulling the handcart.

Even though Caroline felt strong, she was glad for the big Swedish girl, Pauliina Halverson, who labored in the harness beside her. And for Sophia and Ruth pushing in the dust at the rear of the handcart. Together, as a team, they matched the pace of the caravan, up to twenty miles between daylight and dark on a good day.

The *Sioux* had arrived at Florence in the dusk of the evening of the second day after leaving St. Joseph. The Mormons had set up their tents by lantern light near the cemetery of Winter Quarters. Caroline had heard of the much respected place, where the Latter-day Saints, fleeing from the persecution by the Gentiles, had spent that terrible winter during the exodus to Utah. She and Pauliina had walked through the cemetery in the frail light of the dying moon. They had spoken not one word. None were needed to know the suffering that had occurred there. The number of graves told it all.

Anton blew a series of light, lively notes on a bugle he possessed to rouse the people at five o'clock in the morning of the first full day in Florence. By seven o'clock breakfast

125

had been cooked and eaten. Immediately the converts assembled for a song, a prayer, and instructions for the day from Mathias and Anton.

The missionaries weighed the articles the people were allowed to take with them—twenty pounds. Everything else must be discarded. There was much moaning and complaining from some of the people, for though they had known of the limit, nevertheless they had brought some prized possessions—dishes, books, and one person a feather tick. Now they were forced to abandon those cherished belongings, throw them down on the ground for the rain and sun to destroy.

Provisions of flour, bacon, rice, dry beans, dried apples, and sugar—enough for ten days—were distributed. The converts followed the missionaries into the adjacent meadow, where fifty-five handcarts stood in eleven rows of five.

Caroline, Sophia, and Ruth slowly circled around one of the handcarts, examining it from all angles.

"It doesn't look too heavy to pull," said Sophia.

"Not standing there empty," Caroline said.

"Is that the one you young ladies choose to take to Salt Lake City?" asked a man, drawing near.

"It should be as good as any of the others, since they all appear to be alike," Caroline said.

"They are all solidly made," said the man. "I'm one of the carpenters who built them. I heard you talking about its weight. Well, it weighs sixty pounds and rolls easy. The wheels are four feet tall and the iron rims one quarter inch thick and two inches wide. You'll be glad for the width of the rims, for that keeps the wheels from cutting into the dirt or sand, making the cart hard to pull.

"The axles are of hickory and have iron skeins on the hubs for the wheels to bear on. They'll last all the way to Salt Lake City if you grease them three times a week. The wooden side bars extend out forward as shafts and have that crossbar in front to push against. The box bed is three feet wide, four feet long, and nine inches deep. The cart will haul more than you might think. There's a piece of canvas to cover everything to keep off the rain. With all your belongings and the food and water you must carry with you, the total weight will be more than two hundred pounds."

"What's that?" Caroline asked pointing at two contraptions that looked like halters made of leather straps and hung from the front of the box bed.

"That's a pair of harnesses. The two of you who'll be pulling can put those over your shoulders to make the pulling easier. They have straps that buckle around your chest and under your arms."

"We must wear harness like horses?" Sophia said.

"Yes, like horses." The carpenter's eyes were clouded with compassion. "You are beginning a most difficult journey. There will be many times when you'll wish you were as strong as horses, and just as dumb in your feelings."

The carpenter left as Anton, accompanied by one of the Swedish girls, approached Caroline and her two companions. "This is Pauliina Halverson," Anton said. "She would like to join you and be the fourth girl with your handcart. She wants to learn as much English as possible before she reaches Salt Lake City. The best way for her to do that is to travel with some of you who speak English."

Caroline evaluated the Swede, measuring her probable strength against the thousand-mile journey that lay before them. Ruth was small of stature and fine boned. Sophia had approximately the same small to medium build as Caroline. Neither of them were horses, as the carpenter had said they might at times wish they were.

Pauliina was dressed in men's clothing, as was Caroline, with sturdy leather shoes and a hat with a brim. She towered nearly a head above Caroline. Her hips and shoulders were broad. A long, thick braid of silver-gold hair hung down her back to the waist.

"I strong," Pauliina said. She smiled and her sky-blue eyes sparkled as she answered Caroline's unasked question.

Caroline hesitated a moment, then said, "I *am* strong. That is the way you correctly say it."

"I *am* strong," Pauliina repeated. Her smile broadened as she recognized by Caroline's words the fact that she had been accepted into the group of English girls.

Caroline raised her view from the dusty trail and wiped at

the sweat on her face with her shirt sleeve. The handcarts were strung out in a line stretching more than a quarter of a mile across the greenish gray of the land. The winter had been long and had treated the northern Nebraska prairie harshly. Caroline had seen many rotting carcasses of buffalo and wild horses. Vultures fed on the carrion of some of the most recent dead. The growth of spring grass had been much delayed, but finally the tiny green shoots of life were poking their heads into the sunlight. The gaunt steers and mules grazed late into the night on the nutritious new feed.

The caravan followed the Platte River Trail, which paralleled the river on the northern edge of the broad, flat floodplain. The Mormons had forded the Elkhorn River, the Loup River, and many lesser streams flowing down through the brushy breaks to empty into the Platte. The route was the same one used by immigrants trekking west to some far-off place called Oregon, on the shore of the Pacific Ocean.

She frequently saw graves beside the trail. The Mormons had added to the number, for they were three people fewer than when they had left Florence. The Pattersons' two little sons perished of whooping cough within hours of each other in the night. Sacraments were said and the small bodies were buried in the prairie soil.

Brother Anders Fjeld died of exhaustion in the heat of an afternoon. After the funeral his widow dashed away her tears. She sorted through their scant belongings and transferred a few articles to the handcart of people who had agreed to accept her with their group. The caravan journeyed on, the widow pushing at the rear of the vehicle. Her own cart had been left behind on the plain.

The possessions of Mathias and Anton were carried in one of the wagons. Thus freed, the two missionaries moved along the converts, pushing where needed on one handcart or pulling on another. At the stream crossings where the banks were steep and difficult to negotiate, they helped every cart to cross. Then they hurried to overtake those who had gone on ahead and continued to lend strength to the weak.

The three mule-drawn supply wagons, driven by three of

the larger male children, led the way on the much used trail. The herd of fourteen steer came last. There had been fifteen animals until the previous evening when the first had been butchered. The steer had provided each of the people about two pounds of meat each. Another steer would be slaughtered every week until the travelers reached Salt Lake City.

Mathias halted the caravan of Latter-day Saints for the night in a grove of trees beside the creek. The tents were pitched in a huge circle enclosed by the handcarts. Two men drove the mules and cattle out to graze. One of the men carried a rifle.

After her tent was erected and supper eaten, Caroline left the camp and walked up the creek, in the opposite direction from which the livestock had gone. She was worried about the few weapons the men of the caravan possessed. They had passed the edge of civilization a hundred miles back. Now they were in a land that had no law, where only the gun and the war lance ruled. Yet only six men had firearms. Mathias and Anton each had a rifle and a pistol. Three of the converts had been given rifles by the church officials in St. Joe. Another man had a shotgun, an old antiquated weapon he had traded a watch for in St. Joseph. That was the entire array of armaments to protect two hundred and fifty innocents in the wilderness.

Caroline had questioned Mathias about the lack of weapons. He had explained that few of the converts had ever fired a gun. And even fewer had ever owned one. The purchase of a gun was a low priority to a family living in poverty. However, she should not be alarmed, for armed men were coming from Salt Lake City to protect them from the Indians and white renegades on the long journey across the prairie and the mountains. Also, he added, there had been only two minor attacks on travelers on the Platte River Trail in the past year. Mathias seemed confident of their safety. Caroline was not.

She stared to the west across the limitless gray prairie. The vast, flat emptiness inspired a disconsolate feeling about a woman's insignificance, that she did not matter at all. However, she still felt her destiny lay in that direction. But was the destiny of death to be hers?

She entered the woods and found the creek. She bathed and then sat silently on the bank near the water as the daylight leaked away into the heavens.

The slow wind died. The whispering leaves of the trees above her ceased their movement and hung without a rustle. Complete silence reigned. Caroline held her breath to better hear this rare intervals of utter stillness.

Several seconds crept by. The only thing that moved was the last of the daylight abandoning the prairie. The water of the creek became as smooth and black as a pool of tar.

A series of melodious bird warbles, sweetly trilled and quavering, sounded from the treetop directly over Caroline's head. She cocked her ear to listen to the tuneful song.

The bird song stopped for a moment, then came again, an enchanting medley beginning low, rising to full-throated volume, then sliding delightfully downward in a succession of perfect, lovely notes. And lower still, until it could only be heard in Caroline's memory.

She remained very quiet, waiting, hoping for the lovely song to come again. But the total silence reigned.

Why had the bird sung at night? Had it been meant for her alone? Foolish thought. Only a coincidence.

Still, it had helped her to conquer her bout of melancholy. She climbed to her feet and turned toward the camp. Destiny was destiny and could not be changed. She would go and meet hers. Even if that meant dragging that contraption of a handcart for a hundred days—yes, even for a thousand days.

17

SAM ROSE FROM HIS BED IN THE COLD, DISMAL, darkness of the early morning. Without lighting the candle, he washed in the basin of water that sat on the stand in the corner of his room in the boardinghouse. As he always did each day before he pulled on his buckskin clothing, he felt the bulging cyst in the top of his stomach. The thing had stopped growing; he was fairly confident of that. But it was a hateful, threatening thing waiting to rupture, to spill its poison and kill him.

He dressed and went out into the dark street. He felt much troubled. The days had sped past as he searched St. Joe for the river pirates. The probability that the men had left the town, if they had ever been there, was becoming almost a certainty. Trappers often went overland to St. Louis on the Mississippi, or downriver to New Orleans.

Sam moved slowly along the street through the growing morning twilight. The brisk wind blowing over the town was chilly, for the temperature had fallen below freezing during the night. The ground was frozen as hard as stone.

The covered wagon of an immigrant family came by, its iron wheels jolting and rattling on the hard earth. The man and woman sat bundled in heavy coats on the high seat. The woman held a crying baby in her arms. The wagon turned down Francis Street to the ferry.

A group of men rode by on trotting horses. Sam peered intently at them. No, none of them were the men he sought.

He scrutinized the patrons eating breakfast in a restaurant. Disappointed, he went on.

A big brown dog came out of an alley and began to trail noiselessly behind Sam. He ignored the beast, and after half a block it loped off. The double doors of a blacksmith shop swung open, and the smithy began to rekindle the fire in his forge.

The twilight brightened to full daylight. More wagons moved toward the waterfront. A wagon train must be forming upon the west side of the Missouri River. Pedestrians came into the streets, as well as more men on horseback. St. Joe was coming awake.

Sam halted in front of the office of a fur buyer. Perhaps the proprietor would know the men for whom Sam searched.

Ruth Crandall raised her gaze from her father's business ledgers and looked across the office and out the window. She had been at the office for more than two hours, for she liked to work in the quiet morning before the town noise began. It was a safe, comforting feeling with the soft yellow light of the lamp shining on the pages of the ledgers and the black ink recording the purchases and sales, and the profits her father always made. Since the arrival of the railroad in the February just past, the profits were even greater.

Another hour and all business transactions would be recorded. Her father would be pleased. However, there would be no more ledgers to work on. She would leave St. Joe this morning, for she had decided to go with the Mormon converts to Salt Lake City. Her father would not like that.

Though she would miss her father terribly, and her life in St. Joe, the new religion was like a fever in her blood. She must go where it lived, where the people practiced it and thrived. Her hands trembled and her heart felt ready to burst in anticipation of joining the immigrant converts in their journey to the place called Zion.

A gaunt man in buckskins came into sight on the street. He was bent forward as if carrying a heavy load on his back. Each one of his steps was carefully placed upon the ground, as if his legs were fragile and might break.

He halted and looked up at the Crandall Fur & Hides sign on the face of the building. He crossed the sidewalk. The tiny bell fastened to the front door tinkled as he entered.

Ruth watched with growing surprise as the man came

closer. She had thought him an old man, ill and frail, from the manner in which he walked. However, he was not but two or three years older than she was. His eyes were an intense tan color, the color of flint, and glowed with a fierce inner fire. A pistol was in a holster on his belt. It seemed to belong there. She wondered if he had killed, and sensed that he had. Yet, strangely, even with that thought, she felt no fear of him. His hand swept the new, stiff-brimmed felt hat from his head.

"May I help you?" Ruth asked.

"I would like to talk with the fur buyer," Sam said. He cast a scanning look around the office. The young woman could not be the buyer. He saw a door open in the rear, exposing a huge storeroom. The storeroom was empty.

"My father is in New York selling the furs he bought this spring."

"When will he return to St. Joe?"

"In ten days to two weeks. He had no set schedule. I'm Ruth Crandall, his daughter. Is there something I can do for you?"

"Maybe so. I'm Sam Wilde. I'm looking for three trappers who probably sold a large quantity of furs here in St. Joe in the past three or four weeks."

"Many trappers have sold pelts to my father. I keep the records. What are the trappers' names? I can look and see if they traded here."

"That's the problem. I don't know their names. I was hoping the fur buyer, your father, could help me find out their names."

"I'm sorry. I don't deal directly with the trappers, so therefore I can't help you."

The sincere kindness of the girl reached Sam. He focused his attention on her. Their eyes touched for a few seconds, and his cramped, angry heart expanded and beat pleasantly. A rare event in his murderous quest to find the fur thieves. He silently thanked her for her unintentional lessening of his misery.

Ruth saw the change in the young man's gaze as he looked at her, the angry fire in his eyes dying and a gentleness flooding through their depths. A most pleasing expression.

"Is there something else I can help you with?" she asked.

"No. But I do want to thank you," Sam said.

"You're welcome."

As the man turned away, Ruth saw the gentle expression begin to fade from his eyes and the harsh, burning light creep in. He moved toward the door.

Sam stopped midway across the office. God! How beautiful the girl was. He could not erase her face from his mind. It held center stage against all his images of how he would kill his enemies. Or be slain himself. The thought came that she might well be the last beautiful female he would ever see.

He turned around and retraced his steps. He halted in front of her desk and stood staring down into her face. The lamp light and the morning light from the window seemed to compete for the most pleasing way to illuminate the planes and curves of her face and her delightful gray eyes.

A powerful urge came over Sam to touch, to caress, the girl's soft skin. His hand reached out part way toward her before he could stop and freeze it in midair. He allowed his eyes to do what his hand could not. To trace the contours of her face, of her lips.

Sam knew the girl understood his emotion. Still, she did not stir but instead looked steadily back at him.

He sighed without sound. In other times, other situations, he would have spoken to her of things other than murderous trappers.

Sam turned once again to the door and, forgetting for the moment his illness, hastened with a quick stride from the fur buyer's office and the girl, Ruth.

18

NATHAN DUG WITH THE SHOVEL AT THE SPRING
on the side of the low hill ten miles north
of the ranch house. An area some twenty
yards across was a quagmire of mud, trampled and pawed
by buffalo and wild horses in search of more water than
naturally surfaced at the weak spring.

Surrounding the muddy zone, cottonwoods, willows, and
water-loving grasses covered nearly an acre of land. The fact
that all of the plants liked their feet wet told Nathan a
considerable quantity of water lay hidden below the surface,
on top of the bedrock. He had only to dig down to it. On
the side of the hill the depth to it should not be great.

After the spring was opened and flowed freely, he would
drive half a hundred cows and a couple of bulls to it. The
cattle, once they had drunk the water, would remain in the
vicinity to graze. The year-round water supply would open
up another four to five thousand acres of new grassland for
his hungry livestock.

He ceased digging and his head lifted quickly. The rapid
staccato of the hoofbeats of a running horse sounded from
the woods to the east. He dropped the shovel and, stepping
to his gray horse, jerked the rifle from its scabbard. Leading
the mount, he vanished into the nearby grove of cottonwoods.

The Comanche warrior, Crow, riding his black mustang,
broke from the woods and raced across the meadow to the
spring. He dragged the mustang to a sliding halt.

"Nathan," Crow shouted, "you are being robbed!"

Crow watched Nathan come out of the cottonwoods with
the rifle resting in the crook of his arm. The young white
man moved swiftly, yet silently, like the mountain lion with

135

its soft, padded feet. Like the mountain lion, his eyes were cold and observant, seeing everything. Crow had closely studied Nathan during the days they had shared the land by the spring near the ranch house. Nathan was a man beside whom Crow would fight, and have no fear he would be deserted in the battle. Perhaps one day Crow might even come to like the white man.

"Who's stealing what?" asked Nathan.

"White men have killed one of your cows."

"Where?"

"There." Crow pointed to the southeast. "Five of your miles."

Nathan shoved his rifle into the scabbard on the gray horse. He yanked himself astride. "How many white men?"

"Five."

"Let's go and take a look at them," Nathan said.

The gray sprang away at Nathan's low command and in three strides was running. Crow pressed his mustang's ribs with his knees and the animal leapt ahead, running slightly in the lead to guide the way.

Nathan had seen no white men since the Texas Ranger had left. Nor an Indian after Crow's arrival. The presence of either color of men on his land most probably would mean trouble, and Nathan did not want more trouble. He wanted only to be left alone, to work and watch his herd of cattle increase.

The running horses crossed a range of rough, steep hills capped with trees. New buds were bursting from the tips of every limb. The spring grass was half a hand tall, cloaking this southern land in a blanket of green. A startled white-tailed deer burst from a clump of oak. Nathan watched after the deer as it bound away in magnificent leaps. The world was good. That could change swiftly if he had to fight the strange men who had butchered his cow.

Crow motioned at Nathan, and both men drew their mounts down to a walk. They rode quietly on around the side of a hill. Nathan smelled wood smoke and maybe, just for a whiff or two, cooking meat. The hill fell away and the camp of the white men came into view in the edge of a woods beside a small meadow.

The five men around the fire climbed to their feet as Nathan and Crow came into sight. The men moved apart, and their hands swung to hang near the holstered pistol each carried at his side.

Nathan noted the quick, ready way the men reacted to their sudden appearance. They were all young, but on the frontier, a man learned early in life to be wary. Or he did not live to be old.

Nathan primed himself for battle. If one of the men reached for his pistol, Nathan would grab his rifle. At the more than one-hundred-yard distance still separating them he would have all the advantage with his long-range killing weapon.

He glanced beyond the men to the carcass of a half-grown heifer. Its rear legs had been roped, and the animal hoisted partway up on the limb of a tree until only its head lay on the ground. The skin was peeled back from the hindquarters to the middle of the ribs.

Nathan led on down the slope of the hill. He dismounted fifty feet back from the strange riders and let the reins fall to ground-tie his gray.

"Stay with the horses," Nathan said to Crow. "Be ready with your musket."

He angled off slightly to the left of the band of men to give Crow a clear line of fire. He halted across the fire from the strangers.

Crow pulled his musket as he swung down. He held the weapon ready in his hands. Perhaps he would get the opportunity to kill another white man.

Nathan nodded his head at the men. Which one of them was the leader? he wondered. That important bit of information must be discovered immediately. Then he must watch the man closely for his signal to the others to draw their guns.

"Hi," said a thin fellow who was hardly more than a boy.

You're not the leader, thought Nathan as the man started to smile, then stopped, unsure of himself. You're too young. Nathan swept his eyes over the remaining seven.

"What can we do for you?" asked a second man, who

appeared to be the oldest of the bunch. "Why is that Indian standing out there with a rifle in his hands?"

"I expect old Crow would like to shoot another white man to add to his score," Nathan said. "As for what you can do for me . . . well, tell me why you butchered one of my beefs."

The thin-faced fellow glanced worriedly around at his companions. Nathan knew what he was thinking. Where there was no law, stealing a cow was a hanging crime.

"Drum, I told you—"

"Shut up, Charlie," Drum said. He spoke to Nathan. "Who said we killed one of your beefs?"

"I'm willing to take back the words if that dead heifer hanging there in that tree doesn't have the Double T brand on her left flank," said Nathan.

The group of men stirred uneasily. No one spoke.

"From the way you fellows act, I'd guess it's my heifer. That'll be ten dollars. Two from each of you." Nathan gestured down at several skillets of steak sizzling in the edge of the fire. "Looks like damn good meat and should be worth that much."

Nathan shifted almost imperceptibly, preparing himself to fight if it came to that. He had given the strangers a way out. Would they take it? Were they bandits, or honest cowhands passing over his range?

An edgy moment stretched as Drum studied Nathan. One of the men on Drum's left moved his hand.

Nathan reacted without conscious thought. His hand swung, lifted, catching the butt of his revolver. As the gun rose, his thumb eared back the hammer and a finger tightened on the trigger. The open black bore of the gun barrel came level, pointing at the center of the man who had moved. The expression on Nathan's face was deadly, the intent to kill plain.

"No! No!" cried the man. He staggered backward, as if the bullet had already struck him. His hands flew into the air above his head.

"Just getting my money."

Nathan halted the press of his finger on the trigger at the last possible instant. "God," he exclaimed. His breath sucked in and he gave an involuntary start of disbelief at how near he had come to shooting the man. The hand that held the pistol shook twice before he controlled it.

Nathan snapped his head to the side. Crow was sighting down the iron barrel of his rifle at the group.

"Crow! Don't shoot!" Nathan shouted.

Crow jerked with the sudden effort to stop the action already ordered by his mind. He seemed to lose his balance for a split second and took a step forward to regain it. Then the musket lowered.

Nathan's eyes jumped back to the man standing with his hands thrust up. "Damn you," he said raspily. "I almost shot you. So did Crow."

"I only wanted to give you my two dollars," said the man in an apologetic voice. He slowly lowered his hands and took his wallet from a rear pocket.

Nathan held his gun as he ranged his view over the other men. "Are all of you going to pay two dollars?"

A chorus of agreement came from the band of men. Nathan let his attention settle and focus on Drum, who had not answered. "And you?"

"Yes, I'll pay," Drum said. "We're not thieves."

"In that case, if you ask me to join you for dinner, I'll give you the heifer."

"Eat with us," Charlie said in a relieved voice. "You can share my steak with me. It weighs more than two pounds and is plenty for two."

"Crow's hungry too. He'll need some meat."

"I'll not eat with an Indian," Drum said in a surly tone.

"This time, Drum, I guess the rest of us will go our own way and eat with this fellow and his Indian," said the man Nathan had almost shot. "My name is Ash Brock." He held out his hand to Nathan. "Crow can have half of my steak."

"I'm Nathan Tolliver." He shook Ash's hand.

"I'm Charlie Morse," the thin young man said. He continued on to introduce the other men. "This is Les Jamison and Jake Payne. And this is Drum Shadley, who got us to leave Austin and ride north."

Nathan acknowledged the introductions. He beckoned the Comanche. "Crow, come and eat with us."

Crow walked up still holding his musket. Nathan thought
he appeared disappointed that there had been no battle.

Ash and Charlie divided their meat. Crow and Nathan
speared their portion from the skillets with their skinning
knives. Drum squatted on the side of the fire most distant
from the Comanche. His expression was dark as he watched
Crow eat.

"Good beef," Charlie said, ceasing to chew long enough
to speak. "Much better when you don't have to pay for it."
He laughed good-naturedly.

Nathan evaluated the saddled horses tied in the edge of
the woods nearby. Every one was an excellent mount. Each
saddle had a rifle in a scabbard. There were two packhorses.

"Where are you fellows headed?" Nathan asked.

"Up north to find us some wives," Ash replied.

"Wives," Nathan said in surprise. "There are no settlements with white women to the north. Even if you rode
clear to the North Pole."

"That's where you are wrong," Charlie said. "Drum, tell
him what you told us."

"You tell him," Drum said curtly.

Ash spoke. "Drum just got back from St. Joe, Missouri, a
few days ago. He saw hundreds of beautiful women there."

"Just a hundred or so," interjected Drum.

"Okay, Drum, you tell Nathan what you saw, and don't
be so god-awful mean," Ash said. "We're all friends now.
What happened before was just a misunderstanding and is
past."

"Yeah, you tell him, Drum," Charlie added.

"All right," Drum said. "I was up to St. Joe just traveling
around and seeing the country. I was about to leave when a
Mormon missionary coming from Europe arrives in the town.
He had a passel of converts with him, nearly all young
women. I saw them marching through town toward a tent
camp they had set up. I asked some questions about the
women and learned that old Brigham Young, the polygamist in Salt Lake City, sends out hundreds of men who go
all over the world turning people away from their own
religion and to his. Then these missionaries bring back with
them all the people who will come. This missionary in St.

Joe had some of the prettiest blond-headed girls I ever did see. I expect he plans to marry about half of them."

"No man can take care of fifty women," Charlie said.

Drum ignored Charlie and continued to speak. "The spring is the time of the year when the Mormon missionaries return to America with their converts. They congregate in St. Joe until there is a group of two or three hundred. Then all of them gather into what they call a handcart company and go marching off over the plains to Salt Lake City. They've been doing it now for three years."

"What's a handcart?" asked Nathan.

"The Mormons have carpenters at Florence just up the Missouri River from St. Joe. There they build high, two-wheeled carts that the girls and men use to haul their belongings to Salt Lake City."

"That's many hundreds of miles," Nathan said.

"Over a thousand miles across the prairie and the mountains. Now, the way I figure it is that this religion thing with the girls is not very deep, that they mostly want to get married, and pretty bad. Well, we're going to go find them. We'll pick a pretty one for each of us and ask her to come back to Texas with us."

Nathan shook his head in wonderment. "How long ago did you see these pretty girls?"

"About a month ago," Drum answered.

"Won't they have left St. Joe long before you can get there?"

"Sure. And they travel fast for people on foot. It's told that some days they cover more than twenty miles after they get toughened up. We'll catch them on the trail before they can reach the old polygamist himself, Brigham Young, in Salt Lake City. He'll probably take all the young girls that the missionaries don't take for wives."

"Your going to ride twelve, maybe thirteen, hundred miles and then all that long way back to Austin on the off chance of getting a wife? You're a handsome lot, but that's a wild plan. Every one of them may turn you down, and then everything would have been for nothing."

"Just pick the one you want and carry her off," Crow commented, speaking for the first time.

"Sure. The Indian's right," said Ash. "What's to stop us from doing that?"

"Probably get yourself shot by the Mormon men," Nathan said.

"There's only a very few men with the women," Drum said.

"We can get wives," Charlie said with certainty. "Are you married, Nathan?"

"No," answered Nathan.

"Then why don't you come with us?" Charlie asked.

"We could use another gun," Les Jamison said. "We're bound to run into some Indians that won't let us go through peacefully."

Jake Payne spoke. "The winter was late in ending, but the spring grass is coming now and there's plenty of water. So your livestock should be all right for the six weeks or two months you'd be gone."

Nathan fell silent at the unexpected suggestion that he should ride with the band to find a wife. He looked to the north, where the women must be at this very minute, toiling at the handcarts. If Drum told the complete truth.

Jason, his brother and friend, was dead and never could be replaced. Crow provided some companionship, but he was often absent, and even when at the ranch house, he would sit for hours and not utter a word.

However, a woman, a wife—that was a thought. He had known girls as he had moved along the frontier. Each one had provided an enjoyable interlude, a pleasant moment in a rough life.

With a grand clarity Nathan knew he wanted a woman, for she could give him more than friendship. She could give him children. Without his own family, all his labor, land, and cattle, no matter how much he acquired, would have little meaning.

Nathan wondered what kind of woman would travel the tremendously long distance from Europe to America and then drag a handcart a thousand miles. Surely she must be a very special person. Nathan would go and find out for himself. Perhaps they were also as pretty as Drum had said.

"I'll go with you if Drum swears he tells the truth," Nathan said.

Drum bristled at Nathan's statement. "I don't lie. It's just like I said. There's many good-looking women somewhere on the prairie between Florence, Missouri, and the mountains east of Salt Lake City. That's big country, but they always travel the same route, west from Florence along the Platte River to Fort Laramie, and then southwest to Utah. We can go north until we strike the trail. Then see if they've passed that point or not. We'll go either east or west, depending on whether they are ahead of us or not, and catch them."

"All right," said Nathan.

"Then you'll come with us?" Charlie asked.

"Yes. I'll go home and get my gear."

"We're not waiting for you," Drum said.

"Ride on," Nathan said. "I'll overtake you tomorrow or the next day."

"Whether or not you come means nothing to me," Drum said. "Charlie, go get the horses. We're traveling."

Nathan climbed erect. "Crow, let's go," he said.

Crow selected a horse from the remuda in the corral. He put a packsaddle on the animal and led it to the door of the house. The Comanche stepped inside the door and watched the white man gather provisions for the journey.

"Take extra guns, for there are many bad Indians where you go," Crow said.

"I intend to," Nathan replied. He examined the weapons that had belonged to the men who had murdered Jason. He chose a rifle and pistol of the same caliber as his own two weapons so that the ammunition would be interchangeable. When he returned, he would take the guns to Austin, as he had promised the Ranger.

"Kill some Kiowa for me if you get the chance," Crow said.

"I'll do that."

Nathan swiftly loaded the packhorse. He mounted the gray.

"Take care of the cattle," Nathan said. "Keep the springs open so they can get water."

The Comanche reluctantly nodded his agreement. Nathan, like most white men, thought only of work.

"Crow, sleep in the house and wear Jason's clothing."

"The clothes would be too long for me."

"Wear them, anyway. Some white men might come past. You'll be safer if you are here at the house and wearing a white man's clothing. They'll know you are not a bad Indian but a tame one."

Crow looked sharply at Nathan, his black eyes sparking. "I'm not a tame Indian." Then he relented and laughed his low, guttural laugh. "I'll not wear white man's clothing. But I will be careful. All your possessions shall be safe until you return."

"Do you want me to bring you a woman?" Nathan asked.

"Yes. But not a white woman. Bring me a brown-skinned one so that I can beat her sometimes."

"You truly are a bad Indian," Nathan said.

Nathan was laughing as he left the yard. He spoke to the gray horse, and the cow pony broke into a swift, rocking-chair-gallop.

◆ 19 ◆

IN THE GRAYNESS OF THE EARLY DAWN, THE SPHERE of the sinking moon, white as a grizzly's tooth, hung low on the western horizon. All was quiet, except for the muffled thump of iron hooves striking the ground and the swish of grass upon the legs of the horses.

The six horsemen rode at a gallop, the legs of their mounts swinging easily after a night of rest. The immense, flat Llano Estaco, the Staked Plain, surrounded them and stretched away mile upon mile on all sides. The north wind cooled them and tossed the fast-growing prairie grass of the plains into thousands of waves, crests pursuing troughs as though they were part of the surface of a great green sea.

Nathan rode on the right edge of the line of horsemen. His heart beat nicely as he contemplated the fresh morning and the journey over new country. Possibly he would accomplish his quest to acquire a woman. That last thought lay quite pleasantly in his mind.

He ranged his sight out over the limitless prairie. A man could get on a horse and ride it forever at a run across the grand land. How glorious life was.

It was the beginning of the fourth day since he had left his ranch on the Red River. He had caught the group of young Texans on the second day. The band had now come one hundred and fifty miles and was north of the Canadian River. Each evening they had traveled late into the dusk, until darkness threatened. Then, rolled in their blankets, they slept. The first hint of dawn found them up and riding again.

Drum Shadley set the pace. The direction was always straight north. Nathan followed. He was the outsider, the stranger in the group. He would say nothing unless the band took some action that could cause him harm.

Drum was in his early thirties and was the band's eldest. He was a wanderer, a hard, morose man. Les Jamison had a ranch he was developing on the Colorado River. Charlie Morse was the son of a gunsmith. He said his father would soon make him a partner. Jake Payne was a blacksmith. He had rented out his forge and shop to one of his brothers for the time he would be gone. He was well over six feet tall, with large biceps from pounding iron. Ash Brock was a wild horse wrangler, or rather had been. He said he now had enough money to start a horse ranch when he returned.

Nathan understood the desire of the men for wives, except for Drum. Why would a drifter want a wife? More importantly, why would a woman take a drifter as a husband?

The men pulled their mounts down to a trot, a rougher, less comfortable pace but one the horses could keep up for a long distance.

When the sun had climbed a third of the way into the sky, a broad, dark swath of land came into sight a few miles ahead. As the men drew nearer, the dark zone seemed to be moving, drifting off to the west.

"Wow! Look!" exclaimed Charlie. "Buffalo. Thousands of them!"

"More like tens of thousands," Ash said. "We'll have fresh buffalo hump for supper tonight."

"Don't shoot until we're almost through them," Nathan said.

"Yeah, don't shoot," said Ash. "I've never seen such a big herd. Let's see how close we can get to them before they stampede."

The riders pulled their mounts down to a walk. Closer and closer they came to the herd. The nearer buffalo looked up from their grazing to inspect the approaching horsemen. A young calf, still retaining its tannish orange color and not dark like the adults, ran in a frolicking light-stepping way out toward the men. The cow sounded a warning and the calf, its tail arched upward, wheeled and dashed back to the herd.

The buffalo drew back both left and right from the horsemen, like the parting of a black surf, to let them ride through. Two large white wolves, part of the large packs that followed and fed off the buffalo, watched from a distance. The horses of the men warily eyed the buffalo and the wolves.

For more than an hour the men rode through the countless thousands of buffalo. The herd gradually closed in behind and resumed grazing. Nathan never had seen the huge beasts allow men to approach so close. The wolves again took station on the herd, their keen eyes searching for an unwary calf, or an animal weakened by injury or sickness.

The edge of the sea of buffalo came into view. Drum pulled his rifle. "We all need some practice with our guns. Let's shoot a few of the critters."

"Good idea," Ash said.

"Charlie, you hold the packhorses while the rest of us go hunting," Drum called.

"Ah, Drum, I want to shoot a buffalo too."

"Hold the packhorses like I told you to," Drum repeated in a rough tone.

"The packhorses are trained well enough to stay put," Nathan said. "Let him ride with us."

Drum looked at Nathan with a hard expression.

"I don't think they'll run off, either," Ash said.

"All right," Drum said grudgingly.

The men leading the packhorses dropped the lead ropes. All pulled their long guns from the scabbards.

"Let's get to shooting," Drum called. He charged at a huge bull nearby.

The other men, whooping and spurring, sped toward their selected prey.

Nathan chose a yearling male and raced up beside him. The animal veered away. The gray horse swerved to follow. In three jumps he was again alongside the yearling.

Nathan raised his rife and swung the barrel. There was no possible way to miss, with the animal barely fifteen feet distant. The gun roared. The buffalo went down tumbling end over end, as if tripped.

He swung the gray horse around and brought it back to stop by the carcass of the yearling. He stepped down. With a few strokes of his skinning knife, careful to keep the hair off the flesh, Nathan laid back the skin from the ridge of the animal's back, then cut eight to ten pounds of tenderloin from the yearling.

Nathan sliced off a bite of the meat and shoved it into his mouth. He chewed contentedly as he peeled a section of the thinner hide from the buffalo's stomach and wrapped the remainder of the meat in it. In the evening he would make jerky.

Shots were still ringing out, though now at a distance. Some of the men, their single-shot rifles empty, were continuing to pursue the buffalo, riding up quite close and shooting them in the head with their pistols.

The firing dwindled away, and Nathan assembled with the other men on the now vacant prairie. The buffalo had stampeded at the crash of firearms. The animals were a black mass, fast disappearing on the far-flung horizon. The rumble of their hooves was a distant thunder.

The men retrieved the packhorses and struck out on their course to the north. Behind, on the prairie, lay the bodies of thirteen buffalo. On the green grass the carcasses looked

like dark brown boulders thrown down randomly by some
playful giant.

Orrin Grueling rode his jaded, mud-splattered horse into
Temple Square. The night was full of the mixture of falling
snow and rain. The dark form of the partially constructed
Temple of the Church of Jesus Christ of Latter-day Saints
was barely visible on his left.

Construction of the grand temple had begun in 1853, but
the walls were little taller than Grueling's head. Brigham
Young, president and church prophet, had set back the
construction substantially. During an inspection he had judged
the foundation to be too narrow and weak. He railed at the
master builder, telling him the temple must stand for a
millennium, for a thousand years. He ordered the entire
structure to be torn down and started anew, with the foundation doubled in thickness. Grueling hoped he would live
long enough to have the privilege of viewing a ceremony
there.

Grueling passed among the mounds of cut stone waiting
to be placed in the walls, and went on toward the office of
Brigham Young, which was located on an adjacent street.
The hour was late—near midnight, he judged. Still, the
Prophet's orders had been specific: to see him immediately
upon his arrival in Salt Lake City.

Young's office came into view. Yellow lamplight shone in
the window. A horse was tied at the hitching rail. The
presence of the mount told Grueling that the president had
a visitor. The prophet always walked to his home, only a
few blocks distant.

Brigham Young waited for Michael Combers, a bishop of
the Church, to sit down and begin his report. Strife within
the family of high Church officials was a very bad thing.
Young had directed the bishops to go to Richfield, one
hundred and fifty miles to the south, to evaluate and in
some manner resolve the conflict.

The prophet was of stalwart build and in his late fifties.
His face was broad, dominated by large brown eyes. He was
weary. Worst of all, he had missed his usual evening with
his wives and children.

Without removing his coat Combers seated himself across the desk from Young. He rotated his hat in his hands.

"Good news or bad?" Young said, wanting to hurry the discussion.

"That depends on whether you were the son or the father," the bishop said. "For the Church, the news is mostly good. However, this case does point up one of the problems of plural marriages."

"Give me the important information," Young said. There was a hint of sharpness in his voice. He did not want the conversation to become one on polygamy.

"John Bartley married Elizabeth Browning a little more than a year ago. She's one of Irving Browning's daughters. A very lovely young woman."

"I know the Brownings," Young said.

"Elizabeth was Bartley's ninth wife. She was a dutiful wife and got along well with the other wives. For a time. Then she fell in love with Bartley's oldest son. A son by his first wife. Both men wanted the pretty woman."

"What did Elizabeth want?"

"She wanted the son."

Brigham had young wives, and sons old enough to wed them. He felt the sadness of John Bartley as if it were happening to him. "What was the solution? I assume you did find one?"

"The son offered to go off on a long mission. Then, when he returned to Utah, he would find work far away from his home, and the woman."

"Something tells me that was not the final solution."

"That's correct. John Bartley did not want to lose a son. He agreed to divorce Elizabeth so that she could marry his son."

"You had the authority. Did you tend to that?"

"I assisted in the divorce and then performed the wedding ceremony for the young woman and the son."

"Well done. You have not spoken of your role in Bartley's decision. But I'm certain it was substantial. I thank you for resolving a very difficult situation. I shall tell the Twelve Apostles of your good work."

"The Church business must be done," the bishop said.

"Yes. And there seems to be more and more of it each day as our numbers increase."

A knock sounded on the door and both men ceased talking. "It's Orrin Grueling," a voice said from outside.

"I shall be going," Combers said to Young. He put on his hat and opened the door.

"Hello, Brother Rowley," Combers said to the man on the stoop.

"Hello, Bishop Combers. Good to see you," Grueling replied.

Combers stepped past Orrin and went on toward the tethered horses.

"Come in, Orrin," Young called.

"Your messenger told me that I was to come and see you immediately upon arriving in Salt Lake City," Grueling said, advancing into the room.

"That's correct. Please be seated."

"I would've been here sooner, but I was in the Sevier Desert west of Fillmore, after wild horses. The messenger had trouble finding me."

"I'm glad you have come," Young said. "We have brothers and sisters that may be in danger and need protection. Please sit down and let's talk."

Young studied the black-haired, strongly built man of forty or so. He knew of the man's strength, as well as his skill with weapons. The prophet had heard of some of Grueling's exploits, and that some of the people called him the Avenging Angel. His band of compatriots was known as the Sons of Dan. Young believed the man meant to do only those things that would protect the Church. But the time for chastising a member of the Church for some perceived wrong without the sanction of the proper Church official must come to an end. Orrin and his group of followers would soon be called to heel. The congregation numbered nearly one hundred thousand souls and controlled a huge land area. Some dissent from the strict teachings of the Church could be tolerated, but only within reason. The prophet would set those limits, not some self-appointed avenger.

Grueling seated himself in the chair in front of the desk. He remained silent as the prophet began to sort through a stack of papers. He wondered what urgent matter would cause the Church's president to send for him instead of using his regular helpers.

Grueling had great respect for Young, who was the leader of the Church, powerful in all civil matters of the territory, and had been temporary commander of the Army of Saints that had marched out in 1857 to fight the Army of the United States. In addition, Young was the owner of many businesses, running the gamut from ranches and farms to gristmills, sawmills, barbershops, coal mines, a nail factory, and even the Salt Lake City Theatre and Social Hall.

Young was a visionary, a nation builder who had declared the existence of the State of Deseret. His enemies said he was power-hungry and a land grabber. The State of Deseret was an expanse of land comprised of nearly one sixth of the United States.

His doctrine of Outer Cordon had a boundary that extended from the Columbia River on the north to the Gila River on the south, and from Fort Lemhi on the Salmon River, San Bernardino, California, Carson Valley, Nevada, to Grand Valley at Moab. His plan was to hold this Outer Cordon by making settlements at every canyon mouth where water flowed and the land was arable.

In addition, there were many settlements in Canada and Mexico. The Mormons had bought many Indian children out of slavery in Mexico and returned them to their own people.

In 1850, Young's vision had been shattered. The United States government established the Territory of Utah, shrinking Young's empire to but a tenth of what it had been before. A federal judge came to Salt Lake City to sit on the judicial bench. Young had given no outward sign of the sorrow he felt at the death of his dream. Grueling wanted to do what he could to help the saintly man protect the church and what was left of his State of Deseret.

Young lifted a paper and looked at Grueling. "This message arrived from St. Joseph, Missouri, a week ago. By now there is a handcart company far out on the plains en route to Salt Lake City. Deacon Moeller has requested we send armed guards to escort these new converts safely here. Bad

feelings are running high against us in St. Joseph and Florence. He fears white renegades may attack the converts. Or
there may be trouble from the Indians. Though there have
been no reports of attacks by them, who knows what may
have happened during the winter that could set them raiding
when good weather comes."

Young dropped the paper to the desk. "I want you to go
and meet our new brothers and sisters and bring them
unharmed to our valley. Let none of them be taken from
us."

"When should I leave?"

"Tomorrow. We must not delay longer. Go home tonight
and rest with your family. Tomorrow gather twenty men.
See that they are mounted on good horses and are well
armed. Leave as soon as possible that day."

Grueling was pleased that he had time to see his wives
and children. He had been gone for two weeks. Young
knew of a man's needs, for he also was very much a family
man. The prophet had eighty people in his household. They
were domiciled in a three-story house with twenty gables,
called Lion House. It was located nearby.

"I can get half that number of men from those I know,"
Grueling said. "But the remaining men may be hard to find.
We'll be gone at least forty, maybe fifty, days. The season
for plowing and planting will be far past by the time we
return. The men must get their crops in the ground and
irrigated properly. Otherwise they will go hungry next winter."

Young noted that Orrin had made no mention of his own
crops, which also must be planted. "Select the men who can
ride and shoot the best. Tell them that I've ordered it. Also
tell them their fields shall be plowed and seeded by their
brothers, and they will be done before any others. Leave
the information with their first wife as to what each field is
to be sowed with. On your way out of town, bring the men
by my office so that I may speak to them."

"Sir, what should I do if the handcart company is threatened or attacked by Gentiles? How much force may I use?"

"Whatever force is required to halt the attack. Bring
every convert safely to Salt Lake City."

Young saw the black eyes of the man grow hard like

spheres of obsidian. It would be very dangerous to an enemy if Orrin Grueling were to fight.

"Yes, sir," Grueling said.

"Thank you for being so ready to give your assistance," Young said.

"I shall always be ready," Grueling told the prophet.

Young watched Orrin as he left the office, and then he continued to stare at the closed door for a time. This was the first time the Church president had called upon the Avenging Angel for help. It must also be the last. Now that Young had acknowledged the existence of the group of men and its leader, he must destroy their organization. There was a very remote valley in the southern part of the Arizona Territory where he would send Grueling and his wives.

With a sigh Young climbed to his feet. The banishment of Grueling would be a severe punishment on the man and the members of his family. And it was happening only because of Grueling's dedication to the safety of the Mormon Church.

◆ 20 ◆

"BETTER RIDE WITH THE WINNER," DEBREEN called, laughing and looking around at the throng of gamblers and onlookers gathered near him. He held his big hand high in the air and rattled the pair of dice cupped in his palm.

He stood at the end of one of the crap tables in Bouchard's Gambling Emporium in St. Louis. During the ten days since his arrival he had won steadily, four to five hundred dollars each night. But tonight alone he was five thousand dollars ahead, and the wild bird of luck was still perched on his shoulder with talons of steel. He would break Ivorson, the professional gambler who banked the craps game.

DeBreen raised his head to view the entire gambling parlor. News of the grand opening of the lavishly furnished establishment had reached him in St. Joe. He had left at once, catching the train to Hannibal and then a steam packet for the short run down the Mississippi to St. Louis.

The brick-walled Emporium was located on the waterfront with its hustle and bustle. Here it could catch the river traffic, and also the trade of the uptown people out for excitement along the docks. The building was huge, some two hundred feet long and half as wide, and with a ceiling twenty feet high it was supported by elaborately carved wooden columns. A dozen crystal chandeliers blazing with gaslight hung from the ceiling. A thick, plush wool carpet covered the floor.

Bouchard had installed many games of chance—roulette, faro, blackjack, poker, craps, and others. All of the equipment was of the finest construction. He rented the games out by the week. Only the most well-known professional gamblers could acquire the right to spin a wheel or shuffle a deck in the emporium. The reputation of the gamblers as well as the opulent furnishings of the establishment, would make Bouchard a very rich man.

DeBreen decided at that moment to build a similar gaming place in St. Joe. He needed only a few thousand dollars more. The way his luck was running, he might win the money tonight.

DeBreen placed his bet of three hundred dollars on the line. Other gamblers quickly followed suit. He rattled the dice again in his hand and flung the ivory cubes across the table. They bounced back, tumbling and spinning. They came to rest, a three and four spot faceup. A wild, jubilant cry rose from the players.

Ivorson's face was stony as he reached out with his stick and, with its curved end, hooked the dice and drew them to him. He had lost seven thousand dollars in but a few hours to the loudmouthed man and to the other players riding on his luck. Should the losses continue to mount at the same rate, he soon would be bankrupt. He picked up the dice and tossed them back to the end of the table in front of the loudmouth.

DeBreen's laughter and his calls to the people around him was part of the pleasure of winning, but his mind was intent upon the game. He watched the table banker pay off the bets and then rake in and pick up the dice. Why had the man not simply shoved the dice toward DeBreen, as he had always done before? And what was that? Was there a slight, unnecessary bending of the man's fingers?

He looked at Ivorson. The gambler was rubbing his jaw and watching him. In the back of his eyes was the incipient grin of a joker who had pulled a trick. Bastard, thought DeBreen, you grin too soon. You should not try to play tricks with the king of tricksters.

Without removing his sight from Ivorson, DeBreen pulled half of his last winnings from the table and picked up the dice. He shook them briefly and tossed them at the raised backstop at the far end of the table.

Immediately DeBreen moved, shoving several players out of the way and lunging along the side of the table. Before the dice came to rest, he was opposite Ivorson and reaching for him. He caught the craps banker by the wrist in a viselike hold.

"What the hell are you doing?" Ivorson growled. He tried to wrench free, but DeBreen held him like iron.

"I just wanted you and me to see at the same time what comes up on the dice," DeBreen said. "Now, let's take a look at them."

He twisted his head and glanced down. Snake eyes stared up from the green felt of the table.

"Hah!" DeBreen said. "That proves you palmed the dice and switched with loaded ones. You were afraid of my luck."

"You're crazy. Let go of me."

DeBreen raised the man's wrist and slammed them down on the sharp raised edge of the craps table. The man's hands flew open.

"God damn you," Ivorson cursed in pain.

"So the dice ain't in your hands," said DeBreen. "Then let's search a little farther."

The players stood transfixed, watching the two men. Players at other tables ceased playing and turned. DeBreen saw

Bouchard hurrying across the room toward the disturbance.
Two of his armed bouncers fell in beside him.

DeBreen jerked powerfully on Ivorson, pulling him onto
the craps table. He caught the tail of the man's coat and
yanked it up over his head and down and off his arms. He
ripped open the man's right shirt sleeve.

"Now ain't that cute," DeBreen said, pointing at a small
pouchlike device made of leather and strapped to Ivorson's
lower arm. "A little trap with a springed mouth to hold the
dice when there're dropped in." He tripped the spring and a
pair of dice rolled out onto the table.

"What's happening here?" Bouchard demanded to know.

"He cheated by switching loaded dice for the pair that
had my luck in them," DeBreen said.

Ivorson's eyes were murderous. His hand inched toward
his vest pocket.

DeBreen saw Ivorson's movement and jerked the man
the rest of the way across the table. The moment Ivorson's
feet hit the floor, DeBreen slapped him left and right,
hitting savagely, rocking his head back and forth.

"A fellow like you would need a hideout gun," DeBreen
said. "Let me take a look at that pocket. Ah, just as I
thought," he said, extracting a Derringer.

DeBreen's hand snaked out again. The openhanded blows
on Ivorson's face cracked like the firing of the little pistol.

"Hold! That's enough!" Bouchard said. "This is my place
and I'll do what's necessary to keep all the games honest."

"Then do it," DeBreen said testily. He tossed the Derringer to Bouchard.

"Hold the cheat," Bouchard directed his two bouncers.
He faced the other people in the gambling parlor and called
out in a voice loud enough for all to hear. "What should we
do with a man who does not play honestly?"

"Horsewhip him," cried a man.

"Run him out of town on a rail," said a second man.

"First tar and feather him," called yet a third.

A score of other suggestions for the type of punishment
Ivorson should receive came from the crowd.

"What do you say we should do?" Bouchard asked
DeBreen. "You caught him."

"It's simple. Shoot him," DeBreen said.

"We can't kill him," Bouchard said. "There's law in St. Louis."

"I didn't think you would," DeBreen said in disgust.

He scooped up his mound of chips and walked through the crowd to the cashier's cage. "Cash me in. Give me half gold and half paper money," he told the cashier.

DeBreen pocketed his winnings and left the Emporium. He crossed the moonlit street and took up watch in the blackness of a recessed doorway. He leaned against the doorjamb. He would wait.

The side door of the emporium opened and Bouchard's two bouncers dragged Ivorson into the alley. One bouncer held Ivorson's arms behind him while the second methodically struck him with his fist. The blows came swiftly, one to the stomach and then one to the face, and then repeated.

DeBreen did not stir. The beating was thorough, but all the blows were designed to hurt and maim, not to kill.

"I think that's enough," said the bouncer holding Ivorson.

The second bouncer stopped slugging Ivorson. "All right," he said. "Let him go."

The first bouncer released his hold, and Ivorson fell to the ground.

"You shouldn't have all the fun," said the first bouncer. "I should get one chance at him." He drew back his foot and kicked the fallen man in the side. "I think I broke one of his ribs," he said with satisfaction.

Both bouncers turned and entered the emporium. The door closed.

A couple of minutes passed and Ivorson stirred. He groaned as he struggled to his hands and knees. He raised his head and looked around.

"Please don't hit me again," he said through his bloody, broken mouth. He lifted his hand as if to ward off the man coming along the alley toward him. "I'll leave town soon as I can walk."

"No need for you to do that," DeBreen said. "You can die just as easily here."

He caught the gambler by the belt and collar. He hoisted

the man from the ground and, holding him like a battering
ram, made a charging run at the brick wall of the emporium. The gambler's skull struck with a crunching sound.
His body went limp.

"There, that's payment for breaking my winning streak,"
DeBreen said. He walked from the alley, laughing. Bouchard
and his bouncers would have some tough explaining to do as
to why Ivorson had died after they had beaten him.

DeBreen stopped by his hotel and packed his clothing. As
daylight broke, he boarded a river steamer for the day-long
trip up the Mississippi to Hannibal, Missouri.

The train bound west was on schedule. DeBreen bought a
ticket for St. Joseph.

Albert Crandall was seated in the end of the car reading a
newspaper by the light from the oil lamps swinging from the
ceiling. He nodded briefly at DeBreen and went back to his
reading.

DeBreen nodded back at the well-dressed fur buyer. Without a doubt Crandall had made a tremendous profit on the
furs he had sold in the East. Trappers ran the risk of being
killed by Indians, or freezing to death, or dying in uncountable other ways. Crandall only needed to sit in his warm
office and reap the great reward. Come the next spring,
DeBreen would take his own furs to the market in New
York.

The railroad coach was but half full. DeBreen selected a
row of empty seats and lay down, stretching out as best he
could. He slept away the entire journey to St. Joe.

"DeBreen, I want the bastard polygamists dead," Albert
Crandall said, his voice a coarse, hate-filled growl. "I want
you to kill every one of the Mormon missionaries, for they
are the spawn of hell. They've tricked and enticed my daughter Ruth away from me and to that hell of a brothel they call
Salt Lake City."

Crandall sat with DeBreen in a remote corner of the
lobby of the Patee House. The train had carried the two
men across Missouri during the night and had arrived in St.
Joe in the early-morning daylight. Crandall had found the
note from Ruth upon his return to his home. Her statements

had staggered him. At first he could not believe that in a few short days she had been converted to an entirely new religion. She had left him, walking away from his love and the wealthy life-style with which he had provided her. Already she must be far into the wilderness of the great plains on the long trek to Utah.

"Catch the Mormons before they reach Salt Lake City and bring my daughter safely back to me. I'll pay you very well for your efforts."

"Why have you come to me?" DeBreen asked. Crandall had searched him out within an hour after the train had pulled in to St. Joe. Now the fur buyer sat clenching a wadded paper in his hand, probably the message from Ruth. A damn pretty girl. He could understand why the Mormons would want her.

"I've made a judgment about your capabilities," Crandall replied. "You are the man that could run the Mormons down and remove them from this earth."

"Suppose I am? It'd be expensive. I'd need more men than just myself."

"Hire as many men as you think you'll need. There must be plenty who hate Mormons."

"Plenty. But I'll want men who can travel fast and fight hard. I'd want mountain trappers."

"Then get them. Leave St. Joe at once, before the Mormons get too much of a head start."

"How long ago did your daughter leave?"

"Eleven days. Her note says the Mormons will catch a steamboat upriver to Florence. There they will form a handcart company for the travel west to Zion. That means Salt Lake City."

"That's a big lead. But men on horseback can travel more than twice as fast as the Mormons can on foot and pulling those handcarts. We can probably overtake them in ten days to two weeks. Easily before they make it to Fort Laramie in the Wyoming Territory."

"Then you'll do it?"

"First a question before I answer that. Are you sure you want the Mormons killed?"

"I'm very certain. Kill every man."

"Even the male converts from Europe? I saw the Mormon camp before I went to St. Louis. There were twenty to twenty-five of them with the group."

"They are just as bad as the missionaries. Destroy them also."

"How about the kids, twenty or so, and the rest of the women?"

"I don't give a damn about them. Do what you want. There are plenty of husbands for the women here in St. Joe, if they would return. I just want my daughter back with me, and unharmed. Do you hear me, DeBreen? Unharmed!"

"How do you propose that I kill so many people and not get hung for it?"

Crandall eyed DeBreen steadily for a moment. "The nights are black on the prairie. Kill them then. Or catch a few of them at a time when they are separated from the others. I don't think I've misjudged you. You'll find a way to do the killing in a manner not to bring danger to yourself."

DeBreen's mouth stretched into a grin as white and as dead as a bleached bone. He had only been badgering Crandall. DeBreen had no doubt of succeeding in his task. "It'll be expensive," he said.

"Name your price."

"Five thousand dollars for me. Two thousand for each of ten men."

Crandall blinked only once. "Agreed," he said.

That'd been easy, thought DeBreen. He could easily get the men for a thousand dollars each. In fact, some of the men he could select would kill Mormons for nothing. DeBreen's total pay could be ten thousand or more. Once this was completed, he would have enough money to build a gambling emporium here in St. Joe that would rival Bouchard's in St. Louis.

"Payable in advance," DeBreen said.

Crandall shook his head. "Half now and half when Ruth is safely back with me."

"Payment must be now," DeBreen said. His voice had hardened. "When the killing is done, the men will scatter and not return to St. Joe for a long time. That's the way I'm going to run the operation. They'll want the money in their hands before they do the deed."

"All right. I also think they should not come back to St. Joe anytime soon. But there is one condition that must be met without fail. Nobody must ever know that I've hired you. Absolutely nobody. Make the killing of the Mormons seem as if a band of renegades slew them."

"People will want to believe that, for there are many who hate the Mormons and their ways," DeBreen said.

"When can you leave?"

"I know the men I want. But it'll take a little time to round them up, unless I'm damn lucky. But I can leave by tomorrow for sure. When can you have the money available?"

"The bank will be open at ten o'clock today. Meet me at my office shortly after that."

DeBreen nodded. Without another word he strode from the Patee House. He was smiling. He had been wanting to kill some Mormons. Now he would be paid to do it. His smile broadened. He would also have the girl, Ruth, before he returned her to her father. *If* he ever returned her. He could tell Crandall she'd gotten killed in the fighting. Just the thought of possessing her made his blood race.

•◗ 21 ◖•

SAM FELL IN AT THE END OF THE LINE OF PEOPLE waiting in the ticket office to buy passage on the steamboat leaving in an hour for New Orleans. He had not discovered the river pirates in St. Joe. Perhaps the brothels and gambling parlors of New Orleans had drawn the men. If he had no luck in the coastal city, he would then travel back up the Mississippi to Saint Louis. In the fall, if still not successful in his quest, he would return to St. Joe and check the trappers as they outfitted and left for the mountains. He would never relinquish the search for his enemies.

The line shortened as tickets were sold. Sam shifted his bedroll, his few articles of clothing wrapped inside, from one arm to the other and moved ahead. More travelers formed up at his rear.

The rumble of the hoof falls of several galloping horses sounded from outside the street. A man shouted out in a loud voice, "Keep up! Keep up! The boat is about to leave the dock!"

Sam froze at the call. A tingle ran up his back, as if a feather had been drawn along his spine. Hadn't he heard that voice before? From a man with snow-white skin calling for help from the bank of the Missouri River?

Sam whirled about and ran from the ticket office and onto the sidewalk. A block distant, a band of eleven horsemen dressed in buckskins were racing away along the street.

A narrow lane opened up through the pack of running horses, and for a few strides the man who rode in the lead was visible. He twisted to look behind him at the riders following him.

Sam recognized the big, black-bearded river pirate. At last one of the killers had been found and was in sight. Sam broke into a trot, his heart thudding against his ribs.

The man must not escape. Sam threw his bedroll onto the sidewalk. He increased his pace to a run, the hard lump of the cyst pounding his guts with each step.

The band of riders swerved off Main Street and onto Francis Street. They disappeared, running their mounts down the slope toward the Missouri.

The blast of the northbound steamboat's whistle cut the air before Sam reached Francis Street. He rushed on. The vessel was two hundred yards upstream when he pulled to an exhausted halt at the edge of the river.

"Damnation," Sam cursed. The man had escaped him, at least temporarily.

He was surprised at the speed with which he had covered the distance to the waterfront. His strength was returning. His hand felt of the lump in his stomach. The cyst had not burst. He had been very lucky. However, it could rupture the very next time he exerted himself, and the poisonous corruption would flood out into his body and kill him.

"Miss your boat?" asked a man who had stopped loading a dray with crated cargo from a pile on the dock and stood watching Sam.

"I missed catching those men on horseback. Do you know where the boat is heading?"

"To Florence. There'll be another boat in the morning, early."

"Did you get a look at the riders? Do you know any of them?"

"Yep. Recognized some of them."

"How about the big man who acted like the leader? Know him?"

"That's DeBreen. Why'd you want to know?"

"Wanted to meet him in a bad way," Sam said.

"Any particular reason?"

"Yes." Sam did not elaborate. "Looks like I'll have to go to Florence."

"And farther, too, I'd guess. DeBreen and those men with him were outfitted with bedrolls and grub and all had both pistols and rifles. I'd say they were bound west on the plains."

"I'll catch them," Sam said.

"I don't know what you want with those fellows, but DeBreen is a mean one. And DeBreen would only take along men with him that were equally ornery. A young fellow like you would be eaten alive by the likes of them. Steer clear of them, that's my advice."

"How do you know that much about DeBreen?"

"Last summer I saw him kill two men at Garveen's Saloon with a knife. Sliced them up, easy as you please. And then this spring I was right here on the docks when he came in with two rafts loaded down to the waterline with furs. He paid me two dollars to haul them furs up to Crandall's Fur and Hides. When I asked how he came by so many furs, he got downright hostile. Yes, sir, I know DeBreen firsthand. And I've heard a lot more."

"Like what?"

"Like he does whatever pleases him out there, thievin' and murderin'." The man waved a hand, indicating the flat plains lying west of the river. "So take my warning and stay away from them."

"Can't do that. You seem to know a lot about the folks of St. Joe. Who's got the best riding horses in town?"

"That'd be Orval Tomkins. But his prices are high as hell, one hundred and fifty dollars to three hundred a head. If I was looking for a tough mount that'd catch DeBreen, then I'd go across the river and trade. About half a mile below where the ferry lands, is a camp of friendly Sioux. You can see their tepees from here if you look close. They've got some good horses for only a small fraction of the cost for one of Orval's." The man looked knowingly at Sam. "The Sioux are partial to whiskey, so take some of that as part of your trading stock."

"I think I'll go and see what Tomkins has," Sam said.

Crandall cursed under his breath as DeBreen and his band of trappers raced past on Main Street, in front of his place of business. He hurried to the doorway and stared after the men. Horses running on the street was not unusual, but DeBreen should have left quietly on a side street and drawn absolutely no attention to his departure.

Crandall had thought the trapper was the best choice for the task of bringing back his daughter. He was a violent man, and the strands of his mind within their mental crypt were twisted into an evil, cunning fabric. But perhaps his intelligence was too much warped and drove him to reckless action. Crandall felt a surge of black doubt. Had he made a mistake in hiring the man? Would he ever see Ruth again?

As he watched after DeBreen, a young man in buckskins ran from the steamboat ticket office and, tossing aside his bedroll, tore after the horsemen.

Crandall did not move until the riders and the man on foot disappeared from view. Then he walked dejectedly back to his desk. For a very long time he sat and looked at the neat, precise script created by his daughter's hand on one of his ledgers. He believed at that moment that he would never see Ruth again. He had released DeBreen to kill the Mormons, with no gain for himself.

Sam walked up from the docks and turned along Main Street. He scanned the thoroughfare, looking for his bedroll. He spotted it in the arms of a boy, eight or nine years old, sitting on the edge of the sidewalk.

"Looks like you found something that got left behind," Sam said, coming up to the boy.

"I saw you throw it down. Knew you'd most likely be coming back for it."

"So you kept it safe for me?"

The boy bobbed his head. "That's right. I'd been long gone if I was going to steal it."

"You look like an honest fellow to me," Sam agreed. He took some coins from a pocket. "What would make an honest boy feel good?"

"A dime would be nice," said the boy. Then a wistful expression came onto his face. "But a quarter would be a whole lot better."

"Then a quarter it is," Sam said. He handed the boy a coin. "And I'll give you another quarter if you carry that bedroll and show me where Orval Tomkins, the horse trader, does business."

The boy jumped up spritefully. "That's a deal, mister. Follow me." He led off briskly, the bedroll over his shoulder.

A few minutes later, on the edge of town, the lad gestured ahead at a large pole corral and a one-room office nearby. "That's the horse trader's place. But watch out for him. My dad says he's a slippery one and will cheat you out of your rear teeth."

"I'll watch out for him," Sam said. He gave the boy the promised quarter.

"So long," said the boy. He took to his heels back toward the center of the town.

Sam shouldered his possessions and went on toward the corral. A horseman in buckskins overtook and passed him. The man halted and dismounted in front of Tomkins's office.

The rider lifted a hand in greeting, and his steady black eyes surveyed Sam from a weathered, brown face. The man was neither young nor old, a seasoned man of the plains and mountains. "A fellow carrying a bedroll and walking toward a horse trader's place of business might mean he wanted a horse."

"Well, it sure could mean that," Sam replied.

The door of the office opened and a fat man stepped out onto the stoop. "Howdy, gents," he said.

His eyes swept the pair, then came to rest on the man with the horse. "I saw you come first. How can I help you?"

"Maybe not at all. I was just talking to this young fellow who might be needing a horse. If he does, we may strike a bargain and not need your services." He held out his hand to Sam. "Name's Mitchell."

"I'm Sam Wilde. Maybe we can do business."

"Now see here," Tomkins said. "You can't come to my place and then sell your horse to one of my customers."

"Are you one of his customers?" Mitchell asked.

"Not yet," Sam said.

"That's good," Mitchell said, turning his back to Tomkins. "I'm quitting trapping and going back east to Pennsylvania. Going to get married. So I've got a horse to sell. He's not been gelded but still he's gentle. He's a fast walker for every day traveling, and a fast runner when the Indians get pressing you close. He's tough and has never been fed grain like the city horses. He can live on cottonwood bark in the winter and grass in summer. So he's not spoiled and can survive wherever you can. Sam, what do you offer me?"

"What do you want?" Sam asked. The reddish-brown horse was a fine-looking mount, with long legs and a deep chest. He stepped to the animal, caught its head, and pulled the big mouth open to check the wear on the teeth. About an eight-year-old, Sam judged.

"I wouldn't ride anything but the best," Mitchell said. "Therefore I want top dollar."

"I probably don't have what you would call top dollar. And I have others things to buy right away."

"I'll make this a bidding game," Tomkins said. "I'll give you seventy-five dollars for the animal."

"Would you sell the saddle and bridle too?" Sam asked, ignoring Tomkins's bid. Both pieces of equipment were well used but still quite serviceable. Actually the gear was better than new, for it was broken in just right to be comfortable to man and horse. A Sharps carbine hung in a leather scabbard on the saddle.

"I'd do that. Without a horse they're not much use."

"A hundred dollars for the horse and the gear that's on him," Sam said.

"One hundred fifty," Tomkins said.

"Stay out of this, Tomkins," Mitchell said. "Something tells me this young fellow needs the horse worse than you do. And I believe he'd take good care of him."

Sam placed his hand on the stock of the Sharps. "Is there a chance that you'd let the rifle go too?"

"It's a mighty fine weapon." Mitchell checked Sam's buckskin-clad body. "But where's your rifle? You've been to the mountains, where a man's got to have a gun."

"River pirates," Sam said shortly.

"You look puny, like maybe they might've punched a hole through you."

"Right through the middle." Sam touched his stomach.

"Did they get all your furs?"

"Every one. And killed my five partners."

"I was robbed once, so I know the feeling. Do you know who did it?"

"I found out just a few minutes ago."

"You're going after them?"

"Just as quick as I can get a gun and a horse."

"It's bad to sell a horse you've had for years. It's even worse to part with the rifle that's saved your life many times. But I'm considering it. Take a closer look at it if you want."

Sam pulled the weapon from the scabbard. It was .52-caliber, similar to the Sharps he had lost on the Missouri. All the metal surfaces were clean and lightly oiled. The gun came up nicely to his shoulder, and his eye fell naturally directly down the sights. He slid the rifle back into the scabbard.

"Two hundred dollars for your whole outfit," Sam said.

"Make it two fifty and it's yours," Mitchell came back. "That's still a good bargain."

"I know that it's a fair price." Sam knew the rifle alone was worth fifty dollars. I'll pay it if that includes the powder and shot you got for the rifle, and the bullet mold."

"Those items go with it."

Mitchell handed the reins of the horse to Sam. "He'll outrun most anything you'll ever meet. And his step is as

soft as the bounce of a woman's teat. If you're hurting
inside like I think you might be, that'd be of interest to
you." He slid his hand lovingly along the animal's neck and
then over the stock of the rifle. His thumb hooked for a
moment over the hammer of the gun. He sighed deeply.
"Like parting with old friends."

Mitchell stepped away from the horse. "Kill the river
pirates with my blessing," he said.

"I'll surely try to do that," Sam said. He reached for his
wallet.

"Sure I saw some men in buckskins," the dockworker at
Florence told Sam. "Eleven fellows looking like trappers
came off the steam packet yesterday evening. They hardly
waited for the gangway to touch the shore before they came
riding off. I thought it strange that trappers were going back
to the mountains in the spring."

Sam had just left the deck of the steamboat that had
carried him upriver from St. Joe and stood holding his
horse. He had asked his question of the first person he met
in Florence who might have knowledge of DeBreen.

"Was a thick-chested man with a heavy black beard leading the men?" Sam said.

"Yep, and shouting for all the others to hurry."

"Which way did they head?"

"Like I told you, west."

Sam looked across the town of Florence, three short
streets running parallel to the Missouri River. "Show me
where you last saw them," he said.

"Over there on the prairie." The man pointed. "They
were the last to ride west from here, so their sign is the
freshest."

"Thanks," Sam said. He mounted the roan horse and
rode up the slight bank of the river to the first street. A
minute later he was on the outskirts of town. The tracks of
DeBreen and his men were plain in the dirt. The pursuit
was finally beginning, after all the long days of searching.

Sam pressed his moccasined heels against the ribs of the
horse. He left the small town on the riverbank at a gallop.

The roan warmed to his work and his pace grew swifter.

Soon he was running with a swift stride. The animal's step was as soft as Mitchell had said; still, the bulging lump in Sam's stomach was like a rock bouncing and jarring his guts.

The last two hours of the day passed pain-filled and long. The sun fell from the sky, hemorrhaging a crimson red as it sank below the horizon. Was the blood color an omen that Sam would soon kill DeBreen? Or perhaps it meant that he was riding to his own death.

Sam pushed on until night shadows masked the trail. He halted near a clump of trees beside a small stream. He swung down slowly, carefully. His stomach ached and his weakened muscles trembled with fatigue. He leaned against the horse for a few seconds to collect his strength.

At the creek he watered the horse. As the roan stretched its neck to drink, Sam lay down just upstream and slaked his own thirst. He unsaddled the animal and, taking a picket pin and staking rope from a saddlebag, tethered the mount in a grassy spot.

No fire was built. Sam spread the bedroll and placed his rifle and pistol within easy reach. Pulling his grub sack to him, he fished out a chunk of cheese, part of a loaf of hard bread, and some dried apples. He was not hungry but forced himself to eat a little.

The roan came to an end of its picket rope and sniffed at the man's food. "Here," Sam said. Reaching out, he gave the roan a piece of dried apple. The animal swallowed the sweet tidbit, then lowered its bony head to sniff again at the food.

"Go eat grass," Sam said. He stowed away the remaining food.

Sam slid into his blankets. He consciously did not touch the lump in his stomach. The last thing he heard as he went to sleep was the dry branches of a nearby tree rubbing in the wind and sounding like a cat scratching.

The morning was clear and crisp. The path of DeBreen and his band of men through the winter-killed grass was as obvious as a highway. Older, and rained on at least once, were the wheel marks of several vehicles. Sam wondered if DeBreen was trying to overtake those people.

Well rested, the roan wanted to run. But Sam held him to an easy gallop. The day would be long and hard, so Sam would have to ration the horse's strength and his own as well.

He ate a few bites of food as he traveled. He stopped once to water the horse and fill his canteen. He forded the Elkhorn River at the same crossing DeBreen and the wheeled vehicles had used. Sam made a weary night camp on the bank of the Loup River a short distance upstream from where it joined with the silt-laden, slow-flowing Platte River.

A flock of crows flapped in to land in a tall cottonwood beside the Loup. The crows, hanging to the limbs like the black boils of some awful disease, made Sam think of his own illness, the deadly cyst within his sore stomach.

He believed the gulf that separated him from death was a narrow one. As he contemplated that thought he was surprised that he had no fear of death. Perhaps death would wait until he found and killed DeBreen.

Sam lay down on his bedroll. He fretted, feeling very unsettled. After a swift day of riding, he knew he had not gained on his enemy. DeBreen was pushing just as hard as Sam was. Why was that?

•◆ 22 ◆•

TO CAROLINE, PULLING DOGGEDLY ON THE HAND-cart, each mile the caravan covered looked no different from the one before. The rise and fall of the sand hills had the elemental sameness of the broad ocean. Time could have been flowing backward and she would not have known the difference. Except for the frequent deaths.

On the fourteenth day out from Florence, the caravan

had reached the junction of the Platte River with the North
Platte. The Mormons veered to follow the North Platte.
Within half a day they had entered a land of low, rolling
sand hills, a desolate terrain of sparse grass and little
live water. For seven days now they had fought the sand
hills.

The wheels of the handcarts cut into the sandy soil and
brought heartbreaking labor to the people. Mathias and
Anton moved among the converts with encouraging words.
They added their strength to help those most in need of
assistance to mount the steep upgrades. Still, the weak
began to die from exhaustion and the heat.

Hardly a day passed that someone did not fall upon the
earth and not rise. Bad days saw two deaths. The company
halted barely long enough to bury the dead in shallow
graves.

Caroline no longer cried at the funerals. She had used up
all her tears. Other people, she noted, had also grown numb
to death and had ceased crying when it came.

Mathias had told the people the sand hills stretched for
one hundred and fifty miles. Caroline feared for the converts that would die before the far boundary was finally
reached.

A large dust devil whirled through the caravan, spinning
up the sand and the old tattered grass of the past summer in
a little storm. Caroline closed her eyes and stopped breathing until the rotating funnel had passed. Bending and twisting, the dust devil swept away over the prairie.

The day wore on, the yellow orb of the sun climbing to its
zenith and walking slowly down along its ancient path in the
sky. As the sun neared the horizon it threw its sharp,
slanting rays to pierce the eyes of the Mormons like needles.

The night came fuming up from the eastern rim of the
world. Nathan called a halt, and the creaking wheels of the
handcarts ahead of Caroline stopped. She sagged across the
cross bars.

The carts that trailed at the end of the column straggled
up and gathered with the others. Caroline and Pauliina
positioned their cart in the usual circular pattern and stepped

from inside the cross bars. Ruth and Sophia came from the rear and they all stood silently catching their breath.

"Not one sign of water," Caroline said. She stared out over the sand hills to the limits of her vision. There would be rationing of water and no chance to wash away the day's sweat and dirt.

The night seemed to fall upon the tired travelers with unnatural swiftness. Caroline and Pauliina hurried at setting up the tent. Ruth and Sophia gathered buffalo chips for fuel. They built their evening cooking fire on the outside perimeter of the handcarts, where it was not so congested and there was only the smoke of their own fire to contend with.

The four prepared their simple meal of dried apples cooked with rice, fried bacon, and bread. They ate quickly and assembled with the others for the evening religious service.

Nathan told the people they had made fifteen miles that day, a great accomplishment in the sand. He spoke a short sermon of encouragement for the hard days still to come, led the people in song, and ended the ceremony.

Caroline rummaged through her possessions and found a piece of cloth. She wiped her face to remove the gritty rime of salt crystals left by the drying of her sweat. She badly wanted a bath.

But now that the sun was gone, there was a growing chill in the air. Caroline pulled on her coat and went to sit with the other three girls by the small fire of buffalo chips they all had built.

"It will freeze tonight," Ruth said, buttoning her coat.

"That's better than rain," Caroline replied.

"Tell me, what is this freeze?" Pauliina asked.

As they had done for nearly every evening since the trek over the plains had begun, the three girls began to teach Pauliina the pronunciation and meaning of English words and phrases. The Swedish girl was quick to learn. Her laughter at mastering another piece of the foreign language brightened the days for the other girls. Pauliina was an enjoyable addition to the group. Never once had Caroline seen the girl angry, or difficult to get along with.

The flames died. The girls' conversation ceased. They sat looking at the dying fire, a tiny red glow in the darkness. Then, one by one, they climbed to their feet and went off toward their tent.

Caroline remained by herself and stared into the darkness that lay dense on the awesome, lonely void of the prairie. There was no moon and the stars glittered like ice shards flung across the ebony sky. America was very different from crowded, rainy England. But different or not, here she would stay and make her home.

Mathias came through the ring of handcarts and approached the fire. "Good evening, Caroline," he said.

"Hello, Mathias."

"May I sit with you for a moment?"

"Certainly." She watched his shadowy form sink wearily down on the opposite side of the glowing coals.

Mathias pulled up a handful of dry grass and tossed it onto the coals. The grass caught fire easily and bright yellow flames flared up.

"Was there something special you wanted to say to me?" Caroline asked. The conversations between them always had been about the business of the journey, or a short discourse on religion. Yet at times she had noticed him watching her. She felt that pleasure all women feel when handsome men look at them in that certain manner. Tonight his face seemed more than normally strained. He removed his hat and absently began to rotate it in his hands.

"Are you and the other girls all right?"

"Like the rest of the people, we're tired and food is short. But we have no complaints."

"I didn't expect any complaints from you. In three days we'll butcher another steer. Then everybody will have a few meals of fresh meat."

"I saw some Indians at a distance today. They worry me. When do you think the men from Salt Lake City will arrive to protect us?"

"We are more than three hundred miles along the trail. I had hoped the men would have met us by now. The farther west we get, the more likely the danger from Indians. On the other hand, there should be less danger from an attack by white renegades."

"Can we make it through if the men don't come?"

"We must." Mathias threw another handful of grass on the fire, and the flames leapt up, renewed. He looked intently at Caroline.

"Almost every man marries shortly after returning home from a mission. I think that I will also."

Caroline was surprised at the sudden turn of the conversation. Why was he telling her this? "That should be nice for you," she murmured.

Mathias turned his head and swept his eyes over the dark outlines of the handcarts and the blurred forms of the people sitting tiredly around the score of low-burning fires. "Once the people are safely in Salt Lake City and no longer my responsibility, then I shall ask a woman to be my wife."

He looked at Caroline. "Until then I must wait. And also the woman I would ask must wait."

Caroline thought Mathias's face had become flushed, but in the ruddy yellow light of the fire she was not sure.

"Does that seem like a reasonable plan?" he asked.

"I suppose so."

"Good." Mathias climbed to his feet. "There are some sick people I must visit before it gets too late. I think one of them will die. Good night, Caroline."

"Good night." She thought the conversation had ended very abruptly.

Mathias moved away from the fire. His form became mingled with the murk of the night as he went back inside the circle of handcarts. Her heart was beating rapidly. Had she just been proposed to? What would her answer be if the direct question was put to her? Without doubt, he was a handsome man and intelligent and gentle.

Then the bone-chilling remembrance came to Caroline of her slaying Varick, the captain of the *African Blackbird*. Mathias had refused to kill the man when she so desperately needed protection.

There were many long days of travel ahead. She would have plenty of time to think about marriage and Mathias Rowley.

She felt the cold deepening. She pulled her coat around her and walked to the tent.

Ruth sat close to the single candle that lit the tent. She studied The Book of Mormon, holding it so that the feeble light fell upon the pages. She read from the religious book every night. Her head rose as Caroline entered.

"Ruth, are you sorry that you came on this journey with the Mormons?" Caroline asked.

"Oh, my, no. I'm sure they have the true religion. It gives me strength for the hard work of pulling the handcarts, and it will surely take us all to heaven. Don't you think so too?"

Caroline did not answer the question. She wished she saw things as clearly and simply as Ruth did. "How does a man fit into your religion?"

"I can have both," Ruth said. Her eyes sparkled and she smiled. She closed the book of Mormon.

"That's the way to talk," Sophia said with a chuckle from her blankets.

"Amen," Pauliina said.

"I guess that says it all." Caroline joined in the burst of laughter.

Removing only her shoes, she snuffed out the candle and wrapped herself in the blankets. So Mathias wanted to marry her—or at least that was her interpretation of his words. All in all, perhaps that was not a bad thought.

Sleep came to Caroline's weary body within a handful of heartbeats.

◆◆ 23 ◆◆

NATHAN CAME AWAKE WITH THE SOUND OF A MOAN
lying on the wind. He sat bolt upright, his
hand scooping up his pistol.

The moan came from the darkness again off to his right.
In the faint light of the star shine he saw Charlie sitting in
his blankets.

"What's the matter, Charlie?" Nathan asked.

"I'm sick. My stomach is cramping like hell. Must've
eaten something bad yesterday."

"Anything I can do for you?"

"If you were a doctor, maybe then."

"Can't help you there."

"Then I'll just have to bear it," Charlie said. He lay back
on his bedroll. "Sorry I woke you."

Nathan checked Polaris in the north sky, and the Big
Dipper. The Dipper rotated like the hand of a great celestial
clock around the polestar once each twenty-four hours, measuring off the passage of time. Nathan judged daylight was
an hour away.

He lay resting, watching the slow drift of the stars across
the black dome of the heavens. The band of men had
crossed the Canadian River and the Cimarron River. The
Arkansas River lay probably less than a hundred miles
ahead. Then another six or seven days and three hundred
miles would bring them to the Platte River. There they
should find the trail of the Mormons, or so Drum said.

Nathan thought of Jason. Time should have lessened his
sorrow at his brother's death but it had not, and the poi-
gnant memory of what his brother had meant to him con-
stricted his throat and tears came to his eyes. Perhaps a wife

176

would occupy his time in the evening, when Nathan's mind most often tended to remember Jason.

What would Jason have said about Nathan taking a wife? Nathan smiled at the thought. Jason would have laughed his gentle laugh and hugged the new member of his family.

Gradually the dawn chased the blackness from the prairie. The stars winked out one by one. The sky began to turn blue.

One of the horses nickered and stomped the ground. A second whinnied an answer.

"Roll out," Drum called. "Let's ride. There's pretty women waiting."

The men began to climb from their beds. Charlie rose last, his face pale and pinched.

Charlie looked at Nathan and grinned weakly. "I'll be all right once I'm in the saddle."

"Okay, Charlie," Nathan said, and walked toward his picketed horse.

"Charlie, go get my horse," Drum called across the camp. "The brute has slipped his hobbles and is off over there half a mile or so."

"I don't feel up to doing that, Drum," Charlie said. "I was sick last night and I'm not much better this morning. I'm just barely able to take care of myself."

"Go get the damn horse," Drum ordered. "Saddle up and ride over there and bring it back. It's too far for me to walk."

Drum's harsh commands to the ill man scratched Nathan's nerves. "Go get your own horse, Drum. And stop ordering Charlie around."

The camp instantly became silent as every man ceased what he was doing and turned to look at Nathan.

"What's that you said?" Drum asked in a belligerent voice.

"You heard right. Leave Charlie alone."

"What business is it of yours?"

"Every man should take care of his own needs."

"I'm leading this outfit, so I'll give the orders."

"You can lead all you want," Nathan said. "But that's just as long as what you do is right for all of us."

"I'll put you in your place," Drum said. He advanced toward Nathan, his booted feet thudding on the ground.

Ash spoke. "Drum, we don't want fighting in the group."

Jake Payne, the blacksmith, intercepted Drum and caught him by the arm. "Let it drop. You two fellows beating each other up won't do us any good."

"I can take him easy," Drum said.

"I'm not so sure you could. I suspect Nathan's been in some fights, and probably won most of them. Besides, you have been riding Charlie and that's not right. We're all equals regardless of how old or young you are. And if the strongest man was the leader, then that'd be me, for I can whip any one of you. So let's get traveling north."

Les came to stand beside Ash and Jake. Without any communication among themselves they blocked Drum's path toward Nathan.

"Jake said it straight," Les said. "We should've stopped you before now from ordering Charlie around like a slave."

"We've got women to find," Ash said. "Let's not allow anything to slow us down."

"It's too early in the morning for fighting," Jake said. "And on an empty stomach too."

Drum looked past the men at Nathan. "If all of you are going to protect him, then maybe you should choose him to lead you. I'm turning back to Austin."

"You don't have to do that, Drum," Ash said. "We've all just got to get along with each other."

"I'm leaving," Drum said. He pulled loose from Jake's hold on his arm and struck out over the prairie for his horse.

"Damnation," said Ash in disgust. "Well, I'm going on with or without Drum. How about the rest of you?"

"Drum's turning back doesn't change anything," Jake said.

"That's what I say too," Les said.

The other men swiftly began to prepare for travel.

Drum returned with his mount and flung the saddle upon its back. The remainder of the band of men, sitting astride their mounts, silently watched him tighten the cinch and tie his gear behind the saddle.

Drum swung up and gathered the bridle reins in his hand.

He touched spurs to the horse's ribs and without a word left the camp at a trot.

The south wind shoved the band of four riders north under the domed sky of endless sapphire blue. The flat plains unrolled monotonously before them. Within Nathan's view a score of prairie hawks riding their brown wings hung penned against the sky. Their heads were turned down, the keen-eyed hunters searching the grass-covered earth below. Now and then one of the aerial gliders would fold its wonderful wings and plummet like a dart to the ground, then launch himself again upward, climbing the soft ladder of air. Often a mouse or a small bird, and once a wiggling snake, hung clutched in a hawk's sharp talons.

Nathan pulled his horse to a halt and twisted to look to the rear as a new sound became audible. He stood erect in his stirrups and shaded his eyes. A horseman was spurring his mount at a dead run, directly toward the group.

"That's Drum," Ash said, beside Nathan. "Must've changed his mind about going with us. But he'll soon kill his horse at that pace."

"Look behind him about a quarter of a mile," Nathan said. "There's a bunch of riders chasing him."

"Could be Indians." Jake had ridden up on Nathan's side. "And there's a hell of a lot of them."

"We're in Kiowa country," Nathan said. He recalled Crow's request that he kill some Kiowa for him. *Looks like I'll get that chance, old Crow. But whether or not I'll live to tell you about it is another matter.*

"Must be thirty-five or forty of them," Ash said.

"More like half a hundred," Jake said. "Why, for God's sake, did Drum lead them down to us?"

"He's only thinking about his own hide," Ash replied.

"We're his only chance to survive," Nathan said.

"But will any of us survive?" Jake said quietly, as if he were speaking to himself.

"Do we fight or run?" Ash said.

Nathan swept his view around in every direction. There was only the prairie, flat as a board with not one boulder or sinkhole to seek for protection.

"The horses of the Indians are partly used up," Ash said. "We can outrun them. Let's ride for it."

"They'd catch Drum for certain if we did that," Nathan said.

"Better him than all of us," Les said.

"We can't leave him," Nathan said. "Everybody dismount! Quick now! Throw your horses down on the ground in a circle. Tie their legs. Build a fort as best you can with their bodies. Hurry, for we've got only a minute!"

Nathan sprang down. He spoke to the gray horse. Then sharply again when the gray hesitated to obey. The animal rolled its eyes at Nathan, then obediently dropped down on its knees and fell onto its side. Nathan bound the animal's legs so that it would not rise when the shooting started.

Nathan's packhorse was not trained to play the game. After three failed attempts to make the horse fall, Nathan hastened to tie off the front leg with the end of his lariat. Then abruptly he jerked the rope powerfully, pulling the horse's leg under it, and, an instant later, threw himself with all his strength against the brute's shoulder. The horse crashed down, pack and all. Nathan threw a loop and caught the two front legs, tied them. Then the two rear legs.

Nathan saw the other men had their riding horses thrown and legs bound. None of their packhorses were yet down.

Drum was within two hundred yards and was driving hard. Sweat covered the racing horse and was flung from the driving legs like dirty clods of snow. To his rear rode forty miniature painted warriors on miniature running mustangs aimed with deadly purpose upon the white men.

Drum pulled his mount to a sliding stop. He leapt down.

"Throw him there," Nathan shouted, and pointed at a large gap in the makeshift fortress of horse bodies.

Near Nathan, Charlie and Les were struggling with one of the packhorses. The brute, its ears laid back and fighting them with teeth and hooves, refused to go down.

Nathan pulled his Colt revolver. When the uncooperative packhorse was in approximately the correct position to add to the defense, Nathan shot it through the head. The fatally wounded animal collapsed.

"You killed my packhorse," Charlie cried.

"Better it than you," Nathan replied. "Now, you and Les grab its tail and swing its rump around in line with that other horse." Nathan leapt forward and helped them to move the heavy body.

Nathan called out for all to hear. "Check the loads in your guns. Have your extra ammunition handy."

He reloaded the firing chamber of his pistol as he watched the Indians charging inexorably upon them. He heard their war cries, the blood roar of a hunting pack, deep and savage. They came at the top of their speed, the miniature men becoming full-sized, hardened warriors with painted faces, and weapons of bow and arrow, battle lance, and a few rifles.

Ash came to stand beside Nathan. "Okay if I fight here?"

"Glad to have you," Nathan said.

"How do you think they'll attack?"

"Looks like they plan to ride right over us," Nathan said, eyeing the war party. He raised his voice. "Wait until they get close. We can't afford any misses."

The men dropped down, some to kneel and others to lay behind the bodies of the horses.

Nathan saw the war chief riding in the center of his braves. The man was dressed in riding chaps, beaded gauntlet, breastplate, and an eagle plume blowing in his hair. As Nathan watched, the chief shouted something. About half of his warriors slowed and formed a second rank about fifty feet behind the first. Nathan understood the chief's plan. The lead wave of warriors would draw the white men's first shots, then the second wave would face only empty rifles.

"Pick your targets," Nathan directed. He brought his rifle up to bear on the war chief, who was rushing straight on. *You are a brave man,* he thought. *But foolish. I do not want to fight. Yet I'm going to kill you.*

"Fire!" Nathan shouted.

A shattering roll of rifle fire roared out over the prairie. Nathan never felt the kick of his exploding weapon. His eyes and mind were locked on the Indian chief. The large-caliber bullet struck the chief high in the chest and slammed him from the back of his mustang. He vanished under the hooves of the horses of the second wave of riders.

The volley of rifle fire blasted open a gap in the center of the leading rank of Kiowa. Riderless horses raced onward with the rest of the charging animals. As the Kiowa at both ends of the line sped past, they fired with their bows and arrows and rifles down on the white men.

Nathan pulled his revolver and shot a warrior in the second rank. The man continued to grip the back of his running mustang with his leg for a few lunges. Then he leaned to the side and fell, slack muscled and jumble legged, to the ground.

Nathan rotated the barrel of the pistol and fired. Another brave fell, rolling in a cloud of pale dust.

A feathered shaft with a jasper joint zipped past Nathan from the side, slicing his cheek. He ignored the wound. A rider was bearing down upon him from less than twenty feet away. Their eyes locked. Time seemed to slow to a crawl as the Indian pulled his bow to full draw.

Nathan thrust out his pistol and shot the man through the heart. The hot hostility in the Kiowa's black eyes faded, was replaced by surprise, and then by death. The horse rushed on, carrying its dead master from Nathan's sight.

The other white men were firing and yelling wildly. Nathan saw Ash shoot. The bullet struck the head of the horse instead of the man on its back. The animal fell heavily upon its rider, crushing his ribs and the air from his lungs in a short, shrill wail.

The last of the Kiowa sped past. They raced on beyond rifle range and halted. Nathan heard their calls as they gathered in a milling, angry group.

Ash shouted out with relief and triumph. He looked around, excited and happy, joyous that the battle was over and he was still alive. Then abruptly he fell silent as he looked down.

The other men's view followed Ash's eyes. Charlie lay across his horse. His face was a bloody specter. A heavy rifle ball fired at close range had torn through the front of his head from side to side, exploding and tearing away part of his forehead.

"Anybody else hurt?" Nathan asked into the silence.

"I am," Drum said. He sat leaning against the back of his horse, his hand pressed tightly to his chest.

"Bad?" asked Nathan.

Drum tried to answer, but his voice came as a gurgle as blood rose in his throat. Red bubbles burst on his lips. He coughed, and a crimson stream gushed from his mouth. His chest heaved convulsively as he tried to breathe. The stream of blood from his mouth increased. His chest made one last gigantic heave, then moved no more. Drum slid sideways to the ground.

Ash knelt quickly beside Drum. He felt for a pulse in his throat. "He's dead," Ash said.

"Well, by God, at least, we got some of them in payment," Les said, and gestured around with his hand.

The bodies of several Kiowa lay strewn about the small fortress of horse bodies. Three Indian mustangs lay dead. Several riderless mustangs were drifting off over the prairie.

Jake spoke. "Looks like we killed about nine of them, and they killed two of us. I don't like that kind of a trade."

"They killed two of our horses too," Les said. "Mine and Drum's."

"You take Charlie's mount," Nathan said.

Nathan saw the body of the war chief move, and a hand rose feebly in the air as if he were beckoning to somebody. Nathan walked to stand over the Indian. A steady flow of blood leaked from the big hole in the chief's chest, where Nathan's bullet had entered. Nathan knew an even larger hole would be in his back, where the bullet had torn free.

You should already be dead with such an injury, thought Nathan. But the Kiowa lay staring up at him with keen human intelligence and the natural animal ferocity that refuses to die easily.

Then the last drop of blood drained away. Death clouded the war chief's black, angry eyes.

Nathan returned to the other men. "Reload. Get ready for another charge."

They reloaded in grim silence and Nathan watched the Kiowa warriors talk and gesticulate among themselves. Without the war chief to lead them, they seemed uncertain whether or not to continue the battle.

The voices of the Kiowa quieted. Some consensus had been reached. They moved, riding in a wide circle beyond easy rifle range around the entrenched white men. Reaching the side from which they had made their assault, the Kiowa dismounted and stood holding their mustangs.

"Now what does that action mean?" Ash said.

"They're telling us they don't want to fight anymore and are waiting to pick up their dead," said Nathan. "Or it could be a trick to get us more out in the open, for they still greatly outnumber us."

"I know that I don't want any more fighting," Ash said.

"Let's gamble they've had enough killing for today," Nathan said. "Get the horses up and let's travel. We'll take Drum and Charlie with us. Bury them later in some secret place where the Kiowa can't find and mutilate them."

Jake spoke. "It's strange that Drum and Charlie out of all of us were the two to get killed."

"Some men are born with bad luck," Les said.

"Charlie didn't live long enough to find a wife," Ash said.

"And Drum won't have to make the long journey back to Austin," Jake said. "But he and Charlie have a long journey to make together. I hope they get along better where they're going than they did here on earth."

Warily watching the Kiowa, the band of white men untied their horses and got them onto their feet. The bodies of Drum and Charlie were lashed across the backs of two of the packhorses. The band moved out to the north.

Nathan looked at Charlie's body. In some ways the young man had reminded him of Jason.

"God, how useless both of those deaths were," Nathan said. He spoke so low that only the uncaring south wind heard the words.

ORRIN GRUELING AND HIS BAND OF TWENTY ARMED Mormons halted their horses near the gate set in the long, log palisade wall of Fort Laramie, in the Wyoming Territory. The small, remote outpost had been constructed at the confluence of the Laramie and North Platte Rivers twenty-five years before, in 1834.

"Wait for me here," Orrin Grueling told his followers. "Stay close to the horses, for I'll be gone only a few minutes and we'll be moving on." He did not want his men to enter the stronghold of the Gentile enemy because trouble often occurred when the two sides met.

Grueling reined his mount toward the gate. He glanced at the thirty or so tepees squatting on the open grassland north of the fort. Friendly Cheyenne, at least friendly for the moment. A pack of curious Indian children had stopped their play to stare at the white horsemen.

Grueling passed through the open gate, waved on by the lone guard. He had been to Fort Laramie before, and now he swept his gaze around to refresh his memory of the isolated outpost of the U.S. Army. A wide parade ground dominated the enclosed area of the fort. On his right a squad of mounted troopers drilled under the sharp-tongued orders of a sergeant. Beyond the soldiers were the enlisted men's barracks. The officers' quarters, five small houses, were on the opposite side of the compound.

Directly ahead was the commandant's office and the duty officer's room. Flanking that structure on the left were the armory, a blacksmith, and several other wooden buildings that Grueling did not know the purpose of. On the right was a store and trading post combined. Grueling knew that business was operated by a civilian with a contract from the army.

Three men dressed as civilians sat in the shade of the porch of the store. They watched Grueling as he crossed the compound.

A lieutenant emerged from the commandant's office. The officer started toward the officers' quarters, then, noticing the approaching rider, halted.

"Good day," Grueling greeted the lieutenant. "Are you the duty officer?"

"Yes, sir," replied the lieutenant. "How may I help you?"

"Have you heard of any Indian trouble to the east between here and Florence?"

"We received a report that some Sioux attacked a riverboat that had run aground about a hundred miles upriver from Florence. Luckily there were enough men with weapons to drive them off."

"How about Pawnee along the Platte?"

"A small wagon train came through a week or so ago. They said a man was lost along the Platte. He went out to hunt buffalo and did not return. They never found out what happened to him. I've heard nothing else."

"Thanks for the information."

"Did you come in from Oregon?" asked the officer.

Grueling wished the lieutenant had not asked where he was from. Only a few short months before, armed Mormons had faced the U.S. Army, ready for battle. That would not be soon forgotten by either the Gentiles or the Mormons.

"No. From Salt Lake City."

The officer scowled, then said, "Any trouble in that direction?"

"None. All is peaceful."

"That's good." The lieutenant said brusquely. He pivoted on a heel and walked off.

"Are you a Mormon?" asked one of the men sitting on the porch of the store. "I heard you tell that lieutenant you're from Salt Lake."

Grueling almost turned away without responding to the question. But the tone of the man's voice rankled him.

"I belong to the Church of Jesus Christ of Latter-day Saints, if that's what you mean," Grueling said.

"Saints! Did you say Saints?" cried the man. "No man can be a Saint who lives with whores. He's not a Saint but a whoremonger."

"You tell him good, Ezra," a second man called in encouragement.

"I've been told that old Brigham Young had to build a big three-story house to hold all his whores," the third man said.

The men grinned at Grueling with grim humor. Ezra spat a stream of tobacco juice in Grueling's direction.

"Polygamists are a filthy stain on the earth," Ezra said. "They're lower than breeding dogs."

Grueling's hand jumped to the butt of the pistol buckled to his waist. He caught his red burst of anger before he could draw his weapon. "If we weren't in this army post, I'd teach you stupid bastards a hard lesson," he said through slitted lips.

"Stupid bastards!" Ezra's voice rose steeply. He came to his feet and jumped down off the porch and onto the ground.

"Yes, and cowards," Grueling said.

Ezra's face became mottled with red. "Maybe you'd like to go outside the gate and say that again?"

Grueling's eyes were half closed, hiding his thoughts. He laughed low in his chest. *I knew you were stupid.*

"Yes. I'd like to go outside the fort and have this out. Bring your two friends with you. I'll see that they get a lesson too."

"Come on," Ezra said to his two cohorts. "I'm itching to get to this Saint with my fists. I'll fix him so that he's absolutely no use to any woman in bed, let alone a dozen of them."

Grueling's laughter deepened as he rode across the parade ground. He looked back once, to be sure the three followed. Perhaps they needed another insult or two, to draw them from the protection of the army. But they walked close behind them, their hands already balled into fists.

The Mormon men had dismounted and moved into the shade of the fort's log wall. When Grueling came through the gate, the men pushed away from the logs and stood waiting.

Ezra and his comrades came into sight behind Grueling. Their steps slowed, then stopped, as they saw the band of silent, armed men.

The Mormon leader swung quickly down from the saddle. He spoke to his men. "Fellows, these bastards called our wives whores. I think we should have a little talk with them. Block the way back into the fort."

The Mormons swiftly formed a hard-eyed circle, surrounding the three men.

"Now you!" Grueling cried. He lunged forward and landed a ferocious blow on Ezra's face. Then, almost too fast to see, Grueling's fists swung again and again, hammering the staggering man.

Grueling ceased his attack as Ezra collapsed. "That's enough for him. I think we should give those other two a few licks to teach them respect and to hold their insulting tongues."

As if waiting for the word, the Mormon men fell upon Ezra's comrades. Hard fists struck the two from every direction, smashing faces, stomachs, backs. The two fought back savagely, but they were hammered down to the ground.

"Hold! Stop!" Grueling ordered. He plunged into the melee to protect the fallen men. The Wyoming Territory was under martial law, and he did not want murder committed so close to the fort. The soldiers would arrest the entire band of Mormons and lock them away.

Grueling felt a stab of pain on the side of his head as a Mormon accidentally hit him while trying to get past to the men on the ground.

"Stand back!" Grueling ordered sharply. He shoved away the man who had struck him and motioned the others back.

The men grudgingly stepped away from the bodies lying limply on the ground.

"Bolsom, Travers, carry those three unholy Gentiles over there and set them against the wall. Hurry it. Make it look like they are just sleeping, if you can. The rest of you, mount up."

The band of Mormons rode out from Fort Laramie and

crossed the nearby Laramie River at a gravelly ford. They lifted their horses into a trot along the North Platte River, then toward the gray, hazy horizon in the southeast.

The handcart company was a string of slow, clumsy bugs toiling over the sandy plain. The blazing yellow sun scorched the prairie and the people. Weary children cried in thin voices, venting their complaints of the heat, and the hunger, gnawing in their bellies.

A woman stopped shoving at the rear of one of the handcarts. She let her arms fall to her sides. She turned from the line of vehicles and stared vacantly around over the land. Then, unsteady and tottering on her feet, she walked away.

The three women remaining at the handcart felt the increased difficulty in making it move. They lifted their eyes up from the dusty ground. "Alice has stopped helping," the woman said at the rear.

From the handcart behind, Caroline saw Alice moving off stiff-legged like a sleepwalker across the sand. Alice stopped and stood for a moment, her hands rising to hold her head. She crumpled to the ground, boneless as a rag doll.

"Oh, God! Something's wrong with Alice," Caroline cried. "Pauliina, come, let's go help her."

They dropped the front of their cart down, jumped over the pulling bars, and ran out to Alice. Caroline knelt beside the still form.

"Has she fainted from the heat?" asked Pauliina in a frightened voice.

Caroline could not feel a pulse in Alice's throat. She dropped her head and pressed her ear to the quiet chest.

"She's not breathing and there's no heartbeat," Caroline said in a stricken voice. "I think she's dead."

Sophia and Ruth and the women from Alice's cart came running up. From farther back in the line Ellen walked up slowly, almost fearfully. All gathered around the gaunt form lying so quietly in the sand.

Caroline gazed down at the dead girl's face, raw from the wind and sun. The cheeks were hollow from hunger and toil. Caroline felt her sorrow as she straightened the raggedy tail of Alice's dress, pulling it down to the tops of her worn, dusty shoes.

"She is the seventeenth person to die since we left Florence," Sophia said sadly.

"I want no more funerals, no more deaths," Caroline said. Yet she knew there would be many more.

Mathias and Anton came hurrying down the string of handcarts. The remaining heat-tortured humans simply slumped down and sat by their carts. Too weary to go and see for themselves, they waited for Mathias to announce the cause of the delay. Both missionaries knelt beside Caroline.

"What happened?" Mathias asked.

Caroline looked at Mathias sadly. "Alice simply quit pushing and walked out here and fell down. She's dead."

"It's an exceptionally hard pull today through the sand, and awfully hot," Anton said.

"We're all going to die," exclaimed Ellen, her voice high and tinged with hysteria. "We're not yet halfway to Salt Lake City and the steep mountains are still ahead of us. Every one of us will perish in this godforsaken land."

"No, we shall not," Mathias said. "The Lord will strengthen us. We will soon be across the sand country. The steep mountains will be but gentle grades to our feet. We shall reach Zion."

"Amen," Ruth said, her face bright with true belief.

"You are both fools," cried Ellen. "We're dying and will continue to die. We must turn back."

"We can't turn back, Ellen," Caroline said. "There's nothing to turn back to."

Ellen looked back in the direction from which they had journeyed so laboriously. A crafty smile stretched her lips, and an expression of incipient madness came into her eyes. Without another word she went toward her handcart.

"I'll put Alice in the supply wagon," Anton said.

"All right. We'll hold the funeral this evening," Mathias said.

Anton gently lifted Alice's slight body. Cradling her in his arms, he walked away.

Mathias looked at Caroline, his eyes full of misery. "The Church must have a larger relief fund so that there will be more wagons to haul the possession of the converts. They should not have to drag those handcarts and burst their hearts."

"If we had only to walk, few of us would die," Caroline agreed.

Mathias sighed and came to his feet. "We'll rest a quarter of an hour before we start again."

•◆ 25 ◆•

WHEN WOLF VOICE SAW THE CARAVAN OF strange two-wheeled vehicles moving over the prairie, he knew the gods were looking favorably upon him. He called out to Man of Stone and the ten other Pawnee braves with him. "Let us go and see what the white men and women possess. They may have many things of value for us to take."

"They will probably shoot at us," said Man of Stone.

"Come, do not be a coward," Wolf Voice replied.

"I'm not a coward." Man of Stone snorted.

"Then come with me," Wolf Voice said. "Let us see if they will take up their guns and fight."

Wolf Voice warily watched the people pushing and pulling the handcarts as he led his band on a course that gradually drew closer. The white people turned their heads to look at him, but they did not stop or reach for their rifles. They appeared to have no fear of the approaching Pawnees.

"Don't touch your weapons," Wolf Voice told his followers. "I don't think these white people want to fight us."

He raised his short leather whip and struck his mustang. The entire band raced at a gallop up one side of the train of handcarts, turned around the front vehicle, and tore back along the other side. Wolf Voice saw the wide, frightened

eyes of the women. Oh! So many pretty women. He raised
his voice in a loud shout. His braves began to howl and
hoot. The women became more afraid. Wolf Voice laughed
at that and ran his mustang faster.

The yelling riders wheeled their wild mounts around the
tail end of the string of vehicles. The herd of ten steer being
driven by a man and two boys almost stampeded. The older
boy yelled angrily at the Pawnee and ran to head off the
steer. The man shouted for the boy to shut up.

Caroline watched the arms of the Pawnee rise and fall as
they flopped their mustangs down on the handcart company. With their stringy muscles and long, tangled hair, they
appeared as wild as the mustangs they rode.

She felt alarm as the Pawnee came ever closer. Other
groups of Indians had been seen along the trail, but always
they had sat their horses at a distance on the prairie and
merely watched them pass.

All of the Indians were dressed in buckskin breeches,
moccasins, and leggings tied high as their knees. They rode
on saddles made of blankets or on pieces of buffalo hide
with the hair still on them and tied to the backs of their
mounts. Strong war bows were across their mahogany shoulders, and quivers of arrows and war shields were fastened to
the sides of the horses. The Indian in the lead had a fourteen-
foot-long lance with a slender iron bladed point. The butt of
the lance was inserted in a leather scabbard and the point
extended up behind the rider.

The Pawnee braves spread apart and began a second,
slower circle of the moving column of handcarts. The Indians rode silently by staring down from their mustangs at the
four or five people working to roll each cart. Wolf Voice felt
his excitement rising as he gazed into the faces of the white
females.

He came up even with a cart and the women turned
hastily toward him. The nearest female pulling in front cast
her round, green eyes upon him.

Wolf Voice was astounded at the green color of the woman's large eyes. And the expression on her face, not one of
fear as he had expected but one of challenge, as if she dared

him to bother her. *Well, I just might do that,* thought Wolf Voice.

He examined the big woman with the long silver-gold hair working beside green eyes. Man of Stone would like her. The two women pushing were also very pretty. In fact, a man could come in the dark and take either one of the four women and not be disappointed in what he found when daylight came.

Caroline gave a short, quick gasp as the Indian jumped down from his horse almost against her. With an abrupt motion of his hand the man ordered Pauliina from inside the cart's crossbars and took her place. He turned his brown face and stared at Caroline for a moment.

"Push," Wolf Voice said in his own language, and leaned into the bar.

Caroline did not understand the word, but she did comprehend the Indian's action. To keep the handcart from bumping into her, she began to push on the bar.

The Indian said nothing more as the caravan rolled over the prairie. One mile passed, then a second. Frequently he glanced to the side at Caroline. At first she always looked back into the glittering black eyes in their deep sockets. Then she realized that was what he wanted, so she gazed steadily ahead.

She saw that several other Indians had dismounted and were helping the women to propel their carts. Still mounted, two other Pawnee had tied braided leather ropes to the bars of the carts and around the necks of their mustangs, and the animals pulled the vehicles along. One of the mounted braves, hardly more than a boy, was smiling broadly as he gazed down at a girl about his own age walking beside the cart he towed.

Wolf Voice felt cheated when the woman would no longer look at him with her wondrous eyes. He slid his hand along the pulling bar toward Caroline's fingers.

Seeing the brown hand creep upon her like a large brown spider, Caroline released her hold and ducked under the side bar and away from the cart.

Wolf Voice gave a guttural chuckle at Caroline's action. He halted and motioned for the yellow-haired woman to take his place. Then he leapt astride his mustang. He sent the mount in a run to the front of the caravan.

Pauliina motioned to Caroline. "Come help me."

Caroline again took her place beside Pauliina.

"He scared me," Pauliina said with a worried expression.

"Me too," Caroline said. "But now he's gone." She called behind her to Sophia and Ruth. "Are you two ready to go again?"

"Yes" came their answers.

The cart began to move. Then, abruptly, the cart in front stopped. To keep from colliding with it, Caroline and Pauliina jerked their vehicle to a halt.

"What's wrong now?" Sophia called.

"We don't know. Everything up ahead is stopping," Caroline said.

Mathias and Wolf Voice came into sight, walking down the line of handcarts. The Pawnee motioned for Mathias to stop in front of Caroline's cart. He began to speak and gesture.

Mathias shook his head, perplexed. Wolf Voice saw that neither his words nor the sign language of the plains was being understood. The man was stupid. Everyone knew the signs. He thought for a moment. He raised ten fingers and pointed at his horse, then at Mathias, and last at Caroline. Then he slowly repeated the series of motions.

A worried expression crossed Mathias's face. He spoke to Caroline. "The Indian seems to think I'm a chief here. He's offering me ten horses for you."

Caroline also had understood the simple signs. She shook her head. "Tell him no."

Wolf Voice had understood Caroline's reply. Before Mathias could communicate with the Pawnee, the man responded, raising both hands twice and again pointing at his horse, at Mathias, and at Caroline.

"No!" exclaimed Caroline. "I'm not for sale for twenty horses, or at any price." She swung her hand angrily in a flat cutting motion. She turned her back to the Pawnee warrior. Every man knew what that meant.

Wolf Voice's blood boiled with rage at being denied what he desired. He spoke in a wrath-filled tone. "Green-eyed woman, you will be mine. And I shall keep all my mustangs."

He vaulted upon the back of his mount and gave a shrill, keening call. He struck the mustang savagely with the whip. The hurt animal sprang away, throwing dirt and grass behind it.

At Wolf Voice's cry the other Pawnee warriors ceased their efforts to help the women. They sprang astride their mustangs and darted away, falling in behind their leader like iron filings to a magnet. They raced over the prairie in the direction from which they had come.

"I think we will have much trouble coming from that bunch of Indians because you turned down his offer," Mathias said.

"Should I have agreed to being sold like a brood mare?" Caroline asked in a cold voice.

"No. Certainly not," Mathias said quickly.

"Well, then!" Caroline said.

Anton's trumpet woke the sun. And the converts. Caroline lay listening to the familiar notes until they ended. She wondered if there was some special tale to be told about Anton and his trumpet. She must remember to ask him.

She stretched and stood up to put on her dusty men's clothing. After combing her hair a few times she donned her battered hat with a rueful grimace. Perhaps today they would reach a stream where she could bathe.

Caroline left the tent as the other girls began to dress. Only three people had risen before her. Anton and Mathias were striking their tent. Ellen was rummaging through the bed of the handcart she shared with three other girls. Caroline was not surprised to see Ellen. The woman was often up at odd hours, wandering about the camp.

Caroline walked a few paces away from the circle of handcarts and stared out over the prairie in the direction in which they would travel. The land lay nearly flat, with only slight undulations in its surface near the shallow, dry watercourses. The wild grass was growing rapidly and was now above the tops of her shoes. The dark green carpet stretched away to infinity. Within the range of her vision there was not one sign of life.

She squared her shoulders and looked the empty, lonely

land full in the face. For a brief moment she saw beauty in the simple landscape. Then the remembrance of all the deaths and the thoughts of the heartbreaking labor that lay ahead today and for many days beyond that obliterated her budding emotion toward the great prairie.

"The cattle are gone!" a man shouted from the far side of the camp.

Others took up the shout. The voices swiftly rose to a hubbub of questions and cries of consternation. The people hurried from all parts of the camp and gathered near the man who had made the discovery.

"Where's John?" asked a man. "He relieved me on guard at midnight."

"Out there! What is that in the grass?" a woman asked excitedly. Her arm shook as she pointed.

The crowd surged onto the prairie. They halted and stared down at the man lying on the ground.

"It's John," said Anton. He knelt beside the still form and opened the shirt. "He's been killed with a knife."

"The Indians must've done it," a man said. "They must have come back during the night and killed John and stole the cattle."

"What a calamity," a woman said. "John's son is now a complete orphan. The poor little lad had already lost his mother. Who's going to take care of him?"

"He can travel with Anton and me," Mathias said. "We'll find a home for him in Salt Lake City."

Anton spoke in a low voice to Mathias. "We were lucky to have kept the mules hobbled and inside the ring of handcarts. Losing the steers is bad, but without the mules we would've been in a very bad fix."

"We are in a bad fix," Mathias said, looking around at the approximately two hundred and forty men, women, and children. Their gaunt faces were creased with dismay. He felt the heavy burden upon him to feed and keep them safe. He certainly wasn't doing a very good job of it. The hand-cart company was ill equipped to make the journey to Salt Lake City. Where in God's name were the men Brigham Young should have sent?

"Should we go after the cattle?" Anton asked Mathias.

"No, we might be able to track them and catch up, but we would be no match for the Indians in a fight. And besides, we can't leave the women by themselves."

"Today would've been the day for slaughtering a steer for meat," Sophia said to Caroline.

Mathias heard Sophia. He knew others were thinking the same thought. He raised his voice so all the people could hear him. "We'll have to ration our food even more strictly. But we shall reach Zion, for the Lord will help us. There is no hunger in Zion."

"We will find buffalo to kill for food," Anton added. "We can make an early camp, and Mathias and I will hunt."

"Anton is right," Mathias said. "Now we must hold a proper funeral for our brother John and bury him. Two of you men dig a grave here near where he lays."

The grave was dug. Mathias spoke the words of the burial ritual and led the people in song. The body, wrapped in a blanket, was lowered into the earth. The excavation was filled and the prairie sod placed over the mound of dirt.

"Prepare to travel," Mathias told the gathering.

Caroline turned away with a heavy heart. The people were in great peril. She sensed a catastrophe sweeping toward them.

She walked to her tent. Silently she worked with the other three women to dismantle it and load their possessions on the handcart. They finished the task and waited for the call to move out.

Caroline saw Mathias and Anton circling the camp from different directions. The two met near Caroline.

"Have you seen Ellen?" Mathias asked. "The women at her cart are complaining she's not helping them pack."

"I saw her first thing this morning but not since then."

"We've looked everywhere among the carts," Anton said. "I don't believe she's in camp."

"Then I think she may have started back to St. Joe," Caroline said. "She spoke several times of wanting all of us to turn back. John's death and the loss of the cattle could have made her decide to do just that."

"I remember her saying that at Alice's death," Mathias said. "She'd be a fool to try to make such a dangerous trip alone."

"She's been acting odd lately," Caroline said. "She may not be thinking correctly."

"If she is heading to St. Joe, she'd follow our old trail," Anton said, looking east across the plain. "I don't see anyone."

"Ellen is a fast walker," Caroline said. "If she left soon after we found John, she could be three to four miles away and not in sight."

"I'll go and find her," Anton said.

"Force her to return with you, if you have to," Mathias said.

"All right. I'll pack my bedroll and some grub."

"Take your rifle and ride one of the mules," Mathias said. "We'll get along with just three mules hitched to one of the wagons until you get back."

"I'll catch back up to the handcart company in a couple of days."

"We'll be watching for you," Mathias replied. "But, Anton, if you don't find her soon, come back without her. We need you and the mule. The safety of our people here must come before Ellen."

"I understand," Anton said. "But I shall not fail to find her."

A smile of great joy wreathed Ellen's face as she strode along. She was free of the handcart company whose people were dying from exhaustion and Indian knives in the dark. And now that Indians had taken the cattle, more people would soon die from starvation. She was returning to civilization, to the streets and safety of St. Joe.

As she walked, she kept a close watch to the rear. Someone from the handcart company might try to find her and force her to return.

A film of sweat gradually formed on her forehead as the sun climbed its high arc. She took a drink from her canteen and put it back inside her pack.

Near noon, Ellen spotted a figure coming across the prairie far behind her. She hastily went off the trail. After a couple of hundred yards she found a buffalo wallow. Smiling slyly, she lay down in the depression and watched the trail.

A man riding a mule passed and drew away to the east. She recognized Anton. When he was only a tiny, blurred form, she rose up from her hiding place. She could no longer follow the trail because he might be lying in wait someplace ahead and catch her.

She turned south and paced off. She would outsmart the missionary by going in a different direction. She laughed a lunatic's laugh.

·◆ 26 ◆·

DEBREEN SAW THE FORM OF SOME ANIMAL PENNED against the red disk of the evening sun. Gradually, as the band of trappers traveled on, the figure took distinct shape, a man riding astride a bareback mule. He held a rifle across the mule's back in front of him.

"Hello," the man called out as he came near. He lifted a hand and smiled at the band of trappers. "I'm glad to see some white men."

"Howdy," DeBreen relied.

"A woman wondered off from our group. Have you seen her along the trail?"

"Nope," DeBreen said.

Anton was dismayed at the answer. "Have you been on the trail all day?"

"Today and every other day since we left Florence," DeBreen said. "What outfit are you with? Where are you bound?"

DeBreen saw the man hesitate to answer as his eyes

examined the faces of the trappers who fanned out across the trail in front of him.

"To Salt Lake City," Anton said.

"I see. You're one of the Mormon people," DeBreen said in a friendly tone.

"Yes."

"How many women you got with you?"

Anton knew the question was not innocent. The men's countenances were hard. The horses they rode looked worn from fast traveling. Had the men come hunting for the Saints?

"A few," Anton said. He rested his hand on his rifle, a finger curved over the hammer, ready to ear it back. He felt the hand tremble. He had never fought with a gun in his life. "Are you sure you saw no sign of a lone woman walking east?"

DeBreen ignored the question. "How far away are the rest of your Mormons?"

"I'll guess I'll get on my way," Anton said, as if DeBreen had not spoken. He gathered the reins and started to turn the mule to go around the men and horses on the trail.

"Wait a minute," DeBreen ordered. "Leave the mule with us."

Anton looked at the trapper in surprise. His hand gripped the rifle. "No, I need the mule to ride."

"Dead men can't ride," DeBreen said. He drew his pistol swiftly, pointed it at Anton, and fired.

The bullet smashed through the bridge of Anton's nose, tore on through his skull, and exploded out the rear of his head. The heavily charged ball of lead rocked Anton back onto the rump of the mule. His legs came loose from the animal's ribs. He fell, landing hard upon the ground.

"One Mormon polygamist sent on to his celestial kingdom," DeBreen said. "As young as he was, he probably didn't have any wives there. He'll have to live forever without a woman."

"Only a couple of dozen more Mormons to shoot," added Stanker.

DeBreen began to laugh. The other men joined in, and the band's laughter swelled to an uproarious gale that could be heard for a mile across the prairie.

As the laughter quieted, Stanker spoke to DeBreen. "Did you really want the mule?"

"Sure. We'll take it with us and return it to the Mormons. That'll give us more of an excuse to talk with them."

DeBreen gestured at the body. "Phillips, throw a loop around that dead fellow's leg and drag him over there, away from the trail a quarter of a mile or better." He chucked a thumb to the north. "We don't want him found anytime soon."

"Sure thing, DeBreen," Phillips said. He stepped down to the ground with his rope.

Wolf Voice halted his mustang. It was time to turn back. They had driven the white travelers' animals hard for two days. Now the village of the Pawnee lay but a day ahead.

"Stop," Wolf Voice called out to the other braves. "We must talk."

"What is the trouble?" Man of Stone asked.

"It is time for me to go back and take some other thing more valuable than these animals from them."

"What is that?" man of Stone said.

"Something that has not left my memory since I saw her. The pretty white woman with the green eyes."

"What of the rest of us?" Man of Stone asked.

"Go with me and steal your own woman."

Man of Stone laughed. "That would be a pleasant task. I shall ride back with you. I think it would be easy to take one of their women. Their guards act as if they are deaf and are not difficult to kill."

"How about the rest of you?" asked Wolf Voice.

The remaining Pawnee warriors were silent, cogitating on Wolf Voice's proposal.

One spoke. "I have two women now. That is enough."

Another said, "It is time to return to our village."

The other braves voiced their agreement with the last man's statement.

"Then take their animals and go," Wolf Voice said. "Our people will like the new kind of meat."

Wolf Voice spoke to Man of Stone. "Let us travel fast, for I am anxious to lay with the fair-skinned woman." He kicked his mustang into a full run to the southwest.

Man of Stone lashed his mount and raced away beside
Wolf Voice.

The two Pawnee journeyed throughout the day. Near
dark, they approached the trail the white people had traveled.

Their course dipped down into a depression deeper than
they were tall. The surrounding prairie was lost to view. The
rays of the low evening sun did not reach the bottom of the
sink, and the Pawnee rode in shadow.

A half mile later the depression began to grow shallow.
Little by little the wide plain came back into sight.

"Back! Back!" Wolf Voice said quickly. He wheeled his
mustang and rode it to a lower stretch of land.

Man of Stone retreated with Wolf Voice. "What did you
see?" he asked.

"A white man riding toward the falling sun."

"Should we slay him?"

"He has a horse. Surely he will have a gun. Maybe two,
one for each of us. I think we should kill him and take those
things from him."

"If he has a gun, he can shoot us before we can get close
enough to use our bows."

"We must follow behind until he makes his camp. Tonight, while he sleeps, we shall slay him."

Man of Stone grinned. "He will be dead when the new
morning comes."

The afternoon waned, the sun sank, and then it was night.
Sam hounded the trail until the last bit of daylight had faded
into the shadows of black night shadows. He halted where
the darkness overtook him. His enemy had matched his
pace, and he was no closer to him than when the day had
begun.

He staked the roan out to graze. He spread his blankets
and dug out provisions for a cold supper. Silently he ate, a
hunched form in the gloom lying on the prairie grass.

His thoughts were dismal. He felt the bulk and the weight
of the cyst in his stomach. He saw no future for himself
beyond catching and reeking revenge by killing DeBreen
and the other two men who had been with him on the
Missouri.

Sam lay down. He stared into the darkness. He begrudged every hour when travel must stop.

Sometime late in the night he came awake in one fractional tick of time. What had awakened him? Was it something threatening in a dreamworld he could not remember, or was it something real?

Some primal instinct told him real enemies were near. His hand closed on the butt of his pistol.

He raised up slightly and looked over the top of the grass. The half-moon had fallen below the horizon and he stared hard into the black fabric of the night. There was only the flat form of the prairie, more felt than seen, surrounding him on all sides. The wind sighed and the roan made low, tearing sounds as it cropped the buffalo grass at the other end of its tether. A peacefulness seemed to pervade the earth. Sam believed it to be a false peace.

He took his long-bladed skinning knife into his other hand and waited in the murk of the moonless night. Enemies could have watched him make camp and stolen close. They would know that he would be very near his horse but might not know exactly where he lay.

The stars drifted west, across the black dome of the heavens. Gradually the night wasted away and the first almost imperceptible light of dawn arrived. The enemy had to attack soon or retreat. Otherwise his advantage over Sam would be lost.

A soft thud sounded off to Sam's left. He raised his head quickly to look.

Immediately he knew he had made a mistake. Someone who had slipped upon him so quietly would not now make a noise. The noise was a trick to cause him to show himself. He twisted back to look to the right.

A dark form had risen from the prairie grass and was hurtling forward not three long paces distant.

Sam thrust out his pistol and fired at the center of the figure. The charging man shook under the impact of the bullet, but his momentum carried him onward. He drove into Sam's extended arm, knocking the gun from his hand, then he crashed down on Sam.

Sam lost his breath with a swish. He thought his ribs had

cracked. He thrust strongly upward into the body with his skinning knife.

Even as the blade entered the man Sam knew the half-naked thing lying upon him was lifeless. He shoved the corpse away and rolled hastily to the side.

Wolf Voice rushed in at a right angle to the approach Man of Stone had made. He had seen Man of Stone fall at the firing of the white man's gun. His rage at the death of his comrade gave speed to his driving legs.

As Sam rose to his feet he heard the man's racing footsteps coming up fast behind him. He dodged to the side.

Wolf Voice reached out his full arm length, trying mightily to cut Sam, who was moving swiftly out of the way. The knife missed. The Indian halted and spun, his knife ready to strike again.

Sam lifted his blade and held it out in front of him. He hoped there was not yet another Indian, for then he surely would be beaten.

The two men stood for a bit of time, studying each other in the light of the false dawn. Sam had seen how the Indian moved, lithely and quickly. He would be difficult to kill with a knife.

Sam's breath came shallow and ragged. He had escaped being killed, but only by the miracle that the attack of the two Indians had been miscoordinated by some tiny part of a second. He did not think there would be another miracle.

The Indian moved forward, his steel blade poised to stab and cut. Sam gripped his knife and prepared to defend himself as best as he could. He knew that in a prolonged battle he would lose. Already his breath was short, his muscles weak.

Wolf Voice sprang across the few feet separating him from the white man. His knife flashed out. Then he leapt away, for the white man had blocked his strike and slashed back at him. Then, swiftly, Wolf Voice advanced again on his foe.

The two men fought with their knives, thrusting and parrying, leaping in and out. They danced in the pale dawn, two lethal creatures, scorpions with deadly stingers.

A passing white buffalo wolf that had made its own kill in

the night saw the fighting men. It halted to watch the strange tableau of the two-legged creatures with their single fangs.

A minute slid past. Then two. Sam's strength was gone. The next attack, or surely the one after that, could not be turned aside, and he would die.

Wolf Voice darted in. Sam started to spring back, but his moccasined feet slipped on the mashed green grass and his retreat was slowed. His hands rose as he tried to catch his balance.

The Indian sensed the moment when the white man's guard was removed. He closed the distance between him and his foe with a bound. His blade stabbed out. The sharp point entered the white man's stomach.

Sam, as his foot slipped, knew he was doomed. He was off-balance, half falling backward. But just maybe with luck he could take his assailant into the other world with him. He was already raising his hands. He added force to the one holding the knife, thrusting out at the Indian closing in on him.

The honed steel met the neck of the advancing Indian, drove inward to grate off the hard bones of the spinal column in the back.

The Indian's knife had struck Sam like a fist to the stomach. He fell onto his back. His head smacked the ground. Stars exploded in his brain and spun in a yellow and red whirlpool.

He rolled to his stomach and tired to rise. Hurry! Get up! Where was the Indian?

Sam halted on his hands and knees. The Indian lay without movement a few feet distant. Somehow Sam had won. A cold wind blew through his stunned mind and cleared it.

He looked down to see how badly he was wounded. Liquid was streaming from a cut in his deerskin blouse. He lifted the tail of the garment and peered closely at his midsection. In the weak light he saw pus and corruption gushing forth from a hole in his stomach. Unbelieving, he realized the Indian's knife had pierced the huge cyst where it pressed so tightly against his skin. Now the poisonous liquid that had been contained within was pouring forth.

Sam watched as the cyst diminished in size. He pressed on the last of the bulge to assist in the ejection of the last of the vile material. Finally the pus ceased to flow and only pale, watery blood oozed out.

He lay down on his stomach in the prairie grass. He was exhausted, his whole body quivering. Later he would sew up the knife wound. For now he would let it stay open to ensure that every possible drop of poison drained from his body.

The curious white wolf waited in the perfectly still dawn and watched the place where the two men lay. After a while, when nothing moved, the wolf stretched and trotted away.

•◆ 27 ◆•

THE TALL ROAN STOOD MOTIONLESS BENEATH the sun. Its head drooped tiredly. It was hungry and thirsty, yet it did not stir.

Sam lay on the ground in the shadow cast by the horse. Hour by hour the strength had flown back into his body. The Indian's knife had cut an inch-long hole in a layer of stomach muscle, but the blade had not penetrated beyond the diameter of the cyst, thus not injuring anything deeper within his body. Now his stomach was flat, and the wound would probably heal quickly. He had not felt this well in weeks.

The patient roan tossed its head and looked down at the man. Sam regarded the inquisitive black eyes of the animal. He knew the horse wanted to be moving, but they would wait a while longer.

"Stand," he said to the horse. He closed his eyes and slept.

Sam awoke with the sun's slanting rays shining in under the roan's belly and striking him. He climbed to his feet and slapped the big horse fondly on the neck. "Time to find a water hole," he told the horse.

The mounts of the two dead Pawnee had drifted off only a short distance from their fallen masters. Both lifted their heads from feeding on the grass and watched Sam. Good-looking animals, he thought. He would take them with him. In a chase they would be very valuable.

Sam caught the mustangs, tied lead ropes around their necks, and rode off leading them.

The prairie spread out before him with not one rise of land to halt or slow the blasts of winter's arctic wind, not a tree to break the burning rays of the sun. He loved it. Almost as much as the high mountain valleys of the Rockies with their golden aspen and deer browsing the cliff on the slopes above.

Two hours later, at the edge of the night, he dropped down into the valley of the Blue River, a tributary of the North Platte River. He chose a camp beneath the spreading limbs of a giant sycamore. He tethered the roan near his bed. After cutting lengths of rope he hobbled the Indian ponies and turned them loose to graze.

He started to whistle, for it was okay to whistle when a man felt so damn good. Even if he did plan to do murder.

"We've caught the Mormons," DeBreen said, staring at the procession of handcarts winding over the prairie a mile ahead.

"They've made better time and are farther along than we thought they would be," Stanker said.

"I've been told the men and women pulling the handcarts can travel faster than a wagon train," Phillips added. "Now I believe it."

"And they lose more people too," Stanker said. "Back a couple of years ago, a handcart company started out late for Salt Lake City, got caught by winter weather, and three people out of every ten died."

"This one is going to be more dangerous than that one," DeBreen said. "Here's our plan. Phillips, you and Taylor

stay behind and out of sight. At night, come in close, kill
the Mormon guards that are posted, and haul them far off
so that they won't be found. Do the same the second night.
And if any Mormons go out on the plains during the day,
kill them too. The rest of us will ride in, acting friendly, and
see what kind of outfit they run. We'll help you do some
killing if we get the chance.''

"You'll get to the women before us," Phillips growled.
"How about me and Taylor?"

"You'll both get your share of the women. More than you
can handle, so just wait a little."

On their galloping horses, the band of nine trappers swept
up behind the handcart company. DeBreen slowed the pace
and led the men past the people toiling at the vehicles. The
Mormons looked badly worn, and their gaunt bodies showed
they were starving.

Mathias stopped the cart he pulled for a lame man. The
carts to his rear stopped in a chain reaction. He walked to
meet the new arrivals; perhaps they had news of Anton or
Ellen.

DeBreen reined his horse in beside Caroline's cart. He
looked her up and down; and then at Sophia, in harness
with her; then at Ruth and Pauliina, at the back. His eyes
lingered a moment on Ruth.

DeBreen touched the brim of his hat. "Good day, young
ladies, we meet again," he said.

"It appears that way," Caroline replied. She glanced at
the mule being led by one of the men. Her heart sank. What
had happened to Anton and Ellen?

"How is your journey going?" DeBreen asked.

"Couldn't ask for an easier trip," Sophia said tartly.

"I'm glad to hear that. But I'm surprised. I would've
supposed those handcarts would be hard to pull."

"They almost roll themselves along," Sophia said.

DeBreen cast a short look at Pauliina, standing with her
big hands on her hips and strong arms akimbo. "Well, with
a horse of a woman like she is, I guess the cart does go
easily."

Caroline hated the man, for she knew the words had hurt
Pauliina. She stared hard at him. There was something

malevolent in the back of his eyes. He was one of those men who liked to hurt people.

DeBreen touched his hat brim again and rode forward, leading the mule.

"I don't like him any better now than when we saw him in St. Joe," Caroline said to Sophia. "Let's go and listen to what he has to say to Mathias."

"I don't think that man being here is an accident," Sophia said.

"I saw him once before too," Ruth said. "When he sold furs to my father."

"Would your father hire him to come and take you back?" Caroline asked.

Ruth bit her lip as she considered the question. "I don't know," she replied with a worried expression. "I thought my father acted afraid of him that one time I saw them together discussing furs."

"Why would nine men be needed to take Ruth back?" Sophia asked.

"Be quiet, we don't want him to hear us," Caroline cautioned as the four girls hastened forward with several other people.

DeBreen dismounted near Mathias. "Are you the leader of this group of people?" he asked.

"I suppose I could be called that," Mathias answered. He recognized the mule. "My name is Rowley."

DeBreen noticed Mathias's scrutiny of the animal. "We found the mule grazing beside the trail a day's ride back," DeBreen said. "I thought it had probably strayed, so I brought it along, hoping to return it to its rightful owner. Is it yours?"

"Yes. It's ours. You didn't see the man who was riding it?"

"Saw nobody. Only the mule."

"No woman, either?"

"Like I said, nobody."

"One of the women wandered off and Anton Lund went to find her," Mathias said in explanation.

"Sorry, but I can't help you with either of them. My name's DeBreen. Me and my men are heading for Fort

Laramie to offer our services to the soldiers there and to help kill some Indians."

As DeBreen spoke, he casually pivoted around, raking a calculating look over the gathering of Mormons. Caroline thought he seemed to be counting them, measuring them, especially the few men. The other buckskin-clad men, still sitting their mounts, roamed their eyes over the women, looking at them from top to bottom. Caroline sensed something sinister and threatening in their intense appraisal. She felt a chill of apprehension.

"I don't see any guns except your pistol," DeBreen said to Mathias. "That's not much protection from Indians."

"We have some men with rifles who can use them. We lost a man two nights ago. He was killed when Indians took our small herd of steers."

"That's too bad," DeBreen said. "We're in no hurry to reach Fort Laramie. If you want us to, we can ride along with you for a few days. Maybe you need some meat. We'll kill you some buffalo."

Caroline wanted to shout out to Mathias to refuse DeBreen's offer. She believed he was lying, a dangerous man.

"Losing the cattle has made us short of provisions," Mathias said. "A couple of buffalo would be most welcome. Then you can go on your way."

"We will do some hunting for you yet today," DeBreen said. He faced his men. "Stanker, you and Ross ride on ahead and kill two or three buffalo."

"Right. We'll meet you along the trail with the meat," Phillips said.

"Mathias was a fool to have accepted the help of that bunch," Sophia said under her breath to Caroline.

"I agree, but I can understand why. The people are starving, and those men have horses and will know how to hunt buffalo. Our empty stomachs are Mathias's immediate concern."

Phillips lay in the prairie grass in the early night and watched the camp of the Mormons. The aroma of frying buffalo meat wafted to him on the slow, evening wind.

DeBreen and the trappers were eating and talking with the polygamists. Some of the women sat near him, listening intently and apparently interested in what he was saying. DeBreen had given Phillips the meanest job.

"I wish I was there instead of here," Taylor whispered as he reclined near Phillips.

"Well, you're not," muttered Phillips.

The evening meal ended for the Mormons. Two men left the camp. Walking in opposite directions and carrying rifles, they went into the dark prairie just outside the handcarts.

"There go the guards," Phillips said. "You take the fellow going north and I'll take the one heading south."

Taylor pointed up at the sky. "That moon's making a little light, and it'll be hard to get close enough to knife the Mormons without some fuss and noise."

"Naw, it won't be. The moon's almost gone. Here's how we'll do it. Crawl up between the man and the camp. Then just stand up and walk toward him. He won't be able to see your face in the dark and will think you're just one of the trappers he saw before. He'll think you're coming out to talk with him. Get close and knife him quick and quiet."

"That's a good plan," Taylor said. He crawled off through the grass on his stomach.

"It's a woman," Ash said, standing up in his stirrups and staring over his horse's head and out across the prairie. "I can see that she's wearing a skirt."

"I believe you are right," Nathan said, also standing up in his stirrups in order to see better.

The woman walked steadily along through the grass, which whipped and danced to the stiff wind. Her head was bent down as she looked at the ground. A blanket roll was tied over her shoulder.

"I can't tell if it's an Indian squaw or a white woman," Ash said.

"We'll ride on and talk with her," Nathan said.

A few minutes later, as the band of Texans closed the distance to the figure coming over the plains, Jake said, "Looks like a white woman to me. At least she's wearing a white woman's clothes."

"It's mighty strange for her to be out here and traveling south," Ash said. "There's no white people for a thousand miles in that direction."

"She must be lost," Jake said.

"Most probably," Nathan said. "I wonder if she might be one of the Mormon women. We're getting close to the route Drum said they would use along the Platte River."

The woman lifted her head. She immediately halted as her eyes spotted the approaching horsemen. She spun to the side and darted off over the flat grassland.

"Woman, we mean you no harm," Nathan called out to her.

"I'll catch her," Ash said. He touched his mount with his heels and the animal broke into a gallop after the fleeing figure.

"I'll help him," Jake said. He hurried his horse up beside Ash.

"Don't scare her," Nathan called out. His voice was drowned out by the pounding hooves of the two men bearing swiftly down on the woman.

She cast a look behind and then back to the front. She increased her pace to an all-out run, her feet kicking the tail of her skirt and the blanket roll bouncing on her back.

Ash shouted out. "For God's sake, woman, stop. We just want to talk to you."

Nathan jumped the roan forward into a full running stride. "Ash, she's frightened. Don't chase her!" he shouted.

The woman looked again to the rear. Closer now, Nathan saw her face twist with fear. She bent forward, her arms pumping as she desperately tried to outrun the men on horseback.

"Head her off, Jake," Ash yelled. "Make her stop."

Jake drove ahead of the fleeing woman, jerked his horse to a stop, and leapt down. Ash stopped behind the woman and swung to the ground.

The woman slid to a halt. "I'll never go back! Never!" she shouted.

Jake moved toward the woman. She screamed in a shrill voice, peaking at an intensity of hate and fear that was not human. She launched herself at the big blacksmith.

Jake backed away from the woman's attack. He had not expected that. She bore in on him, her hands clawing at his face. He retreated, shielding his eyes.

The woman sensed Ash coming up behind her, and her crazed eyes darted to the rear. She whirled, screamed her wild scream again, and rushed at Ash.

"Damnation!" Nathan exclaimed as he sped forward. He was very afraid she would hurt herself in the fitlike state she was in.

Jake lunged toward her, grabbed her in a bear hug, and pinned her arms to her side. "Please. Please," he said, trying to calm the wildly struggling woman. "You don't have to go back."

Nathan reined in his horse close to the struggling pair. He heard the woman's breath sobbing in her throat and she fought Jake at the extreme limits of mortal strength.

Abruptly she stiffened, then, coming from the very core of her, a tremor ran through her body. She collapsed in Jake's arms.

Jake hastily knelt and laid the woman down in the grass. Nathan and Ash hunkered down beside him. Her glance moved from one worried face to the other.

Nathan saw a strange light of awakening come into her eyes. Her lips moved but no sound would come. She breathed once, and then the life went out of her as smoothly as a lamp ceases to burn when the oil is all gone.

"She's dying!" Jake cried. His hands shot out to clutch the woman by the shoulders. He shook her. "Don't die! Please, don't die!" he pleaded. She was as limp as cloth in his hands.

"Let me have her," Nathan said, taking the woman from Jake and bending quickly to put his ear next to her mouth. Nothing—not one sign of a breath.

"She's dead," Nathan said, looking into Jake's anguished face.

Les came up and knelt with the other Texans beside the still body.

Jake looked from one face to the next. He was responsible for this tragedy. A soul-bending sadness brought tears to the blacksmith's eyes. "I only wanted to help her, and in the end I killed her," he said.

"Not you alone," Ash said. "I was part of it. We didn't know this would happen. We meant only good toward her."

"That's right," Nathan said. "It could have been any one of us who had hold of her when she died."

Ash laid his hand on Jake's shoulder. "I once roped a beautiful little mare running with a band of mustangs. Well, I pulled her down as gently as I could, and walked up the rope to get acquainted. The moment I touched her, she just trembled and died. She'd simply scared herself to death. This woman's fright killed her, not you. We don't know why she was so afraid of us. But she surely would have died out here on the plains all by herself."

Les reached for the woman's bedroll and pulled it off her shoulder. "Let's see if she has anything that will tell us who she is." He unrolled the bedding. "There's nothing but the blanket and an empty canteen. Not a speck of food. She couldn't have survived for long."

"Wrap her in the blanket," Nathan said. "We must bury her."

Jake gazed at the woman's face. "I hope she knows how sorry I feel."

The four Texans began to dig in the prairie grass with their knives.

28

THE TEXANS RODE SWIFTLY, SENSING THE GOAL of their long journey was near. They did not talk and made no stop for food. When the sun reached its zenith, they slowed their mounts to a walk.

As the day burned down to evening, the prairie ended, falling away before the horsemen in a series of short, steep gullies down into a river valley. The meandering river flowed off to the east in the center of a two-mile-wide floodplain. Brush and giant trees bordered the river. From their elevation, the men could see black, dead swamp water in several abandoned oxbows of the river.

"The North Platte at last," Nathan said.

"We can be across the river in an hour or less," Jake said.

The Texans touched their mounts with spurs and, leading the packhorses, went into the valley. There they found a gravel-bottomed riffle and forded the river, the water lapping at the horses' bellies.

An awful stench assailed their noses. Half a hundred buffalo had fallen through the ice during the winter. Then, in the spring thaw, the rotting carcasses had been washed, along with much brush and tree trunks, into a huge drift. The men seemed to be riding through a lake of putrid odor.

They hurried their mounts past the dead buffalo. In the next two miles they had climbed up from the valley and onto the plain again.

Nathan reined his mount to a halt. "Take a look, fellows," he said, pointing down at a wide, dusty trail full of wheel marks and footprints.

Ash flung his eyes left and right along the worn path. He jerked off his hat. "Yahoo," he yelled at the top of his voice. "We've found them."

"You're right," Nathan said. "The tracks show that handcarts have passed here." He scanned to the west. There was only the prairie, empty and silent as far as he could see. Without another word he turned along the trail that stretched all the way to Salt Lake City.

In the black ash of night the riders approached a small, wood-lined creek which ran in from the right and onward across the trail toward the river lying some four miles south. The men stopped their weary mounts. They sat silently in their saddles and peered into the dark woods.

"What's that?" Nathan said. "I think I hear voices." He cupped his hands to funnel more sound to his ears and listened intently. The voices of women drifted to him on the soft wind.

"I hear it too," Ash said.

"Could be the women of a wagon train heading for Oregon," Jake said.

"I feel we have found the Mormons," Ash said.

"Whoever it is, is about a half mile to the west on the other side of the stretch of woods," Les said.

"There's only one way to find out for sure," Jake said. "Let's go and take a look."

"Maybe we'd better wait until daylight," Ash suggested. "They'll have guards posted. They might take a shot at us coming out of the dark."

"We can take a look from a distance tonight," Nathan said. "Then tomorrow go and talk with them."

Nathan moved slowly through the woods and turned left. They may have found the Mormon women, and he felt his excitement growing. Yet at the same time he was reluctant to take the final step and approach the camp. He noted that nobody else hurried. They must have the same emotion as he.

The Texans crossed through a projecting finger of woods, and two scores of tiny fires appeared before them on the distant prairie. They stopped and surveyed the lights, and the outline of vehicles was silhouetted against them.

"They're the people with the handcarts," Ash said.

"It's the Mormons," Nathan agreed.

"Now we'll soon know if Drum told the truth and all the women are pretty," Jake said.

"Drum never said all of them were pretty," Les said, correcting Jake.

"All right. But that doesn't matter," Jake said. "All we need are four pretty ones."

The Mormon camp was quiet. The people could be seen gathered in the center of the circle of handcarts. Fragments of a man's voice could be heard now and then.

Nathan studied the ruddy, flickering glow of the lights. How feeble the fires seemed in the immense cave of the black night.

A chorus of women's voices arose, saying amens. The man must have completed a prayer. The women began to sing. Their higher pitched tones easily spanned the distance to the listening Texans. The chirp and twitter of the insects ceased, as if they felt outdone and were also listening to the women.

Nathan leaned forward, endeavoring to catch every word and syllable of the women's song. How brave and beautiful their voices sounded singing against the dark emptiness of the prairie. He listened to the lovely female voices down to the last vibration.

"I hope they sing another song," Ash said in a hushed tone.

"Sure is more enjoyable hearing them than men's voices," Jake said.

"Amen," Les said, imitating the women's words of concurrence of what had been said.

The congregation in the Mormon camp dispersed, their forms passing in front of the fires like dark ghosts. The light from the fires, blocked off for brief periods, blinked on and off like distant fireflies.

"No more songs tonight," Les said, disappointed.

"We'll ride back a ways and cross to the other side of the creek and make camp," Nathan said. "Tomorrow we'll see how pretty the women are."

The Texans made a fireless camp. They did not speak as they staked out their horses.

Nathan lay on his blanket for a long time, watching the yellow half-moon falling to the west. He and the other three travelers were reaching the end of a long journey. When this search for women ended and they rode south, would they still be lonely men?

Nathan heard a man's voice calling the morning wake-up at the camp of the Mormons. He pulled on his boots and stood erect. The eastern sky showed a faint graying, heralding the sun's imminent arrival from below the horizon. The Mormons were early to rise.

Taking his only extra shirt and trousers, Nathan walked to the creek. As he bathed, the other men came to wash themselves and don clean clothes. They were a hairy-faced, wild-looking lot. Nathan wondered if he looked as wild as the others did. What would the women think of them?

The men ate without speaking, each pondering on his own private thoughts. They packed, saddled, and rode out under the blue bowl of the sky that pressed down on the prairie in all directions. They recrossed the wooded creek and turned toward the camp of the Mormons.

Caroline helped the three girls load the cart. She tried not to think of the countless steps she must make that day. Already the sun, just barely above the horizon, hit her with its heat. The day would be a scorcher. And still ahead were scores of other days and thousands of steps that must be made before she finally could rest.

She tossed the end of the tie line across the cart, so Sophia could use it to lash down the canvas covering the items in the bed of the handcart. Sophia ignored the line and stared out across the prairie with a surprised expression on her face.

Caroline twisted to see four men were riding toward the camp. They halted and sat with easy grace upon their big horses a few yards away. Their eyes scanned out from the shadows under the broad brims of their hats at the four young women.

Nathan felt his breath catch as the green eyes of the nearer woman fell upon him. His heart shifted within him and began to race. His breath came again, quick and shallow. It was glorious to be a man and looking at such a beautiful woman.

A hot blush flamed on Caroline's cheeks. It seemed the man's intense look had a palpable force that touched her. Her anger flared as hotly as her blush.

"What are you staring at?" Caroline said sharply.

Nathan jerked off his hat. He would tell the woman he meant no disrespect by looking at her. That his intentions were honorable, that he wanted only to meet her, to talk for a few minutes.

But before he could utter a word, she spoke again. "Well, speak up. What do you want?" Caroline asked angrily.

Nathan, stung by her tone, lashed back. "A wife. But surely not a sharp-tongued one like you." His eyes had turned cold.

He reined his mount away, his jaw rigid. Hell, there were bound to be more agreeable females than this one.

The other horsemen, casting surprised and somewhat chastened glances at Caroline, moved after Nathan. They strung out, riding slowly past the women readying their handcarts for travel. One by one the men stopped to talk with a woman.

"Caroline, why in God's good name did you talk to that man like that?" Sophia asked. "He meant you no harm, and you scared off the others."

"I'm sick and tired of men looking at me like I was some cow waiting to be bred," Caroline shot back.

"Well, aren't we waiting to be bred?" Sophia said, her eyes sparkling mischievously. "Though we would prefer to call it making love."

Pauliina and Ruth had come forward and stood nearby. Ruth spoke. "Sophia, you shouldn't talk like that."

"Why shouldn't she?" Pauliina asked. "It's true."

Pauliina and Sophia began to laugh. Ruth watched them for a few seconds. Then she shyly joined in.

"You're all quite correct," Caroline said. Suddenly she was laughing with the others.

Nathan heard the girls laughing. They were making fun of him. He pulled away from the Mormon camp, leaving his friends behind in conversation with some of the women.

He dismounted in the shade of a tree near the creek. He squatted on his haunches and broodingly watched as the circle of handcarts broke apart and strung out in a line two abreast. He felt only gloom at the green-eyed girl's harsh words. Her laughter made it worse. She was a cruel person. Or had he been too direct? Had he somehow unknowingly insulted her?

Nathan watched the procession pass, the women, actually most only girls, toiling at the vehicles. Their heads were down as they leaned into their harnesses or pushed at the rear. A woman called out in a scolding voice for a child to keep up. Here and there a wheel made a grinding noise on its axle.

There was a splendor in the women, in the female strength, grace and will. Nathan's spirit rose again. Among all the women there must be one for him to take back to Texas.

The cart of the girl who had spoken so brusquely to him rolled past. Three of the girls glanced sideways at him. But not the sharp-tongued one.

To the north a short distance, a band of nine horsemen in buckskins came out of the trees by the creek and rode along the caravan. Several of the men spoke to certain women and tossed the ends of short ropes to them. The women made the ropes fast to the pulling bars of their carts. The men walked ahead, leading the horses towing the vehicles. Then the women joined the men and talked with them.

Nathan was surprised at the presence of the riders. The fact that they had camped off by themselves indicated they were not part of the Mormon party. What were they doing here? Were they competitors for the women?

Ash completed a circle of the caravan. The most lovely girls were those at the first handcart the Texans had approached. He guided his horse near Sophia. "My name's Ash Brock," he said. "May I look at you without you yelling at me?" He threw a meaningful glance at Caroline. "Maybe we could even talk a little."

"I think I can stand that," Sophia said with a smile. "My name is Sophia Applewhite."

"I'd be pleased to help you pull the cart," Ash said.

"That's a kind offer," Sophia replied. "I accept for all of us. Toss me the end of your rope."

"It's called a lariat," Ash said, uncoiling the lariat.

"All right. Lariat." She fastened the end to the crossbar of the handcart. "Where are you from?"

"Texas." Ash threw a loop of the lariat around the horn of his saddle and took up the slack.

"How far away is that?"

"About thirteen hundred miles to the south. I live near a town called Austin."

"Thirteen hundred miles," Sophia said in amazement. "Did you come all that long distance for the same reason as your friend?"

"Like Nathan said, we're looking maybe to find wives." Ash's voice was firm and his eyes steady as he looked at Sophia.

"Do you have to leave Texas to find wives?"

"No. But we all thought it a good idea. We wanted some pretty ones like you."

"So you think some of us are pretty?"

"Yes." Ash looked around at the other three girls. Every one of them was watching him. He felt embarrassed, but he could not weaken now.

"Do you expect a woman to leave and go back to this Texas with you?"

"I might ask some special girl to do that."

Sophia thoughtfully studied the somber face of the Texan. Then she put her head down so he could not see her face.

"All of us are going to Salt Lake City," Ruth said. "We're Mormons now."

"I expect each girl will make her own decision about whether or not she would go on to Salt Lake City if she's asked to go to Texas," Ash replied.

Everyone became quiet. They trudged onward, the horse pulling the cart and the girls walking beside it. Ash wished Sophia would talk with him some more. Or just look at him again. Men and women did not have to talk to communicate.

Jake rode up and fell in beside Ash. "Are any of them friendly?" Jake asked.

"That one there on the right is," Ash replied. "Her name's Sophia. Try one of the others yourself."

"I'll do that." Jake slowed his horse and took station beside Pauliina.

"Hello. I'm Jake Payne." He looked down at the big blond girl.

"My name is Pauliina Halverson." She was surprised that one of the men would choose her to talk to. The man DeBreen had called her a horse. That still made her heart ache.

"Can we talk?" Jake asked.

"I can no talk English good," Pauliina said.

"I think you'll do just fine." Jake dismounted and fell into step beside Pauliina.

Caroline cast a short look over the cart at Pauliina. A bright, pleased expression wreathed the face of the Swedish girl. Caroline was glad. The big Texan was a fitting match for her.

Nathan rode to the front of the caravan to talk with Mathias Rowley. One of the men pulling a handcart had pointed the missionary out as the leader.

DeBreen quickly galloped up and reached Mathias at the same time as Nathan. He cast an inquisitive eye at the Texan. Nathan knew the man's sudden appearance was intentional.

Nathan spoke to the missionary. "My name's Nathan Tolliver. May my friends and I travel along with you for a spell?"

"If you are going in the same direction, then I don't see how I could stop you," Mathias said. "Where are you from?"

"Texas."

"Where are you heading?" DeBreen interjected.

Nathan evaluated the buckskin-clad man. "Are you with these people?"

"Yes," DeBreen said.

"DeBreen has been with us for two days," Mathias said. "He has killed meat for us. Some Indians—DeBreen said they must have been Pawnee—ran off our small herd of steer. We're short of food."

"You didn't answer my question," DeBreen said, his voice tight. "Where are you heading?"

"Yes, I'd like to know too," Mathias added.

Nathan ignored DeBreen and turned to speak directly to the missionary. The Mormon was the only person who had the right to question him. "About right here where we are."

Mathias cocked his eye, questioning Nathan's response. "I don't understand."

"We heard there were some pretty women crossing the prairie. We came to see for ourselves."

"The women are Mormons. They're not up for grabs by any Gentile who rides by," Mathias said coldly.

"I reckon that'd be up to the women to decide. At least those not married."

"You heard what Mathias said," DeBreen said in a gruff tone. "Maybe you and your friends had better ride on."

"I don't think we'll do that." Nathan studied the trapper closely. "My friends and I have come a long distance to talk with the pretty women."

"Maybe I'll make you leave," DeBreen said.

Mathias watched the Texan's face, checking to see how he would respond to DeBreen's threat. He saw no fear, only a quick hardening of the man's eyes.

"Now, DeBreen, this man has a right to journey along this trail," Mathias said quickly. He did not like the Texans being here, but he was also worried about the intentions of the trappers. Did they pose a threat? The two groups of men might balance each other and thus keep his people from possible harm.

Nathan nodded at Mathias. "Thank you. We'll stay out of your way."

He reined the gray horse back along the caravan. He felt DeBreen's eyes on his back. The sensation was disturbing.

Near the center of the caravan four young women labored at their cart. Nathan stopped and offered his assistance. It was readily accepted. He fastened his lariat to the vehicle. As they moved on, he talked to the pretty redheaded woman who walked nearest to him.

•◆ 29 ◆•

CAROLINE SMEARED THE BLACK GREASE ON THE left axle and wheel hub while Pauliina held up the side of the handcart. Finishing quickly, Caroline shoved the wheel back on the axle. The locknut was screwed on and tightened to hold the wheel. The two girls moved to the opposite sides of the cart and began to repeat the process.

Caroline saw other people in the camp performing the thrice-weekly ritual of greasing the wheels of their vehicles. The task must be accomplished that day. The next day was Sunday, the Sabbath, and absolutely no work could be done on that holy day.

Ruth knelt and cooked supper over a small fire of dry brambles she had carried from the woods along the creek west of camp. Mathias had pushed the caravan hard until almost dark to reach a stream he called Brush Creek, where there was water and fuel. Sophia was arranging the canvas and poles on the ground in preparation for raising the tent.

The four Texans walked in between the handcarts and into the light cast by the cooking fires. Caroline saw Ash and Jake immediately turn to head toward Sophia and Pauliina. The remaining Texans separated and went off to two other groups of women. The man she had rebuffed, whose name she had learned was Nathan, began to talk with the redheaded Emily. The woman smiled most pleasantly at the Texan.

For the first time Caroline wished she were clothed in a dress and bonnet, as were Sophia and Ruth and nearly all the other women. Still, Pauliina was wearing a man's trousers and shirt, the same as Caroline, and Jake apparently found her attractive.

DeBreen and three of his men came into the circle of carts. Caroline disliked the trapper leader, for she was certain he was a rogue and a scoundrel.

DeBreen wound his way near to Mathias, who was in conversation with some of the men of the handcart company. The other trappers fanned out among the women.

Caroline looked one last time at Nathan and then went back to greasing the wheel of the cart.

Jake came up, spoke to Pauliina, and took the side of the cart from her hands. He held it lightly, as if it were a matchstick.

"Texan, come help me set up the tent," Sophia said to Ash.

"That would be my pleasure, handcart woman," Ash responded with a wide grin.

Nathan felt at ease as he sat and talked with the redheaded Emily. Her smile was pleasant and infectious, often causing him to smile in return. Now and again she would reach out and touch his hand to emphasize what she said. Nathan found the contact stirred him in a manly way.

One of DeBreen's men, a sour-faced individual, came and started a conversation with one of the women in an adjacent group. Nathan noted the man's arrival and then continued his conversation with Emily.

He saw Jake and Ash finish helping the women rig up the tent. Then the two men and the four women began to talk by the fire.

A whisper of sound came from beyond the circle of hand-carts. Nathan came instantly to his feet, twisting to look, his hand reaching for his pistol. A figure was materializing from the night, black from black.

A gaunt young man rode his horse into the light near Nathan. The horse halted. The man's eyes swept over the assemblage, slowing to study each man in buckskins.

Nathan saw the drawn, taut features of the rider. Nathan had seen that expression before—cold, hard hate.

The horseman looked at Nathan. "Is that DeBreen over there?" He spoke in a flat, emotionless voice and nodded across the enclosed area to where DeBreen was talking with Mathias.

"Yes," Nathan said.

"How long has he been here?" Sam asked.

"I only just arrived, so I don't know for sure. But I've been told he's been here two days or so."

Without another word the rider swung down. He dropped the reins of the horse to ground-tie it. He loosened his pistol, in its holster on his side, and started across the camp.

Sam walked steadily, closing the distance to his enemy by half. "Are you DeBreen?" Sam asked, his voice ringing throughout the camp.

All the conversation ceased and the people turned to see who was calling so loudly.

DeBreen whirled around, his hand swinging to hang near his pistol. A new arrival, a man he didn't know, was coming straight at him. DeBreen heard the antagonism in the stranger's voice, saw it in the way he walked. Who was he?

"I'm DeBreen."

"You were on the upper Missouri in early March." It was a statement, not a question.

DeBreen shrugged his big shoulders. "Maybe I was. And then again, maybe I wasn't. What's it to you?"

Sam said nothing. He stopped to stare unblinkingly at DeBreen. Several seconds passed.

"What do you want?" DeBreen's voice rose belligerently. "Are you deaf?"

Sam made no response. His eyes bore into DeBreen. He was holding his anger at bay, savoring this moment of finally seeing his foe eye to eye. In a few seconds he would pull his revolver and empty every cylinder into the white skin of the murderous river pirate.

"I think the fellow's crazy," DeBreen said in a mocking tone.

Mathias knew the man was not crazy. But the light that burned in his eyes told that violence was near. Mathias spoke. "My name is Rowley. This is my camp. I don't want the women or children hurt."

Sam glanced to the side and looked into Rowley's worried face. The man's request was a fair one. Sam could not fight DeBreen here. "I'll not do anything to cause harm to your women and children," Sam said. He wheeled around and started back toward his horse.

Abruptly Sam halted. He recognized Ruth Crandall sitting by one of the fires. Her sensitive features were full of apprehension. He veered in her direction.

Ruth remembered the frail young trapper who had come to her father's place of business in St. Joe. He still seemed old beyond his years, but his step was firm and he seemed stronger.

"Hello, Miss Crandall," Sam said, removing his hat from his head.

Ruth climbed to her feet and straightened her dress. "Hello, Mr. Wilde. I'm surprised to see you."

"Not as surprised as I am to find you this far from St. Joe. Where are you bound?"

"To Salt Lake City."

Ruth saw Sam's sudden understanding of what that meant. She did not like his look of disapproval.

"You have joined up with the Mormons?"

She nodded without speaking.

Sam shuffled from one foot to the other. He would like to continue a conversation with Ruth, but nearly every person in camp was listening, and he did not know what to say. However, he should tell her what kind of man DeBreen was. "May we talk tomorrow?"

"Certainly, if you want." Ruth recalled how he had looked at her when they had last met. That same expression of awe, as if he were viewing something of great value, was in his eyes now. Most pleasing.

"Good. Until then. I'll look you up."

"I won't be hard to find." Ruth smiled at the serious young man.

Sam moved to his horse and picked up the reins. He spoke to Nathan. "You are not with the Mormons or DeBreen?"

"That's right. I came up from Texas with some other fellows." Nathan evaluated the man. Obviously he was a foe of DeBreen. That just might make him a friend of Nathan's. There was going to be trouble with DeBreen; Nathan was sure of that. The Texans were outnumbered, and he did not think the Mormons could be counted on to fight. Another gun would be valuable.

Nathan spoke. "You're welcome to camp with us tonight. After that little meeting with DeBreen you may need somebody to watch your back."

"All right. I've got two Indian ponies out there on the prairie that I must pick up first."

"I'll show you where our camp is," Nathan said.

The two men went into the darkness.

Sam spoke as they walked along. "I saw only three of DeBreen's men. Do you know where the other seven are tonight?"

"You mean the other five?"

"No, seven. I've followed them all the way from St. Joe, and from Florence, rode on their tracks. I can count. DeBreen has ten men riding with him."

"I've seen only seven. I think we'd better talk about this."

*   *   *

At the Texans' camp Nathan kindled a small fire for light. Then Sam and he sat and talked across the flames.

As Sam told his story the other Texans came one by one, emerging from the dark and seating themselves. They listened silently.

"I plan to kill DeBreen," Sam said, ending his tale.

"Then why did you face him there at the Mormon camp?" Nathan said. "He will soon figure out you survived the river ambush and be warned."

"I had planned to shoot him on the spot. But that Mormon fellow asked me not to start a fight. So I had to back off."

"I think DeBreen will be coming after you."

A twisted, contorted smile came to Sam's face, his hate making him an ugly young man. "That's all right too," he said.

"I've learned something else," Ash said. "Sophia told me three Mormon men have vanished since DeBreen came. Two were on guard duty and could not be found when the reliefs came. Their rifles were gone too. Now the Mormons have just one rifle and one pistol. The third man went off to fetch wood and never came back. DeBreen tells Rowley the Indians must have taken the men."

"Sam says DeBreen has two other men around someplace," Nathan said. "They could be responsible for the disappearance of the Mormons and not the Indians. I have a feeling that DeBreen plans to destroy all the Mormons."

"I agree," Nathan replied. "And that explains why he tried to run us off. But why does he want the Mormons dead?" Nathan tossed some wood on the fire and thoughtfully watched the shower of sparks rise straight up in the still air.

"Maybe he just hates Mormons," Sam said into the silence.

"We can't let anything happen to the women," Jake said. "We may have to take on DeBreen and his men."

"We now know there would be eleven men against us in a fight," Nathan said. "Even with Sam to help us, we'd be outnumbered nearly two to one."

"From the looks of them I'd judge they would be tough

fighters too," Les said. "Especially DeBreen. But even so, we can't let them kill the Mormons.

"The answer is simple," Sam said. He extended his empty hand, as if it held a pistol. He slowly pulled the trigger on the imaginary weapon. "We'll catch them apart from each other. I'll kill DeBreen, and then, when they no longer have a leader, we can kill two or three at a time without too much danger to us."

"Start our own war?" Nathan asked.

"Exactly," Sam replied.

"I don't know about that," Nathan said. "Let's sleep on it."

Nathan awoke as the half-moon slid below the horizon. He heard Sam arise and move off in the darkness. He thought he knew where the man was going.

Nathan lay and mulled over what Sam had said about starting a war to whittle away at DeBreen's larger force. There was logic to that proposal.

An hour later Sam returned, coming through the darkness as silently as a shadow.

"Are DeBreen and his men still in their camp?" Nathan asked.

"So you're awake and thinking the same thing as me?" Sam said. "Yeah, they're still there. There'll be no trouble from them tonight."

The morning was bright with light when Nathan awoke. This was the latest he had slept in days. He looked toward the Mormon camp, located some two hundred yards away. On this Sunday the people were late in rising.

He buckled on his pistol and ambled toward the creek, lined with big sycamore, oak, and walnut trees. In the sky a hunting hawk came gliding down from the north, its head angled down and its keen eyes scouring the grass-covered ground for prey. Just as the hawk reached the creek it banked steeply away, and its wings pumped hard for a few swift strokes. Something in the trees had frightened the bird.

Nathan stole upstream, then into the woods. The band of trees was not more than fifty yards wide, growing only on the narrow floodplain, where the creek water supplied moisture to their roots.

He moved stealthily from one silent morning shadow to the next. The sound of splashing water and a woman's voice humming a song came to him.

◆ 30 ◆

CAROLINE GATHERED A CLEAN CHANGE OF CLOTH-ing, left the camp, and aimed her steps toward Brush Creek. A cool bath in the morning and a day of reprieve from the cruel harness and handle of the handcart was an event she would thoroughly enjoy.

She bent to pick a stalk of the new buffalo grass and chewed on it as she walked along. All around her the prairie was becoming gilded in bright sun colors. Hidden in the grass, a meadowlark trilled its short series of notes. A bumblebee droned over the ground, checking the emerging flower heads for nectar.

She entered the woods as the top limbs of the trees began to tremble to the first faint puffs of the morning wind. The creek came into view, flowing among the gray boles of the trees.

She walked slowly up the stream until she found a pool of water some forty feet long and three feet deep. She stripped, tossed her soiled clothing into the water to soak, and waded in. She began to hum and leisurely bathe herself.

A blue jay came flapping in, the white sections of its wings like little semaphores signaling its arrival. The bird landed on the high branch of a sycamore and chattered away as it cocked its head from side to side and watched her with first one black eye and then the other.

*   *   *

Nathan's eyes probed out ahead as he crept through the grove of walnut trees. The sound of the woman humming came from directly ahead. He left the walnuts and entered a stand of sycamores. A blue jay darted away with a call of alarm.

Nathan stopped instantly, listening intently. The humming continued, the woman taking no warning from the bird's cry. And she was close, only a few feet in front of him.

Nathan peered past the trunk of a big sycamore. His breath caught in his throat. A nude woman stood knee-deep in a pool of water in the creek. She was bathing, scooping up the water in her double hands and splashing her body, then rubbing. It was the green-eyed woman. She was humming to herself, altogether a most pleasant voice.

He pressed against the tree, staring at the ivory-white body of the woman, at the swell of her hips, the bounce of her bosom as she moved. The beauty of her mesmerized him. Was she real or something dreamed?

Nathan had made love to pretty girls twice before as he had roamed the frontier. But never had he encountered one he craved as much as he craved the green-eyed girl. He felt his mood brighten to a glorious exhilaration as he watched her.

The girl knelt in the water and started to wash her hair. Her humming ceased as she worked on her long, tawny mane.

Nathan knew she would hate him if she knew he'd spied upon her. Yet he'd spied, and he felt no more guilt than if he were looking at a beautiful flower. But what flower could attract a man the way a beautiful young woman could?

Caroline finished her bathing. She scrubbed her clothes. The wet garments were wrung out and hung on a branch extending out over the creek. She waded to the shallow end of the pool and began to peer down into the water.

Her two hands were inserted into the water, then quickly brought together. She lifted a crayfish some five inches long into the air. Its strong pincers snapped at her, trying to catch her fingers. But she held it safely by the back. With a happy laugh Caroline tossed the crayfish into the grass on the creek bank.

Nathan saw the grass jerk and tremble as the crayfish tried to fight its way back to the water. The stiff stems held it imprisoned. Caroline bent again to peer into the water.

Her wet tangle of hair fell around her face. She straightened, twisted her hair into a thick braid, and tied it in one loose loop at the rear of her head. She went back to catching crayfish, tossing them one after another on the bank.

Nathan could not get enough of watching the nude huntress. Believing herself all alone, her every action, every movement, was beautifully uninhibited, pure animal, young and graceful. He knew he was viewing a jewel, a jewel of incalculable value to a man in this lonely land. With such a woman a man would be complete. Never again to feel wanting wherever he journeyed in the universe.

It was a grand day to find a woman he wanted as a wife. However, it might be very difficult to get her to agree to that.

The girl froze in mid-motion, bent at the waist. Her head rose, questioning. Nathan could see her testing the air for sound. Then her eyes swung to the far side of the pool.

She seemed to shrink into herself. She cowered down in the water, sinking as deeply as the shallow water would allow but still only barely to her waist.

Nathan crept forward a foot so that he could see around the trunk of the tree and determine what scared her. Two men in buckskins and flat-crowned trapper hats stood on the creek bank and stared at the girl. Each man wore a pistol and a knife on his belt. They were men Nathan had never seen before.

"Come out of the water, pretty girl, and give us a little lovin'," one of the men said.

"Go away," Caroline replied sternly. "Leave me alone."

"We can't do that," said the men. "We haven't had a girl for a spell. We're not going to pass up this chance at a pretty one."

The second man nodded his head in agreement. He licked his coarse lips in anticipation.

"If you don't go away at once, I'll scream."

"Well, if you do, it'll only be a short one," said the first man. "For I'll jump out there and bash you in the mouth."

The second man spoke. "You don't want my friend to get his moccasins wet, now do you? Come on out of the water. Here on the bank the grass is nice and soft for you to lay on."

Nathan felt sorrow at the frightened expression on the ashen face of the girl. His anger flared bright and cold.

"Never!" cried Caroline.

"Then I guess I'll just have to carry you out," said the first man. "If I have to do that, then I'm not going to be as gentle as I would be if you would love us willingly."

Caroline's hands frantically searched the bottom of the creek for a weapon. They closed upon two fist-sized stones. She gripped one in each hand and stood up, the water dripping from her body.

"Damnation, ain't that something," said the second man, his eyes devouring the girl.

"I'll brain the first man who gets near me," Caroline threatened, cocking her right arm.

God! Nathan liked her spirit. He pulled his revolver and cocked it under his cupped hand to deaden the sound. He stepped from behind the tree and stood in the open.

Intent on the girl, the trappers did not see Nathan appear. They laughed derisively at Caroline and her rocks. "Here I come," said the first man.

"If you do, you're a dead man," Nathan said.

The two trappers jerked at the unexpected challenge. They spun a quarter turn to face Nathan.

Caroline twisted to look in the direction of the voice. The Texan called Nathan stood in the shadows at the edge of the woods. He was so still, he seemed cast of stone. He leaned slightly forward, a half-raised pistol in his hand.

How long had he been there watching her bathe? She did not care. An overwhelming relief flooded her being. Then a sickening thought came to her. There were two trappers against him.

Nathan took three slow paces off at an angle to get the girl more out of the line of fire. These men would fight.

"I want you two to get out of here and let the girl alone." Nathan's voice was hard.

"What you want doesn't mean spit in the wind," the first man growled.

"Make them go," Caroline cried to Nathan. She shivered at the thought of the two trappers alone with her in the woods. How brave was the Texan? Was he like Mathias, afraid to fight and kill? Her eyes scoured Nathan's face. The rims of his nostrils were ice-white and his eyes burned with a controlled fury. She sensed no fear in him. The sun sent a ruddy glint from the iron of his pistol as he shifted it ever so slightly. She could not imagine a man more ready to fight.

"We're not leavin', he is," said the first man.

"You're wrong," Nathan said. "I'm staying." His words were flat and ugly.

"Do you plan to fight both of us and die for a woman?"

"I'm not going to be the one who dies. However, if it should by some miracle be me, then that is all right too."

The trappers looked at Nathan's pistol, pointing at the ground just in front of them. Only a slight lift, a tiny fraction of a second, would be needed to bring the weapon to bear on them. Their weapons were still holstered.

"Let's go, Phillips," Ross said. "She's not worth gettin' killed for."

"We can take him," Phillips said.

"I don't think so. He's too ready. I'm leavin'."

Phillips studied Nathan a moment longer. "All right," he told Ross.

The trappers wheeled around and walked from the creek and into the woods.

Nathan waited for the count of five, then he dashed across the creek and entered the woods upstream from the men. He had seen the implacable malevolence in the men's faces. They must be the last two of DeBreen's band. That meant they could not leave him or the girl alive to tell of their presence.

Caroline was greatly surprised at the Texan's sudden disappearance. He had driven the trappers off. Why hadn't he waited for her to thank him? She hastened from the water and began to dress hurriedly in her fresh clothing.

As she buttoned the shirt over her breast she caught movement in the woods. The trappers were returning, slinking warily forward at the border of the trees. Their pistols were gripped in their hands. Their hard eyes scuttled about in all directions.

Nathan moved quietly into the woods a score of paces, then turned left and slipped onward. The course of the trappers should lie just ahead.

He heard whispered voices and slowed. The men came into his view. They nodded in agreement to some plan and pulled their revolvers. They crept back in the direction of the creek. Nathan trailed behind.

The men halted to peer out into the opening surrounding the pool of water where Caroline had bathed. Nathan raised his Colt and aimed it between the men.

Nathan hissed like a cat. Both men whirled.

He shot the man on the right because he moved most quickly. The barrel of Nathan's gun swung the short arc and came into alignment with the second man. He squeezed the trigger. The speeding ball of lead tore into the man, shattering his throbbing heart. Caroline heard the explosions of the pistol in the woods and the crushing sound of bullets striking flesh, a sound she would never forget. The first man was flung back. He dropped his pistol and his hands rose to hold his chest. He fell half into the water. The second man crashed down beside him.

Nathan stepped out of the woods. Gunpowder smoke still curled up from the wicked black barrel of his pistol.

"My God, you killed them." Caroline was stunned by the roar of the gun and the violent deaths.

"Just what they planned to do to us," Nathan said. "Hurry and finish dressing," he told her.

He stepped to the grass where the crayfish lay, and rapidly began to snap off their tails.

"Put your wet clothes over your shoulder to free your hands," he said, and scooped up a double handful of crayfish tails.

Caroline, puzzled, did as directed. The Texan's tone brooked no delay or argument.

"Here." He placed the crayfish tails in her hands. "Hurry out of the woods. Keep everyone from coming here. Show them the crawdads and tell them what a good meal you will have. Explain the gunshots by saying a Texan was showing you how he fired his pistol."

"Why not tell what happened?"

"Nobody must see these bodies. I'll explain later, when we have time to talk. Go now. I've got to get rid of these dead men." DeBreen must be kept off-balance. He must not find out about the deaths of his two men.

Caroline trotted through the woods and broke onto the open prairie. Mathias was walking swiftly from the camp. DeBreen and two of his men were riding toward her. She put a smile on her face and held up the double handful of crayfish tails.

Nathan slung one of the bodies over his shoulder and hustled off with it down the stream. When he judged he was far enough away from the killing ground that no one would come to search, he dumped the corpse in a dense patch of briars. A few minutes later the second body lay with the first. He pulled the tangled briars over the two still forms and laid some brush over that. He hoped the buzzards did not find the dead men before the handcart company moved on. He returned and obliterated all sign of the men at the creek.

Blood from the corpses had stained his shirt. He removed the garment and began to wash it in the creek. He was worried. The battle between the Texans and DeBreen's gang had started. How many of his friends, how many Mormons, would die before the fight ended? Who would win in the end?

31

CAROLINE SAT ON HER SLEEPING PALLET AND ATE the fried crayfish tails with Sophia, Pauliina, and Ruth. She chewed slowly, savoring the new tasty food as she watched the Texans' camp. Nathan had walked from the woods and begun to talk with his comrades. She thought he would soon come to explain why she should not tell Mathias and the other Mormons about the two strange trappers who had threatened her in the woods.

"What's happening with the boys from Texas that's so interesting?" Sophia asked, noticing Caroline's frequent glances across the prairie.

"Oh, nothing," Caroline replied. "Nathan said he wanted to talk to me. I was just looking to see if he was coming." She felt guilty at deceiving her friends.

"So you are getting friendly with him," Sophia said.

"Don't leave us and go off to Texas," Ruth said. "There will be no Mormons or Mormon churches there."

"There are some things that are more important than churches," Pauliina said.

"What could that be?" Ruth asked with a puzzled expression on her face. "Aren't we risking our lives and working like slaves to cross the plains and mountains for our religion?"

"A good husband is more important," Pauliina said in a solemn voice.

"My religion comes before men," Ruth said. "Doesn't yours?" Ruth looked at Caroline and Sophia.

"I haven't been put into a position where I have to decide that," Sophia said.

Caroline did not reply. Nathan had climbed astride his

237

horse and, leading a second mount, was riding toward the Mormon camp.

Nathan halted the gray horse near the four young women. His eyes fastened upon Caroline. He removed his hat with a sweep of his hand.

"Would you like to go for a ride?" he asked. "I've borrowed Les's horse. He's gentle."

Caroline looked up at Nathan. His eyes were flat and noncommittal. He was on guard. Did he think she would hurt his feelings again?

"All right, I'll try it," Caroline said.

Saddle leather creaked as he stepped down. "I'll help you to mount."

Caroline walked to the horse, a tall black animal, and lifted her foot to the stirrup. She grabbed the saddle horn and pulled. Nathan's strong hand caught her beneath the arms and lifted. She swung up on the back of the horse.

"Do you know how to ride?" Nathan asked as he placed the reins in her hand.

"I've ridden a plow horse."

"Well, this is different. Hold both reins together in your hand. If you want to go right, then swing the reins right so that they touch the left side of the horse's neck. To go left, just do the opposite. All the rules are simple. For now, just do as I do."

He stepped astride his gray and touched its ribs with his spurs. The black horse moved along by Nathan's side without Caroline having to do anything.

They rode west from the encampment over the sun-drenched prairie. Caroline ranged her sight across the grass-covered, slightly rolling topography, which stretched away to a hazy infinity beneath an opal sky. A puff of wind flowed past, riffling the grass and whispering the reeds together. She felt lighthearted. She could get to like this America. Then she recalled the deaths of the two men in the woods by Brush Creek.

"Why didn't you want me to tell about those two men who threatened me and you?"

"I think DeBreen plans to stop you from reaching Salt Lake City and that those two are the ones who killed your guards. Why else would they be skulking about? You and the other Mormons might be safer if DeBreen doesn't find out right away that his men are dead."

"If you are right about DeBreen, then he probably killed Anton too. He came to our camp with the mule Anton was riding when he left."

"Who's Anton?"

"He was one of the missionaries. He went back along the trail to find Ellen, who had started to return to St. Joe. Anton just simply disappeared. And Ellen was never seen again.

"You're missing a woman?"

"Yes."

"We found one south of the Platte River."

"Where is she now?"

"She died when we tried to help her. She became so frightened of us that she scared herself to death."

Caroline saw the sadness in Nathan's face. "Did she say anything to you?"

"She kept screaming that she would never go back. We didn't know what place she didn't want to go back to. Then she just simply died. We buried her there on the prairie."

"I'm sorry for Ellen. I'll tell the others."

They rode in silence for a time, the horses walking side by side. The wind increased and it was warm. The human figures and vehicles at the camp shrank, seemingly sinking into the prairie. Then even those miniature forms vanished, and for the first time Caroline was completely out of sight of all other humans. Except for the strange man from some faraway place called Texas.

She sensed the vast emptiness of the mighty prairie. There was nothing before her but the green land, the grayish-blue heavens, and the one merging into the other at some distant boundary that only could be guessed at.

Finally Caroline spoke to the silent Nathan, who seemed intent on riding on forever. "Maybe we should turn back. We've come a very long way." She swept her sight to the rear.

Nathan leaned on his pommel and looked at her for a moment before he spoke. "Are you afraid?" he questioned.

Caroline shifted her eyes to Nathan's. She wondered if he was asking if she was afraid of him or the prairie.

"No, I'm not afraid." She meant it. She owed a great debt to this man. "I wish to apologize for yesterday. I was rude for no reason. Will you forgive me? And accept my thanks for helping me today in the woods?"

Nathan looked into Caroline's green eyes, wide and luminous as moons as she awaited his answer. His heart raced as it had the first time he'd seen her. He wanted to have her as his wife, to ride to Texas with him and live in the stone house Jason and he had built. He reflected upon the Mormon religion and had a greater respect for their concept of Celestial Marriage, one that would endure on earth and in heaven for all eternity. He would want that kind of marriage. But there was the problem how to convince Caroline of the earthly marriage.

"I accept your apology, though none is needed. And those two men deserved to be killed."

"Had you been watching me before they came?"

"Yes," Nathan replied simply. He held his eyes steady. This was no time to act like a bashful boy.

"I'm glad you were there."

"So am I." Let her wonder whether he meant to be there to help her or only to see her in the nude. He smiled at the recollection of the sight of her young, womanly body.

They reined their mounts around and headed back in the direction of the Mormon camp.

"Tell me about your Texas. What kind of country is it?"

"The land is big—bigger than three or four other states. It has many hundreds of miles of ocean coastline. I want to see that someday. There are broad plains, hills, and rivers. Most important, it has millions of acres of grazing land."

"Where do you live? On the hills or the plains?"

"In the hills by a river."

"What do you do for a living?"

"I have a ranch, more than two hundred thousand acres on the upper Red River, a fork of the river called the Salt Fork. That's in northwest Texas."

"How can one so young own so much land? Did you inherit it?"

"I inherited nothing but life. I laid claim to the land by marking off the boundary of what I wanted. I picked land with grass and water. I have some cattle now. One day I'll have a grand ranch."

"A person can own land merely by marking it off and saying it is his?"

"No, that's not all. A formal, written claim must be made in the state capital for the few hundred acres each man is allowed. That lets you own land free and clear. Then you can graze all the surrounding public land that you can hold against the Indians and white men who try to take it away from you." Nathan smiled ruefully. "Even if you have to kill them."

"Can a woman claim land in Texas?"

"I know of no law against it."

Caroline thoughtfully considered Nathan's answer. "Have you killed to hold your land?"

Nathan saw a ghost of something in the back of Caroline's eyes, something he could not decipher, but it was something sad.

"Yes. There are times when a man must kill to keep what is his. Or simply to go on living."

"And a woman too."

"I'm sure that is right, though we don't think of a woman killing somebody."

Caroline tossed her head to rid herself of the terrible remembrance of the deaths aboard the *African Blackbird*. "Tell me more about your Texas," she said.

Sam talked quietly with Ruth in the shade of a tree at the edge of the woods. Jake and Ash sat nearby, with Pauliina and Sophia. Ash was actually holding Sophia's hand. Sam wished he had the courage to take Ruth's hand.

"DeBreen ambushed my friends and stole all of our furs," Sam said, concluding his tale. "Now I've found him. I'll take my revenge when it's possible and not hurt innocent people."

"You must have been wounded in that fight," Ruth said, recalling how ill Sam had appeared that first day she had seen him.

"I thought I would surely die from that rifle shot," Sam said. "It went clear through me." He touched his stomach over the spot. He grinned. "Then an Indian cut me with his knife and started me on the road to healing."

"There must be a good story there," Ruth said. "Tell it to me." She leaned toward the young trapper. Being near him was very pleasant.

Sam began, talking slowly and describing the event in much detail. He wanted the interlude to last a very long time.

Sophia's knee pressed against Ash's as they sat in the shade facing each other. She had made the contact and held it, and Ash knew it was deliberate. He had been too slow in making the first move. *Well, girl, I'll not be slow again.*

"How many wild horses have you caught?" Sophia asked, continuing on with the conversation.

"More than five hundred. I break them to the saddle and to a man on their back. Then I sell them. The new owner must train them for whatever special use he wants."

"Are there many wild horses?"

"Thousands of them. But I catch only the best, and they bring a good price. I've saved most of the money. When I get back to Texas, I'm going to start a horse-breeding ranch. I'll select the very best brood mares and studs, and I'll sure keep the tough spirit of the wild ones."

Mathias left the Mormon camp and walked to the group of people sitting at the edge of the woods. He looked down in a disapproving manner at Sophia, who was sitting and touching the Texan.

Ash thought the missionary was going to reprimand Sophia. He primed himself to tell the Mormon to go to hell.

Mathias's expression changed and he knelt near Ash. "I'd like to ask a favor of you," he said. "One of our men left early this morning to find a mule that had strayed. He's been gone for hours. Far too long. Would you ride and look for him?"

"Sure," Ash said, glad not to argue with the Mormon. "I see Nathan coming. He's also a good tracker. I'll ask him to go with me."

Mathias looked in the same direction as Ash. His face became strained at the sight of Caroline with Nathan.

Ash caught the Mormon's expression. The missionary was very possessive of his female converts. *That's too bad, fellow*, Ash thought, *for we Texans plan to take some of them from you.*

"That's generous of you to help," Mathias said.

"Which way did the man and the mule go?"

"Northeast," Mathias replied, pointing. He climbed erect and walked off as Caroline and Nathan drew closer. He did not look at Caroline again.

•◆ 32 ◆•

ATHAN AND ASH RODE AT A TROT. THE TRACKS of a mule and a man walking upon its sign were plain on the sandy ground. The broken broken stems of grass made the trail visible for several yards ahead.

"The mule's path is as straight as a string," Ash said. "You'd think he'd stop to graze some. He must've had some special place to go or was being rode hard."

"I think he had a rider," Nathan said.

"Yeah. That'd best explain his behavior."

"I'll be damned," Nathan said, halting his horse and staring down at the grassy ground.

The tracks of two shod horses came in from the east and turned to follow the sign of the mule and the man.

"Nathan, the mule did have a rider. Now here's a man bringing an extra horse. It's all a trick to get a Mormon off by himself."

"So he can be killed without anyone knowing what happened."

"We'll be too late to help him, but let's ride," Nathan said. He kicked the gray into a full run on the path of broken grass.

Two miles later Nathan called out to Ash and pointed at the sky ahead. A buzzard was circling, working up the wind on the scent of something dead. As the riders drove in under the buzzard, the carrion eater began to pump its wide black wings, scooping air, pressing it down as it climbed back into the sky.

The horsemen stopped. A brown mule and a blond man of forty or so lay motionless on the ground at their feet. The blood was black and congealed around a wound in the man's chest.

"The shooting is hours old," Ash said. "It was a trap. The poor bastard never had a chance. The killers rode off on the two horses."

"DeBreen means to kill all the Mormon men. And he's killed the mule to slow them down so he'll have plenty of time."

"Why does he want the men dead?"

"I don't know. I'll bet it has something to do with the women. It's obvious he doesn't want them to find out what he's doing."

"Then he must have some plan for them, or else he wouldn't care."

Nathan speculated on what should be done next. "We must warn Jake and Les not to be caught out alone. And Sam, too, but he'll be on guard. DeBreen will see all of us as a threat to his plan."

"The Mormons must be warned too," Ash said.

"I don't believe we should do that. Let this man's death be the warning. That'll scare the Mormons enough to keep them in camp. We'll not tell about the shod horses and the two men. We don't want DeBreen to attack in force before we figure a way to beat him."

"We've got to whittle down the number of DeBreen's men."

"Right."

"You reduced the number by two this morning."

"I thought that would've stopped the killing of the Mormons. I was wrong. DeBreen has sent other men after them."

"We can put the dead man across my horse's back," Ash said. "I'll ride double with you."

The funeral was held under a baking heaven in the late afternoon. Nathan stood on the outside of the congregation of Mormons and listened to Rowley's eulogy for the dead. The order was given to fill the grave. Several women gathered around the widow to comfort her.

Sam spoke to Nathan. "If I'd shot DeBreen yesterday, maybe this man would still be alive."

"You were correct in not starting a fight in the middle of the camp," Nathan replied.

"Maybe."

Mathias led the people from the gravesite and they reassembled within the camp. He began the evening sermon, dwelling upon the need to remain strong.

DeBreen and his men, their hats in their hands and their heads bent piously, had gathered with the Mormons. They quietly listened to the religious service. DeBreen kept his eyes away from the Texans, banded together on the side opposite the Mormons.

The Mormons began to sing "Rock Of Ages." The voices of the large number of women drowned out the voices of the few Mormon men. Nathan would have liked to join in the hymn. But he did not know how to make music, how to sing the right song. In fact, he did not know all the words to any song. His life on the fringes of the frontier, isolated from family and church, had left him lacking in some ways. He resolved to correct that once he had returned south.

The singing ended and the assemblage of people drifted apart. Nathan noted the silent dejection of the Mormons. He felt sorry for them.

Ash was talking to Sophia. Jake moved toward Pauliina. Caroline was winding a course to the perimeter of the circle of handcarts. Nathan strode after her.

Caroline saw Nathan drawing close and halted, waiting for him.

"Would you like to go for a stroll?" Nathan asked.

Caroline glanced at the sun, swelling as it touched the western horizon. Already the yellow sphere was weakening, turning orange.

"Yes, I would. There is daylight left."

"Good. Let's walk by the woods."

"All right."

The shadows of the trees ran out to meet them as they walked away from the camp. Nathan felt a new and strange thing was about to happen to him. He wondered about his sense of expectation.

Caroline turned her eyes upon him. He saw tiny glints of orange sunlight reflecting from the green orbs, a beautiful combination of color, cool green and hot fire.

"Talk to me," she said.

"What about?"

"Not about danger and death. About something that will make me feel good."

As Caroline ceased speaking, a wolf howled far off to the south, a weird and lovely sound.

"Even the wolves sound sad and lonely," Caroline said. "Must all life be that way?"

"Many times it is. I once knew a young man who often laughed and saw the most wondrous sights in the common things of this world."

"That is a lucky man. I would like to talk with him."

"You can never talk with him. Border thieves killed him."

Caroline looked quickly at Nathan. "I'm sorry to hear he is dead. Who was he?"

"My brother, Jason." Nathan lifted his face to the sky so that Caroline could not see the depth of his sadness. For a moment he watched the heavens. Time should have softened the memory. It had not. He dropped his gaze back to earth.

He told Caroline of gentle Jason and their life together. He described his battle with his brother's killers.

Caroline told Nathan a little of her life. She said nothing of the death of the captain of the *African Blackbird*.

They walked slowly along the fringe of the woods. The air lay still and heavy with memories of the day's heat. The daylight drained from the sky, spilling over the western horizon, leaving a blue-black heaven speckled with stars and a half-moon. A cloud moved across the moon and darkness flooded over the land.

A silence fell upon Caroline and Nathan. Neither broke it, letting the quietness extend as they walked on.

A rustling noise came from a short distance directly in front of them. Nathan caught Caroline's hand with his left and drew his pistol with the right.

The weak light created an eerie silhouette of something on the ground. They crept closer to see. Whispered voices reached them. They halted and peered into the darkness.

The whispers ceased. The rustling sound became rhythmic. Caroline recognized the sound. Nathan felt her hand stiffen within his.

The moon tore free of the cloud. Its silver light fell upon the prairie.

Sophia and Ash lay upon the grassy ground. They were locked in each other's arms as they took their love in the heat of the moonlit night. In their passion their strong young bodies thrust quick and hard, as violent as a knife fight.

Caroline clutched Nathan's hand and drew him backward. Lovemaking was a private thing and should not be viewed by others. They stole away, their presence unknown by Sophia and Ash.

"I must return to the camp," Caroline said. She extracted her hand from Nathan's grip.

"Must you?"

"Yes."

They crossed through the night's silver-blue moon glow. Just outside the circle of handcarts, Caroline stopped. Nathan halted beside her.

She turned to him, raised her face, and kissed him. Nathan felt her lips, soft, parting, caressing his. His spirit soared at the wonder of her touch.

Then she pulled away. "That was for your kindness to me. But I shall never go to Texas."

Before Nathan could speak, Caroline hastened in between the handcarts.

Nathan's feeling of exhilaration crashed, breaking like thin glass upon rock. Wretched, he walked into the night shadows.

◆ 33 ◆

NATHAN WAS THE LAST OF THE TEXANS TO BREAK camp. Leading his packhorse, he rode toward the Mormon handcart company which was already lined up two abreast and moving out to the west.

Near the front of the caravan a man called to his small son to get behind the handcart and push. A baby cried somewhere farther back, and a woman spoke soothingly to it. The journey was hard on the old and the very young.

The day was hazy. The air lay still, heavy and humid. The trees on the floodplain of the North Platte River three miles south were barely discernible. Nathan judged it would rain before the day ended.

He checked for DeBreen. The trapper was with his men, riding in a group on the right side of the caravan. Unlike the day before, they were offering no assistance to the Mormons. Nathan marked that fact and it worried him. He knew that the uneasy, unspoken truce that existed between the trappers and the Texans would soon break. However, Nathan doubted DeBreen would attack in front of the Mormon's. But some plan would soon be put into motion.

He spotted Ash, who had hooked his horse to the handcart of Sophia and her three comrades and was towing it along. His packhorse was tied to the rear of the vehicle. Jake walked beside Pauliina. His horse was pulling the handcart of four women just behind.

Sam, with his two Indian ponies, rode out of the woods by Brush Creek. He scanned the long double line of carts and then offered the ponies to certain groups of people who were having a hard time keeping up.

To Nathan's surprise, Les had fastened his mount to pull the cart of the redheaded Emily, and was in earnest conversation with her as they walked. As Nathan approached, Les broke off from Emily and came to meet him.

Les seemed uncomfortable as he looked up at Nathan. He spoke directly to the subject on both their minds. "Yesterday I saw you go off with Caroline and judged you were more interested in her than in Emily. So I asked Emily out. We seem to have hit it off real well. I hope that's all right with you."

"That's fine, Les. She's a nice person, and pretty. Good luck to you. Watch DeBreen and his men. They might start trouble."

Les breathed a sigh of relief. Then he nodded. "I'll watch out for them."

Nathan touched the gray with his heels and trotted him up the string of carts. He saw Mathias pulling on one family's handcart. The husband pushed with his wife at the tail end of the cart. Nathan fell in beside Mathias.

"If you want me to, I'll ride on ahead and kill a buffalo for the people."

"The brothers and sisters would be very grateful to you for that," Mathias said. "They are without meat and need more nourishing food than what we have."

"Then I'll do it." The Mormon's expression was not friendly, and Nathan wondered what the reason was. "Here, tie my packhorse to that cart. He can carry his load and pull the cart too."

Nathan handed the lead rope of the animal to Mathias and galloped off ahead. He passed DeBreen and his band. Their hostile eyes followed after him. Enemies could not hide from each other on the flat prairie.

Nathan rode on at a gallop. South a mile, the terrain fell away in rough breaks to the North Platte. To the north, the last remnant of the long stretch of sand hills was sliding to the rear. A lone antelope stood on the crest of one of the more distant hills and watched the single horseman go by.

An hour later Nathan spotted a herd of several hundred buffalo, but they were far off to the north. Though he could easily ride to them and kill one, the Mormons would have to veer off their route quite a distance to retrieve the meat. He let the herd go by.

The two young bull buffalo drank their fill of the river water and ambled away on the trail that climbed back up to the prairie. They had separated from the herd and roamed about during the night. Now they wanted to rejoin the herd. They merely glanced at the wolf that rose up from the brush beside the trail. In their young strength the bulls did not fear a lone wolf. And he would know they were not to be trifled with.

Nathan spotted the bulls plodding up the worn trail from the direction of the river. If they held their course, he could kill them right on the caravan route. He pulled his rifle and dismounted. He moved to the far side of the gray and out of view of the buffalo. The sight of a horse would be a familiar one to the buffalo and wouldn't frighten them.

As the bulls drew close, they lifted their heads and eyed the horse, standing motionless and watching. One of the bulls tossed its head and snorted at the horse. Both buffalo continued on.

Nathan waited until the bulls reached the trail not fifty paces in front of him. He moved from behind the horse, raised his rifle, and fired.

The farther bull grunted at the slam of the bullet. It sank to its knees, struggled to hold that position, then rolled onto its side. The second bull thundered off in a surprisingly fast gait.

Nathan sprang astride and spurred the gray. He shoved the single shot rifle into its scabbard and drew his pistol. The gray pounded ahead, easily drawing even with the running buffalo. Nathan extended the pistol until it was not two yards from the bull's head. At the crash of the gun the bull's legs folded, and the giant body struck the ground, sliding along for a few feet before coming to a stop.

Nathan reined his horse in and looked back over his kills. He decided not to field-dress the big animals. The Mormons would reach this point in a couple of hours and could carve them into hundreds of pieces right where they lay. He turned the gray back to the east.

The sun reached its burning zenith and the handcart caravan halted for rest and the noon meal. Many of the people, those that could, crowded into the shade cast by the beds of their carts. They began to eat their scant rations.

DeBreen and his band sat in the shade of their horses and chewed on jerky. Every man's eyes were on the Mormons, sitting or lying on the ground near their carts. The Texans could be seen talking with some of the women.

"Those goddamn Texans have spoiled our plans," Stanker growled. He nodded at Sam, off by himself on the prairie and sitting half under his horse. "And that fellow, Wilde, I wonder which one of the men on the rafts he was." He looked questioningly at DeBreen.

The trapper leader shrugged his big shoulders. "That doesn't make any difference. There's something more important. Did he have anything to do with Phillips and Ross disappearing?"

"Maybe they just gave up and went back to St. Joe," Stanker said.

"They wouldn't do that without telling me," DeBreen said.

"What are we waiting for?" Taylor said. "I'm getting damn tired. We came to kill Mormons. Let's do it."

"There's enough of us to take the Texans," Stanker said. "Then we can do whatever we want with the Mormons. I'm itching to get at some of those pretty women."

A rumble of approving voices broke from the other men. They looked expectantly at DeBreen for his answer.

"Killing the Mormons would be easy," DeBreen said. "They don't have guns and they're not fighters. The Texans would be some harder to kill. We could do it, but they'd sure as hell take a few of us with them."

DeBreen swung his small gray eyes to examine each man. "Still, I agree it's past time we did something."

DeBreen made one brief gesture toward Wilde, then looked at Stanker. "Wilde should be killed first. He would be suspicious if I went over there. But he hasn't seen you up close since he found us. Maybe he wouldn't even recognize you after all this time. Why don't you go over there and shoot him? That would stop him from joining with the Texans against us.''

Stanker ranged his gaze over Wilde. DeBreen was a tricky man. Was he now putting Stanker into the most dangerous position, as he had seen DeBreen do with other men? Stanker thought so. But he was confident he could kill the bothersome young fellow. Start a little argument that the Mormons could hear, then pull a gun and shoot Wilde. The thought felt good to Stanker.

"I like the idea," Stanker said. "You keep the Texans off me when Wilde is down.''

"We'll do that," DeBreen said.

"Then count him dead." Stanker rose to his feet and walked toward Wilde.

Sam watched Ruth, sitting beside Pauliina near their handcart. She looked very small and defenseless compared to the big Swedish woman. Sam would try to stay close and keep her safe from DeBreen. But how long could that continue? He had now been with the Mormons two days. He would not delay much longer before he killed DeBreen. Ruth probably would despise him if she saw him commit murder.

He caught movement with the corner of his eye and twisted to see what it was. One of the trappers had left his comrades and was coming in Sam's direction. The man's step was strong and purposeful.

Sam loosened his pistol in its holster and climbed to his feet. He did not think the man intended to make idle chatter.

There was something familiar about the middle-aged trapper with the long, hairy face. Sam had seen that horselike countenance somewhere before. Then full recollection rushed into Sam's mind. The man was one of the river pirates.

Sam swept his eyes around. The Mormons and three of the Texans rested at the handcarts. The fourth Texan, Nathan, was within sight and returning at a trot on his horse. DeBreen's band of men watched Sam. The tense, expectant attitude reinforced Sam's belief that the approaching man meant trouble.

Sam smiled icily. He smelled death on the wind. Farrow, old friend, I'm about to keep my promise to you and shoot one of your murderers.

He rested his hand on the butt of his revolver. He remembered Farrow's advice: If you are certain there is going to be a fight, then start it yourself. The fraction of time an enemy would waste in reacting to your move could mean the difference between life and death.

Stanker stopped and set his feet. "My name's Stanker. DeBreen said you were trying to accuse him of some crime that happened this spring on the upper Missouri. Well, I was with DeBreen then, so tell me what we were supposed to have done."

"No need for me to tell you, for you know what you did," Sam said, his voice coming savagely between his teeth. Without the slightest warning he drew his pistol, aimed it at Stanker, and fired.

Stanker shuddered at the impact of the bullet. His eyes flared wide, showing much white in great surprise. God! He had not expected Wilde to attack him so early in the argument. He reached for his own pistol.

A second lance of fire and smoke exploded from the end of Wilde's gun. Stanker staggered backward, trying to hold his footing. His legs crumpled and he fell, his face plowing into the grass-covered prairie soil.

Nathan heard the shots ahead, near the string of handcarts. His eyes jumped the distance and he saw a man fall. A second man stood looking down. Nathan recognized the thin form that was upright—Sam Wilde.

Nathan shouted at the gray and slapped it on the neck. The brute bolted in the direction of the camp. Nathan saw DeBreen and his men walking toward Sam. Ash, Les, and Jake were closing in on him from the opposite direction. The Mormons were talking and gesturing uselessly.

Nathan reined his horse to a sliding stop and sprang down near Sam. "What happened?" Nathan questioned.

The three remaining Texans came up hurriedly. They gathered around Sam.

"That man was one of then, Nathan." Sam pointed down at Stanker's corpse. "He helped kill Farrow and the others. Now he's dead. And here comes DeBreen. He'll be just as dead in a minute." Sam gripped his pistol hard. The blood lust strummed through every particle of his being. His mouth closed with a snap and the muscles ridged along his jaw.

"Take it easy," Nathan said, looking at the fierce lines of Sam's face. Never had he seen a man more eager to do battle. "We'll stand by you, but don't provoke a fight with DeBreen now. They outnumber us. We'll all be shot to hell. Fight him later."

"It's now! I'm going to do kill him now," Sam said in a grating voice, and his eyes locked on DeBreen.

"No, not now," Jake said. He stepped closer to Sam and grabbed him by the shoulder. He squeezed, and Sam winced at the pain that was building under the hard fingers. "Nathan's right. We'll back you. But if you say one word to start a fight, I'll hit you so hard, you'll not be able to talk for a week. You say only something that'll keep DeBreen off us. Or let Nathan do the talking."

"Sam has to talk," Nathan said. "He did the shooting. Do it right, Sam," he warned.

The four Texans turned to stand beside Sam, and waited.

DeBreen and his band of seven halted not ten yards distant. "Why in hell did you shoot Stanker?" DeBreen asked in a belligerent voice.

Sam glanced at Jake. He saw the warning glint in the man's eyes. His right hand was clenched into a sledgehammer fist.

"Stanker came over here to shoot me, DeBreen," Sam said. DeBreen had been too far away to hear what Stanker said. Sam began to lie. "I don't know why. He called me a son of a bitch and dared me to fight. I had no choice. He was god-awful slow."

DeBreen's eyes squinted until they seemed to have vanished into their sockets beneath the bony brows. He measured the Texans. Every man was poised, primed to reach for a pistol and fight. Wilde and the one called Nathan watched him closely. If DeBreen signaled to his men or grabbed for his gun, both opponents would try to kill him.

DeBreen did not think he could kill the two of them before one put a bullet through him. At such short range there would be little possibility that they would miss.

"It doesn't make any sense that Stanker would jump you for no reason," DeBreen said in a disbelieving tone.

"It's crazy, all right," Sam said. "I haven't the foggiest idea why he jumped me. Was he okay in the head?" Give DeBreen an excuse to back down, thought Sam. His lust to kill DeBreen was lessening as he realized that he did not want the Texans to die because of him. Further, they had come to stand with him as friends. If they had not, Sam would be dead by now.

DeBreen knew Wilde and the Texans had to be removed as impediments to his plans. But to accomplish their destruction with some degree of certainty and safety, he would have to wait until they were not expecting his attack. It was obvious his adversaries were also hoping to avoid an immediate fight.

Nathan saw DeBreen's eyes come halfway open, and the man seemed to relax slightly. "Stanker was an ornery bastard," DeBreen said to Sam. "Maybe he just didn't like your looks because you're so damn ugly."

"That's probably the reason," Nathan interjected hastily, wanting to prevent Sam from making some angry retort. "Come on, Sam, let's get out of the hot sun and into some shade."

Jake, not removing his attention from DeBreen, took hold of Sam's shoulder as a reminder of his warning.

Nathan spoke. "Sam—and the rest of you—let's go. This is over."

Warily the Texans began to back away. At a hundred feet Jake removed his hand from Sam's shoulder. "You did that right," he said.

"Yeah," Sam said disgustedly. "But I'm still going to kill that damn murderer." Yet he was glad for the reprieve to have time to devise a situation where he would have more advantage. He would need it if he was to survive DeBreen's men.

Ruth's trembling slowly subsided as Sam and the Texans drew away from DeBreen. "Oh, God!" she said. "A man killed right before our eyes. And the men with their big guns argued. I thought there would be more killing."

"It appeared to me that the man came to threaten Sam and got what he deserved," Sophia said. "Sam was sitting and bothering nobody. Just looking at you now and then."

"There's no reason for one person to kill another," Ruth said.

"You're wrong," Caroline said. "We live in a violent world, and there are times when a person must become violent and kill merely to keep from being severely hurt or killed themselves. You should be thinking of Sam. I believe he's sweet on you. Did you worry about him, that he could be killed?"

"Yes, I thought of that. I was afraid DeBreen would shoot him. Do you really think Sam likes me?"

Caroline looked intently at Ruth. "You're not that innocent. Don't play games with me or with yourself. Women are born with the ability to read a man's eyes and their emotions toward them."

"She had better do it often too," Sophia said, "for sometimes a man is too bashful to say what's on his mind."

"I truly believe Sam much wants you," Pauliina said. "Or I am not understanding what Jake feels when he looks at me." She smiled a large smile.

"I like to see that certain expression in their eyes that they would like to jump on me," Sophia said. "Ruth, what would you do if Sam asked you to go off with him to the mountains or maybe to Texas?"

Ruth skimmed her eyes from one of her friends to another. "I'm going with the Mormons to Salt Lake City," she answered. "Aren't all of you?"

"I am," Caroline said.

Neither Sophia or Pauliina answered. They were looking off in the direction of the Texans.

---•◆ **34** ◆•---

FAR AWAY, MIRAGES OF LAKES, OF STRANGE, CON-
torted landscapes, formed on the hot prairie
ahead of the handcart caravan. The mirages
weakened and died as the toiling, snaking stream of humans
drew nearer. As the old false images vanished, new ones
continued to appear on the flat distant plain.

Nathan pushed at the rear of a handcart. Every hour or so
he would drop back the line and lend his strength to another
group of struggling people. His two horses were elsewhere,
one pulling at a cart ahead, the other where he had left it
with Mathias.

He felt obliged to assist the Mormons as long as he
traveled with them. But he had begun to believe he was not
destined to find a wife among them. He was greatly sad-
dened by that thought.

DeBreen and his band were another worry. They rode in
a line on the right side of the caravan. Frequently they
threw measuring looks at the women, like a pack of preda-
tors sizing up their prey. Nathan knew that if the Texans
left, DeBreen would destroy the Mormons. He still did not
know why.

The caravan reached the two buffalo Nathan had slain
earlier in the day. Mathias and two other Mormon men
skinned the animals and began to carve the carcasses.

The travelers, holding pans or pieces of oilcloth in their
hands, queued up in front of the men to receive their cut of
the bloody meat. Then, smiling, their step lighter, they
returned to their carts.

The caravan moved out, having stopped for less than an

hour. Of the two buffalo, only the heavy, wet hides and the bony skeletons remained behind on the prairie.

A new image formed among the mirages ahead on the prairie, a jagged hill rearing up above what appeared to be a sheet of water. As the handcart company labored on, the water mirage thinned and finally melted away. The hill became more solid in form, darker in color, and grew until it rose a thousand feet above the plain.

Scott's Bluff was in sight about twenty miles ahead. The word came down the chain of handcarts from Mathias. A major milepost had been reached.

Nathan watched the sun fall to the west on a long sliding trajectory, like a great, hot cannonball seeking a target. It intersected high, thin, white clouds, like a giant swan's tail, scudding across the sky from the northwest. An hour later the swan's tail had sailed on past to the southeast. Behind came a long storm line of dark cumulus clouds, created by moisture sucked up to tremendous heights in the warm elevator shafts of summer's thermal updrafts. The thunderheads drove in beneath the sun.

Swiftly the storm clouds piled up, towering in livid cliffs five, six miles to touch the heavens. They came striding like giants across the plains. Misty fingers of rain hung down from the broad, black bottoms of the thunderheads.

The storm front charged ever more closer to the handcart people. The rain thickened, turning to long dark streamers touching the ground.

Wind rushed out ahead of the storm, whipping the prairie grass and buffeting the toiling men and women. Dust fell upon them like dry rain.

Nathan saw the storm's imminent arrival. He collected his packhorse and hastened forward to find the gray.

"When are you going to stop?" Nathan questioned Mathias. He pointed at the boiling black cloud mass bearing down on them. "The storm's right on us and it'll get dark early."

"Right now," Mathias replied. He turned and held up both hands. "Make camp!" he shouted.

Nathan untied the gray from the crossbar of the cart. He looked around for the other Texans as the carts came in and started to form their usual circle. Les and Emily arrived. Shortly Ash and Jake came into sight with the cart they helped pull.

Nathan's view fell upon Caroline. Her hat, blown from her head by the wind, hung down her back. Her hair had broken free of its bindings and the wind blew it out in a long tawny stream. God, she was beautiful! His heart hammered in his chest, as it had the first time he'd seen her. Never had he felt the ebb of his life running so strong and vital, and it was all because of this woman. Yet he could not possess her. A hellish, bitter piece of knowledge.

Jake wheeled the handcart into position between two others. The women immediately unlashed the tarpaulin and removed the tent poles and canvas. All hands began to raise the tent.

Nathan rode near the group. He dropped the reins of the horses. Without consciously planning what he meant to do, he caught Caroline by the shoulders and turned her toward him. Her hands came up quickly in a defensive manner, as if to ward off whoever had grabbed her. Her green eyes were tinged with feline yellow.

"What do you want?" she said in astonishment. Her head lifted defiantly.

"I came for this," Nathan said. He crushed her to him and kissed her roughly. He tasted her, smelled her female perspiration, felt her hair whipping around his face. God, he loved it.

Caroline remained totally rigid in Nathan's arms. She did not struggle against him. It would be useless, for his arms were like steel bands holding her.

Nathan released Caroline and stepped back. He had hoped to kindle some feeling, some response in her, but there had been nothing, not one sign that she shared his feelings.

"Why did you do that?" she asked.

"That was good-bye. I'm leaving for Texas tomorrow." The thought had only just occurred to him, but the instant he uttered the words, he knew it was true.

"Leaving? Tomorrow?"

Nathan nodded his head. "Will you go with me?"

"No. I'm going to Utah."

Nathan felt shattered. But he had expected nothing else. She had already told him she would not go with him.

"Then this is truly good-bye." He snatched up the reins of the horses, threw one quick look around at the surprised faces of the Texans and the three other girls, and walked stiffly off in the wind.

Nathan moved away from the Mormon camp. He halted on a slight rise of ground and began to unbuckle the straps of the packsaddle. He felt only gloom. Perhaps he should make a search yet tonight for another woman. He could sort through them and in a straightforward manner ask the prettiest to marry him. If she refused him, then he could ask the next prettiest. One might eventually say yes. Even as the thought came to him, he knew he would not do it.

He looked up as a horseman rode by close on his side. DeBreen stared down at him with a malignant glance, the hatred ageless and ugly in his eyes. Go to hell, Nathan thought. He was tired of all of them, the Mormons and DeBreen alike.

Lightning flashed and thunder rumbled. It would be raining in half an hour.

He staked out the two horses. His gear was piled on the topmost point of the low rise of land. Over this he spread his tarpaulin and anchored it down at three corners.

Jake, Ash and Les came and made similar camps nearby. Finishing their task, they hunkered down by Nathan.

"It's kind of sudden to be deciding to go back to Texas, isn't it?" Ash asked.

"No more sudden than deciding to come north with you," Nathan replied.

"I reckon about the same," Ash said.

"How about DeBreen?" Les asked. "You know what he'll do to the Mormons if we leave."

"You fellows don't have to leave just because I do," Nathan said.

"We couldn't stop DeBreen alone," Jake said.

"He can't be stopped even if I stayed. The first time our backs are turned, he's going to shoot the hell out of us."

"Here comes Sam," Ash said. "Let's get him in on this palaver."

Sam stopped and climbed down from his mount. "Nathan, Ruth said you were leaving tomorrow."

"That's right. How did she come to tell you that?"

"She looked me up. She was scared that all of you would leave. Then DeBreen would be left here to do what he pleases. The women are all frightened."

"She's got it right," Nathan said.

"I wouldn't want Ruth hurt," Sam said. "I say we strike DeBreen now. A hell of a storm is coming, and we can catch him off-guard while he's holed up to stay out of the rain."

"I wouldn't be surprised if he plans the same trick for us," Nathan said. He looked to the west some three hundred yards away and beyond a shallow, brushy gully where DeBreen and his men were making their camp. "If we could lay a trap for DeBreen and get in the first shots, we just might kill him and most of his men."

"I'd like to get that done without us getting all shot up ourselves," Ash said. "I'd hate to think of not being around to take Sophia back to Texas."

"Has Sophia said she would go with you?" Nathan asked.

"I haven't directly asked her, but it's kind of understood that she will. But it's now time. I'll do it tonight."

"I'll ask Pauliina too," Jake said.

"I've already asked Caroline," Nathan said. "You know her answer." He spoke to Les. "How about you and Emily?"

"She said yes today. We're just waiting on you fellows."

"Sam, why don't you take Ruth and come to Texas with us?" Ash said.

"She'd never come with me," Sam said wistfully. He yanked his hat down more firmly on his head and stared into the wind at the Mormon camp. "But I'd sure like that."

"All she can do is turn you down," Jake said. "I imagine that hurts, but Nathan is still living after Caroline told him nothing doing."

"I'll think on it," Sam said. "Nathan, do we fight DeBreen?"

"I have a plan," Nathan said, pivoting back to face them. "If you fellows think it's a good idea, we'll try it tonight."

The men gathered closer together. They talked as the

clouds threw lightning bolts and sent them skittering across
the prairie. Thunder shook the earth. And the men talked
on as an early dusk came and darkened the world.

They finally nodded in agreement. In the dimming light
their shadowy faces were stark with the realization that
none of them might see the morrow. Jake and Ash rose and
walked toward the tent of Sophia and Pauliina. Les went off
to find Emily. Sam hurriedly began to make his camp near
the Texans.

Nathan climbed erect and stared into the whistling wind.
The storm was gaining in intensity, the clouds boiling and
churning directly above his head. The thunder deafened
him; streaks of lightning blinded him. He felt as agitated
and unsettled as the storm.

Ash and Jake returned. They smiled and called out happily to Nathan and Sam. Les came running and dived in
under his tarp.

The rain came—giant, cold drops falling from a very great
height, that had barely melted from ice. The storm fell upon
the prairie like a mean, wet dog.

Caroline lay and listened to the drumming rain and the
keening banshee of the wind. The mighty wind snapped the
canvas against the guy ropes, and the center pole bent and
jerked. The flame of the single candle flickered and danced,
barely staying alight. The tent seemed about ready to fly
away.

Shortly before the storm struck, Sophia and Pauliina had
gone outside and talked with Ash and Jake. After a time the
two girls had reentered the tent, their faces bright with joy.

"We're going to Texas tomorrow," Sophia said. "We've
been asked and we said yes." She laughed and hugged
Caroline.

"I think Jake and Ash will make fine husbands," Caroline
said. "Congratulations to both of you."

"How about your religion?" cried Ruth.

"Well, what about it?" Sophia asked.

"You can't give it up."

"Sure I can, for a good man."

"But you don't have to, for you can find a husband in Salt
Lake City," Ruth said.

"Maybe so, but this way I get to pick the one I want," Sophia said. "Most likely I wouldn't get that chance in Utah. And besides, any man who chooses me might already have ten wives or more."

Ruth looked imploringly at Caroline. "Tell them they must go with us."

"They must make their own decision," Caroline replied.

"This is awful," Ruth said in a plaintive voice.

"I sure don't think so," Sophia said happily. She snuffed out the candle.

The young women grew still, resting on their sleeping pallets and thinking their private thoughts. Outside, the storm raged on.

Caroline climbed up from her bed. She knew the girls were still awake, but there was something she must do. She moved toward the tent flap that opened to the outside.

Lightning flared, like a sun exploding. The inside of the tent became bright as day.

The light winked out and black night once again filled the tent.

"Caroline, where are you going?" Ruth called out above the storm.

"I'm going to properly thank a man who did something very brave for me, and to say good-bye to him," Caroline said in the darkness.

"What do you mean?" Ruth asked.

"Shut up and grow up," Sophia snapped.

Caroline untied the flap and stepped out into the storm. The rain struck hard, wetting quickly with its ice-cold deluge. The howling wind sucked away her breath. She shivered, and her lungs pulled hard to catch the swift air.

She tied the tent flap back into place and turned, her eyes probing the blackness. Lightning struck the ground somewhere close to the south. In the glare the mounds of the Texans' tarpaulins became visible, glistening like wet oilcloth for a brief moment. She moved into the night, walking the dark world with the wind and the rain.

Nathan sat up quickly when the wind began to claw at the corner of his tarp. One corner was jerking and seemed ready to come free from the saddle that held it down. He put his hand on the tarp to hold it in place.

"Nathan, let me in," Caroline said, her voice coming as thin as a ghost's from outside.

"My God!" exclaimed Nathan. He jerked the tarp loose and lifted it.

Caroline ducked down and slid in beside him. She trembled from the cold wetness and from what she was about to do.

"Is it all right that I am here?"

Nathan looked at her in the almost constant flashes of lightning. Her face was taut, questioning.

"Very much all right," Nathan said. He replaced the tarp under the saddle to hold it against the violent bursts of the wind. "You are freezing. Let me put my blanket around you."

"Shouldn't I take off my wet clothes first?" Caroline said.

Without waiting for an answer she began to unbutton her shirt. She had to remain seated, for the height of the tarp was low, limited by the length of the packsaddle set on end to act as a center pole.

She saw him there in the frequent lightning flashes, silently watching her as she disrobed.

"Now cover me," she said, lying down nude on Nathan's bed.

Nathan started to cover Caroline with a blanket.

'Wait," she said. "Won't you lie down, too, and help me get warm?"

Nathan felt a tremble in his hard muscled body at the meaning of her words. He stretched out beside her. "If I hold you, that would help you to get warm faster."

"Yes. Do that."

Nathan wrapped Caroline in his arms. He was surprised at the thinness of her body. He easily could count her ribs with his fingers. And they seemed fragile, giving way under the slightest pressure. Her bright eyes and brave face made her seem a larger woman. His hands found the firm mounds of her breasts.

"I'm still going to Utah," Caroline whispered.

"I know. You told me that."

Nathan held her close, feeling her cool flesh against him from her head down to her toes. In the pure happiness of the moment he forgot all the lonely tomorrows that were to be his fate. He kissed her soft lips gently. His hands explored the planes and the curves of her body.

She grew warm. He entered the delicious, moist womanhood of her.

●◆ 35 ◆●

"**N**ATHAN, THE RAIN HAS NEARLY STOPPED." Sam's low voice came from outside the tarpaulin covering. "It's time to get into position."

Nathan had been awake for some time, lying quietly with the sleeping Caroline's breath softly fanning his cheek. He had made love to her, slept, and then loved her again. He did not sleep again as the night wore on. He wanted to store as much memory of this time with her as possible.

The storm with its lightning and thunder had worked its way off to the east. Its noise was only a distant echo. The wind had ceased. A drizzle tapped lightly on the tarpaulin. Sam was correct: The time for the battle was near.

"I'm awake," Nathan said. "Tell everyone to keep their rifles and pistols covered. We must not have any misfires. And tell them to leave their spurs behind."

"What's happening?" Caroline whispered, awakened by the voices.

"Tonight we fight DeBreen."

"Why do you risk your life? You and the others have only to ride away and you'll be safe."

"We can't leave DeBreen alive. We know what he'll do to all the Mormons."

"There are too many of them for you to win."

"We have a plan that may even the odds some."

Caroline touched Nathan's face with her fingers. Then she drew away from him. "I must go back to my tent."

"Yes, I understand. It's not safe here."

Caroline tossed the blanket aside and pulled on her still damp clothing. "Good-bye," she said.

Nathan heard the finality in her voice. "Good-bye," he replied.

She slid from under the tarp and was gone.

Nathan dressed and wrapped his rifle and pistol in pieces of oilcloth. He went into the night.

The drizzle had slackened to a cold, falling mist. To the west a thin slice of the sky with many stars showed against the black velvet of the heavens. With the clouds moving east, the moon, now nearly three-quarters full, would soon be in sight.

The three Texans and Sam quietly approached Nathan. They did not speak, awaiting his directions. They had accepted him as their leader. He felt the weight of his position and thought about how to keep them from getting killed and still win the battle.

"It's late," Nathan said, his voice barely above a whisper. "If DeBreen and his men are coming, it'll be now, before the moon shows through the clouds. Let's move."

He led them into the murky night toward DeBreen's camp. A soft rustling of wind on feathers swept past, an owl hunting the night's darkness. They reached the shallow gully and silently crept down into the brushy bottom. By standing erect, they could see over the top and out across the prairie.

"Spread out about twenty feet apart," Nathan said. "If none of DeBreen's men comes directly at you, then shift positions to fight where they are. Wait until they get close before you shoot."

"I hope the moon is clear of the clouds so we can see them," Ash said.

"Nathan, and the rest of you, listen to me," Les said in a hushed voice. "If anything should happen to me, tell Emily my ranch is hers. She has said that she will marry me. So as far as I'm concerned, she's already my wife. Do all of you bear witness to what I've said?"

"We hear you," Nathan replied. "But you'll come out of this okay."

"Maybe so. Still, don't any of you forget what I've said."

Les went to Nathan's left. Ash followed. Jake and Sam moved right. All sound of their steps stopped. The night lay black and heavy in the gully and on the prairie.

The seconds ticked past, adding to one minute, two, three. The distant muttering of the storm faded to near silence. The clouds continued drifting to the east on the high, invisible wind. Nathan thought the trailing edge of the clouds was beginning to brighten as the moon drew ever closer to it.

The misty drizzle stopped altogether. Nathan unwrapped the oilcloth from around his rifle and pistol and let the covering fall to the ground.

He breathed deeply, smelling the wet grass and the brush and the mud in the gully bottom. He thought of his love-making with Caroline and his heart beat nicely at the memory.

He looked out across the wet prairie and reevaluated his plan. Nothing stirred within the range of his ears, and his eyes saw nothing in the cold, leaden light. He fully believed DeBreen would steal upon the Texans in the dark. Their position in the gully was the best he could do. He knew the men with him would stand fast and fight. However, Les worried him with his premonition of death.

His nerves tightened up a notch. He sensed the aura of something hostile there in the darkness on the prairie. Then he heard the slow, cautious footsteps on the sodden ground. DeBreen and his fighters were coming.

Nathan checked the clouds, which still obscured most of the sky. *Hurry, moon, hurry. Give us light to shoot by.*

The enemy was closer, now easily within range of both rifle and pistol. Nathan sank lower in the gully, trying to catch silhouettes against the strip of star-studded sky. The trailing edge of the clouds looked no brighter. Where was the moon?

A patch of stars vanished. One man located, thought Nathan. A second group of stars was blocked out to the right of the first. A second man. But the stars were not enough to shoot by, and he dare not miss, for then DeBreen's larger force would overwhelm them.

An incipient crack broke through the layer of clouds. The crack became a gap that widened swiftly. The moon hung in the opening and spilled its rays down to the earth. The prairie became bathed in pale silver.

The men in front of Nathan suddenly halted, pinned to the prairie by the light.

Nathan raised his rifle and fired into the dark center of a figure of a man. The form collapsed. Instantly Nathan dropped the rifle into his left hand and drew his pistol. He fired at the second man. The man staggered, seemed to trip, fell.

Other gunshots rippled along the draw to Nathan's left. DeBreen's band had approached slightly off center of the position of the men waiting in ambush. Nathan crouched and moved left through the brush to support Les and Ash.

A gun crashed on the prairie. Nathan heard the whizzing pass of the bullet. He saw the flash and shot back quickly.

Les and Ash were firing rapidly out of the gully. Answering shots were even heavier. Nathan joined them in a savage fusillade at the shadowy, moving forms.

Sam and Jake ran up. "Have you seen DeBreen?" Sam shouted, catching Nathan by the shoulder.

"How in hell could I tell which one is DeBreen?" Nathan said, shaking off Sam's hand. "Kill all of them."

Sam and Jake began to blaze away at the muzzle flashes. A shrill cry rose, and was quickly cut off. DeBreen, thought Sam. That sounded like DeBreen's voice. He marked the spot in his mind.

The firing stopped abruptly. Nathan saw a man run toward DeBreen's camp. A second form laboriously climbed up from the ground and limped away in the same direction. The fight was shot out of DeBreen's men. They would not stop running until they reached the Missouri River.

"Stay in the gully," Nathan called to his comrades. "A wounded man can kill you. Anybody hit? Les, are you okay?"

"Yes."

"Ash?"

"Just a scratch on my ribs."

"Sam?"

"Okay."

"Jake?"

"That was one fine ambush," Jake called back. "Caught them with the moon behind them."

Nathan knew that cold, black chance had won the battle for them. Neither DeBreen nor he could forecast the position of the moon exactly. Had the moonlight not come through, there could easily have been a different group of men celebrating a victory.

"It won't be daylight for an hour or so," Nathan said. "We'll wait until we can see, then take a look at DeBreen's men."

"Somebody should tell the women we are all alive," Ash said. "They'll be worried after all the shooting."

"Let Les do it," Nathan said. So much for premonitions.

Grueling awoke when the night was still dense and black. He had driven his men and horses every day since leaving Salt Lake City. He ignored the few complaints uttered by the men. But the horses were weakening, and that was important. Three were limping from strained tendons or hooves bruised by stones.

He rose and knelt on his blanket. Silently he prayed that the women of the handcart company were safe and that he would reach them soon. Nothing must happen to them, for they were necessary to help mother the race of Saints that would occupy and forever hold the Mormon empire the Prophet called Deseret.

Grueling seated himself and watched the eastern sky. He thought of taking another wife. He would closely inspect the women of the handcart company. It would be best if he made his selection before they reached Salt Lake City. Once they reached there, they were given a day to rest. Then the women would put on their prettiest dresses and line up in Temple Square. The Mormon men desiring wives would come and walk along the line, each one choosing the woman he wanted. Sometimes they would take two or three wives at a time. Often the men's first wives helped him to select the new ones.

Scott's Bluff gradually took form in the morning light to the east. Grueling stood up.

"Roll out!" he shouted. "We ride in ten minutes. The handcart company can't be far."

In five minutes the men had broken camp, packed their bedding, saddled, and sat on their horses. Several chewed food as they awaited Grueling's order to ride.

Good men, thought Grueling, every one. They obeyed like soldiers. Good soldiers for the Prophet. Grueling had not been wrong in his selection of those who should make the journey with him.

"Let's ride," Grueling called. He kicked his horse to a trot through the faint, uncertain light of the dying night. The rumbling of the horses' hooves of his twenty fighting men held close station behind him.

They rode into the new day, during which they would do the Prophet's work.

Morning came. The night unraveled reluctantly, giving up its dominion over the prairie.

The Texans and Sam walked warily through the damp grass, examining the corpses lying almost in a line along the gully.

"Five men dead," Nathan said. "And I saw two making off for DeBreen's camp. Where's the eighth man?"

"I'm looking for him now," Sam called. "I think I know where he fell." He moved on ahead in a slight zigzagging pattern.

He found the thick-chested body of DeBreen, lying face-down and unmoving. Yet DeBreen was not to be trusted, even when he appeared dead. Sam held his pistol ready as he cautiously drew near.

He dropped his knee in the center of the broad back to prevent any sudden movement. "Are you still alive, DeBreen?" Sam asked.

The body stirred weakly and tried to roll. Sam pressed down harder, holding DeBreen against the ground.

"Now don't do that," Sam said. "Let me see both of your hands." He put the barrel of his pistol to DeBreen's temple.

DeBreen, ignoring the gun, turned his head to look over his shoulder at Sam. His face was a bloody mask. Sam's bullet had blown away part of his cheek and one eye. The shattered face split open and smiled horribly.

"You goddamn bastard," DeBreen croaked.

"A dying man shouldn't use the Lord's name in vain," Sam said.

"There is no God, only death." DeBreen's croaking voice almost broke.

"It's time you found out. And Farrow and the others are waiting for you."

"I need a little help."

"Sure," Sam said. "I'm glad to oblige you. It's been a long trail, and I want it to end."

DeBreen locked his one good eye on Sam. "Then do it," he said.

Sam put the barrel of his pistol against DeBreen's back, directly over his heart. He squeezed the trigger.

The Mormon men came with shovels, and graves were dug for the dead in the ground where they died. Mathias spoke a short prayer for their souls. The earth was closed over them.

Sam and the Texans remained behind as Mathias and the other Mormons walked off toward their camp.

"I'm ready to travel south," Nathan said.

"I'm ready too," Ash said. He looked at Les and Jake. "How about you two? Ready?"

"The sooner the better," Les said.

"I'm more than ready," Jake said.

"Sam, what are you going to do?" Nathan asked.

"I'm broke, except for maybe a hundred dollars. So I'll go to the mountains again come fall and do some trapping. Until then I'll work in St. Joe to get enough money to buy an outfit."

"You're not broke," Ash said.

"What do you mean?"

Ash extracted a heavy pouch from the front of his shirt. "I went through the pockets of DeBreen and his men. I collected more than seven thousand dollars in gold coins. You helped kill them, so we'll split the money five ways."

The men looked around at each other. Their reluctance to agree with Ash's proposal showed on their faces.

Ash shook the bag, making the coins jingle. "Well?" he

asked. "We've earned it. What's the old saying? 'To the victor goes the spoils'?"

"Oh, hell, why not," Nathan said. "These men tried to kill us, and Sam needs the money. Give him my share."

"Nothing doing," Sam said. "I'll take just my own share."

They gathered in a circle and divided the coins. Sam hefted his portion in his hand and thoughtfully cast a look at the unseen mountains to the west.

"You could go to Texas with us," Ash said.

"I'd go if Ruth would go with me. But I don't think that's in the cards."

"Go ask her," Nathan said. The other men voiced their encouragement.

"I'll think on it," Sam said.

"DeBreen had some good horses," Jake said. "We should take enough of them for the women to ride, and give the rest to the Mormons."

"I'll get them," Nathan said. "You fellows get your women ready to travel. Sam, go ask Ruth to go to Texas with you." Without waiting for an answer Nathan went off with a swift step toward DeBreen's empty camp.

Grueling held the horses to a ground-devouring trot along the North Platte River. Scott's Bluff slid past on the opposite side of the river. The band of men climbed up through the breaks onto the prairie.

The sun climbed twice its diameter above the horizon as the band hastened to the east. The air had been washed clean by the night's rainfall, and objects at a great distance were clear and distinct. To Grueling's satisfaction he saw dark shapes moving on the prairie ahead. He recognized handcarts forming into a double line for travel.

"We have found the company of converts!" Grueling shouted out to his men. He raised the pace of his band to a gallop.

•◆ 36 ◆•

AM DISMOUNTED AND TIED HIS HORSE TO ONE wheel of the women's handcart. He removed his hat and held it tightly in his hand as he walked toward Ruth, standing with Caroline. Both women were watching Sophia and Pauliina take their personal possessions from the cart.

"Ruth, would you walk with me a little?" Sam asked.

Ruth studied Sam's face for a few seconds. "All right," she said.

They went off from the camp, neither speaking, feeling an important moment had arisen in their lives.

Sam looked sideways at Ruth's beautiful face as they walked. His desire for her was a great ache in his heart. "Ruth, Nathan and the other Texans have asked me to go south with them. There's land aplenty just for the taking in Texas. A man could make a good home for a woman. Will you go with me?"

Ruth halted and turned toward Sam. "I like you, Sam, very much. But there are no Mormons or Mormon churches in Texas. I asked Mathias about that. I could not leave my church."

"You would have Sophia and Pauliina near you. They are Mormons."

"I know. But I don't think their belief in our religion is very strong. And I still want a place to worship the Lord."

"There are other good religions in Texas."

"I am a Mormon and I want a Mormon temple to worship in. I want to see the Prophet. These things can only be done in Salt Lake City. I must go there." She looked steadily into Sam's eyes. "Why don't you come to Salt Lake City with us, with me?"

273

Sam silently considered the proposal. Then he spoke. "I couldn't live among the Mormons, for I would always be an outcast."

"Join the Church. Become one of us," Ruth said hopefully.

"I believe all churches are to some degree false. I know I could never be a faithful Mormon."

"I'm sure the religion of the Church of Jesus Christ of Latter-day Saints is the true one. I have enough faith for both of us."

Sam shook his head. "I can't go."

"I shall go on with the others to Utah," Ruth said firmly.

"Then I wish you well, Ruth. May all good things come your way."

"God will always look after and protect the Mormons."

"I don't care about the Mormons," Sam said. At that moment he hated the religion. "I hope God, if there is one, takes good care of you." He turned away.

He did not see the tears in Ruth's eyes, nor hear her muffled sob.

Rowley gave the order for the company to assemble into marching formation. He pulled his wagon to the lead position, then walked back along the line of handcarts to the Texans and the three women preparing to leave.

He looked at Caroline. She was thoughtfully observing Sophia, Pauliina, and Emily sorting out the items they would take to Texas with them. Mathias felt a great joy that Caroline was going on to Salt Lake City with him. He had seen Nathan's expression when he looked at Caroline, and their walks together had bothered him.

Mathias spoke to Sam and the Texans, who stood holding several horses, some with saddles and others carrying pack-saddles. "I'd like to thank all of you for what you have done to help us."

All the men except Nathan voiced their acceptance of Mathias's thanks. Nathan only briefly nodded. He did not trust himself to speak. He hated leaving without Caroline. Her words in the night that she would not go with him had left no doubt about her intentions, no room for Nathan to hope. He would not ask her again.

"Are you about ready, handcart woman?" Ash called to Sophia in a lighthearted tone.

"Nearly so, Texas man. But I'm no longer a handcart woman." She laughed happily. "I'm Texas bound."

Nathan heard the drum of running horses approaching from the west. He turned. A large band of riders was hurrying toward the Mormons.

Rowley broke away and walked out to meet the newcomers. He raised his hand in greeting. "Grueling, I'm very glad to see you."

"I'm glad to have found you. Is everybody all right?" Grueling dismounted. His men swung down behind him.

"Everything is fine now that you are here," Mathias said.

Grueling barely acknowledged Mathias's reply. He was studying the three pretty women, who were packing what appeared to be their personal possessions, the four men seemingly waiting for them.

"What's going on there?" Grueling gestured at the Texans. "Who are those strangely dressed fellows?"

"Some Texans who came north to find wives."

"Are those women making ready to go with the Texans?"

"Yes. They're about ready to leave. Then we can be on our way."

"No women are deserting the company," Grueling said harshly. "Why would you permit it? The Prophet told me to bring every woman to Salt Lake City. That same order applies to you."

Grueling brushed past Mathias and called out in a strident voice, "Where do you women think you're going?"

Nathan watched Rowley welcome the band of men. The long-expected Mormon guards from Utah had finally arrived. Caroline would now be safe during the remainder of her journey. That thought did little to allay his deep sadness at their parting.

Nathan was surprised at the loud, blunt question of the man called Grueling. He had no right to speak to the women in that tone. Nathan felt his instant anger. Jake, Ash, and Les grew tense, and their faces became bleak.

Grueling jabbed his finger at the three women, one after the other. "I ask again: Where do you think you are going?"

"To Texas," Sophia replied, the first of the women to overcome her astonishment at the rough question coming from the stranger. She lifted her head challengingly.

"No Mormon women are going off with apostates," Grueling said, his voice hard. "There are good husbands waiting in Salt Lake City. You can probably find husbands right among these men who came with me."

"I don't know what an apostate is," Ash said. "But these women are going with us Texans. You go hunt yourself some other women."

"I don't think so," Grueling said. He motioned with his hand.

The twenty Mormon men moved quickly to flank Grueling. They stared belligerently at the three Texans.

Sam came up beside Nathan. "What's happening?" he asked.

"Trouble." Nathan stepped up and stood beside Ash.

Sam followed on Nathan's right. "Goddamn Mormons want all the beautiful women," Sam said.

Mathias saw the coming battle. The Texans would not go without the women. "Grueling, you don't understand. These men risked their lives this morning by fighting a battle to keep this handcart company safe. Let the women leave with them."

"Absolutely not. My instructions are to bring every one of the women to Salt Lake City. I intend to do exactly that."

"I've heard of your actions, Grueling," Mathias said angrily. "This time you are going too far."

"Tell that to our Prophet, Brigham Young, when you get back. For now we've ridden too far to stand idly by and let those, or any other women, leave."

Caroline's voice cut into the conversation like a sharp knife. "Do you mean you'd use force to prevent them from going with the men of their choice?"

Grueling looked at Caroline. "You're not wanting to go, so why are you getting into this?"

"Because it's important to me to know how I'll be treated in your much-bragged-about Zion."

Mathias felt his alarm at the confrontation between Caroline and Grueling. He spoke quickly. "Caroline, this man is different from other Mormon men," he said. "We are not dictators or mean to our women."

"You say that," Caroline said sharply. "What does he say?" She jabbed her finger at Grueling as he had jabbed his finger at her friends. "And what do all these other men say?"

"My wives do as I say," Grueling said.

"And how many wives do you have to order around?" Caroline questioned.

"I have five good wives."

"Five wives. And I bet they're very obedient wives too," Caroline said, mocking Grueling. She spun to look at Nathan. "What have you to say about a woman who would be your wife?"

Nathan looked into Caroline's eyes, sparkling like jewels with her emotion. She was grand. "I'd say she deserved a husband all to herself."

Caroline smiled at Nathan, the most beautiful thing he had ever seen. He would give his soul to spend the next hundred years with her.

Caroline's smile became a happy laugh, as if she could read his mind. With this man she would never be afraid of what the future might bring. In Texas she could claim land fit for a king; better, a queen.

"Will that horse carry both of us?" she asked Nathan.

"Yes. But we have plenty of horses."

"Give me a minute and I'll be ready to travel."

"Stop!" ordered Grueling. He moved in front of Caroline and made to take hold of her.

"Hold there!" Nathan's voice was like thunder. No man could touch his woman with force. His anger was so cold, it seemed to burn him. He moved with unnatural swiftness upon Grueling.

Mathias was closer. He lunged at Grueling. The Avenging Angel was going too far. "You stupid bastard!" Mathias cried, his voice full of anguish. "You have caused me to lose something very valuable to me." Mathias struck Grueling a savage blow to the face.

Grueling staggered backward. He lifted his hands in defense.

Mathias charged forward, beating aside Grueling's guard, striking him powerfully with his fist, left and right.

Grueling's legs buckled and he fell hard. Mathias bent over him, his fist cocked to strike again. Grueling did not stir.

Mathias straightened, breathing hard. He shot a fierce look at Grueling's men. "This handcart company is mine. I'll give the orders. Do all of you understand me?"

A few of the men nodded in the affirmative. Most stared back, obviously unsure of which side to choose. One man spoke. "Orrin can settle that with you when he comes around." There was respect for Mathias in his voice.

Mathias turned to Caroline. "Don't go. Come with me."

"It is too late for that. I'm going with Nathan," Caroline replied. "I would never fit into your land of Zion. I must have the freedom to breathe, to be myself."

Mathias's face became tortured. "Are you very sure?"

"Yes." Her voice had an unshakable certainty.

"Then go now," Mathias said sadly. "Go before Grueling becomes conscious and there's more trouble."

Caroline hastened to the handcart and rolled her scant possessions into her blankets. She returned with the bundle. Nathan added it to the load on the packhorse.

The four Texans helped the women to mount their horses. They took up the lead ropes of the packhorses.

Sam guided his mustang over to Ruth. "Here, take one of these ponies to help you get to Utah."

"Thank you, Sam," Ruth said. "I shall never forget you."

Sam leaned down from the saddle. He brushed Ruth's cheek with his fingertips, then slowly ran them along the delicate skin and bone of her jaw. That was all he would ever receive from this lovely girl. Soon she would be someone else's wife. He felt as if a picket pin had been driven through his heart.

"Good-bye," Ruth said.

"I shall remember and dream of you for as long as I shall live," Sam said. He reined his horse away.

Nathan spoke to the sad man. "What are you going to do?"

"I'm going to the mountains in the fall to trap."

"Remember that you have friends in Texas. Come to see us there on the Salt Fork of the Red River and maybe stay."

"I'll surely do that. So long for now."

Sam lifted his horses in a swift pace to the east. He cast one long look over his shoulder. Then he faced the front again.

Nathan led off. Caroline guided her horse in beside him.

After a time she glanced back. One lone handcart sat forlorn and abandoned on the empty prairie.

Author's Note

The Mormon migration by handcart lasted five years, from 1856 through 1860. In total, ten handcart companies containing 2,962 converts and 653 handcarts crossed the wilderness of the great prairie and the Rocky Mountains to Salt Lake City.

The converts, mostly young women from England and Scandinavia, bent their backs in heart-bursting toil to pull the handcarts through the wilderness. Meager food rations and fierce storms falling upon the unprotected people added to the misery. Many weakened and died and were buried on the prairie.

The most terrible loss of life occurred in the fifth handcart company. The company was poorly organized and started late from Iowa City, Iowa. Dressed in summer clothing, and with their food gone, the Mormon converts became stranded by a winter snowfall in the high mountains far north of Salt

Lake City. Three out of every ten people perished from exhaustion, hunger, and the cold before a relief party of young Mormon men, sent by Brigham Young from Salt Lake City, could reach them.

The handcart companies of 1856, 1857, and 1858 began in Iowa City. The journey was 1,300 miles and took approximately four months. With the completion of the railroad to St. Joseph, Missouri, in February 1859, the route was shortened to 1,000 miles and took about three months. The Mormon immigrants organized at St. Joseph, then caught riverboats up the Missouri River to begin their handcart trek from Florence, Nebraska. (Florence is now part of Omaha.)

The Mormon Church halted the use of handcarts after 1860. Thereafter the new immigrant converts traveled by wagon train, until the completion of the transcontinental railroad on May 10, 1869. The journey that had required three to four months of great hardship could now be accomplished in relative comfort in less than two days.

The construction of the Salt Lake City Temple was completed in 1893 and became the center of the far flung Mormon Religion.